What others are saying about

The Prophecy:

The final installment of The Children of Lilith is a fitting conclusion to the story of Carl and Moira Morgan. The story doesn't waste time getting to the action. In spite of the knowledge that they will all die whether or not they succeed in their efforts to kill Lilith, the main characters all move forward resolutely. Mistakes are made, judgment is clouded, human frailties muddy up the process, but they press forward with assurance they are doing their best to do the right thing. David Belt explores the issues of human fallibility with the thoughtfulness of one who has experienced the impact of his own weaknesses. Carl, the leader of the vampire resistance, wrestles with the power he holds over the others in his team, even knowing that by so doing, he is at the mercy of their fallibility. Tony Lupescu faces the unintended consequences of his past choices and the devastating effects they have. The newly penitent vampire Sergei, struggles with the difficulty of overcoming the deeply engrained habits his long years of deliberate sin have created within him. Through all this, the only way to succeed is to completely place their lives at the mercy of Father in Heaven.

It's a great end to a great story and a good lesson for each one of us as we fight our own Liliths.

Trevor O'Donnal, Springville, UT

It had been a while since I'd read *The Penitent*, but there were enough references in *The Prophecy* to the main events in *The Penitent* to get me back in the story.

So now it's war. And war is ugly. And painful. And you lose people you care about. And it seems unfair. And hopeless. And because of the prophecy, Carl and Moira know that if they lose, they die and if they win, they die because all Lilith's children will die with her.

C. David Belt doesn't hold much back as he shows how evil Lilith is. I really like the part where Tony breaks the rules and is in contact with the enemy even though Carl warns his followers. But the rules don't apply to Tony, he's too smart and ends up paying the price. It was hard reading about the consequences of Tony's actions, but Belt managed to find the perfect balance of horror without going over the line with graphic details.

There will be readers who will disagree with me and think Belt *did* cross the line and think it was too horrible for words. But that was the point—Lilith is capable of acts too horrible for words.

Belt adds two new groups of players in the war against Lilith—the Marines and The People of Esther. Both play an integral part in the conclusion of the story. And while in one way the story ended the way I expected, I was surprised by how Belt handled The People of Esther and the future of life in this world without Lilith.

Overall, the three books were well written and it was a really good story with a satisfying ending.

Deborah Carl, Nashua, New Hampshire

Tonight I am reviewing *The Prophecy* by C David Belt. His writing style is impeccable as always, and his book is very gripping from the start. He stays true to his characters and plot points through the book. I must give a warning that this book does have darker elements to it than the others touched on. I give this book 5 stars!

Book Junkie Reviews

Let's imagine that everything you have ever been taught to believe in any religion has just been altered, and a new theory has been brought to your attention, making you question the realm of its possibility. Then you add in a few thousand vampires, and boom, there it is sitting right in front of you making perfect sense right? Wrong! This is the mind-blowing experience I had while reading *The Prophecy*. I found myself more than a couple of times wanting to cover my eyes as the scenes in the book played out before me in my mind. In *The Prophecy* Lilith will stop at nothing until she has what she wants, and she doesn't care what she has to do or who she has to kill to get it. You will not be let down by *The Prophecy* if horror is what you seek. This is one story I wished I hadn't taken to bed with me to read. 5/5

Tammy Hall, Tammy's Tea Time Reviews

The Prophecy, while arguably the darkest volume in this trilogy, does ultimately culminate in a very satisfactory manner. I didn't think I'd enjoy this series as much as I have, but now I am hooked on the products of Mr. Belt's creative juices. I can't wait to see what he distills for us next.

Michele Dugdale, Springville, UT

The Prophecy

The Children of Lilith
Volume III

The Prophecy

C. David Belt

ISBN: hardcover

ISBN: paperback

ISBN: 978-1-3016-8555-4 e-book

Cover design: Ben Savage

PARABLES
10829 Dublin Road
Walkersville, MD 21793
www.parablespub.com
parables@parablespub.com

For Cindy,
now and forever.

Yea, when this flesh and heart shall fail
And mortal life shall cease,
I shall possess within the veil
A life of joy and peace.

John Newton

Cowards die many times before their deaths;
The valiant never taste of death but once.
Of all the wonders that I yet have heard,
It seems to me most strange that men should fear;
Seeing that death, a necessary end,
Will come when it will come.

William Shakespeare

The truth will set you free, but first it will make you miserable.

James A. Garfield

Author's Note

Once more into the breach, dear friends, once more," said the Bard. The central theme of this final book is courage, specifically the courage to do right in the face of certain death.

When I was a cadet in the AFROTC program at Brigham Young University, I once had the privilege of hearing Colonel Bernard F. Fisher, USAF-retired, give a speech. Colonel Fisher is a genuine war hero of the Vietnam War, the first *living* Air Force recipient of the Congressional Medal of Honor. As cadets, we all knew the story, how he landed a prop-driven A-1E close-air-support aircraft, call sign Hobo-51, on a cratered runway, under heavy fire, in the A Shau Valley. Dodging shell holes and debris, he taxied his two-seat aircraft to the hiding place of downed fellow A-1 pilot, Major D. W. "Jump" Myers, loaded Myers aboard the aircraft, and managed to take off again, all the while suffering numerous hits on his aircraft.

I didn't know it at the time, but Bernard Fisher had been awarded the Silver Star for bravery only the day before the dramatic rescue of Jump Myers.

To say that we cadets were inspired by Bernard Fisher's courage under fire would be like saying that a hurricane is a bit breezy. We all sat in awe and listened as this humble man from Clearfield, Utah, made light of his heroism. He recounted the incident, sure enough, but then he got really quiet.

He said that he wasn't the true hero of that day. The true hero, he said, was a Marine who fought on the ground at A Shau that day. Sadly, I cannot remember the man's name. This Marine lost both legs when a shell hit his gunnery position, slaughtering his entire squad. He removed his belt and the belt of a fallen comrade and improvised tourniquets around the ruin of his legs. Then he manned the machine gun and provided cover fire for Colonel Fisher and other embattled Marines, allowing them to withdraw.

He died at that machine-gun post.

I wish I could remember his name, but I can't.

But our Heavenly Father knows who he is.

One note about the locations used in this story: those locations and facilities mentioned by name are real, as improbable as that may be to those unfamiliar with them. I did not make them up.

The story of a certain WW II Marine captain related in the narrative is also factual, as incredible as it sounds.

Truth really can be stranger than fiction.

And finally, as this trilogy comes to its conclusion, to all of you who have traveled on this journey with me through the story of Carl and Moira Morgan, I must say that it has been a pleasure and a joy. I sincerely hope you are pleased and that you enjoy the destination as much as you have the road.

C. David Belt
February, 2012
cdavidbelt@hotmail.com

Chapter 1

Tony

*S*ons of God! Brood of Light-Bearer who fell!' That is how I would render the first half.'"

The message is in plain text. The email address looks like a random mix of letters and numbers, and the email provider is one that supports anonymous accounts.

I've been collaborating with colleagues across the country and in the U.K., Israel, and Egypt for more than a week. We've been trying to decipher the twenty-four syllables of Adamic (at least I *assume* it's Adamic) that Lilith uttered at the battle at the farm. My colleagues are experts in Hebrew, Arabic, Egyptian, Greek, and Latin. We've been exchanging emails ever since I asked for their help.

Of course, I've told them I'm not at liberty to reveal the *source* just yet, but I'm certain it's a language that predated all others, a protolanguage. In the beginning, some refused to collaborate on the project because I wouldn't reveal my source, because I was being cryptic. But eventually, most couldn't resist the lure of the *puzzle*. That's something we all share in common, my colleagues and I: we can't resist the potential, the lure of hidden knowledge.

And of course, I can't tell my academic friends that the source is a *native speaker*. I also can't tell them that the text is an outburst from a six-thousand-year-old vampire after she'd been impaled by the very spear that once pierced Christ's side, a spear being wielded by a former Nazi assassin who is now a *repentant* vampire.

In other words, I can't betray my *friends*.

My colleagues and I have been exchanging a veritable whirlwind of email messages for days, with theories, postulations, and outright guesses about roots, word endings, and syntax. It's a fascinating puzzle, but we have so little to go on. So, a *puzzle* is all it is and all it's likely to remain, unless I meet Lilith, the ancient Mother of Night, the mother of all vampires, face-to-face.

And that would be an encounter I'd be unlikely to survive.

I've survived one such encounter with her already . . . and *that* only because she had more immediate concerns to occupy her attention than one mortal *stupid* enough to embroil himself in a battle between factions of vampires.

God may watch over imbeciles and fools, but *nobody* has that much luck.

I'm no warrior, like Carl. I'm not a master of the sword, like Moira, Carl's wife. I'm just Tony Lupescu, scholar, professor of ancient scripture at Brigham Young University. I'm just an academic . . . and a *mortal* one at that.

I've made up my mind that I'll just have to make do with the sample, *just twenty-four syllables*, that I have. But, hey, it's a heck of a lot more than I knew about the language of Adam *before* I witnessed the Penitent vampires of the "Vampire Stake," led by Carl Morgan, the world's first and only Unwilling vampire, forced into battle with the minions of Lilith.

Twenty-four syllables. It's not a Rosetta Stone with a dead language carved beside a direct translation in a *known* language, but it's all I have, and I'll have to be content with that.

And it's *knowledge*!

And a fascinating *puzzle*.

And I *was* content with the *seeking*, even if I might not find the answer . . .

But now . . . this almost-anonymous email. And a *piece* of the puzzle that *fits*. I can *feel* it. This is the *correct* translation. I don't know *how* I know it, but I *do* know.

So, with a jumbled mixture of eagerness and trepidation and a dozen other emotions that I barely understand, I reach for my mouse and click the "Reply" button.

"*Who are you?*" I type. "*How did you get this address? What makes you think this is correct? And why on EARTH would someone say both of these together? It makes no sense: sons of God AND spawn of Satan (that would be 'Light-Bearer who fell') in the same breath. How can someone be both?*"

I sit there for a bit, debating with myself the wisdom of responding. Once I click the "Send" button, there'll be no turning back. I *could* simply ignore the anonymous message, but then I'd never know what the sender knows. And what could be the harm, so long as I don't reveal anything that would betray my friends?

Impulsively, I click "Send" before I can change my mind.

There. It's sent.

I've crossed the Rubicon. "*Alea iacta est*," as Caesar said: *The die is cast*.

"Tony!" Kathleen calls from the living room. "Lorenzo's here!"

Speaking of points of no return . . . The coming meeting is something I'm looking forward to with anticipation and dread. *How will my wife react?*

"Coming," I call back. I glance once more at my email. I click the "Send-Receive" button. No reply. *Of course not. It's too soon.*

I get up and walk into the living room.

Kathleen's sitting on the loveseat, and Lorenzo and Rolf are seated, their backs to me, on the sofa,. Of course, *Rolf's* here: Lorenzo has taken Rolf with him everywhere since Rolf was injured. The kids have been in bed for an hour, so it's just the four of us. Lorenzo and Kathleen are talking in low voices. Rolf, of course, says nothing.

I pause at the entrance to the room and take a deep breath. No sense in putting this off any longer. Kathleen needs to know what we're facing, the danger I've placed our family in.

I glance at the front door. Kathleen usually insists that Lorenzo and Rolf leave their swords at the door. *Surely they didn't come unarmed!* I round the corner of the couch and look at Lorenzo. My concern must be plain on my face because he glances down at his lap and pats the basket-hilted claymore lying across his thighs. Rolf's hand rests on the handle of the broadsword in his lap. His gaze catches mine and he nods in greeting.

Kathleen's allowing them to hold on to their swords? Does she have some sense of what's coming? Did Lorenzo use Persuasion on her? No way! That would be a complete violation of my trust! He wouldn't do that, would he?

One glance at Kathleen lays *that* suspicion to rest. She does *not* look happy. She's sitting, but her back's ramrod straight.

"Tony," she says, her tone reflecting her irritation, "they insisted on keeping those . . . *things* with them."

"My apologies, dear lady," Lorenzo says, his Italian accent more pronounced than usual, "but I fear that we must stand ready at all times, especially after dark." He turns his face toward me and says, "The Morgans intercepted another scouting party last night." He looks at me meaningfully and then adds, "In the *south*."

By that he means Lilith's scouts were here in the Provo area.

I'm about to ask what happened, but he says, "The engagement was a success."

And by that he means that the scouts are dead . . . and that Moira and Carl are still alive.

"That's the third such intercept since the *incident* at the farm," Lorenzo says. "And this time, there were *six* of them."

My eyes go wide at the number. The previous two scouting parties consisted of only two vampires each.

"She's either getting bolder or more desperate . . . ," I say, but Kathleen interrupts me.

"Will you *please* tell me what in the *heck* all of you are talking about?"

"Kat," I say, trying to calm her. I don't need to see the angry look in her eyes to realize I've just made a *huge* mistake: she hates when I use that pet name in public. *This is* not *going well*. But it doesn't matter. I have to tell her anyway. I cross in front of the couch and sit beside her. I take both her hands in mine and look into her angry and fearful blue eyes.

"You do need to know what's going on," I say. "Do you remember my family legend about my great-great-grandfather Laurentiu?"

"Yes," she says with a quick nod, which is followed immediately by a shake of the head, "the so-called vampire."

"Not 'so-called,'" I reply, my voice gentle. "He really *was* a vampire. Only, he didn't die in the sunlight, like we all believed."

She pulls back from me a bit, but leaves her hands in mine. Her beautiful face is a mask of skepticism. "What? You mean . . . like he's still alive? Sweetie, I *never* believed those stories. I know they're part of your family history, but vampires aren't real. I know that's one of your hobbies, but . . ."

"No, honey," I say, cutting her off, "it's all very real. I know it's hard to swallow, but vampires are very real . . . and so is my great-great-grandfather." I glance over at Lorenzo, and Kathleen follows my eyes. She glances at him and then back at me. Her eyes fix on Lorenzo, and then her jaw drops.

"No!" she cries suddenly and rises to her feet.

Lorenzo rises also, extends his sword behind himself, and bows deeply at the waist. "*Si, signora mia,*" he says, rising, "I was born in 1490 in Roma. I was Converted and became a vampire in 1513. For more than a century I . . ."

"Stop it!" Kathleen cries, and now I can see she's *really* furious. "This is *not* funny!"

Lorenzo nods quickly and says, "Dear lady, please forgive me." He looks at me. "If I may, Tony?"

"Please," I say. It's the only way, and we both knew it would come to this.

Lorenzo locks eyes with Kathleen and then rises into the air about a foot or so. Kathleen gasps and puts both hands to her mouth. I raise a hand and lay it on her arm.

She doesn't flinch away.

"Please do not be frightened, granddaughter," Lorenzo says, his voice calm and apologetic. "Please observe my teeth." He opens his mouth, and I see his upper canine teeth extend until his fangs are quite obvious. He remains that way for several moments, hovering in my living room with his fangs extended. Then his canines retract, and he settles softly to the floor.

Kathleen swallows several times and begins to tremble. "M-m-monster!" she cries at last.

Lorenzo bows his head. "I was *indeed* a monster for more than a century," he said, "but I have been a Penitent, a seeker of forgiveness and redemption, for the better part of four hundred years. I have given my life to God. I serve Him now."

First Rolf's head and then Lorenzo's snap to the left. Lorenzo grimaces. He turns his face back to Kathleen. "Forgive me, dear lady, but we seem to have awakened Abigail."

I can't hear anything.

"Mommy!" It's Abby's voice from her room upstairs. Now I can hear her crying.

Kathleen immediately begins to move. She's off like a shot, out of the room and up the stairs.

I hear the door shut behind her. After a moment, Abby quiets down.

There's nothing we can do now except wait for Kathleen to return.

I sit on the loveseat. Lorenzo sits as well, placing the sword back across his thighs.

"*That* could have gone better," I say with a grimace.

"Abby OK," Rolf says, startling me. I haven't heard him speak since he took some bullets to the brain at Müller's farm nine days ago. Moira told us his speech centers were probably destroyed. The tissue regenerated quickly, but the *knowledge* was lost. He has to learn how to speak and understand speech all over again. Just like a baby.

Only this is a lot faster than I expected.

"He's been doing better," Lorenzo says. "Aren't you, Rolf?"

The German, who now sounds more Italian than German, looks annoyed and a bit irritated. "Not baby," he says. "I . . . I'm learning"—he slaps the side of his head twice and then shakes his fist in frustration as he struggles to find the word—"fast. I'm learning fast."

I notice for the first time that the sword he's gripping so tightly is Sarah's Scottish broadsword. He has abandoned his own Teutonic hand-and-a-half sword and taken Sarah's sword for his own. He knew her for such a short time before she was killed by Müller, but he fell hopelessly in love with her. Lorenzo told me that he often finds Rolf silently weeping, clutching the sword to his chest.

"Yes," Lorenzo says, "you're doing remarkably well . . . better than any of us thought possible."

"I learn fast. I fight. Must understand . . . commands. Must understand Carl's commands. We kill Lilith." He glances back to the left. "Kat comes."

"*Kathleen*," I whisper. "Don't let her hear you say that!"

I can hear Kathleen's footsteps on the stairs. She stops at the bottom, plants her feet, and folds her arms.

"Tell me one thing." Her tone brooks no evasion. "Are my children in danger?"

"Not from *me*, my lady," Lorenzo says. "Nor from any of my friends. I would never hurt my grandchildren. I . . . we are *reformed*. We are Penitents, seeking the grace of God."

"There are *more* of you?" Her expression is stern. Apart from noting her all-business, protect-her-children-at-any-cost bearing, I can't tell *what* she's thinking or feeling.

"Yes, Kathleen," Lorenzo says. "There are forty-seven of us . . . forty-seven Penitents, that is. More are joining us almost every night. There are so many of us now, we must leave the state in order to Feed . . ."

"But," I say, interrupting him, "we *are* in danger, honey."

"You played with my children," Kathleen says, her eyes staring daggers at Lorenzo. "And they were never in any danger?"

"Not from me," Lorenzo repeats. "I haven't killed a mortal in nearly three centuries. And I would *never* harm my own flesh and blood."

"What about *you*?" she says, turning her intense gaze on Rolf. "You, Rolf, the creepy, silent guy! Are *you* going to hurt my kids?"

"I not hurt Abby," Rolf says. "Not hurt . . . Little Tony. I'm not . . . bad vampire."

Kathleen looks shocked. She's never heard Rolf speak before.

"He took a bullet to the head," I explain quickly. "His brain is completely healed, but he has to learn to talk all over again. He's made incredible progress. He's not retarded or slow or a . . . *pedophile* or anything like that. He's one of the *good* guys."

She shifts her gaze to me. "I'll deal with *you* later."

Yep! I'm in real *trouble!* But I can't leave it there. *I'm an idiot. I don't know when to just keep my mouth shut.*

"They've been *protecting* us," I say. "There are others . . . many, *many* others who're *evil*, and they *are* looking for us . . . well, for *me*."

"Why?" she said. "What did you *do*, Tony?"

Yep! Somehow this was going to be all my *fault! Well, to be honest, it is.*

"He brought us together," Lorenzo says, "organized us, taught us the gospel of Jesus Christ. He *was* our leader."

"You?" she says, her eyes wide.

"You know me," I say, shrugging sheepishly, "I just can't seem to keep my big mouth shut."

"You *were* the leader?" she asks.

"Yes," I reply. "Actually, I was more of a teacher. But now they have a *new* leader. He's a vampire *and* a member of the Church. And he has never killed . . . never killed a *mortal*, that is. There are even a couple of prophecies about him and his wife. You've met them. They're the Morgans . . . Carl and Moira Morgan."

"Moira is a . . . a . . . ?" she stammers.

"Vampire, yes," I finish for her.

"But . . . I *like* her!"

"Don't you like *me*?" Lorenzo says, a fake pout on his face.

"I . . . *used* to," Kathleen says. She hasn't moved from her place, her arms folded. She's still guarding the stairs, still guarding her children.

"I see," Lorenzo says.

"Oh, my heck!" She unfolds her arms and places her hands over her eyes. Then she drops her hands. "I do, I guess. It's just a lot to take in!"

Then she steps away from the stairs and gives Lorenzo a quick hug. She pulls back and says, "You're really his great-great-grandfather Laurentiu?"

"That I am, granddaughter," he replies. "But come, we must discuss the very real dangers." He gestures toward the loveseat. "Please sit down."

She walks over to the loveseat and sits. Lorenzo and Rolf both take their seats again, placing their swords in their laps. Cautiously, I join my wife on the sofa.

She reaches over and takes my hand.

I breathe an audible sigh of relief.

Both Lorenzo and Rolf smile at this, although Rolf's smile is tinged with sadness.

"You see, Kathleen," Lorenzo begins, "there is a war of sorts going on . . ."

◢ ◢ ◢

Lorenzo does most of the talking, but Kat asks a lot of questions. *Do they know where we live? Do they know who we are?* The answer to both is, *Apparently not so far, but they are looking.* Lorenzo informs her that there are at least two Penitents guarding our home each night from the air now, and during daylight, there are two stationed outside in Carl's minivan, ready to cloak themselves in darkness and come to our aid in an emergency.

Then her questions shift to inquiries about vampires in general, but she's most captivated by the love story of Lorenzo and Mara, my great-great-grandmother. Lorenzo weeps as he recounts the tale, and Kathleen goes over and hugs him when he's done. Lorenzo talks about how he wanted the two of *us* to have the two of *them* sealed in the temple after he's gone.

"Why can't you just wait until you can do it yourself?" she asks.

"Ah, dear lady," he says, shaking his head sadly, "it may have been centuries, but, long ago, I was a murderer. Even if I *could* get a clearance from your First Presidency, such things take time. And I expect that I . . . all of us . . . the Penitent vampires, I mean . . . all of us will be dead shortly."

"But, you're immortal, aren't you?" She's obviously distressed.

"Yes, I'm immortal, but you see, this war among the Children of Lilith can end in only one of two ways: either in victory or defeat. Either way, we will die."

"You see, Kathleen," I say, "the Prophecy . . . the newer one, at least . . . states that, once Lilith falls, all vampires will die. So, win or lose, Tony, Rolf, Carl, Moira, and all their friends will be dead."

Lorenzo smiles sadly. "But we'll have rid the Earth of the evil of Lilith and her Children."

"But," she says, "can't you . . . I don't know . . . put it off for a while?"

"Every . . . night," Rolf interjects, and all eyes go to him, "people die. Every night Lilith kill people."

Lorenzo nods. "Yes, as much as I cherish life, the longer we delay, the more innocents will die to Feed Lilith and her minions. And," he adds, his eyes moist with new tears, "I have hope that the Lord will have mercy on me and I will see my Mara again."

◢ ◢ ◢

It's nearly midnight before my great-great-grandfather and Rolf leave. Kathleen goes upstairs to check on the kids, while I go to my office to shut down my computer for the evening . . . and check my email.

I sit down at my desk and click the "Send-Receive" button. I wait anxiously, my fingers drumming on the desk beside my mouse.

There's one message.

It's a response from the anonymous sender. I open it hurriedly and read the plain-text message:

How did I get your email address? Let's just say that I have people who have been sniffing around, looking for messages such as yours.

How do I know the translation is correct? Let's just say that I have some knowledge of the First Tongue.

Why would anyone lump the Sons of God and the Brood of Lucifer together? Well, that depends on your perspective. What if the speaker considered both to be insulting, both to be two sides of the same coin, so to speak?

And as for who I am?

I think you know the answer.

So tell me: what do you want to know?

Chapter 2

Moira

T his is a Fox News breaking alert!" The drawling voice on the television has that odd mixture of alarm and world-weariness that seems common to so many TV anchormen.

I'm sitting at a table in the break room at LDS Hospital, sipping blood mixed with tomato juice from my thermos. (Truth to tell, 'tis mostly blood, but one must do *something* to disguise the scent.) There are three others in the room. John Tolman, one of my fellow trauma surgeons; Eric Heller, an intern I barely know; and Alicia Simmons, a pediatric nurse.

None of them so much as glance at the TV.

"Amazing video footage has surfaced of an aerial swordfight between two flying . . . that's right . . . *flying* people," the announcer says.

All eyes snap to the TV, including my own. I watch the face of a man in his early thirties as he intones:

"Last month we brought you a story about reports of a battle between two so-called 'angels' in the sky above downtown Salt Lake City, Utah. At the time, there were some conflicting eyewitness accounts, but no other evidence. Witnesses described two people, a man dressed in a white, gold, and red robe and sporting white angels' wings, and a woman, dressed all in black, *flying* and fighting with *swords* in the air above the heart of Salt Lake City. Video footage has now come to light and it appears to show the conclusion of that battle."

My blood runs cold. *This cannae be!*

The announcer continues, "What you are about to see, folks, is video from inside the cavernous Conference Center of the Church of Jesus Christ of Latter-day Saints, what most of our viewers know as the Mormon Church. Many of you will recognize it as the place where the Mormon Tabernacle Choir sings."

Behind him, an image of the Conference Center appears.

"Now, folks," he drawls on, "before we show you this incredible footage, we want you to know that our video experts have verified that this is *unaltered* and *unedited* video. I repeat: this is *unaltered* video. We're going to pause it, speed it up, and zoom in on occasion, but we're going to show the entire film with no other edits."

Black-and-white video of the Conference Center interior replaces the announcer's face. The choir loft and the pipes of the great organ are visible, but nothing moves. Then Gunther Paul Müller appears from the left side of the screen and flies toward the top and center of the great hall, his huge wings beatin' furiously, his broken sword in his hand. He pauses and then hovers for a moment. His back is to the camera, there's nae mistaking his blood-stained white ceremonial robe. The picture freezes, and the announcer says, "Our experts have confirmed that there are no wires holding this man in the air. He appears to *actually* be *flying*, just as you see here, folks." The image begins to move again, and Müller flies up and out of the view of the camera.

"Now, folks, wait just a few seconds, and you'll see the second flying person," the announcer says as the video shows only the pipe organ and choir loft again.

And suddenly, there I am on the screen, flying into the center of the hall, wearing tattered, charred, and soaked black sweat clothes. I'm wingless and carrying my schiavona, my black "sword of truth." My hair is drenched, and my back is to the camera as I halt in mid air.

At least ye cannae see my face and, with nae color, ye cannae see that my hair's red.

But, just as that thought passes, and I begin to hope my face was nae captured on film, my image turns about and faces nigh straight at the camera. The image freezes and zooms in on my face. The expanded image is grainy, but *I* recognize myself . . . as could anyone who knows me well.

"The remainder of this video is somewhat graphic," the announcer says. "You may want to have small children leave the room."

And the image remains a frozen close-up of my face.

I wait for gasps of recognition from the others in the room, but there are nae any.

Uncomfortable seconds tick past, but I cannae look away from the screen. I can only stare at my face. On the screen, water streams from my hair, my mascara's running. *What an odd thing to notice with my whole world falling apart before my eyes!*

"At this time," the anchorman says, "we can only speculate as to how these two people are able to fly, why one has wings and the other doesn't, or even why they're fighting."

After what seems an interminable, excruciating length of time, my face is replaced by the moving image again. I'm shown spinning about in the air as I look all around for Müller. He was speaking, ranting to me at the time. He was above me, hidden in the network of catwalks, speakers, lights, and wires at the apex of the great hall, but I did nae ken that at the time.

Mercifully, there's nae sound to accompany the video . . . nae sound, that is, save the voice of the newsman.

"As you can see here, the woman appears to be looking around for the man. He'll reappear shortly. Watch closely, now. The action moves rather quickly."

I watch in horror as Müller dives at my image from above. He swings his broken blade, and it slices into my image's neck. There's an initial spurt of blood. My video-self puts her free hand to her neck and wheels about as Müller turns in mid air and flies back at her. I see him hack at her side. My image flails about, tryin' to stay aloft and keep him in sight. She clutches her hand to her side. 'Tis another mercy that ye cannae see on the screen that at this point I was holding my intestines in with my free hand while the Seed repaired the damage.

Müller continues his flight up and over the choir loft. Framed against the pipes of the organ, he turns and flies back toward the camera. On the screen, I'm still clutching my side, hovers, waiting for him. The two come together, Müller swinging his broken sword. I dodge his blow, and catching hold of his robe, swing him around. He becomes entangled in a dangling wire, and his wings vanish. I thrust the black sword into Müller's heart. For a moment, our images appear as lovers, or would, if 'twere nae for my sword protruding from Müller's back. His blade falls from his hand.

So far, nobody has looked back at me. 'Tis as a train wreck. Ye cannae look away.

"They remain like this for about a minute," the voice on the television says. "We're going to speed this up just a little until the woman begins moving again." The video does appear to "fast-forward," as they say, though there's little movement.

I was waiting for him to be truly dead.

I see myself pull the sword slowly from Müller's chest. Then I watch as my image pats the back of her head. *I was checking to see that my hair had all grown back since Müller had pulled out a chunk of it. What vanity! Ach, lassie! Ye're exposed for the whole world to see and ye're worried that ye might appear to be a wee bit vain?*

The voice continues, "I don't know what she's waiting for here. Perhaps she's making sure he's dead." *Aye, laddie, ye have the right of that!* "Although, how anyone could survive a sword through the heart, as this appears to be, is beyond me. So we're going to speed this up again for a moment." The video zips by for a bit and then resumes its normal speed.

I watch as the video Moira untangles Müller from the wire, bundles him under her left arm, flies down and out of the view of the camera . . . *I was retrieving his sword . . .* and then back up into view briefly, all before flying out of sight.

"That's it, folks," the newsman says. *He could be discussing the weather forecast rather than the end of my whole world.* "We're going to run the footage again, and we're going to bring on a panel of experts."

He continues, "With us by phone from the University of Utah, we'd like to welcome Dr. Anna . . ."

I stop listening. The film restarts and fills the left side of the screen while the publicity photograph of a middle-aged woman fills the right side of the screen.

'Twas my face . . . my face on the national news.

Me . . . flying . . . fighting . . . killing.

Will the police arrest me for murder?

With nae corpse—Müller's body was burnt to less than ash—will there be any evidence to support a charge of murder? The video is . . .

". . . incredible," a woman's voice says flatly from the television. "And by 'incredible' I mean 'without credibility.' Just because your *experts* have declared this footage to be authentic, doesn't mean this hasn't been manufactured somehow."

"How do we know," a man in an expensive suit—the caption identifies him as "Reverend Dr." *something-or-other*—says in a thick southern drawl, "that this isn't some hoax perpetrated by the Mormon Church? I mean, every *Christian* knows that angels have wings, and it was the *angel* in this . . . *fantasy* that was slain. As you saw, the woman in black kills the so-called angel. How do we know that the Mormons aren't trying to *fool* Christians into believing in *their* version of angels? Many in your audience may be unaware that Mormons claim that angels do *not* have wings . . ."

My face reappears in frozen close-up on the left side of the screen.

"You know who that looks like, don't you?" Eric the intern says. He's staring intently at the screen.

My heart skips a beat, and I hold my breath as I wait in dread of the answer.

"She *does* look familiar," Alicia says, staring at the screen.

"Elizabeth Taylor," Eric says. "Well, a *young* Elizabeth Taylor."

I breathe an audible sigh of relief.

"Elizabeth *who*?" Alicia replies, looking at him puzzled.

"Elizabeth *Taylor*," he says, his voice impatient. "You know . . . *Cleopatra, Father of the Bride* . . ."

"You mean Kimberly . . . what's-her-name . . . Williams? Kimberly Williams?" Alicia asks.

"No, dummy," Eric says in mock scorn, "not the Steve Martin remake; the *classic*. You know . . . Spencer Tracy."

"How old *are* you?" Alicia asks, shaking her head.

"'Bout the same as you," Eric retorts. "I just end up watching a lot of late-night cable. Besides, if I were to talk about somebody more modern . . . I'd have to say Rachel McAdams."

"Not Rachel McAdams," John Tolman puts in his tuppence-worth. "Well, maybe . . . *if* she had a really bad hair day."

I screw the lid back onto my thermos and prepare to make my escape. *What am I going to do? At least they did nae recognize me.*

I'm almost to the door when Alicia says, "No, she looks more like Dr. Morgan than any of those."

I freeze dead in my tracks.

She pauses and looks more closely at the TV. "She *does* kinda look like you, Dr. Morgan."

John looks back at me and grins. "You been doing any flying lately, Moira?" He cocks his head, closes one eye, and looks as if he's seriously considering the possibility. "As I recall . . ." he says, nodding, "you were really *late* that day." He glances around the room and says, "I don't know . . . has anyone ever seen Moira and *Super-Woman* here"—he points back at the screen—"*together?*" He raises his eyebrows as if he's had an epiphany. I cannae tell if he's serious or nae.

I open my mouth to reply, nae kenning what in the world I can say to that.

Alicia snorts. 'Tis a laugh. "Are you *kidding* me? Have you *ever* seen Moira with a single hair out of place or her makeup less than *perfect?* Six hours of surgery and she *still* looks like a super-model. Makes me *sick!*"

That elicits a laugh from all three of them.

I cannae collect myself enough to laugh along with them.

They dinnae seem to notice and all turn back to the TV.

"Seriously, though," Eric says, "she *does* look familiar."

Mercifully, my face disappears from the left side of the screen to be replaced by footage of the fight. The voice of the anchorman says, "And with us now, from our Fox affiliate in Salt Lake City, we have the man who brought this amazing video to our attention. Russell Halloran, welcome."

On the television, the right side of the screen is filled with the head and shoulders of a severe-looking man with a brown crew cut. "It's good to be here," he says and smiles, but the smile does nae go higher than his mouth. His eyes are intense.

"Now, tell us, Russell," the anchorman says, "how you obtained this footage. It's security video, isn't it?"

The man on the TV, Russell Halloran, waits a second to answer, the delay being due to the satellite transmission. Then he stirs and says, "That's right. The video is from the morning of the battle."

"And you work for Mormon Church Security, don't you?"

"Actually, my company supplies the security video equipment to LDS Church Security."

"Isn't the video the property of the Mormon Church?" the newsman asks.

After a small delay, Halloran shakes his head. "There's a provision in our contract with the Church that allows us to use video that has become a part of the public record for our own promotional purposes. The Church supplied the footage to the police who investigated the incident. That made the footage fair game for release. The Church won't be happy about it, but we're within our rights. The police have decided to treat this as an elaborate hoax, in spite of blood and other physical evidence found at that scene."

"So why *did* you go public with this?"

"Because, the truth needs to be told. The word needs to get out: demons walk among us."

What did he say? Demons? I want to leave . . . to escape, but I cannae make myself go.

"Demons?" the anchorman asks. He sounds genuinely surprised.

"Yes," Halloran answers, "demons. They're among us. I belong to the Brotherhood of Tobias. Tobias is best known as the hero of the apocryphal 'Book of Tobit.' Tobias was aided by the Angel Raphael in fighting the Demon Asmodeus. The Brotherhood of Tobias is an ancient order of demon hunters. We *expose* them to the light of day."

What is he going on about? Tobias? Demon hunters? Ancient order?

What difference does it make? My face is on national TV!

I can hear the newsman huff a nervous laugh. "Mr. Halloran, you know that sounds . . . uh, *nutty*, for lack of a better word, don't you?"

"And 'flying people' *isn't* 'nutty'?" Halloran retorts after a second. "If your viewers want to know the truth, they should go to our website: www.theywalktheearth.org. Demons have walked among us for thousands of years. The Brotherhood of Tobias is dedicated to exposing them. Only then can we defeat them."

"Uh, folks," the newsman says with another nervous chuckle, "this is *not* what we expected to hear from Mr. Halloran. Uh, Mr. Halloran, this isn't what you *told* us when we, uh, agreed to interview you. You said that the Mormon Church was trying to suppress evidence of a *murder*."

"Yes," Halloran eventually replies, unfazed, "the she-demon murdered an angel of God, and the Church is covering it up."

"Uh, yeah . . . but you said that the footage was supplied *by* the Mormon Church to the authorities."

"Yes," Halloran replies, "they did turn it over to the police, but they have resisted letting this go public. They don't want people to know that demons exist. They're on the *wrong side* of this war."

"War?" the announcer says. "What war is that?"

After the delay, "The war between Heaven and Hell. The Brotherhood of Tobias is asking the public to help us identify the she-demon. We believe she lives in the Salt Lake City area. And there are others like her gathering here. You can't see it in the video, but she has red hair."

Nae! How would he know that?

"Anyone with any information that could help us identify her," Halloran continues, "please go to our website, www.theywalktheearth.org or call . . ."

"Just a minute, Mr. Halloran," the news anchor says quickly. The image of Halloran and the footage of the battle are abruptly replaced by the face of the newsman. He looks upset. "You may not use this program to promote your organization. You came to us under false pretenses, it seems."

"Dr. Morgan, are you OK?" 'Tis Alicia's voice. She's looking back at me. "You look pale. Are you all right?"

I must be a sight! I try to compose myself quickly and say, "What's that, lassie?"

"Are you OK?" she repeats.

They're all three looking at me now.

"Ach! I'm grand!" I say, waving dismissively.

"We didn't mean anything by it," she says. "We were just kidding around, you know?"

"Yeah," Eric says. "The woman on the news *does* look a little bit like you . . . and that bit about the *red hair* . . . but, you know, it's just a fake video."

"Yeah," Alicia says, "comic-book stuff. Nobody can *fly* like that."

Eric stands up and turns off the TV.

"Hey!" John cries. "I was *watching* that!"

"Sorry, doctor," Eric replies and turns the set back on.

". . . and we'll also look into this Brotherhood of Tobias or whatever he called it," the newsman says. "We'll bring you more on this as it develops. Now back to 'Your World with . . .'"

"Never mind," John says irritably, and he stands and turns the set off himself. "Story's over and so's my break." He turns and starts to walk past me, tossing a paper cup into the trash. He winks at me. "Catch you later, Super-Woman. Your secret's safe with us! But you might want to start wearing glasses or something to complete your disguise." He shakes his head and chuckles to himself. Then he stops abruptly and slaps his thigh. "Or maybe a *wig* to cover that *red hair*." He chuckles again and walks out of the break room, saying, "It's a bird! It's a plane! No, it's Moira! The Redheaded She-Devil!" His laughter lingers in the hall outside.

Eric and Alicia each try to stifle laughs of their own.

Then Alicia giggles, and Eric guffaws.

They smile in my direction and leave the room chuckling.

I'm glad they are nae taking this seriously . . . yet.

But that doesn't mean that everyone *will treat this as lightly as they are.*

'Tis bad enough that Lilith and her minions are searching for us. Now there's this band of mortals, this Brotherhood of Tobias, looking for me.

And that was my face on national TV!

Chapter 3

Carl

I swear fealty to you, Carl Morgan, the Unwilling. So help me God. I will serve you in His name. My life and my sword are yours to command." The voice is crisp, properly British.

I hate this part! I understand why this is necessary, but I just hate it!

The man kneeling at my feet looks up expectantly as he holds his sword, the blade resting on his open palms, presenting the weapon to me. *Maybe he expects me to draw my own sword or take his and tap each of his shoulders with it.* Brown-haired, gray-eyed, somewhat slight of build, Andrew looks to be in his mid-twenties. In actuality, he's three times that age.

At least, that's his story.

"I promise you, Andrew," I say, "that I'll do my best to lead you." I feel the dread weight of command on my shoulders like the world on the back of Atlas. There are seventy-one of us now. Three new recruits tonight. *And the newcomers always seem to expect a speech from me.* "But, in the end," I continue, "all I can guarantee you is, even if we win, we're all going to die. It's one heck of a choice: slavery, death, and damnation . . . or victory, death, and the *hope* of redemption."

"That's enough for me," he says and gets to his feet.

"It'll have to be," I say. I extend my hand and shake his. He's got a firm handshake. I like him instantly. It's stupid to base my impression of any man or vampire on his handshake, but it's like a gut check for me. And I know it's no more reliable than our "wings" test used to be. He could be working for Lilith for all I know, infiltrating the Stake, as Martha did.

Poor, pathetic Martha . . . seduced and corrupted at such a young age.

Like Ben.

I look around the huge Brigham Young University lecture hall. Andrew is the first of our new members to swear the oath tonight.

Two of our scouts brought them in. These three surrendered to them and asked to join us. The new arrivals don't know what to *call* us, of course. They just asked to join the Penitents here in Utah. Or they came seeking the

"Breakers." (That'd be Moira and me, since we "broke" Lilith's power by disbanding and destroying a Cult.) Our scouts, Georg and Dorothea, applied the "wings" test to the newcomers. We know it's not a foolproof test, but, so far, no *Penitent* has failed it. So, it's a preliminary filter at best.

Müller was able to fly winglessly, and he turned out to be one of Lilith's Enforcers, one of her twelve disciples. So did Isaiah Bartlett, but he was under orders from Müller to do anything necessary to convince us he was a Penitent. Because he was ordered to prove himself to us, he was able to "pass" the "wings" test.

After accepting the surrender of the newcomers, Georg and Dorothea took possession of the weapons of the new arrivals (swords for each of them) and blindfolded and hooded them before bringing them to our nightly meeting at BYU. *We have no way to keep hostile vampires prisoner. If they surrender, we'll test them and give them a chance to swear the oath and free themselves of Lilith's control. If not . . .*

Two more recruits are waiting, a man and a woman. Georg and Dorothea stand behind them with drawn swords. These three wouldn't be the first to attempt to infiltrate us (like Martha), so we have to be cautious.

The woman identifies herself as Yasmina, a pretty, twentyish-looking vampire of Middle-Eastern descent. She's well over a century in actual age, and she's been a Penitent for most of that . . . or so she says. The man is one of the *oldest-looking* vampires I've ever met. His name's Sergei. He has rugged features and a strong Russian accent. He appears to be in his forties. By contrast, he's been a vampire for only a decade or so. His *repentance* began less than two years ago.

Of course, those're the stories they've given us. And we have no idea if the stories are true. Until the newcomers swear the oath and are tested, we can't be sure if they're sincere . . . or if they're agents of Lilith.

Andrew gasps. "It's gone!" he cries.

Is he saying what I think *he's saying, what I* hope *he's saying?*

"What's gone, laddie?" Moira asks, her eyes glancing at me.

She's thinking the same thing I am.

"The Call!" Andrew says in wonder and obvious *delight.* A smile spreads across his face. It's a *glorious* smile of unexpected relief.

He's a Master!

I'm not positive how that works. Is he *still* a Master now that he has taken the oath? *I* was a Master briefly . . . from the moment I slew Michael right up to the moment I dissolved the Cult.

And Ben was murdered seconds after that.

If Andrew's still a Master, even after his oath to me, that could be very useful.

I really, really despise *how I'm thinking of people as weapons or tools. But, we're at war. And in this war, I have to use every asset God sends my way. I've been hoping we'd get a Master ever since we . . . lost Ghalyela.*

There's something I want to try.

"You're a Master?" I ask.

"Yes," he says, "I was. I abandoned my Cult years ago. Ever since then, I've felt Lilith's Call, but she hasn't ordered me to return to her. If she did, I wouldn't be able to resist. Lately, it's . . . the Call's been growing stronger." He chuckles. "Now it's *gone!*"

This seems like the perfect opportunity to try out my new "weapon." *If this even works.* This is virgin territory we're exploring.

I've discussed my idea only with Moira. I look over at her and incline my head slightly in Andrew's direction. She nods. She knows what I'm about to do. She draws her black sword and comes to stand at my side.

I point at the two newcomers, Yasmina and Sergei, and say, "Wait just a minute, you two. If you'll pardon me, I'm going to ask you to wait a bit longer. Are either of you Masters?"

They shake their heads.

I put a hand on Andrew's shoulder. "Andrew, would you come with me, please? I have an assignment for you."

I turn my back on him and start to walk toward the door of the lecture hall. It'd be safer to make him go ahead of me, but Moira's following behind us. She's got my six, so to speak. I catch Tony Lupescu's eye as I go. He's standing over by the whiteboard with Sam Gallagher, the other mortal in the room. I motion for him to join us.

Becoming a vampire means giving up your free will. The Seed compels you to obey Lilith and her Cult Masters. If you're not sworn to a specific Master, you're forced to obey any command from any Master. Masters aren't forced to obey other Masters, of course, but they're still subject to Lilith herself and to her Enforcers. During the battle at Müller's farm, we killed five of them. Moira killed Müller in the Conference Center. So that left Lilith with six Enforcers.

I imagine she's ordained replacements by now.

The oath that our Stake vampires swear, if they swear it willingly *and* sincerely, *frees them from Lilith's control entirely. It breaks their Covenant with her. But the Seed enforces the* new *covenant they make with God: to obey* me. *I hate* that. *I hate having people* forced *to follow* my *commands. I know they accept that condition of their own free will, but I wish . . . I wish there were some other way.*

Once I reach the closed lecture hall door, I turn around. I can hear the breathing and the heartbeats of the guards posted outside.

Andrew halts. Moira stands behind him, her sword pointed at his heart. Tony catches up to us and says, "What's up, Carl?"

"Tony," I say, "lend me that notebook and pen you're always using to take notes."

"Sure." He hands me the requested items.

I flip the notebook to a clean page and begin to write. While doing so and keeping my eyes fixed on the page, I say nonchalantly, "Andrew, close your mouth and sneeze."

He sneezes immediately, and mucus flies from his nose.

I look up at him and smile.

Andrew looks shocked and completely flummoxed.

Of all the involuntary actions your body can force on you, a sneeze is the most difficult to fake convincingly.

There are chuckles from the rest of the Stake. They know *exactly* what just happened.

Sergei and Yasmina, the newcomers, look confused.

Moira lowers her sword.

"Welcome to the family," I say. "You just passed the test. Your oath was sincere."

"What? Because I obeyed . . . ?"

"Yep," I say. "From now on, I'll do my best to phrase everything as a *request* so you have a *choice*. In the heat of battle, I may slip up and give a direct order, but I'll try to avoid that. We need soldiers and friends, not slaves. Your oath to me, in the name of the Son of God, frees you from Lilith's control. Your Covenant with her is broken."

He smiles. "You have no idea what this means to me."

"You're right," I say. "I don't. I've never been bound to her or any other vampire. And frankly, I don't like having people bound to me."

"But you've *freed* me!"

"No, you did that yourself, with the help of God."

As far as we can determine, Lilith doesn't know who we are, Moira and I. And I'm sure she's desperate to kill the prophesied Unwilling and Penitent. She knows what we look like, but other than the fact that we're based in Utah, I don't think she knows anything else . . . not even our names. She's been sending scouting parties to find us, but none have returned. Our patrols have dispatched them all. I've been worried for a while that she might send infiltrators . . . and that we might not be able to detect them.

I show Andrew what I've written on the notepad. Being careful to phrase my words as a request and not an order, I say, "Andrew, if you would, please follow these instructions."

He reads my writing and nods.

Moira turns around and stares on the assembled Stake.

I focus on the two new recruits, Yasmina and Sergei.

Without turning around, Andrew suddenly barks, "Hop on one foot!"

In an instant, Yasmina is hopping on one foot, involuntarily obeying the command of a Master.

A fraction of a second later, Sergei begins to hop vigorously.

No member of the Stake even twitches.

In a flash, Moira is across the room and behind the Russian, her black sword gleaming at his throat. Before Sergei can react, I'm in front of him, my hand on the hilt of *his* sword and my dirk pointed at his heart.

Sergei stops hopping.

"Andrew," I say, my eyes still fixed on the Russian, "please release Yasmina."

"You can stop now," he says.

Yasmina stops hopping.

The rest of the Stake is on their feet, weapons drawn and at the ready.

"Who are you?" I say, my tone ice and steel.

"I am Sergei Ivanov Tupelev," he replies. He's a cold one. There's not even a hint of fear in his eyes.

"Don't play games with me," I say. "Master or Enforcer?"

"I'm a Penitent like you."

"I'm not a Penitent," I say. "I'm the Unwilling. So, Master or Enforcer?"

"Carl," Tony says from behind me, "what're you doing?"

"No Covenant-bound rank-and-file vampire could resist a command from a Master like Andrew. Sergei, here, already told me he's not a Master. Either he lied or he's an Enforcer. And either way, he's a spy."

Sergei's rugged face twists into a sneer. "So, no matter how I answer, you're going to execute me anyway, *nyet*?"

Sam Gallagher, standing over by the whiteboard, laughs nervously. "He's not going to kill you. Are you, Carl?"

"What choice do we have, Sammy?" Moira says, the single edge of her ebony blade pressing against the spy's neck. "We cannae let him return to Lilith and report what he's learned, laddie."

"But that'd be *murder*!" Sam protests. "You can't just *kill* him!"

"Think on it a wee bit, laddie," she replies. "He knows our faces, he knows where we meet. He knows our names. He'll lead a legion of vampires down on this place and they'll slaughter the lot of us. He'll slaughter your family and Tony's as well."

"This is war," I say. *I have to be as cold as the cockpit of a B-52 on winter alert.* "And in wartime, you execute spies."

"Or you take them *prisoner*!" Sam pleads.

"We don't have the means to detain him or the manpower to guard him," I say. "Captain Moroni did the same in the Book of Mormon."

"Yeah," Sam says, "but wasn't that for those who wouldn't take an oath of peace?" His desperation to stop us breaks my heart.

"Sammy," Moira replies, "there's nary an oath that this one'd take 'twould bind him."

"Moira!" Sam begs. "You can't just kill him!"

"She's not going to, Sam," I say. "*I* am. *I'm* the commander, and it's *my* responsibility. The rest of you have enough blood on your hands. Killing in combat is one thing. I won't have you . . ."

"I'll take your oath," Sergei says. His eyes blaze with defiance. "Would that satisfy you?"

"The oath must be taken willingly," I say, "and your repentance must be *real*. Otherwise it doesn't work." *Like Martha.*

"Oh, but my repentance *is* real," the Russian says. "I repent here and now. I renounce my Queen. And to answer your question, I'm an Enforcer. I was ordained shortly after Lilith returned from this place. I'm part of her innermost Circle, one of her chosen disciples. Think of what I could tell you."

"Do you deny you came here as an infiltrator?" I say.

"No, you're correct. I came here to spy on you, to infiltrate your ranks, but that was before I saw the effect your oath had on Andrew." The fire in his eyes hasn't dimmed one iota. He's still as defiant as ever. "I confess as much, but I'm willing to forsake my Queen, my immortality, my *sins*, if you will, to join you. I didn't think it was possible to be free of her."

Could he be telling the truth? Would the oath even work if his repentance isn't absolute?

"If ye dinnae have faith in Christ, 'twill do ye nae good to invoke in His name," Moira says, her sword never moving from his throat. "And ye are nae Penitent. Only in humility can we approach God."

"You mistake my excitement for a lack of humility. I want freedom. I just thought you were a bunch of deluded fanatics. But Andrew is *free*. If he can be freed, then so can I. Doesn't God's mercy extend to all?"

I don't see any evidence of humility in his eyes. I really don't want to kill him, but if he's able to get word back to Lilith, all the people who've placed themselves under my command . . . and the mortals and their families . . . will all die. Am I just not reading him right?

"Georg, Dorothea," I say without taking my eyes off the Enforcer, "would you please, each of you, take an arm? Don't let him move, if you would." The two scouts sheath their swords and move into position on either side of Sergei. They take his arms firmly in their hands. "Moira," I continue, "if he gives you *any* reason, don't hesitate: take his head off." *I don't have to worry about phrasing things as requests with Moira. She's free of Lilith's Covenant without the oath. We've been sealed together in the temple of God. If he makes a move, it's not an execution: it's defense.*

"OK. Tell me something I don't know," I say. My dirk's still pressing against his chest. "Tell me something useful."

"I can't," he says. "Unless your oath can release me, I can't reveal anything."

Lilith's failsafe if he's captured?

"Swear the oath," I say.

"Should I kneel?"

"You're not moving an inch, buster, until I know I can trust you . . . at least until I know you're safe."

"Very well then," he says, his eyes fixed on mine. "I swear fealty to you, Carl Morgan, the Unwilling. I will serve you in Jesus' name. My life and my sword are yours to command."

He glares at me. Nothing has changed. *I'm going to have to kill him. For all my talk of executing spies in wartime, I feel sick at the thought of actually having to . . .*

His steady, defiant gaze falters. His eyes and his mouth go wide. Tears spill down his cheeks. "I don't . . ." His voice is soft, but full of wonder. "I don't . . . I probably never did . . . Nobody could . . ." His voice falters and he starts to sob. "*Mashenka!*" he cries, a heart-wrenching cry. "*Prostee menya!*"

What's he talking about?

"Does anyone speak Russian?" That came from one of the Stake vampires. I don't know who said it.

"I do," Lorenzo Corelli says. "He said, 'Mashenka, forgive me.'"

OK. That's not what I expected. And I still don't know if the oath has bound him . . . and freed him.

He's still being held upright by Georg and Dorothea. Moira still has her sword at his throat, and I still have my dirk at his chest, but his body has gone slack. He continues to be wracked with sobs in spite of his restraints.

"Sergei," I say, "stop crying."

The response is immediate. His sobs cease. The tears stop falling.

It worked! He's with us! We have an Enforcer!

Another "weapon."

I may be sick.

I sheath my dirk. "You can release him," I say to Moira and the two scouts.

Moira puts her sword at her side, but keeps it in her hand. Georg and Dorothea let go of Sergei's arms.

He collapses to his knees.

"It's OK," I say as kindly as I can manage. "Let it out."

Released from my command, his sobs resume, shaking his whole body as he kneels on the floor. He doesn't look like a middle-aged man now so much as he looks like a lost little boy.

"Mashenka! *Prostee menya!*" he cries, his eyes toward Heaven. "*Ya nye mog ostanovuitsya sam! Prostee! Prostee!* Mashenka!"

"'Mashenka, forgive me," Lorenzo translates. "I couldn't stop myself. Forgive. Forgive. Mashenka.'"

Moira glances at me. I know what she wants to do. I nod.

She sheaths her black sword as she comes from around behind the grieving man. Then she falls to her knees and wraps her arms around him. "There, there," she coos. "'Tis all right, laddie. Ye're among friends now. Shush, now."

Sergei rests his head on her shoulder. His arms encircle her.

Nobody can give comfort like my Moira.

Lorenzo comes up beside me. I put my hand on the ancient vampire's shoulder.

"'Mashenka?'" I ask.

He shrugs. "It's a form of 'Mary.'"

"He's . . . praying to . . . the Virgin Mary?" I ask.

"No, it's a diminutive, an endearing form of the name. Most likely she's a wife, a lover, or . . ."

"My daughter," Sergei says in a broken voice. His sobs are under control now, but he's still weeping. "My little Masha. I became . . . I became what I am in order to save her. I was going to cure . . ." He pauses, his breath hitching. "She had pancreatic cancer. No cure. She was dying. My *Teacher* promised that I could cure her. But when I Awoke . . ." A huge sob shakes him. "When I Awoke . . . Mashenka . . . was my *Offering*!"

No way! How sick!

"The Teacher . . . she put a slit in my Mashenka's throat. I . . . *I couldn't stop myself!*" He sobs again. "Mashenka! My *malyenkaya*!"

"There now, laddie," Moira coos, stroking his head. "Your Mashenka's with God. We've all been where ye are. We understand. Shush now. God can help ye. Jesus can make ye whole."

He accepted Conversion so he could heal *his child . . . and then ended up* murdering *her? What would guilt like that* do *to a man? It'd break him or it'd* harden *him like flint. Could it drive a man from evil to evil until he rose . . . or sank to become an Enforcer?*

I suppose it could.

"Um, excuse me," a voice says off to my left. It's Yasmina.

I turn to look at her.

"Please, release me!" she pleads. There are tears on her cheeks as well. "Let *me* swear the oath! *I* need redemption too. Please!"

I nod to her.

She kneels and offers me her sword. It's a scimitar, a wicked-looking weapon with a deeply curving blade. Her face is upturned, gazing at me with unmistakable hope. "I swear fealty . . ."

Chapter 4

Carl

I lied to you. Forgive me." Sergei's sitting in a chair at the front of the lecture hall. I'd bet that the eyes of all the Stake are riveted on him. *He certainly has* my *attention.* His head's erect. From his posture and expression, you'd think that he looks *proud* or defiant . . . except for his eyes. They're wells of unfathomable grief. Georg and Dorothea stand on either side of him. Their swords are drawn, but my gut tells me they won't need them.

"I was Converted more than fifty years ago," Sergei continues after a moment. "I was a Master as well. I lied about that too. I killed my Master and my Teacher shortly after my Conversion because of . . . my daughter's death." He swallows hard, and his lips tremble. He clears his throat softly. "Later, I was chosen and ordained an Enforcer because, in mortality, I was a spy. I was GRU, Soviet military intelligence. My Queen . . . I mean, Lilith needed someone to oversee intelligence and infiltration operations, so I got the job. I sent many scouts, but none returned. I assume you . . . *dispatched* them all?" He looks up at me, his haunted eyes boring into mine.

This man is a mass of contradictions. I don't understand *him. On the one hand, he seems indomitable, unbending, and unashamed. On the other hand . . . I knew a woman who accidentally ran over her own toddler as she was backing up the family minivan. How do you forgive yourself for that, even if it was an accident? How much worse would it be if you drank your own daughter's blood, draining the life out of her?*

"As far as we know, we've got them all," I say.

He nods. "Yes, you got them all. At least, I can confirm that none have returned." He lowers his eyes and stares straight ahead. "I undertook this infiltration mission myself." He chuckles. "I never thought I would 'go native,' as you Americans say. Until the moment I was . . . free . . . I didn't really believe it was *possible.*"

He looks back up at me. "I had . . . buried my guilt. I haven't even *thought* about my Mashenka in decades . . . not since I was ordained a Master. My Qu . . . *Lilith* drove all thought of anyone else from my mind. She is . . ." He looks down, shudders, and then shakes his head. "No, she cannot be. No one can."

"She cannot be *what?*" I prod.

"No one can be that . . . *perfect*. She's so . . . *desirable*. She drives all thought . . . I would've done *anything* to please her . . . even *forget* my malyenkaya. But it . . . it wasn't *real*, was it?" He looks into my eyes again.

"The one time *I* saw her," I say, "she seemed to *change*. At first, she made me think of my first wife, Sharon, and then she made me think of my current wife, Moira . . . only *different*. More . . . *sensual*, less *wholesome*. Every other male who was there was affected similarly. It was like we were all seeing *objectified* versions of the women we love or *desire*."

"Sarah," Rolf says, standing near Lorenzo. "She had Sarah's . . ." He waves his hand in front of his face.

"Face," Lorenzo prompts.

Rolf nods. "She had Sarah's face."

"I *loved* her," Sergei says, nodding.

"Tell me something I don't know," I say, hastily adding, "*please.*"

"I don't know how to fulfill that *request* when I don't know what you don't know."

"What does she know about *us?*" I ask. *There's still a small, nagging doubt in my mind about him. Old habits die hard, but I don't want to give up any information a-bout what we know . . . in case it could get back to Lilith.*

"Virtually nothing . . ." he replies. "She knows you are the fulfillment of the . . ." He glances at Tony and Sam . . . at the *mortals*. "This, too?" he says in wonder. "I can talk about the Great Secret in front of *them!*"

I nod.

That's a good sign! Revealing the Great Secret to mortals is strictly forbidden by Lilith.

"She knows that you are the fulfillment of the Curse," he continues. "You and your wife are the 'Unwilling and the Penitent, joined in the House of God in the Top of the Mountains.' That *is* what 'Utah' means, is it not?"

Moira nods.

"Yes," he says, "she knows *that*. She knows your faces, the color of your eyes, your hair. She knows that *you're* American." He nods slightly at me. "And she knows that *you're* Scottish." He nods at Moira. "She knows that you dissolved a Cult, that you broke her power. She doesn't know *how*. She knows you are somehow an unwilling vampire. Again, she doesn't know how. She knows you are here in Utah. She knows you're connected with a college or university . . . most likely a university . . . the University of Utah or more like-ly Brigham Young University."

That makes my blood run cold. *That's too close.*

"You have a scholar among your ranks, a mortal, who speaks Hebrew, Egyptian, Latin, Greek, etc. His name is Tony or Anthony." He looks at

Tony. "That would be *you*."

Tony's as white as a sheet, the delicious blood drained from his face.

"Lilith thinks *you*"—he points to Tony—"are the key to *their* undoing." He gestures to me and then to Moira. "She's desperate to find you, Tony. She wants to capture your family. Yes," he says, looking at Tony's stricken expression, "she knows you have a family. You have a wife, Kathleen, and two children, Abigail or Abby and Little Tony. Their ages are uncertain, but the assumption is they are quite young. If I failed to infiltrate this band of Renegades, I was to locate *you* and Persuade you to join our . . . *her* cause."

"My family . . . Are they in danger?" Tony says. He's trembling.

"Yes," Sergei replies, "but not immediately, I would think. *I* was charged with locating you. What I have told you is, I believe, all that my former Queen knows."

"It's enough," I say. "Too much for my comfort. Tony, I want you to get your family of Utah." Sam Gallagher is now holding Tony up. I don't think Tony's legs can support him. "Tonight."

He nods weakly.

"I'd advise against that," the Russian says. "Once she has your identity, she can track your every move through bank cards, the GPS in your car, your cell phone. If you leave the country, your passport will give you away. She has eyes and ears everywhere. No, it would be better if you stayed here where you can be protected . . . at least at night. I would see about getting protection during the day."

"Protection during the day? Against whom?" Moira asks.

"Lilith has many mortal pawns," Sergei answers. "She has thralls or unwitting dupes in every major government. She has seventy-nine of your senators, more than one hundred of the congressmen in your House of Representatives, agents in your White House, advisors to your president, three of your Supreme Court justices, several generals and admirals (her daytime bodyguards are drawn from your U.S. Marines Corps), highly placed directors of your CIA, FBI, ATF, and IRS. She has her tentacles wrapped around presidents of labor unions, banks, investment firms, and other major multinational corporations. She has agents in the Vatican, the UN, the Hague, the Kremlin, Beijing, London, Paris, Sidney, Tehran, Jerusalem, Pyong-Yang, Baghdad (at least before Saddam fell), Kiev, Tokyo, Brussels . . . Need I go on?"

I'm stunned. Her reach . . . It's staggering!

"What . . . does she have here in Utah?" I ask.

"Surprisingly little," he says, "and she doesn't have time to cultivate and grow a proper network here. She hasn't bothered with state governments, except for a few governors here and there. *Local* governments are more the purview of the local Master and his or her Cult, but there's no Cult in Utah. *You* saw to that. She's managed to get some FBI and IRS assets diverted here to search for you, but that's a recent effort, and it hasn't borne fruit so far, at least not that I know of. They're not the most efficient of investigators."

"How does she know so much about Tony?" Lorenzo says. He's now standing with Sam, and together they're keeping watch over Lorenzo's great-great-grandson. Tony's sitting in a chair between the two of them now.

Sergei shakes his head. "That I don't know. It wasn't in my area of responsibility. I suspect she has a source either in your organization or close to it."

"A source, ye say?" Moira asks. "D'ye mean a *spy*? A *traitor*?"

Like Martha.

The Russian shakes his head again.

"From the *level* of information she has," I say, "I wouldn't think so. If she had a spy, willing or unwilling, her information would be much more *complete*. We talked pretty freely in our staff meetings. No, it's more likely just bits and pieces she's gathering, probably via electronic chatter."

I turn to the assembled Stake. "I cannot stress this enough, people: *please* watch what you say on cell phones, text messages, and emails. If you're posting on a blog or Facebook or some other website, *please* stop. Even *little* details can be assembled into a larger picture like pieces in a jigsaw puzzle. You don't need every piece in place to be able to discern what the larger picture is. I don't know who this 'source' is, but it could be *any* of us. Folks, I was an OpSec officer in the Air Force for a while. That stands for 'Operational Security.' Collecting tiny bits of seemingly innocent information casually spoken or written is one of the most vital ways an enemy has of gathering harmful intelligence."

Sergei nods. "As you Yankees used to say in the Great Patriotic War, 'Loose lips sink ships.'"

"The Great Patriotic War" is what the Soviets used to call World War II.

"Tell me about her forces," I say and quickly add, *"please."*

Sergei laughs bitterly. "You may *command* me," he says. "Now that my eyes are *opened*, I will serve you willingly, with no regrets. After what happened to my Mashenka . . . after what I did . . . This . . . *plague* must cease." He swallows hard and briefly looks like he might be sick, but that passes. "Her forces? Around the world? There are, I would estimate, roughly two thousand vampires. But, *with* her, that she could muster in a hurry? It varies, but I would say less than two hundred. However, she could Call all her Masters and have everyone there, all two thousand or so in a matter of weeks. She could have her Masters Convert all of their Chosen, and that would swell her numbers greatly. But she couldn't *Feed* that big an army. There isn't enough blood in the whole farm to Feed that many. And she keeps only a few dozen immortals in her immediate presence now that she's gone into hiding. She wants you dead, but that isn't going to be done with sheer numbers. She thinks, if she tried a frontal assault, the two of you, the *impor-*

tant ones, would just go to ground as *she* has."

That isn't *what we'd do, not turn tail and run. We're not trying to ensure our own survival at all costs. We wouldn't just* abandon *our people.*

"Do you know *where* she's hiding?" I ask.

"I know where she *was* hiding, but she won't be there anymore. With her link to me *broken . . .*"

"She can *feel* it?" I ask.

"Immediately. She'll assume I'm either dead or captured. We didn't know *how* you were able to break her control over her Children, but she's seen e-nough evidence to know that you *have* done it. She's frantic, *obsessed* with finding you . . . and *killing* you."

No surprise there.

"So," I say, "she'd know you might be cooperating with us?"

"Not *cooperating*," he replies. "*Never* that. She has always thought her pow-er was absolute. She has assumed that you were *forcibly* enslaving her Children somehow. It never occurred to her . . . or to *any* of us that it could be *voluntary*. It means death for all of us if you succeed. And, after all, why would anybody want that?"

"Why would *ye*?" Moira asks. "Ye don't seem to be particularly . . . *devout*, if ye'll pardon me for sayin' so."

"And I never have been *devout*." He looks back at me. "Religion was frowned upon in my country. I believed in the power of the state and the righteousness of communism, socialism, and my revolutionary principles.

"But," he continues, "you spoke of the power of God. I didn't believe that could be all there was to it. I've *seen* the power of Lilith. She commands Lucifer himself. But, you . . . you talked about the power of Jesus, and Andrew swore an oath and he was *free*. He was bound to *you*, but the worst you made him do was *sneeze*. You fumble all over yourself trying to keep from *commanding* anyone. You're a Child of Lilith, and yet you aren't seeking to dominate or corrupt . . . or *murder*. If that's what it means to serve *God*, and it means that no more innocents like my Masha will be murdered, that no more desperate parents like me will sell their souls . . . *That* I would *die* for. Not for my sake . . . there can be no redemption for *me* . . . but, I would die for *them*."

"Ach, ye cannae leave it there, laddie!" Moira cries. "Ye *can* be saved. Ye must *humble* yerself, aye, but Jesus *can* save ye. Ye *can* find redemption, if nae in this world, in the world to come! I can *promise* ye that."

"How could it be possible?" he chokes. "I *murdered* my Mashenka!"

"*All* of us," Lorenzo says, "save Carl and the mortals, have murdered. *All* of us are worthy of damnation many times over. There's no question. But we've all thrown ourselves on the mercy of the Lord. He *will* redeem us. I bear *testimony* of that, as the Mormons say."

"Mormons?" Sergei looks shocked. "What is 'the Mormons?'"

"Some spymaster you are," I say. "You're trying to run espionage operations in Utah, and you don't know who the Mormons are?'"

"You mean the *religion* out here?" He looks utterly astonished. *"That's* what she's been ranting about?"

OK. Now I'm *confused.*

"Yeah," I say, "the *religion* out here. Moira and I and the mortals here . . . we're Mormons. What do you mean, 'She's been ranting?'"

"For weeks now," he replies, and he looks as if some profound understanding is dawning on him, "on occasion, she's been ranting, hysterical. And that *never* happens. She's been spending *hours* on her computer, researching something . . . and *that* never happens. (She has people to do such things for her.) Then, after hours spent researching, she starts screaming, destroying things, lashing out at Children around her, screaming in the First Tongue. Nobody knows what she's saying. She's the only one alive who speaks it."

Out of the corner of my eye, I notice Tony perk up. Something Sergei said has gotten his attention. I glance quickly at him. The color has returned to his face. His eyes look . . . *eager.*

"But," Sergei continues, "one of the words I *have* caught over and over is *that* word, 'Mormon' . . . that . . . and, of course, 'Adam.' She *hates* him. And he's been dead for five thousand years. I know he pronounced the Curse, but I never understood her *hatred* for him."

"She tried to *seduce* him," Tony says. His voice is weak, but, as I look at him, there's a fire in his eyes, as when he's teaching. *And he* loves *teaching.*

"What are you talking about?" Lorenzo asks.

"The rabbis have it all wrong, you see," Tony says. "Lilith is, in Jewish folklore, supposed to have been Adam's *first* wife, or second, depending on the version of the story. She was *before* Eve. Supposedly, she was created of the same earth as Adam and considered herself his equal. As the story goes, she refused to be subservient to him and left him. Then she mated with the Archangel Samael and gave birth to all the demons in the world. That's the legend. But we know it's all fantasy made up by rabbis in the Middle Ages, probably to justify certain attitudes toward women."

He stands up now, waving off Sam and Lorenzo. He's a little shaky, but he's rubbing his hands together the way he does when he's "warming to his subject."

"In reality," he continues, "she was Adam's *granddaughter,* the daughter of Cain *before* God cursed him. After she made her own Covenant with Lucifer, she tried to seduce her grandfather, Adam. And she *failed.* My guess is it was a *spectacular* and *humiliating* failure. That's the *only* time she's failed in a sexual conquest, I'll bet. And it was *before* the Prophecy or Curse was uttered by Adam. That's why she hates him so vehemently."

"How would you know . . . Where did you get this information?" Lorenzo asks. He's staring at Tony in wonder. "I've never heard the part about a botched seduction."

"It's . . . um . . . it's a th-th-th . . ." Tony clears his throat. "It's a *theory* I've been working on." Now he's blushing appetizingly. *I can hear some of the others salivating.* This isn't like Tony. I don't think I've ever heard him *stutter* before.

He has been through a shock, with the revelation that the enemy knows so much about him and his family. I know it'd unnerve me if the enemy were to discover who Moira is.

"Discuss this with me after the meeting, if you please," Lorenzo says.

"S-sure," Tony says as he sits back down. He looks pale again.

"Lorenzo," I say, "*please* see that the guards for the Lupescus and the Gallaghers are doubled at night. And do the same with the mortal body-guards for daytime." *Darn it! I forgot to phrase it as a request!* "I meant, *please* do the same with the bodyguards."

"Consider it done," he says with a grim nod.

"You have *bodyguards* for us in daylight?" Sam asks, obviously astounded. He looks a bit shaken himself now. "I mean, I *knew* about the vampires guarding us at night . . ."

"We didn't want to alarm you," Lorenzo says. "They've been trying to stay out of sight . . . incognito, as it were. They'll have to be more obvious now."

"Those two guys . . . the ones that look like jarheads out of uniform . . . the ones who've been auditing my classes lately?" Sam asks.

"Yes," Lorenzo replies. "Carl and Moira hired a security firm to watch over you during the day."

"They were supposed to be discrete," I mutter.

"Cool!" Sam's face splits in a grin.

Sam Gallagher is the biggest, most lovable geek I've ever known. He thought it was 'cool' when he found out that Moira, his old Primary teacher, was a vampire.

"And I'll be able to get more samples for my research!" he says eagerly.

He looks absolutely ecstatic. Sam's been experimenting with vampire blood and tissue samples to learn more about the Seed and vampire biology. He was supposed to be pre-senting some of his findings tonight, but we got interrupted when Georg and Dorothea brought in our latest additions.

"Speaking of your research," I say, "and since you mortals require *some* sleep and time with your families, why don't you present your findings right now."

"Cool!" says Sam.

A total geek. You can't help but love this guy!

"Laddie?" Moira says, interrupting.

"What?" I say.

"Could we nae hear Tony's research on the Brotherhood?"

Crap! Of course, that'd be foremost in her mind!

"Oh, sweetheart!" I say. "I'm sorry! I completely *spaced* it with all the . . . *uproar* over Sergei."

"Dinnae worry yerself about it, laddie. There's nae harm done." She smiles at me.

How I love her smile!

"Tony," I say, "do you feel up to it?" He looks completely distracted.

"The Brotherhood?" he says, looking confused. Then his eyes go wide, and he seems to lock in on what I was saying. "Of course!"

He gets to his feet again.

"As far as I've been able to determine," he says, sounding stronger, but less sure of himself than before (when he was talking about Lilith), "the Brotherhood has been around for less than six months. On their website, they *claim* to be more than two thousand years old, but there's no record of them prior to the last several months, at least nothing which bears up under even *cursory* scrutiny. Their website is certainly no older than six months and it's hosted in Salt Lake. I happen to know someone in the website provider's office. You'd think that, in this day and age, an *ancient* organization, as they claim to be, would've had a web presence for longer than a handful of months. They claim to have several thousand members worldwide. Their website, however, received very little traffic until the news story today. Now it's been swamped. The hits shut down their servers for a bit. Most of the traffic has been from visitors posting *tips*, 'sightings' of the 'she-demon.'" He looks at Moira and grimaces. "Sorry, Moira."

She nods, her expression tense.

"Russell Halloran's story checks out," Tony continues, "at least as far as I can tell, and I have a friend in Church Security. He was able to verify *how* Halloran obtained the video, etc. *He*, my friend that is, wouldn't comment on the footage, of course, but he verified that such footage, if it existed, *would* have been provided to the police. But, well, I just can't find any evidence that there was a 'Brotherhood of Tobias' prior to six months ago. Halloran's probably a member of the Brotherhood, but he's not the owner of the web . . ."

"The 'Brotherhood of Tobias'?" Sergei interrupts. "I know of this 'brotherhood.'"

All eyes are back on the Russian now.

He snorts derisively. "It's no 'ancient order,' he says. "As you say, it's only half a year old."

"How do you know?" Tony says.

Sergei blinks. "Because I *created* it."

Chapter 5

Moira

Ye created it?" I say.

"Yes. It was a brilliant plan, if I do say so myself," the former Enforcer replies. "We knew that you Breakers and your Renegades were active in this area. Gunther Müller had his plan, and I had mine. He came here and set up his 'church' to try to smoke you out from among the Children gathering here."

He waves a hand dismissively. "*I* decided to use mortals. Think of it: hundreds of eyes and ears searching for you." His own eyes are gleaming. "Maybe one of our recruits might actually *recognize* you. So, I created a website, a back story for a nonexistent 'ancient brotherhood,' complete with an extrabiblical reference to an old tale of demon fighting, a toll-free number, and . . . *Voila!* Instant network of mortal watchdogs searching for a redheaded 'she-demon!' Crazies and useful idiots came out of the woodwork. In a matter of two weeks, I had a couple hundred spies joining up, eagerly sending me tips. Most of the recruits were complete morons, like cattle on the farm. Most of the tips were useless, but the video of you fighting Gunther was very promising. Today alone, the final status report I received after sunset listed another forty-seven applications for membership. You made the national news."

"I know," I say, trying hard and failing to keep the gall out of my voice.

Carl's nodding. This makes perfect sense to him, I'd wager. And, I do have to admit, 'twas an *effective* plan . . . *diabolical*, aye, but effective.

"Can you call them off?" my husband asks.

I feel a desperate surge of hope. But the Russian shrugs his shoulders, and that hope fades.

Sergei's expression is doubtful. "I can *try*. Lilith will know that I'm *compromised* or dead, but I doubt very much that her people have contacted the mortal head of the Brotherhood. (He's also the webmaster.) I might be able to get the website taken down, but *nothing* will stop these pawns from continuing their work. They're a very *suspicious* bunch."

"Conspiracy theorists," Carl says.

"Fanatics," Sergei agrees, nodding. "If anything, this would probably convince them that the 'demons' are behind the disbanding of the group and the removal of the website."

"Why nae tell them the truth?" I ask.

"What?" Carl says, turning to look at me.

Sergei echoes the question.

"Ye have a small army of fanatics that're on the lookout for demons," I say. "Right now they're looking for Carl and me . . . mostly for me. Why d'ye nae tell them, *use* their fanaticism, to have them look for the *real* demons. Have them be on the lookout for flying demons with *wings*. Have them watch the skies at night and report any sightings to *us*. Tell them that the *protectors*, the ones guarding the city, are the ones *without* wings."

Carl blinks at me, and I can see the thought taking hold. But, 'tis Sergei that takes it to heart.

"That might work," he says, nodding vigorously. "If I can turn them *before* . . ." he hesitates as if searching for the right word, "the *enemy* does, we might be able to use them to our advantage. At the very least, they wouldn't be *united* in working against us. Even the confusion might buy us some time."

He turns his face back to Carl. "With your permission, my Lord, I'll . . ."

"Don't call me that!" Carl snaps. Then he shakes his head and clenches his fists in annoyance. "I mean, *please* don't call me that. We have no Lord but Jesus. I'm your *leader*, maybe, your *captain*, for lack of a better word, but *never* your lord. *Please* just call me Carl."

"Yes, sir," the Russian says with a curt nod. "My captain, with your permission, I'll call the head of the Brotherhood and have him take down the video . . ."

"That won't do much good," Sam says. "It's already gone viral."

I cannae suppress a groan of frustration.

"Nevertheless," Sergei continues, "it will be a sign that the Brotherhood has espoused the 'course correction' I'm about to give them. I'll tell them that the Brotherhood has been *subverted* by the demons for their own nefarious purposes. I'll tell them that the *real* demons, as you said, are the ones with *wings*. I'll make sure they report only to me and to *one other*. I'll need a backup, someone to take over if I am killed or . . . if I fall in *other* ways. This . . . change is rather sudden for me. None of the old urges and temptations of just half an hour ago have . . . gone away. It will be . . . a struggle. I haven't restrained even my slightest urge for decades. And I have been a very *evil* man."

"Trust in God," Carl says. "You can do it."

"That's just it," the Russian replies. "I haven't trusted in God my whole life. I don't know how."

"We'll work on it . . . together," Carl says. "But right now I need you to seize control of this network of mortals." He turns to the assembled Stake and looks about for someone in particular. Apparently spying the one he's lookin' for, he says, "In-Tae, will you please take the assignment to be Sergei's backup with the Brotherhood and his senior companion?"

A Korean vampire with boyish features stands and says, "Yes." He starts down the aisle toward us.

"What is a 'senior companion'?" Sergei asks Carl.

"It's a Mormon term," Carl says with a slightly sheepish grin. "It means he'll be your mentor, your trainer, and your *shadow*. Every new member gets one. He'll be with you constantly until you're ready to help someone else . . . to be *their* senior companion." Carl leans in and whispers so softly that even *I* can barely hear him, "He'll also be there to strengthen you when those urges become too much to handle."

To Georg and Dorothea he says, "You two, go with them and find a room where he can call the Brotherhood without the background noise in here. We'll fill you in later." His face twists in a grimace. "I mean, *please* go with them and find a room."

In-Tae, as he passes the table at the front of the room, nods at Lorenzo. The Korean makes a clapping motion and then holds his hands slightly apart as if he's ready to catch a ball, all the while nae breaking stride as he walks toward us. Lorenzo reaches into a box under the table and pulls out a small blue book with gold lettering. He tosses it to In-Tae, who catches it deftly just before he stops next to us. The Korean bows slightly to Sergei and offers his right hand (the one *nae* holding the book) to the Russian. "I am Kim In-Tae," he says in his lightly accented baritone voice.

Sergei takes his hand and shakes it. In-Tae uses that hand to pull Sergei to his feet. He then presents the book to the Russian with the other hand.

"What's this?" the erstwhile Enforcer says, eying the title of the book with curiosity.

"Trust me," In-Tae says. "You're going to need it. It saved my life. Not so long ago, I was a Penitent without hope. I was going to end my life, as so many of our kind do, but I found a copy of this book in a bus station in Seoul. I read it. It gave me hope. It prompted me to come here. It's called the Book of Mormon."

"Sam," Carl says to Sammy, my long-ago Primary bairn, "you're up."

Sammy rises to his feet eagerly and goes to the whiteboard. He uncaps a marker and begins to scribble on the board.

Still facing away from us, he says, "The general consensus is that a vampire can survive on as little as a quart of human blood per week. One quart! And that's even with the amount of activity you do, especially flying or other superhuman feats, such as Healing and projecting your dark shadows. Healing! Don't get me started on that! We're talking about cells dividing and regenerating at incredible speeds! That takes an *enormous* amount of energy!

All of this leads me to conclude that a vampire utilizes energy at a varying rate commensurate with the level of physical, psychic, or regenerative activity." He finishes writing on the board by vigorously underlining the number 682.8.

He turns around and beams his eager smile. He reminds me so much of the wee laddie I taught years ago. "A mortal utilizes between fifteen hundred and twenty-four hundred calories per day, depending on sex, weight, and level of physical activity," he continues. "A quart of human blood contains only about six hundred and eighty calories." He points with his marker at the underlined number. "Thus a quart of human blood doesn't contain enough calories to account for even one day's worth of *normal* activity, much less *vampiric* activity. Scientifically, it makes no sense!"

"Wha' part of the word 'vampire' don't you understand?" Collin, a blonde vampire at the back of the room says in his strong Cockney accent. From what I recall, he's a very young lad, in vampiric terms, having Converted less than a decade ago. "Hello-o! It's called *supernatural* for a reason!"

"That's just my point," Sammy says. "You're only getting a fraction of your energy from the blood you consume. And, even if you consume several times that amount, you don't gain any weight, unless you haven't Fed in a long time, and, even then, you only return to your *normal* weight and *no more*. So the *amount* of blood isn't the most significant factor: it only appears to be important that you consume a *minimum* amount, perhaps as a *catalyst* of some sort. And since you can't consume any *other* form of food, that means the energy has to come from some *other* source!"

"And what would that be, laddie?" I ask.

"I have no idea!" he exclaims and chuckles. "It can't be the Sun, *obviously*, which is the ultimate source of most bioenergy on earth. You don't seem to absorb heat from the ambient air. Cosmic radiation can't be a significant source of energy. I don't know *where* it comes from!"

What's he so giddy about?

"It's a mystery!" he cries. "It's a puzzle, and I'll just have to keep digging!" He shrugs and says, "I'm going to need more samples, folks."

There are a few groans from around the room, but most members of the Stake nod.

"On the bright side," Sammy continues, "I've gathered some hard data on the Seed. It seems to survive for about one hundred seconds or so outside the vampiric host. In your bodies, it is amazingly resilient, but once it's cut off, such as when it's conducted by your saliva into a mortal, it reproduces at a *fantastic* rate, spreading throughout the mortal host, but then it just . . . dies."

"That's the Essence," Tony interrupts. "Once it's cut off from the Essence, it dies."

"Precisely!" Sammy exclaims.

"Could the unexplained energy come from the Essence?" Tony asks. "I mean, if the blood is only a catalyst, as you theorize, could the *energy* actually be coming from the Essence? Could the demonic component of vampirism be . . . I don't know . . . *channeling* the energy from somewhere?"

My cell phone vibrates, taking my attention away from what looks to be shaping up as a lively discussion. 'Tis the ER desk at the hospital. *Why would they be contacting at this hour? I'm nae on-call tonight. And the desk would nae be contacting me after my shift.*

Visions of a bus or train accident with massive casualties run through my head as I step over to a corner of the room. I flip open the phone and answer, "This is Dr. Morgan," while turning the volume down to almost nil. *Hospital business is nae for the ears of the entire Stake.*

"Dr. Morgan!" It sounds like Angie, one of the ER nurses, and she sounds hysterical. "Thank heaven! There's a man here. He's got a *gun*! He's taken *hostages*! He says he wants to talk to *you*! Dr. Morgan, what do I do?"

"Have ye called nine-one-one, lassie?" I say, trying to keep my voice even. *The gunman's asking for me? What would he be wanting with me?*

"Yes! The police are on their way!"

"Calm down, Angie," I say, though I'm far from calm myself. "I'll be right there."

I snap the phone closed and then motion to Carl to join me quickly. He hurries to my side and whispers, "What's up?"

"Trouble at the hospital. I have to go. Now."

"I'll come with you."

"Nae, ye're needed here. Just alert the patrols that I'll be flying." *I dinnae want to alarm him . . . or have the patrols chasing after me.*

"Nobody goes alone, not at night," he says. "I'll send Lorenzo and Rolf."

"Tell them to catch up if they can."

And with that, I run for the door.

◊ ◊ ◊

Lorenzo and Rolf dinnae ever quite catch up. I glance back a few times as I fly as fast as I can go through the night sky. I catch a glimpse of them, trailing a few miles behind me. There's a dense cloud cover tonight and nae Moon to cast a glow.

The wind screams past my ears like a banshee. I squint to keep the gale out of my eyes. My hair whips behind me.

Of all the nights to wear a dress! What was I thinking, wearing a frock to a council of war? Was I just trying to look bonnie for my husband? So much for that! The wind has doomed my hair and makeup. I'll be lucky if it does nae shred my dress.

I'm flying so fast, I can scarcely breathe, and I dare go nae faster. 'Twill do naebody any good for me to arrive hypoxic. I'll need my wits about me. In all my nigh three centuries of life, I've ne'er dealt with a hostage situation.

But, if the gunman's asking for me *specifically* . . .

Why me? Did I fail to save the life of his wife or some other family member? Did I deliver a bairn that was too premature to survive? I wish I had more information!

I can see LDS Hospital in the distance. I'll be there in less than a minute. *How should I go in? Through the ER entrance? Should I try to approach the man by stealth? Would that nae put the hostages at greater hazard?* I dare nae call Angie back. She probably risked her life and the lives of the hostages by calling me.

It's nae like ye to go off half-cocked like this, lassie! What were ye thinking? And why did ye nae tell Carl?

Ach, because 'tis my hospital, and these are my patients. And I will defend them! As much as my dear husband thinks of himself as the defender of our city, this hospital is my place and these are my people. Lorenzo and Rolf'll be here shortly, so I have precious little time. If I were to approach the gunman with them in tow, it could mean the lives of the hostages. If that means putting myself in harm's way, so be it. If the only way I can save them is to surrender myself, then . . .

I'll go in by the front door.

By the time I land in the ER parking lot—and I *hope* 'twas unobserved—the police are already beginning to gather. I see three police cruisers and three officers. They're hanging back, probably cautious of approaching the gunman directly. There are also a number of people in scrubs, most of them hospital employees I know, and a number of others in street clothing, probably patients and their family members. I see Angie, huddling with other ER personnel. I'm glad she's all right. I wish I had time to stop and ask her for more information, but, if I did, it'd be that much harder to get past the police.

The parking lot is too brightly lit for me to use a cloud of darkness to avoid attention. I'll have to walk right past the police and trust to bravado or Persuasion (or both, most likely) to keep them from trying to stop me.

As I walk past the first cruiser, one of the officers cries, "Hey! Hold up, miss! You can't go in there!"

I pay him nae heed and put my left hand on the hilt of my sword.

My sword! Ach, I forgot I had it on! There's nae time or place to hide it. And with things the way they are, we're ne'er without them at night now. Usually, I carry mine to and from work in a long gym bag. But there 'tis, belted at my hip. Nothing to be done about it now.

"You with the sword!" another officer, behind me now, shouts. "Halt!"

I hear the soft sound of the safety being switched off on his side arm.

I stop in my tracks, put my hands in the air, and turn to face him. He's ten feet away from me and walking slowly in my direction. His weapon is pointed at my heart.

But, I can see his eyes clearly. *Can he see mine? Father in Heaven, let it be so!*

"'Tis all right, officer," I say, my voice clear and commanding. "I'm Dr. Morgan. I'm *needed* inside. Ye must let me pass."

Ah! There 'tis. I can feel the Persuasion take hold.

"Right," he says, lowering his weapon. "Dr. Morgan, you're needed inside."

"Are you nuts?" the first officer asks. He looks to be the oldest of the three. "She's got a sword! She could be *with* that guy!"

"Officer," I say to him, fixing him with my eyes, "ye must let me go. I'm here to help. Ye can *trust* me."

He blinks and then nods. "Go ahead, Doctor. You're here to help."

"Aw, come *on*, you guys!" the third officer, a young fellow, says, his gun fixed on me. "You can't be *serious!*"

The older officer walks over to the younger fellow. He places a fatherly hand on the lad's shoulder. "It's all right. You can *trust* her."

The younger man begins to protest, but this takes his attention off me and makes him focus on the senior officer.

That's my cue! I use the opportunity to dash through the ER doors. I hear them slide closed behind me.

The waiting room's deserted. *Of course, they'd have evacuated everyone they could. 'Tis the reason people are all milling about outside. At this point, the only people in the vicinity of the gunman would be* hostages.

I can hear voices coming from down the corridor, from behind closed doors. ". . . if you let the rest of these people go, you'll still have *me* as a hostage." I recognize the voice of Bob Carson, a dear, white-haired security guard.

The brave lad!

"Nobody's leaving! Nobody! Not till I get to see Dr. Mo-ra Morgan!"

I dinnae recognize the voice. He sounds emphatic, *intense*, but nae hysterical.

"What did Dr. Morgan *do* to you?" a frightened female voice says. I dinnae recognize it. Perhaps 'tis a patient.

I can smell the blood of several people. Nary a one of them smells particularly *evil*. I can hear the rapid heartbeats and smell the sweat and body odor of several *nervous* and *frightened* people, but there is nae the sweet corruption of evil.

'Tis very odd.

"Seriously, sir." 'Tis Bob again. "Let them go and keep me. Nobody needs to get hurt. You haven't hurt anybody so far. And I can tell you don't really want to hurt . . ."

"*Somebody's* going to get hurt real soon,"—'tis the gunman's voice—"if Dr. Mo-ra Morgan doesn't have the *courage* to show up . . . starting with *you*."

I hear several people gasp loudly. A woman screams.

I have to act now!

I push open one of the doors and say, "I'm here. Now let these people go."

In a flash, I take in the scene. There are six people sitting on the floor against one wall of the corridor, including Bob and a nurse I dinnae know by name. The rest must be patients. There's one man standing. He's wearing jeans, a polo shirt, and a baseball cap.

And he's holdin' a semiautomatic handgun, pointed at the hostages.

I cannae see his eyes.

He looks at me, and a grin spreads across his face. "*You!*" he says. "I *knew* it!" He glances down slightly. *At my sword?* He nods, and his grin widens.

"Let these people go," I repeat.

He does nae smell evil, and he does nae look daft. I notice he has a small, black, boxy-looking device in his left hand. He slowly pulls it up and presses a red button on the side.

'Tis a small video camera. He points it and the gun at me.

His grin looks to be all teeth, and he says, "Tuesday, September thirteenth, eleven fifty-seven p.m., LDS Hospital Emergency Room." His words are clear, his voice distinct, calm, and *elated*. "Behold the *demon!*"

What? Is he . . .

The first bullet hits me square in the chest.

My heart explodes.

Chapter 6

Moira

*P*ain!
Ach! It itches!
   What happened?
Cannae see!
Brain's cloudy.
Why?
Shot . . . heart.
Seed . . . reconstructing . . .

I gasp loudly as my heart begins delivering blood and oxygen to my brain again.

The itch is still *horrible.* I dinnae ken if the pain or the itch was the worst of it.

I start to sit up.

There's blood everywhere. *My* blood.

I hear screaming.

The breathing comes easier. My vision clears. The colors return.

As I get to an upright sitting position, my hand rests on something sharp. They're wee bits of metal covered in blood. My blood.

Bullet fragments.

He shot me! *That bloody lunatic shot me!*

There are five people cowering against the corridor wall. Some are screaming. They're screaming as two men struggle on the floor about five yards away from me. Bob Carson's trying desperately to wrest the gun away from the madman who shot me.

And the aged security guard is losing . . .

Patients are in danger!

In a flash, I'm on my feet. I close the distance between myself and the struggling men. Just as the madman begins to point the vile weapon at Bob's head, I reach down and snatch it from the gunman's hand. I toss the weapon down the corridor. It goes sliding along the floor and out of my sight. If I dinnae ever see the foul thing again, 'twill be just grand by me.

I wheel around and grasp the gunman under the armpits and slam him against the wall. He's half a head taller than me, but of course, I have nae trouble restraining him. For the moment, he's too stunned to fight back. He drops his video camera, and I step on it, crushing it to smithereens. Nae takin' my eyes off the lunatic, I say, "Bob, can ye walk, laddie?"

"Sh-sh-sure, Dr. Morgan," he says. I can hear him climbing to his feet.

"Get these people to safety," I say. "Leave this one to me."

"Are you . . . ?" Bob hesitates, "I saw you take one in the heart."

"Get these people out of here," I say. "I'm fine. 'Tis nae but a flesh wound. Now, go!" *Like he's really going to believe that! If I had time, I'd see if I could help him and the other hostages to forget, but their safety's my first concern.*

"Let's go, folks!" I hear him say. The others are hysterical.

"He shot her!" says one.

"She was dead!" says another. "I *saw* her!"

"You heard Dr. Morgan," Bob says. "Get moving!"

I hear them getting to their feet and starting to move. I keep my eyes fixed on my assailant's eyes. He's staring back, but I have the *feeling* that Persuasion will nae work on him. If he's of this Brotherhood of Tobias, he's most likely a fanatic . . . and a fanatic can be *very* strong of will.

One of the patients slips, probably in my blood, and screams. I can hear other footsteps coming my way. Three sets. 'Twill be the police officers.

What am I going to do? Even if Persuasion works, there's nae time!

"I'm nae demon," I say with all the Persuasion at my vampiric command. "I'm just a doctor. The *winged* ones are . . ."

"Foul demon of the Pit!" he snarls back at me.

So much for that.

He reaches for my sword.

I keep one hand at his throat and clamp the other with a grip of iron on his reaching hand.

"Touch that, laddie," I say, my voice ice, "and I'll crush your hand."

He glares back at me. There's nary a trace of fear in those intense eyes.

"Break it up!" one of the officers cries. 'Tis the young one, the one I did nae have a chance to Persuade.

I glance at him. His weapon's drawn and pointed in our direction. The other two officers are helping Bob rush the hostages to safety.

Just after they disappear through the doors at the end of the corridor, Lorenzo and Rolf slip through the doors and into the hall. Lorenzo looks at me questioningly as if to ask if I need any assistance. I give a quick shake of my head. He nods, takes hold of Rolf's arm, and the two of them withdraw.

"Break it up, I said!" The young policeman again.

I release my hold on the gunman's neck, but I keep his hand securely in mine.

"Now!" the officer commands.

I let go of the man's hand with reluctance.

"Slowly drop the weapon!" the cop commands.

He means my sword.

"Chuck!" 'Tis the older policeman. He's running back down the corridor now that the hostages are safe. "Stand down! You can trust her!"

"What is *with* you, John?" the younger officer (Chuck) cries. "She's got a flippin' sword!"

"She's a demon!" the gunman yells, and there's madness plainly written in his eyes. "A demon from Hell! She slew the angel of God!"

The older officer (John) steps between his fellow and me. This forces Officer Chuck to point his gun away from me and at the fanatic.

"What are you doing?" Officer Chuck cries.

"Stand down, Chuck!" Officer John says, also aiming his weapon at the fanatic.

"Go back to the Pit from whence you came!" the madman cries. He lunges at me.

Several things happen at once. Officer John begins to pull the trigger on his weapon. I knock the gun aside and the bullet goes into the wall. Officer Chuck fires his weapon also. With vampiric speed, I thrust my body between Chuck and the lunatic and push the madman to the ground. Chuck's bullet strikes me in the back, ripping through my lung before eruptin' out my left breast. A second bullet from Chuck's weapon shatters my right shoulder joint. A third bullet misses me entirely, impacting somewhere down the corridor.

I cannae suppress a cry of agony as I spin round to disarm Chuck, but he's already pointing his gun down and to the side.

My breathing's torturous and my right arm's useless as I turn back to the demented fool on the floor. The Seed's rapidly repairing the damage, but it'll be another second or two before I'll be able to use the arm.

And the itch is horribly distracting.

Ach! I can feel the bullet fragments in my shoulder being pushed out through the skin!

The madman's lying on the floor writhing in pain as he clutches his upper right arm. Blood, delicious and crimson, spurts between his fingers. A bullet fragment must've severed the brachial artery in his arm after it passed through me. He'll bleed out in less than a minute if I dinnae act now.

I drop to my knees, and using my good left hand, I pry his fingers away from his wound. His blood sprays into my face and into my mouth.

I can taste his blood!

Ignore it, lassie!

So sweet!

I clamp my good hand around the wound and lift the arm above his heart. My right arm is beginning to obey me now, so I bring it painfully round, clamp my right hand just under his armpit, and press my right thumb against the brachial pressure point, cutting off the flow of blood.

I need to repair the artery. If I can get enough of the Seed into his wound, 'twould do the trick.

I move my left hand further up his arm, exposing the torn flesh to my waiting mouth. I clamp my lips about the wound. 'Tis a struggle to nae bite down with my extended fangs. *I want his blood so badly!* My mouth is watering already, so there's nae worry about getting enough Seed-laden saliva into him.

The wound begins to Heal.

Gingerly, I release the pressure with my thumb. I can feel the pulse of the artery through my lips. 'Tis strong. There's nary a leak.

Mercifully, he has fainted. He needs blood badly. He lost more than a quart rapidly. He'll be in irreversible shock if I dinnae get him some blood immediately. Fortunately for him, the Seed will cause a momentary surge in the production of blood.

I can still save him.

With a great effort of will, I remove my lips from his arm and force my fangs to retract.

"Freeze!" I hear Officer Chuck's voice behind me. Undoubtedly, he has his weapon pointed at my head.

I dinnae want to end up like Rolf!

"Chuck!" Officer John cries from beside me. "I said to stand down!"

"Officer," I say with a calm I dinnae feel, "this man needs blood. He's lost a lot of it. Now I need a nurse in here and I need ye to let me get him into one of these rooms."

"Lady," Chuck says . . . and I can *smell* his fear, hear it in the slight tremor of his voice . . ."I don't know *what* you are, but I just put two slugs in you and you barely batted an eye. And I just saw you put your *mouth* on that man's wound. I . . ."

"Stand down, Chuck!" John repeats. "You can trust her!"

"Why do you keep *saying* that?" Chuck cries in exasperation. "Do you *know* her?"

"I . . . don't know," John stammers. "I just . . ."

"Officer," I say, "I just saved this man's life, but 'twill all be for naught if I dinnae get some blood into him and that right quickly. Ye stopped shooting at me, and for that ye have my thanks. But, right now, I'm going to lift this man and finish saving him. I would appreciate it if ye would refrain from shooting at me while I'm doing that. That is, unless ye think ye have nae spilled enough blood this night."

Cautiously, I scoop the erstwhile gunman into my arms and stand. The floor is slippery with gore. *Why could I nae wear* sensible *shoes tonight? If I slip and fall, Officer Chuck is likely to shoot me again. And what good would that* do *anyone?*

I turn slowly to face the young officer who has twice shot me tonight. I cannae catch his eyes. He's staring down at the man in my arms. I say, "Laddie, would ye do me the courtesy of looking me in the eye?" He looks up at me. His expression looks ... embarrassed and, aye, *guilty* of all things. I fix him with my eyes and say firmly, "Ye can trust me, laddie. Would ye please run and fetch me a nurse? Tell her I need two units of O-neg packed red cells *stat*. Can ye remember that, laddie?"

The Persuasion works.

Finally!

"'Two units of O-neg packed red cells *stat*,'" he repeats mechanically. He holsters his weapon, turns, and is startled by the sight of Lorenzo and Rolf standing right behind him. Startled or nae, he races off calling, "Nurse! Nurse!"

I hadn't noticed my two friends there before. They must've come back when they heard the shooting. Their expressions are hard to read. When they see me looking at them, they both seem to start. Then they begin glancing round, looking *everywhere* but at me. They look ... uncomfortable.

I dinnae ken what that's *about.*

To Officer John, I say, "Officer, would ye be a dearie and open the door for me?" I lift my chin and indicate the room immediately in front of us.

"Sure, doctor!" he says and slips in the blood on the floor (and very nearly falls) as he hurries to push the door open.

After a flurry of frenzied activity, I emerge from the exam room, leaving behind the patient, two nurses, one of the night docs, and Officers John and Chuck. I find Lorenzo and Rolf waiting for me. When they see me emerge, they look away from me again with embarrassed expressions on their faces.

I must look a sight! I'm covered in blood and my dress is in tatters. And I've still got my sword at my side.

Lorenzo has removed his jacket. 'Tis one of those jackets with leather patches at the elbows that some college professors seem to prefer. The temperature in the hospital would nae bother him as 'twould nae bother any of our kind. *So why does he have it off?* He coughs nervously and hands the jacket to me, still pointedly looking away.

"Thank ye, lad," I say, taking the garment from him.

"You might want to ... cover up a bit," he says. "There's a detective waiting in the lobby to take your statement. Do you want me to Persuade her so she doesn't need to?"

"'Twill nae be necessary," I say as I don the jacket. "There've been too many witnesses this night. 'Twill be difficult enough to explain what happened, at least to the satisfaction of the authorities. If I dinnae supply *some* plausible explanation, 'twould only cause others to question further what happened here."

Lorenzo glances cautiously in my direction and hurriedly looks away.

Is it the sight of the blood? Is it making him hungry?

Ach! 'Twould make nae sense! There's still blood everywhere.

Rolf also glances in my direction and then looks away.

"Moira," he says. 'Tis passing strange to hear a light Italian accent coming from Rolf. "You want to . . ." He cannae find the word he's lookin' for. He makes fists with his hands and crosses one fist below the other across his chest.

What is he doing? What's he tryin to say? Poor lad!

"Holes," he says at last. "Cover holes."

"Holes?" I say in confusion. "They're all healed, laddie."

I look down at my chest and gasp. Quickly, I grab both sides of the jacket and wrap it tightly around me. I can feel the heat rising in my cheeks.

The front of my dress is in tatters, aye! So are my underclothes! My bra! 'Tis all but obliterated in front!

'Tis nae wonder they were looking away! Poor lads!

They're both of them blushing crimson. I'd wager good money, though, 'tis nothing compared to *my* face!

I've been uncovered like this, probably since Officer Chuck shot me. The whole time I was treating and saving the life of the madman who shot me in the first place, I was . . . exposed!

I was so busy, and the smell of the blood on my chest was so distracting . . . and I could nae bear to look at it for fear I'd lose control . . .

I wish 'twere only my modesty that's compromised!

There's an awkward silence for a moment.

"My thanks, kind sirs," I say. "Ye're gentlemen, indeed."

"Maybe I should hold onto your sword for a bit while you talk to the police," Lorenzo says. "And you might want to wash some of the blood off your face."

◢ ◢ ◢

"As ye can plainly see, detective," I say, "I'm *grand*. I can promise ye that my wound is superficial. It's been seen to. And yer officers performed admirably. Nobody else was hurt save the lunatic who started the trouble, and even that deluded man should recover."

I was able to get most of the blood from my face and hands, but there's still plenty on my clothes and in my hair. I'm seated in the ER lobby, conversing with a dour-faced detective from the Salt Lake Metro Police. Other detectives are questioning the hostages. This one does nae seem to believe me.

"Well, you see, Dr. Morgan . . ." she begins.

"Call me Moira." I smile at her. "Please."

"You see, *Dr. Morgan*," she resumes without batting an eye, "I have witnesses who say they saw the suspect," she glances at her notepad again, "one Horace Holdtenschmidt, shoot you in the *chest*. They were certain that you'd been killed. The way one witness, Robert Snow, a retired police officer, put it, you"—she glances at her notepad—"'took one in the heart.'" She scowls as if she has eaten something that disagrees with her. "There's clearly a substantial amount of blood at the scene where you were apparently shot. You're covered in it. Now would you like to explain how you're covered in blood and yet claim to have no more than a 'superficial' wound? Would you please remove that jacket you're wearing so I can see for myself?"

"Am I a suspect?" I ask.

"No," she says, looking more sour and unpleasant with each word, "for now, you're a victim."

"Then I respectfully refuse," I say. "My dress was damaged in the struggle. I'll nae expose myself, if ye please." I stare into her eyes, though I doubt 'twill do any good, and say in a soft but commanding voice, "Ye dinnae need to see my dress."

She blinks, but then her expression hardens.

Ah, well.

"Our forensic team will need to take pictures of you, your wound, and your clothing," she says.

"And if I refuse?"

"I could arrest you for obstruction of justice and impeding an investigation."

"Which am I now?" I say. "A wee moment hence, ye said I was a *victim* and now ye say I'm a *criminal*. Am I to be *victimized* a second time by being forced to flash my breasts in public, detective?"

"Now, just a minute . . .," she begins.

I rise to my feet, pulling Lorenzo's jacket tighter round me. "I've given ye my statement. The madman shot me. I fell. I got up. We struggled. I disarmed him. He . . ."

"Madman, huh?" she says with a sneer. "Is that your *clinical* diagnosis, doctor?"

"Nae, lassie," I say, laboring to hold my temper at bay, "my *clinical* diagnosis is that he's a *loony*. And who would nae be with a name like Horace Holdtenschmidt? 'Twould drive *anyone* over the edge."

She actually smiles a wee bit at that one.

"He lunged for my sword," I continue, "at which point, yer officer shot him. I then worked hard to save his miserable hide so he can be locked up in the psychiatric ward until he's nae longer a danger to society. *The end.*"

She glowers at me.

"Now," I say, "if ye'll excuse me, and even if ye will nae, my husband's waiting outside for me, and I'm certain he's very worried. I intend to go home with him right now, have a long hot bath, and let him pamper me for what's left of the night."

"About that sword . . .," she says.

"'Tis mine. 'Twas a gift from a dear, departed friend. I came here directly from a meeting. And in the meetings of our little group, we carry swords. That's all I intend to say on the matter, unless ye plan to arrest me."

She stares intently at me. Her frown deepens, and then she says, "I like your spunk, doctor. If you weren't impeding my investigation, I'd . . ."

"I'm nae *impeding* yer investigation. Ye have more than enough evidence to lock that man up. Ye just want to have every detail, to solve all the wee mysteries. Well, ye must learn to live with disappointment."

She begins to open her mouth to reply, but I cut her off by saying, "I bid ye good-night, detective."

Then I turn and walk quickly toward the exit, where I can see my laddie standing with Rolf and Lorenzo.

I can hear others talking as I go.

". . . shot her in the heart!"

"She was dead!"

"Did you see her take that creep down?"

"Flipping Super-Woman, I tell you!"

"More like a guardian angel."

"She kinda looks like that woman on the news. You know, the flying woman with the sword?"

From down the corridor I hear the screams of Horace Holdtenschmidt. "The demon! She's a demon! She slew the angel of God!"

"She saved your life, man!" That's Officer John. "Will you give it a rest?"

"The demon! She walks among us!"

With that cry in my ears, I escape the ER and fall into the arms of my dear Carl.

He holds me in a crushing embrace. His breathing is ragged; his hair, wild. He says, "Don't ever do that again! Never alone, especially at night!" Then he bends his face to mine and kisses me fiercely . . . then tenderly. "Never again," he whispers.

"Aye, laddie," I say. Suddenly all the strength has gone out of my knees. "Can we go home now?" At this moment, I would nae protest if he were to lift me and carry me like a bairn in his arms.

Out of the corner of my eye, I see two people approaching us. One of them is a young woman holding a microphone. The other is an older man carrying a large, shoulder-borne television camera. The man presses a button, and a bright light on the top of the camera illuminates us.

"Dr. Morgan!" the reporter yells. "Sheila Hendricks, ABC news. Can you give us a statement? What happened in there?"

Lorenzo steps between the camera and us. Rolf positions himself right in front of the cameraman. "Go!" Rolf says. "Go now!"

Lorenzo says, "Dr. Morgan's been through enough tonight. Please respect her privacy."

Carl turns me away from the camera and puts his arm around my shoulders. We start to walk away. But where can we go? We dinnae have a car here, and we cannae fly away with so many eyes on us.

"We'll get far enough away," he whispers, "duck down between some cars, wrap ourselves in darkness, and get the heck out of here."

The news crew follows us.

"Dr. Morgan!" the reporter calls after me.

We slip behind a dark minivan and envelope ourselves in mentally projected shadows. We continue around to the back of the vehicle.

The news crew walks right past us.

After the reporter and her cameraman pass us by, Lorenzo and Rolf hurriedly join us. *There's nae way the two of them could miss us. The scent of blood is all over me.* Then the four of us shoot upward into the sky, still cloaked in blackness.

"Dr. Morgan!" I can hear the reporter's voice as we fly away. She's still looking for us in the parking lot . . . I hope. "Dr. Morgan! Are you one of the Battling Angels? Can you fly? Dr. Morgan!"

We're out of earshot, but the woman's words echo in my ears.

My life here is over.

What's worse, the enemy'll have my name shortly.

We've been exposed.

I wrap Lorenzo's jacket tighter round myself.

Chapter 7

Tony

They won't answer my calls!" Sam Gallagher sounds hysterical. This is the third time he has phoned me in the last half hour.

"Listen," I say, "I'm sure they're all right. And I'm sure they're *busy*. Lorenzo called about five minutes ago, and he said that they're moving Carl and Moira to their safe house. Then the two of them (Lorenzo and Rolf, that is) are going Hunting."

"*Hunting?*" He's practically yelling into the phone. "But they just Hunted *two days ago*! They should be good for another day at *least*!" He groans in frustration. "Did he say if they were Hunting locally or going out of the area?"

"He didn't say," I reply. "He just said they're going Hunting. But, I'd imagine that they're heading out of the area. With all the Stake activity locally, violent crime is *way* down (tonight's events notwithstanding). Most of our people've had to go out of state lately to find guilty prey. Denver or Reno. Maybe St. George or Winnemucca. At the altitudes they'll be cruising, it's unlikely they'll get cell coverage, and they're *not* going to answer the phone if they're in the act of Hunting."

"But they might not be back for *hours*!" He sounds really upset.

We've got bigger things to think about than where Lorenzo and Rolf are. Lilith knows my name! She knows the names of my wife and children! She's closing in!

"So, what's the big deal, man?" I say, trying to keep the panic out of my own voice. "Paula and Ramón are guarding your house tonight."

"That's not it," he replies. "I just need more samples."

Samples? SAMPLES? I want to scream at him! Samples? Who cares about samples?

Don't panic, Tony, old man. Keep calm. You're not going to do Kat or Abby or Little Tony any good by freaking out.

Lilith knows our names!

Focus on what Sam's saying.

I take a deep breath and say, "Didn't you get any samples tonight?"

"No, everyone was too caught up in the whole *situation* with Moira and

49

the hospital and the newcomers. I was hoping to get some from Sergei, but he's having *issues*. They've tripled the guard over the safe house and doubled the airborne patrols. I asked Paula and Ramón, but they refused. Something about being on a 'heightened state of alert.' I can usually rely on Lorenzo and Rolf for samples, though. But now they're gone . . . probably for the whole night!"

"Have you had any luck freezing the saliva?" I ask.

"No. The virus is dead when I thaw it. Fresh blood or fresh saliva is my only hope."

Hope? That's a weird choice of words.

"Did you suddenly morph into Princess Leia?" I ask, ribbing him. *Anything to take my mind off my own troubles. There's* nothing *I can do about them.*

"You know what I mean!"

Actually, I don't. "I'm just kidding you, Sam!"

"Who's guarding *your* place?" he asks.

"Noriko and . . . Oh, what's her name? Juanita! That's it! Juanita." *And I bet she heard that!* "Sorry, Juanita!" I say a bit louder. *If she heard me before, she's certain to hear that! If not, no harm, no foul.* "Once Lorenzo and Rolf return, they're going to join the others. That'll double the guard. Until then, the airborne patrols are going to back Noriko and Juanita up."

"Could you send one of them over to my place, so I could get a sample?"

"Oh, come on, Sam! You can't really expect me to leave my family unprotected."

"You'll still have three of them. I only need *one* sample."

"Listen," I say. *I can't believe he's asking this!* "With everything that's going on . . . You heard what Sergei said! They've practically found me!"

There's silence on the phone for a moment, and then he says, "OK. Sure. Of course! What was I thinking? I can't believe I asked. I'm sorry."

"Hey, no big deal."

"Yeah, sure. No big deal," he says, but he still sounds . . . anxious. "Hey, if you hear from Lorenzo and Rolf, send them my way, OK?"

"Sure," I reply, "but it could be hours. I'm going to be up for a little while, but it's getting late. I might not be awake when they get back."

"OK," he says. "I'll try Lorenzo's phone in a while if I don't hear from you."

"It's late. It sounds like *you* need to get some sleep."

"Yeah. Sure."

"Hey, Sam, are you OK?"

"Yeah. I'm fine. Sorry. I haven't been sleeping well lately. And after tonight . . . Well, I guess I'm a little on edge. I'm sorry, Tony."

"It's OK, man. Just try to . . . well, *relax* isn't the right word . . . Just try to . . . chill out. Besides, as much as I don't want to *think* about it, there isn't much time left. This is all going to be over soon. I'll never see my great-great-grandfather again . . . or Rolf . . . or Moira . . . or Carl . . . or *any* of them."

"What're we going to do?" he says, the panic apparently back in full force.

"We'll . . . I don't know . . . *go on*, I suppose." *Oh, man! That sounds so corny!* "We'll mourn them, and we'll go on about our lives. I *wish* we had more time. There's so much to learn!"

"Yes!" he cries. "There's so much to learn! If I only had more time . . . if I could find a way to keep the virus alive, I think we could . . . cure any disease! We'd be virtually immortal!"

"I get the feeling that immortality isn't all it's cracked up to be," I say. "It hasn't made our vampire friends happier or, at least in most cases, *wiser*. I think Lorenzo and Moira have gained in wisdom over the centuries, but most of them don't seem to be all that wiser or more mature, in spite of their long lives."

"Why do you think that is?"

"I'm not sure. With the *evil* ones, I think it has to do with not feeling the *need* to improve or progress. They Convert for a variety of reasons: lust for power, immortality, love, revenge, or because they're afraid or vulnerable or insecure, or because they were seduced. Some, because they were just *evil* in the first place, I think. They were drawn to evil, you know? For some, I think it was all of the above."

"I guess you're right, but, if we could cure all disease, people would at least live a lot longer and be productive for more of their lives."

"You could be right . . . at least about the disease part . . . partially . . . but I don't think we'd live all that much longer."

"Why not? If cells can reproduce forever with no genetic damage, why would we age at all? Before the Flood, people used to live for a very long time. Aren't you the one who always talks about how Satan couldn't have *created* the Seed . . . that all he could do was co-opt and corrupt it?"

"I don't think he even did *that* much," I reply. "I think all he managed to do was to supercharge it (for lack of a better term) with the Essence. Maybe that mutated it some, but I think it'd always existed before Lucifer got ahold of it. I think it was always present in the family of Adam . . . before the Flood, that is."

"Well, if you're right, why wouldn't we be able to live longer . . . if I could *somehow* get the Seed to survive without the Essence? Wouldn't we live for hundreds of years, you know, like Adam and Methuselah and the other Patriarchs?"

"I don't think the Seed, even the *original*, nonsupercharged, nonmutated version, could survive today."

"Why not? There's got to be a way to . . ."

"Think about it, Sam. If the Seed was what kept the Patriarchs alive for so long before the Flood, what happened to it? What changed?"

"What do you mean?"

"I mean, something happened at the time of the Flood that changed everything."

"You mean, like water covering the whole Earth?"

"Sam, you and I both know that's impossible. There's not enough water on the *planet* to cover all the land mass at once."

"Ah, come on, Tony! Don't tell me you don't believe the story in Genesis anymore! You haven't turned into one of those the-Flood-was-a-localized-phenomenon pseudointellectuals, have you?"

"No, of course not!" I say. "I believe the scriptures are true. If it was just a local event, there would've been no need for Noah to build the Ark and gather the animals. God doesn't lie, and He doesn't exaggerate."

"Then how do you explain it?"

"I think the water didn't have to cover all of it all at *once*," I say. "What causes the tides?"

"I'm not one of your students, Tony. You don't have to *prove* your theory. Just state it. And the answer is the gravitational pull of the Moon, of course."

"Sorry. OK. Here goes." I take a deep breath and dive in. "What if something larger than the Moon passed by Earth, something like a planet or a massive comet? It didn't even have to be *larger* than the Moon; it just had to be *closer*. Velikovsky postulated something like this back in the fifties. And he wasn't the only one. Such a large body in close proximity to the Earth would cause massive storms and . . ."

"And gargantuan tides!"

"Exactly! Such an event could cause it to rain for forty days and forty nights and cause a massive tide, maybe thousands of feet high. It wouldn't have to cover the whole Earth at once, but I bet it could create tides that would cover thousands or hundreds of thousands of square miles at once. As the Earth rotated, the resulting flood could cover all the Earth by *degrees*. The cataclysm would last for a long time. And it would be a while before Noah would find dry land."

"OK. I'll bite, but could such a flood be high enough to cover Everest?"

"Maybe, but it wouldn't *have* to: there's no life up there."

"Well, strictly speaking . . ."

"You know what I mean. There's nothing up there that Noah would have to preserve in the Ark."

"No? What about the yeti?"

"I'm being serious."

"So am I! Most people don't believe vampires exist . . ."

"Good point," I say. *That sounds more like the Sam I know. I think he may actually believe in the Abominable Snowman.*

"But what does all that have to do with the Seed and the long lives of the Patriarchs?" he asks.

"Well, like I said," I reply, "I *believe* the biblical account. It talks about God placing a rainbow in the sky after the Flood. That means there weren't rainbows *before* the Flood, at least not in the experience of the family of Adam."

"That's impossible," he says. "Rainbows are caused by sunlight passing through raindrops. The laws of physics didn't change. There *must've* been rainbows before the Flood."

"Not if there was no direct sunlight."

"What?"

"What if there were a perpetual, dense cloud cover over the entire Earth (or at least the habitable parts) before the Flood?"

"You mean, like Venus?" he asks.

"Exactly. Then some massive body (comet or whatever) passed by the Earth and so dramatically altered the climate that it broke up the cloud cover or shifted the orbit or the rotation of the Earth or whatever. So, maybe, mankind never *saw* direct sunlight until *after* the Flood."

"You've gotta be kidding me!"

"I'm totally serious. I think that's what happened to the Seed, why people used to live so long *before* the Flood!"

There's stunned silence on the other end of the phone for a moment.

"Wait-a-minute! Wait-a-minute!" Sam says and then he's quiet for several seconds. "That makes total sense! The virus *is* photoreactive! Suppose it *did* have a nonmutated, non-Essence-enhanced version prior to the Flood. We'll call that 'Seed 1.0.' Maybe 1.0 kept you healthy and helped you live a whole lot longer. But, when mankind was finally exposed to direct sunlight, it *died out!* It may have *taken* a while, because people still lived longer than we do today for a few centuries, but it was less effective in the sunlight, and eventually it was just wiped out! The mutated, Essence-enhanced version . . . we'll call that 'Version 1.1 . . . ' *that* version is what the vampires carry."

"That's *my* theory, minus all the 'Version 1.0' stuff," I say.

"But that means . . ." His voice trails off.

"That means that, even if you *could* find a way to preserve the Seed or go back to Version 1.0, there's probably no way to make it work in *mortals*, because of our exposure to sunlight."

He's quiet for a bit. Then he says, "You *do* realize that you just crushed my dream of curing cancer, don't you?"

"Moira says the Seed won't last long enough outside a vampiric host to do more than short-term healing."

"I'm kidding you, Tony. Well . . . sort of. I really *did* hope we could use it to cure cancer . . . but that's probably not going to happen. I guess . . . we'll just have to enjoy it while it lasts."

"Enjoy what?"

"The research!" he says. "I mean, once our friends are . . . gone . . . well, there won't be any more of the Seed to study."

Suddenly, there's a huge lump in my throat. "I'm going to miss them too."

"Yeah," he says. "Me too."

"Listen, Sam. It's late, and I have some research to do, so . . ."

"Are you sure about this cloud-cover thing . . . prior to the Flood, I mean?"

"Actually . . ." I hesitate. *Not yet. I'm not ready to reveal my* source. "I'm not a hundred-percent sure, but I've got . . . at least *one* good source that indicates that might've been the case."

"But," he says, "if there were heavy cloud cover all the time, couldn't the vampires, you know, before the Flood, move about in the daytime? The Prophecy calls Lilith 'the Mother of Night.' Wouldn't she have been able to go outside all the time?"

"Sunscreen," I say.

"What? Sunscreen?"

"They didn't *have* it back then. Cloud cover only protects a vampire for so long. Without sunscreen, any skin that's exposed, even to *filtered* sunlight, for more than a minute or two begins to burn. Even with heavy clothing, they couldn't survive it."

"You sound like you're presenting *facts*, not *theory*, Tony. How can you be so certain?"

"I . . . *can't* be certain." *She could be lying to me about* everything *for all I know.* "But this, at least, fits all the facts we *do* have. Anyway . . . I have to get busy. It's late."

"OK," he says, "but, you *will* tell Lorenzo to call me if you see him, right?"

There's an intense quality to his voice that makes me uneasy, although I can't say why.

"Sure," I say. "Talk to you tomorrow."

"Yeah. 'Night."

I close my phone and plug it into the charger on my desk. I lean back in my chair in the study and turn the computer monitor on. I turned it off when Sam called for the *third* time.

Sam seemed really stressed out. We're *all* on edge right now.

Lilith's searching for me! How on earth did she get my name? And the names of Kat and my kids? Do we have a leak in the Stake again? But, if we did, surely she'd know which university I was at.

Please, Father in Heaven, watch over my family! Keep them safe! And, if I might, please let me have a little more time with my great-great-grandfather . . . and my other friends. I . . .

I hear the *bloop* that indicates a new email has been received.

This is the "research" I was referring to.

There's so little time and so much to be learned! What new tidbit of long-lost ancient knowledge will she dangle tonight? After what Carl said about security at the meeting, I'll make sure I'm extra careful. I mean, I've been careful all along, but it won't hurt to be even more on my guard.

I'm dealing with the oldest living creature in existence, almost as old as mankind itself, someone unimaginably evil and crafty.

And she's after my family! She's closing in!

For the thousandth time, why am I doing this? Why am I chatting *with this monster?*

Because she has knowledge, *knowledge that nobody else on earth has.*

But is it worth the risk?

What risk? I'm not *the one leaking the information!*

I take my mouse and open my email.

It's from her.

As usual, the message has no subject line. I double-click to open it.

"Hello, lover.

"Tonight you may ask any one question of your choice. I promise to answer, no matter what it is."

I hate it when she calls me that. She began calling me "lover" on the second night she emailed me. I don't know if she thinks she's being seductive or if she's mocking me. I suppose, it could be both. Either way, I'm not going to antagonize her. I *need* the knowledge that only Lilith possesses. *Time's running out!*

And there *is* one question I've been dying to have answered. I've asked it before, but she's never answered it.

"Were there humans before Adam?"

I click the "Send" button.

And I wait.

She has skirted this question every time . . . that or flatly refused to answer it.

How do I know if she's telling me the truth? It could all be lies.

But what would be the point of that? What would she gain by lying about ancient history?

Making me look like a fool, that's what! And besides, she lies! That's what she does!

But what she tells me fits all the facts. And it fits with my own theories.

So, in other words, Tony, old man, she's telling you what you want to hear.

And I don't have an answer to that.

Bloop.

I open the response.

"No. My grandparents were the first. All mankind is descended from them."

I stare at the screen. *That* doesn't fit. I really expected her to say something else. I'm not sure *what* I expected her to say, but . . . *that* certainly doesn't fit my theories.

I begin to type.

"What about the fossil record? What about the cave paintings? What about stone tools?"

I click the "Send" button.

I wait less than a minute before I hear another *bloop.*

She was waiting for me. She knew what my follow-up would be.

And she can type at vampiric speed.

I open the reply.

"You mean the BEHEMOT? You asked about HUMANS before Adam. There were no HUMANS before Adam. There were only the beasts that LOOKED like men.

"The children of Adam didn't know about the behemot for centuries. We only encountered them after we began to expand outward from lands surrounding Adam-Ondi-Ahman.

"They had no language, not at first. The sons of God (the descendants of Adam) tried to teach them, but the behemot could learn only a very little. They showed no aptitude or desire to learn the ways of men.

"They were beasts. No more.

"My Children and I could not Feed from them. We tried, of course, but we could derive no sustenance, so they were worthless to us. LESS than worthless.

"Then, many of the idiot sons of God began to breed with them. They produced abominations, the NAPHELIM. The abominations were also not human. My Children could not Feed from them, either.

"And that was when God became REALLY enraged. He sent the Flood to destroy the naphelim and all those who had spawned them.

"The Flood destroyed all my Children.

"I alone survived."

I quickly respond with another question:

"How did you survive?"

I wait. There's no response. *I guess she's done.* In frustration, I reach to turn off my monitor.

Bloop.

"I almost didn't survive. I think Father tried to kill me too. But I bested him! I, Lilith, daughter of Cain the Outcast, I defeated ELOHIM!

"I flew above the raging waters. I found the floating, bloated corpses of the dead. I gorged myself on all I could find. When I could no longer stomach the putrefied blood, I clung to the broken husk of a tree I found floating on the flood. During the day, such as it was during the storm, I hid in a hollow of its broken trunk.

"I nearly gave in to despair, but I summoned the Light-Bearer and forced him to give me of his strength. I drew more upon the Essence during that time than I ever had before or have since. It sustained me, kept the Seed from consuming me, until the waters receded enough that I could find shelter: a cave on the side of a mountain, near where Noah's great barge came to rest.

"I knew there would be no men from which to Feed for many years, not unless I

wanted to consume Noah's entire family.

"And don't think I didn't consider it. That might have been the ultimate revenge. Father murdered my Children and tried to murder me. I could consume all of his. But, no. LIVING would be the best revenge of all.

"So, in my cave, I went to Sleep. I Slept for decades. When I finally emerged, I was little more than a walking sack of bones. I was in agony. Your mortal mind cannot conceive of what I suffered.

"But I DID survive. I defeated God!

"And, once again, I had his children to feast upon. Once again, I had men to satisfy my appetites. Once again, men feared me. They desired me. They worshipped me. They built temples to me. They carved my image in stone.

"Once again, I was the Mother of Night. I was the Goddess of all the Earth.

"I rule the world, though most men think me a myth. They may not even know my name, but my hand is everywhere. I am content to reign from the shadows. I have shaped all human history.

"No man can resist me. No woman can resist me.

"I have seduced emperors, empresses, kings, queens, presidents, generals, ministers, popes, priests, imams, and rabbis. None can resist me.

"YOU cannot resist me. Only I can satisfy your needs. No matter the danger, you cannot resist what I alone can give you. Can you, lover?

"I'm coming for you. And when I am ready, you will give yourself to me. And you will do it of your own free will.

"Won't you, Tony?"

Chapter 8

Carl

Ve have a problem." It's Lorenzo's voice on my cell phone. I can hear the wind howling on the line. He must be flying. And he must be moving pretty fast. "Something's very wrong with Sam."

Curled up next to me on the sofa in our safe house, with my arm around her, Moira stiffens. Her body's as tense as a compressed spring. Sam Gallagher (Sammy, as she calls him) is very special to her.

That's just what we need tonight: another *crisis.* As it is, Moira's been exposed, perhaps not as a vampire, but as one of the "Battling Angels," I doubt we've heard the last from the police about the incident at the hospital, we've got reporters chasing after us, lunatics shooting at Moira and putting mortals in danger, and that crazy Brotherhood of Tobias searching for us. More than likely, neither of us can go back to work. We can't go home. Our lives here in Utah are probably over.

We have a security leak too. Lilith's people are perilously close to identifying Tony.

Like we don't have enough to deal with tonight!

Sometimes I just wish we could take a vacation. Moira and I could just go away for a century or so . . .

"OK," I say, "what's going on?"

"Rolf and I were Hunting in Wyoming," he replies. "We were on our way back to supplement the security at Tony's house when I got a *frantic* call from Sam. We'll be there shortly, but I think Sam needs a *doctor.*"

"So, call a doctor," I say. *Argh! Make it a* request, *not a* command! "I mean, *please* call a doctor." *Why's he telling us this? I like Sam and all, but Moira's gonna be sick with worry. Sam's like a son to her. And Moira doesn't need any more stress tonight.* "*Please* take him to an emergency room, if you think it's that urgent."

"I think he needs a *vampiric* doctor," Lorenzo says.

He's keeping something back.

"What's going on?" I ask. Beside me, Moira seems to be fighting the urge to rip the phone from my hand.

"I've been *uneasy* about Sam for some time now," he says, "but . . . Well, I just think Moira needs to take a look at him."

"We'll be right there, Lorenzo," Moira says beside me.

I look into her beautiful green eyes, eyes that are as hard as emeralds right now.

I nod. "You heard the lady," I say. "We're on our way." I close the phone and Moira gives me a quick, bone-weary smile.

"Give me a moment to change," she says. Then she's off to the bedroom to change out of her bathrobe.

Things are happening so fast. We're running out of time. Lilith's closing in. No matter how many people we have, we'll never have enough to overcome her forces in battle. How in the heck are we going to beat her? I *believe* in the Prophecy, but I just don't know what to do! Every time I pray about what to do, the only answer I get is to have *faith*, to trust in God. I never get an answer about what to *do*.

Moira emerges from the bedroom seconds after entering it. She's now dressed in jeans, a T-shirt, and sneakers. Rather than carrying the stereotypical doctor's bag, she's belting her black sword around her waist. Her expression is grim.

I guess she doesn't need a stethoscope, not with our Seed-enhanced senses.

I belt on my own sword, the Scottish claymore that once belonged to Moira's first love, the long-dead Donald MacDonald. I also belt on my dirk (which used to belong to Moira's father).

"We're moving out," I say loud enough for the six vampires who're guarding the house to hear. Then we're through the door and into the air. I take the lead, and Moira forms up on my right in the Number Two position. The other six stay in pairs and take up position behind us. It's probably not the best tactical formation, four pairs of two following in a straight line, but it'll do.

We head off to the south, toward Provo, at a high rate of speed. We're not moving as fast we *can* go, but we're zipping right along.

"What do you think is wrong with Sam?" I ask as I scan the sky for threats. I have to speak quite loud to be heard clearly above the roaring wind. I spot our scouts, but I don't see any winged bogeys.

"I cannae say, laddie," Moira answers, "but there was somethin' odd about him tonight. He seemed almost *manic*. Can we nae go faster?"

"If we go much faster, it'll be almost impossible to stay together. The last thing we need to do right now is spread out."

Maybe if Moira had let Lorenzo and Rolf keep up with her tonight, things might have gone very differently at the hospital. I'm not going to say that to her, but . . .

"'Twas foolish of me to go off alone like that tonight," she says, eerily echoing my thoughts. "Lorenzo and Rolf might've helped me avoid . . . exposure. I'm sorry, laddie."

"I have to admit, the same thing occurred to me," I say, "but there's no way of knowing for sure. It was only a matter of time before somebody in that stupid Brotherhood identified you. Oh, and I forgot to tell you: Sergei *did* manage to contact the mortal leader of the Brotherhood. Sergei said he *thinks* he convinced the guy that the 'demons' are the ones with the wings and the ones *without* the wings are the good guys. But, even if he succeeded, it'll take a bit to get the word out to the rest of the Brotherhood. Obviously, that Holdtenschmidt guy didn't get the memo."

"He was a lunatic," she says, her shouted voice tinged with bitterness. "'Twould've made nae difference in his case. He's nae one to listen to reason. Ach, Carl! Our lives here are finished! I cannae return to work safely. I'd be puttin' mortals, as well as m'self, in danger. Lilith'll have my name shortly, if she does nae have it already! Then she'll have yers! Our home . . . we cannae go back there. And then there's Sammy and Tony and their families. They're in horrible danger!"

"We knew this day was coming." *Our lives here are the least of our problems. Our immortal lives are over when this conflict's done. When we confront Lilith, we're dead either way.*

I slow slightly and move in toward Moira so I can take her hand in mine. I squeeze it briefly. She squeezes back. Then we let go, and I move back to the Lead position.

"Could we nae go even a *wee* bit faster?"

I signal to the others to tighten up the formation. They move in closer, and, together, we accelerate till breathing is problematic.

"Thank ye, laddie," Moira shouts.

The airstream howls past us.

◢ ◢ ◢

Sam Gallagher and his wife, Nicole—*Sammy and Nikki*—*I wonder if anyone but* Moira *ever calls them that?*—live in a Tudor-style house near the BYU campus. The house is one of the few not converted into student apartments or occupied by octogenarians. Sam inherited the place from his parents. The Gallaghers have no kids; Sam's sterile. So they have a cat (the same cat Sam did his initial experiments on with the Seed). I know Nikki wants a child of her own very badly. Sam wants to adopt, but Nikki hasn't reconciled herself to that idea, at least not yet. So, for now, it's just the two of them and the cat . . . and the two Stake vampires lurking in the shadows, guarding the house.

We make one pass over their home at high altitude and scan for mortal eyes that might observe us as we land. Then we plummet toward the ground and land quietly in the Gallaghers' backyard. Paula and Ramón appear from the shadows, swords drawn.

"Declaration," Paula challenges, her voice flat.

"Proposition," I respond.

She nods, and they sheath their weapons.

In our heightened state of alert, we're using challenges and responses to be certain the vampires approaching us are who they appear to be and are acting of their own free will. There are no exceptions, not even for me.

"They're inside, down in the basement," Paula says.

Moira pushes past me and hurries into the house.

I spin around. "The six of you," I say quickly to the guards who accompanied us, "*please* set up a CAP over the house." A Combat Air Patrol will place them in a position to help us in a pinch and not overwhelm Sam and Nikki. There are enough of our kind inside already.

I hurry in through the back door.

I've been here with Moira a few times to visit the Gallaghers, but I've never been in the basement. It's easy enough to follow the sound of the voices.

"Where's Nikki?" Moira asks.

"I Persuaded her and sent her to bed," Lorenzo says. "She was very upset."

Moira nods. "Tell me precisely what ye observed."

I start down the basement steps as I hear Lorenzo ask, "Just tonight or before?"

Why isn't she talking to Sam? Is he unconscious?

When I reach the basement, I see Moira kneeling in front of Sam. He's sitting upright in a desk chair and staring blankly at nothing in particular. *I guess Lorenzo Persuaded him too. What's going on here?* Lorenzo and Rolf are standing in front of what can only be a lab table. I see a centrifuge, a Bunsen burner, test tubes, and a lot of stuff I can't identify, but it all looks very "lab-ish."

"He's in nae immediate danger, 'twould seem, so start at the beginning," Moira says.

"Very well," Lorenzo says. "I recall him mentioning a few times that he's having trouble sleeping. Also, he seemed agitated. He talked too much."

"He always talks too much," I say.

Moira flashes me a look of annoyance.

I guess I was trying to lighten the mood. Not appropriate, Morgan!

"More than usual, then," Lorenzo says. "Tonight, at the meeting, he seemed positively giddy, oddly so, when discussing his research."

"Aye," Moira says, nodding. She's looking into Sam's eyes, probing him here and there with her fingers. Her head is cocked slightly as if she's listening to his pulse and breathing.

Which is probably exactly what she's doing.

"Then tonight," Lorenzo says, "after the *incident* at the hospital, with all the blood, I needed to Feed."

"Me too," Rolf says, nodding.

That's perfectly understandable. If Moira and I hadn't consumed a couple of bags of blood before the meeting . . .

"So," Lorenzo continues, "we went Hunting. As we were flying back, I checked my voicemail for messages and found more than *twenty* from Sam. I listened to them all. Each one was more frantic, more *emotional* than the last. In each recorded message, he was asking us to come and provide him with samples of our saliva and blood. The tone of the last several messages alternated between anger and conciliation, sometimes both in the same message. Why hadn't we come? Why were we ignoring him? Didn't we know how important his research was? It wasn't like Sam . . . at least, not like the Sam I know."

The look on Moira's face surprises me. The worry I saw on the flight over has been replaced by an intense focus. I've seen that look before, but never on her face.

I've seen that expression on the faces of men who know they're heading into combat.

"Aye," she says, "go on."

"I called him back to say we were on our way," Lorenzo says. "He answered on the first ring, in spite of it being after two in the morning. His tone, however, surprised me. Gone was the anger and desperation that'd characterized his phone messages. He was friendly, chatty, giddy. He didn't even ask if we were coming over at first. He just wanted to talk, it seemed. He asked how the Hunt went. He didn't really listen to my answers, though. He was too quick to move on to the next question . . . and the next."

Moira nods.

"Finally," Lorenzo continues, "he asked, too casually to my mind, if we were going to stop by. If I was uneasy before, this certainly put me on my guard. My first thought was that he was acting under duress, but he didn't use our duress code word. He asked how far out we were, how long we'd be in getting here. I gave him an estimate of half an hour. Then he paused. I could hear him breathing, but he said nothing. Then, abruptly, he said, 'I'll see you then!' and hung up."

He points at Rolf. "Rolf, as you know, keeps the duty roster in his head. He gave me the names and numbers of Sam's guards. So I called Paula. She answered right away and gave the proper authentication, so I knew she was all right. She said the Gallaghers were safe and there were no intruders in the house. She said Sam had been pestering them repeatedly about giving samples. She sounded quite perturbed."

"You got *that* right!" Paula's voice is faint from outside the house, but it's easily discernable to my ears.

"Most annoying!" comes the far away voice of Ramón.

"Folks," I say, noting the fleeting look of pain in Moira's eyes, "this is serious."

In unison, Paula and Ramón say, "Sorry."

"Anyway," Lorenzo continues, "once we got here, Sam greeted us at the back door. He looked terrible. His hands were shaking. His face was pale. His pulse was racing. And he wouldn't stop talking. It was mostly inane small talk, but it was all one-sided. He'd ask questions and then not wait for the answers. He led us down here. And while he continued with his manic, one-sided chat, he prepared syringes and sample dishes."

Lorenzo shakes his head and continues, "His whole manner made me cautious. I felt that providing him with a sample might be . . . well, I didn't think it would be a good idea. I told him so and said we were in a hurry to get to Tony's place. He pleaded with me and then Rolf. When we both refused, he flew into a rage. He threatened us and then he fell to his knees and sobbed. His shouting must have awakened Nicole. She came downstairs, and Sam screamed at her to leave us alone. I used Persuasion to calm him down *and* to help her forget. I sent her to bed."

He pauses and then says, "That's pretty much the whole story."

Moira nods. She takes Sam's face in her hands and forces him to look at her. "Sammy, it's Moira. It's time to wake up now."

He blinks a few times, and then his eyes grow wide. He swallows twice and then smiles weakly. He says, "Moira! What're *you* doing here?"

Moira smiles sadly. "Sammy, I *know*. Ye are *addicted* to the Seed, laddie."

"Wh.. What?" he says. "Addicted? No! It's for my research!"

"Ye've been injectin' yerself with vampire blood and saliva."

"No! No!" he splutters. "Are you *crazy*? It's just legitimate research! Of *course* I've been injecting myself! Why not? I'm the only *test subject* I have! I'm not addicted! I've never taken drugs in my entire life!"

"Sammy. Sammy," Moira coos, still holding his face. "'Tis nae yer fault, laddie. I've heard of this before. In some Cults, Novitiates become so addicted to the Seed that they're available every night for a Feeding, usually more than once a night. Look at ye, laddie! Ye cannae sleep, I'll wager. Yer hands tremble. Ye cannae control yer emotions. When yer source, meaning a vampire, comes nigh to give ye what ye crave, ye talk his ears off to put him at ease. Ye're makin' yerself physically sick, nae doubt."

Sam swallows hard. His breathing accelerates.

"Dinnae hyperventilate, laddie."

"Wh . . . What am I going to . . . ? How . . . ? Nikki! I . . . I *yelled* at her. Moira, I've *never* yelled at her before!"

"Hush, my poor wee bairn. Nikki's just grand. She's asleep. Lorenzo made sure she'll forget what happened this night. The good news, laddie," Moira says, "is that 'tis nae a *physical* addiction."

Sam opens his mouth to say something, but Moira cuts him off.

"Oh, aye, ye've got *physical* symptoms, but the mind can manufacture symptoms when ye've got a *psychological* addiction. But, Sammy, what were ye thinkin'?"

"I don't know!" he wails. "Nikki wanted . . . I'm . . . I just . . ." He starts to moan. It's awful to hear. He sounds so lost. Tears pour down his cheeks.

Was he trying to . . . reverse his sterility so they could conceive a child?

"H-help me," he sobs. He slumps from his chair to kneel on the floor.

Moira takes him in her arms and holds him. She rocks with him from side to side, making cooing noises.

"I . . . I *can't* do this," he sobs. "I don't know what to do. I'm so . . . *ashamed*! Can you make it . . . just go away?"

"Oh, my dearie, if I were to Persuade ye . . ."

"Yes!" he says, like a drowning man clinging to a floating log. "Persuade me! Make it go away! *Please!*"

"Nae, laddie. Hush now. Nae more o' that. Ye need to conquer this on yer own. Ye'll be the stronger for it. I'll help ye. *We'll* help ye. We'll be here for ye. But, we'll make sure ye have nae more of the Seed to tempt ye."

"I can't. I'm not strong enough . . ."

"Turn to the Lord, Sammy. *He's* strong enough. *He'll* bear ye up. He'll nae desert ye in yer hour of need. Hush now. There's a laddie."

Sam sobs quietly into her shoulder.

"Sam," I say, "would you like a priesthood blessing?"

He nods.

"It'll have to be just *me* at this hour of the night," I say. "Is that OK?"

"S-sure," he replies.

"The only person I'd trust to assist me would be Tony," I say, "but I'm sure he's asleep by now."

"Tony!" Rolf says suddenly. "We go *now.*"

"Yes!" Lorenzo nods. "We really must be going."

"Right," I reply. "We've got this covered here."

In a flash, they're up the stairs and gone.

I kneel next to Sam and Moira on the floor. She starts to unwrap her arms from around him.

"It's OK," I say to her, "you can hold him while I do this."

She holds him tightly again.

"Sam," I ask, "what's your full name?"

"Samuel Nephi Gallagher," Moira whispers.

"You . . . remember?" Sam asks, fresh tears on his cheeks.

"I could ne'er forget my wee Sammy," she says, "nae in a thousand years."

I lay my hands on Sam's head and say, "Samuel Nephi Gallagher, in the name of Jesus Christ . . ."

◆ ◆ ◆

"Amen," I say, finishing the blessing, just as my cell phone rings.

I take my hands from Sam's head and pull the phone out of my pocket. I look at the screen and say, "It's Lorenzo again."

What now? More bad news, I'll bet. Can this night get any worse?

I flip the phone open. Immediately, I can hear the wind howling. *Lorenzo's flying somewhere fast again.* Before I can say a word, Lorenzo shouts above the shrieking gale, ". . . Tony . . . 'thleen . . . children! Gone! Noriko . . . 'nita . . . dead!"

"Where are you?" I shout.

"Black . . . 'copter! . . . getting away! Too fast!"

Suddenly the sound of the wind from the phone ceases. I hear a horrible cry of anguish.

"Lorenzo!" I cry. "What's happening?"

"That damnable black helicopter's too fast!" He's breathing hard. "We can't keep up! Noriko and Juanita are dead! Beheaded! *Lilith's taken my family!*"

Chapter 9

Tony

What's your name, li'l darlin'?" The massive vampire's Australian accent is thick, his voice slightly raised to be heard over the sound of the enormous helicopter's twin rotors. His huge hand rests atop Abby's tiny knee.

"*Stop touching me!*" my daughter screams, her six-year-old eyes huge with terror. "*Stop touching me! Daddy! Help me! Make him stop!*"

I strain with everything in me against the handcuffs. My wrists, now slick with my own blood, are shackled to the bulkhead above my head. My feet are shackled below the bench where I'm sitting.

An ordinary seatbelt holds me at the waist as effectively as an iron chain. A simple push of a button on the seatbelt buckle and my body would be free, but I can't touch it.

"*Leave her alone!*" I bellow. "Don't touch her, you sick *freak!*"

"*DADDEEEEEE!*" Abby shrieks. She's belted onto a bench on the opposite side of the helicopter. She kicks at her tormentor. "No! No! *NO!*"

Kathleen's shackled next to Abby, and Little Tony's cuffed and belted in on the other side of Kathleen. Like Abby, the rest of us are dressed for bed.

We were taken as we slept.

Norika and Juanita are dead, and it's all my fault.

My family's been taken by Lilith's vampires, and it's all my fault.

There are almost a dozen vampires, all male, gathered around us, enjoying the obscene spectacle. Their expressions are leering, ravenous.

"*Please!*" Kathleen pleads, her voice hardly rising above a choked whisper. I can barely make out what she's saying. "Please don't hurt my daughter!" Her breath comes in shallow gasps, her face a mask of horror.

Like being in a nightmare when you can't seem to run fast enough or muster enough breath to scream.

Little Tony wails beside her. "*Mommeee!*"

"Don't hurt her!" Kathleen wheezes out. "I'll do anything! *Anything!*"

The brute, with his hand now on Abby's thigh, pauses. His head turns slightly, and he appears to be looking at Kathleen out of the corner of his eye. "*Anything*, darlin'?"

Kathleen looks at him in mute terror, unable to utter a word, her breathing rapid and shallow.

Several of the surrounding vampires chuckle. It's a horrible sound, like the mirth of demons.

"Anything?" the monster repeats.

She nods, unable to speak.

"*No!*" I shout. "*Kathleen! Don't . . .*"

Something, a wad of cloth most likely, is shoved into my mouth, cutting me off mid word. I shake my head and try to push the gag out with my tongue. An incredibly strong hand is clamped over my mouth. A second hand is placed atop my head, holding my head still.

"You'll want to *watch* this, Tony," the owner of the hands says loud enough for me to hear. I can't see much of him . . . just his forearms and the top of the hand over my mouth. I can feel his breath on my ear as he says, "I *love* it when Bo does this!"

Bo, the pervert with his hand on my daughter, laughs softly.

I think I'm going to be sick.

Turning his head back to Kathleen, Bo says with a wicked grin, "Let's see what you're made of, darlin'."

Bo stands, towering over my family. He nods at one of the other vampires. "Larry, go ahead and unshackle her."

Larry, the vampire Bo spoke to, produces a key and moves toward my wife. Bo takes Kathleen's forearms in his huge hands and restrains her while Larry unlocks the shackles at her wrists. The vampire with the key squats down and frees her ankles. Then he unfastens her seatbelt.

Bo releases Kathleen's wrists and takes a step back. He's blocking my view of her face, but I can see enough to tell that she puts an arm protectively around each of our children, holding them as close as their restraints allow. Abby and Little Tony are still sobbing, but they're not screaming anymore.

Bo bends at the waist and appears to offer Kathleen his hand. "Come with me, darlin'," he says, his voice mocking. He pulls her to her feet, grasps her by the arms just below her shoulders, and turns her so I can see both of them in profile.

His leer widens. "So, you'd do just *anything* to save your sweet little girl, wouldn't you, darlin'?"

Kathleen sobs. She shuts her eyes and nods. Tears stream down her face. Her whole body's quaking.

I scream against my gag, but there's nothing I can do. I can only watch.

I've never felt so powerless!

Bo and Kathleen look like a pair of dancers in a slow, obscene tango. Leisurely, suggestively, he turns around in place, holding her, until they're both facing toward the children. They're angled enough for me to see Kathleen's face.

With his free hand, Bo draws Kathleen's hair away from her neck. He opens his mouth wide, and I watch as his fangs extend, trailing strings of saliva. He leans his head in and gives her neck a long, slow lick. Kathleen whimpers. Bo begins to sway from side to side. "We don't have any music, do we, darlin'?" he says. "That's all right." He nuzzles his lips next to her ear. But instead of whispering, he continues to speak loudly. "We'll make our own."

All around us, the other vampires snigger. Their sick grins expose sharp fangs. Many of them have streams of drool running from their lips.

"Pl-pl-please," Kathleen blubbers. "Don't make my children . . . . w-w-watch."

"Ah, now, darlin'," Bo says in a faux whisper loud enough for me to hear, "Don't you worry, now. I want to *help you out*. I'm gonna give you a chance to *save* your little girl. Sweet little sheila, isn't she? I like 'em *young*. I love to hear 'em *scream* . . . especially when they scream for their mommies."

"Mommeee!" Abby screams as if on cue.

"Mommeee!" Little Tony cries, echoing his sister.

"It's OK, sweetie," Kathleen cries. "It's g-g-going to be OK."

"That's right, kiddies," Bo says, his fangs wet, glistening. "Mommy's all right. Everything's gonna be all right . . . for *one* of you."

"Wuh-wuh-one?" Kathleen chokes out.

"That's right, li'l tikes," Bo says. "Mommy's gonna save *one* of you. Just one." He nibbles at Kathleen's earlobe. "Your mommy gets to *choose* which one of you *lives* and which one of you *dies*." He draws the end of that last word out like the hiss of monstrous snake.

"N-no!" Kathleen says, finally finding her voice. "Mommy loves both of you! I love *you*, Abby. I love *you*, Tony."

"No, she don't," Bo says, grinning from ear to ear. "And if she don't choose one, then *both* of you die."

He nods in fiendish glee. "Do you understand me, Abby?" he says, raising the pitch of his voice as you might when talking to a child. "If Mommy says she wuvs *you*, I'll kill Li'l Tony, but *you* get to live. Do you understand? Does Mommy wuv you or Li'l Tony?"

Abby wails, tears streaming down her little face. Her cheeks are flushed from screaming.

"Abby," Bo says, "who does Mommy love? Answer me or I'll *hurt* your Mommy."

"My mommy loves me," Abby sobs.

"Tony," he says, addressing my four-year-old son, "does Mommy wuv you or Abby?"

"Mommy loves me," he wails. His eyes are red.

"Don't *do* this!" Kathleen pleads. "Please!"

"Choose one," he says. "Choose one or I kill 'em both."

I scream against the gag. *No! Stop this!*

I can stop this! I have to stop this! I bear the priesthood of God! I can . . .

"Stop this!"

That voice! I know that voice! Melodious, commanding. Sensuous beyond measure. I've heard it only once before.

How I wish I'd never heard it! Never listened to it! Never been entranced by its words!

Lilith!

The hands that hold my head and mouth release me. I spit out the sodden wad of cloth. I turn my head to the right, toward the front of the helicopter.

And there she is . . . standing in front of a curtained-off area near the front.

Beautiful beyond description.

Terrible as the raging seas.

Evil as the Pit of Hell.

The first time I saw her, that morning at Müller's farm, she looked like Kathleen to me, or at least a highly *sexualized* version of my wife. Lilith isn't having that effect at the moment. *Does that require eye contact?* Her eyes are brown; her luscious, waist-length hair, raven black. Her face . . . physical perfection. She's wearing a floor-length dress of blood red, shimmering silk that hugs every curve and shows too much cleavage.

And I can't take my eyes off her.

My family's in unspeakable peril, and all I can do is *stare* at this woman . . . stare and think . . . unthinkable thoughts.

I'm not even breathing.

I inhale sharply, like a drowning man breaching the surface of the water.

And that breaks the spell.

I tear my eyes away from her and glance around quickly. Bo, Larry, and the rest of the vampires are frozen, staring at their Queen. Kathleen and the children are silent, staring as well.

I look back in Lilith's direction.

She takes a few steps toward us. She walks with a grace that is at once female and feline. The sway of her hips, the swirl of her skirt, the roll of her shoulders, the bounce of her hair, the rise and fall of her . . . I've seen women who've walked seductively before, but they are mere caricatures, pale imitations of *this* woman.

She stops a few paces away, gazing around at us. Even standing motionless, her sensuality seems to permeate the room like a subtle perfume. She still hasn't looked at me. And I don't know which I desire more: to escape her gaze or to be fixed by it.

"I wasn't speaking to you, my Children. Carry on as you were. I was speaking"—she turns her gaze to me, and the air freezes in my lungs—"to *you*, Tony."

She is transformed.

It's not that she looks so *different*. Her hair is still black, her eyes still brown . . . *Or are they blonde and blue?* But now she looks so much like Kathleen, so like *every* woman I've ever thought beautiful, but *Kathleen* most of all. *Is it a pheromone, or something like Persuasion? Maybe it is something like Persuasion. She had to make eye contact.*

"That's right, darlin'," Bo says.

Again, I inhale sharply. I tear my eyes away from the Daughter of Cain. *She's evil, not . . .*

Bo begins to sway once more from side to side, holding Kathleen tight against himself. "Tell your li'l tots which one of 'em gets to *live*."

"Tony," Lilith says, her voice sweet like the promise of forbidden fruit. I turn my face back to her. I can't help myself.

And I hate myself for it.

"Stop this," she says. "You have the power. You bear the High Priesthood of *Son Ahman*. You *can* stop this. Command them, in his name. Surely Father is mightier than all the Legions of Light-Bearer or all my Children."

I open my mouth to speak . . . to *command* them . . . but I . . . can't bring myself to utter the words.

"Why do you hesitate, lover?" Lilith purrs. "Don't you *love* your wife? Your children? She's quite pretty, isn't she, Bo?"

"Nothing compared to you, my Queen," Bo replies, "but, yeah, she's a pretty li'l thing."

"And such lovely children, Tony," Lilith continues. "Don't you want to save *them*, Tony? Stretch out your hand . . . well . . . so to speak. Invoke the name of the Creator of Heaven and Earth and *save* them, lover."

"Go on, darlin'," Bo says and he licks Kathleen's ear. "Choose. And if you don't choose soon, I'll kill 'em *both*."

Kathleen sobs.

I can stop this, can't I? Why can't I speak?

"You're running out of time, lover," Lilith says. "Why *don't* you stop this? Could it be that you know you're *unworthy*, that this is all your own doing? *You* brought this doom on them. *You* were the one who couldn't stay away from me, who kept returning to the fountain of my knowledge for yet another sip. You *knew* you were playing with fire. You *knew* you were walking close to the edge, but you kept edging closer and closer . . . and closer. *Father* hasn't abandoned you in your hour of need. *You* abandoned *him*."

"Ya see, kiddies," Bo says, nibbling Kathleen's ear again. "Mommy don't love neither one of you. She's going to let you *both* die."

"Mommeee!" Little Tony wails.

Abby sobs.

"I'm going to count down from ten," Bo says. "When I get to zero, I'm going to kill 'em both. Unless, of course, you tell me which one to save . . . *or* your worthless husband decides he's got the *stones* to stop me. And you can trust me, darlin', I *will* kill 'em both. And, if you *choose* one, I *promise* that I'll only kill the other one."

Bo winks at me. "Ten."

"*Please!*" Kathleen sobs.

"Nine."

"Don't do this!" she screams.

"Choose, darlin'. Eight."

"Tony! Stop him!" Kathleen pleads.

"Seven."

I can't speak. I can't get my breath.

I have to stop this.

"Six."

"Tony!" my wife screams.

Lorenzo! Where are you?

"Five."

I open my mouth. "In . . . In the name of . . ." *I can't get my breath.*

This is my fault!

"What's that, Tony?" Bo says. "Go on! Cat got your tongue? Four."

"Mommeee!" Abby screams.

"That's right, li'l Abbs!" Bo says. "You keep on screaming *just like that.* That's wha' I like! Three."

I hear lurid laughter from the assembled vampires.

"Stop him, lover," Lilith purrs. She whispers loudly in my ear, "But you *can't*, can you?" Her breath makes my flesh tingle. My body trembles.

My fault!

"Two. Choose, darlin'."

"MOMMEEEE!" Abby and Tony scream together.

"One."

Stop this, Tony!

"T-T-Toh-Toh-Ab-Ab-Abby! *Abby!*" Kathleen's voice is a choked, gurgling cry.

"NO!" I scream.

Bo kisses her ear. "Thank you, darlin'!" His expression is one of ecstasy, of triumph. "That's the *best* I've 'ad all year! And you didn't let me down!"

He nods to one of the other vampires. "Chuck, if you please?"

A vampire (Chuck) takes Kathleen from Bo and holds her tight.

"See, li'l darlin'," Bo says, walking up to Abby. "Your mommy loves *you* best." He bends down and kisses her cheek. Then he turns to my son. "But you, ya little bugger, Mommy *hates* you. She wants you to *die*!"

"Mommee!" he wails.

"I'm s-s-sorry, baby," Kathleen sobs. "I'm so sorry."

"Daddeee!"

Stop this!

My breathing comes in ragged gasps. *Can't breathe!*

Bo lifts my little boy up. Little Tony screams and beats at him with his tiny fists and feet. Bo just laughs. The monster turns my son around in the air.

"S-s-stop!" I manage to say. "In the name of . . ."

"Remember, darlin'," Bo says, looking at Kathleen, but nodding in my direction, "this is all *his* fault, your worthless, unworthy husband." Then he looks me in the eye and laughs.

"I'm s-s-sorry, baby," Kathleen blubbers. "Forgive Mommy."

"He ain't gonna *forgive* you, darlin'. He *hates* you. You picked his *sister* over him. Look at Mommy, li'l lamb." He grins wide, showing his fangs. "Baa-a-a-a! Baa-a-a-a!"

"NO!" I yell.

"I love you, Mommy," my boy says.

Bo sinks his fangs into Little Tony's neck.

♦ ♦ ♦

Bo tosses my son's corpse at Kathleen's feet.

Kathleen retches. Sobs wrack her body. Her legs buckle, and she's held upright only by Chuck, the vampire who grips her arms.

Chuck laughs at her.

She retches again.

The male vampires all seem to think this is hilarious.

Lilith whispers loudly in my ear, "For a moment there, I thought she wouldn't do it. But she did. She *chose*. She chose one child and sacrificed the other." She pulls her lips from my ear and stands. Part of me *mourns* the absence of her lips even as I grieve for the loss of my precious little boy. I feel a deep loathing for myself because of what I let happen here . . . because of what I'm feeling.

I'm worthless. Less *than worthless*.

"I feel your pain, Kathleen," Lilith says. She pulls a lacy kerchief from the pocket of one of the male vampires and gently wipes the vomit from my wife's face. "I, too, had to sacrifice my own babies. I drank their blood. My husband's also. But he was a weak, pathetic man, and I *hated* him. But, you know how that feels, don't you? Your husband is weak and pathetic too. Worthless. He sold you . . . *all* of you. And for what? A few morsels of knowledge from the distant past? He values history and the dead more than he cares for you. He's been exchanging emails with me for weeks, all the while knowing that I was closing in, that he was putting his wife and children in danger.

"And do you know what? He doesn't even know if I told him the truth or lies. He probably doesn't care. He just couldn't help himself. And who could blame him? What man would choose *you* over *me*?"

Kathleen doesn't appear to react, gives no sign that she's even listening.

"And the worst part?" Lilith continues, shrugging. "None of it matters in the end. Because your daughter is going to die too."

Kathleen looks up at her. Her eyes look dead. There's no shock there . . . no outrage . . . just a hollowness.

"But you *knew* that, didn't you?" Lilith says, lifting Kathleen's face in her hands. "You knew that, no matter *what* you chose, both your children were going to die. How did you do it, dear one? How did *you* choose?"

Lilith laughs. "I had three sons and a daughter. Lucifer didn't specify which of them I had to kill first to fulfill my part of the Covenant. So I decided to drink the blood of my oldest boy first, because he reminded me of his father. He was only five years old. I saved my daughter for last. Then I waited until my husband returned from hunting beasts for our dinner. I arranged their bodies so he would think the children were sitting up, waiting for his return. But he soon discovered the truth. Then, when he was sobbing on his knees, I slit his throat with his own obsidian knife. Then I drank his blood."

She smiles. "I feel as if we are *sisters*." She kisses Kathleen on the lips and then lets my wife's head drop.

"Arturo," she says, turning to one of the vampires, "you may have the girl."

"Thank you, my Queen," the vampire says, and he advances on my little girl.

"Daddee!" Abby screams.

Moving very quickly, Arturo lifts my daughter up.

Abby screams and kicks at him, but it does no good. The vampire turns her so she's facing me.

"Daddy! Help meeee!"

Arturo holds Abby close to his chest. His fangs are poised to take my daughter's life.

Kathleen says nothing. She looks weakly at Abby. Kathleen's mouth works, but she makes no sound.

"Tony," Lilith says, smiling sweetly. "Tony, my love, you can *save* her. *Save* your daughter. Go ahead! Command Arturo to stop . . . if you can."

"In . . . the name . . ."

"That's it!" she croons with a malevolent grin that somehow still looks alluring. *Even when mocking me, she's stunning.* "You can do it! This is all your doing, but go ahead! Maybe Father won't let your daughter suffer for your failings."

Abby looks at me in panic. "Daddeee! *Please!*"

Arturo smiles. "Hush, little one," he says.

♦ ♦ ♦

"My babies," Kathleen moans, staring at the lifeless bodies of our children, oblivious to all else.

Lilith comes over and sits beside me. She places a hand on my knee. She leans in toward me and says, "Now, lover, tell me what I should do with your little wife. You're thinking she's all you have left to live for . . . well, that is, except for *me* . . . but she'll *never* forgive you for what you've done."

"What *you* did," I whisper.

"Oh, Tony," she replies, "you knew who and what I was when you decided to . . . engage in *intercourse* with me. Now, don't get me wrong, Kathleen. Tony has never been unfaithful to you *physically*, but he *did* betray you. Tony, lover, you decided that knowing *me* was more important than the safety of your wife and children. That's the very *essence* of infidelity."

She points at Kathleen. "Look at her, Tony. She *hates* you for what you've done. Look in her eyes."

Kathleen lifts her head for a moment. Our eyes lock. *Is that forgiveness . . . understanding I see?*

"How . . . could you?" she says. And then her head falls forward.

I cry out, "Kathleen!"

"Don't worry, lover. Her heart beats still," Lilith says. "You can still *save* her. She'll never forgive you, but you can spare her life. I don't know if her *mind* will survive. In fact, I'm quite sure she'll be quite mad, if she's not already. But, the Seed can cure that as well."

Her finger strokes my cheek as lightly as a feather boa.

My flesh tingles at her touch.

"So, Tony," she says, "I offer you a choice: you can answer my questions as I answered yours, and I'll Heal her. Or you can choose not to help me and I'll drain her myself. And you'll watch and listen as she curses your name."

All my fault. This is all my fault.

"I told you once that you would come to me of your own free will," Lilith whispers loudly in my ear.

"You're *forcing* me," I say. "It's not my choice."

"Ah, lover," she coos. "Of course, it's your choice. Every decision you've made up to this point has led you here. Every branching path you choose leads to a different set of choices. Every choice you make determines the choices you can make in the future. I'm not *forcing* you. I'm offering you yet another choice. That's what seduction is: a hundred little choices, a hundred little lies, seemingly harmless in themselves, until the prey believes that he *must* surrender, that the reward or pleasure of a moment is worth the loss of his eternal soul."

She's right. Of course, she is. This is the path I chose. *I was lying to myself every step of the way, convincing myself the knowledge was worth it, that what I was doing was harmless.*

And the cost . . . *the cost has been the lives of my children . . . and Kathleen's sanity.*

But I can't help *this creature. I can't. I can't betray my friends. I can't!*

Lilith sighs.

"Very well," she says, rising from the bench. "Wake her up and . . ."

"Stop." My surrender is a mere whisper. *To save my wife, all I can manage is a whisper.*

Lilith holds up a hand. "Yes, Tony?"

"I'll tell you . . . anything. Just spare Kathleen."

"Of course, you will, lover. I never doubted it."

Chapter 10

Moira

Ring.

Of all the people in all the world to call me at such a time as this, the last person I'd expect to hear from would be Winnie Morrison. But my cell phone's ringing, and the wee screen's displaying her name. 'Tis barely three in the morning. If she's awake, it could be her Lortabs wearing off. She's still recovering from the injuries she sustained last month at the cruel hands of Müller and his mortal acolytes. But she's weaning herself from the medication. As far as I know, nae being her attending physician now that Winnie's out of the hospital, she's only taking them at night so she can sleep.

Ring.

'Tis a simple ring. I was never one to adopt a silly musical tone as so many people use. The unpretentious ring of an old-fashioned telephone suits me best.

Ring.

In-Tae and I are sitting at the table in Tony and Kathleen's kitchen. We've just finished triggering the calling tree to notify and ascertain the whereabouts and status of all the members of the Stake. Everyone's accounted for except, of course, for the Lupescus. Right now, Carl, Lorenzo, Rolf, and the former Enforcer, Sergei, are combing the house and yard. They're looking for any clue that might've been left behind by Lilith's people. We have nae idea where Lilith has taken Tony and his family.

Lorenzo's bearing up reasonably well . . . . now. If 'twere me, I'd be beside myself with grief and sheer panic.

Ring.

I really should answer it, but I dinnae think I have the strength to deal with Winnie just now.

Once Carl confirmed that Lorenzo was nae longer able to keep sight of that black leviathan of a helicopter, the one that bore our friends away, Carl ordered Lorenzo and Rolf to meet us at Tony's house. (Most times, my laddie does better avoiding giving direct command, which nae vampire in the Stake, other than me, can disobey. This was nae one of those times.) As we flew to the house, Carl did his best to calm Lorenzo.

"*You won't do them any good by panicking and just flying east,*" my husband told him over the phone. *My dearie's voice was calm, belying the haunted pain in his eyes.*

He's blaming himself, *I thought. They placed their trust in him, and he was nae able to protect them. He took precautions, but 'twas nae sufficient to keep them from harm.*

"*We don't know where they've gone,*" *Carl said.*

"*But she'll kill them!*" *Lorenzo's voice was frantic.* "*Tony she'll keep alive, but they'll kill Kathleen and the children! She'll kill them! Or worse! You know what she and her disciples are capable of! And then she'll kill them! You know she will!*"

"*You're right,*" *Carl said.* "*She will.*" *His voice was even, simply stating the facts.*

"*Carl!*" *Lorenzo cried, the agony naked in his voice, but Carl cut him off.*

"*She'll keep Tony alive to get information out of him. She'll either Persuade him, in which case she'll dispose of Kathleen and the kids . . . or she'll use them as leverage. Either way, there's* nothing *we can do to help them at the moment, not if we don't know where they've gone.*"

"*We can't just do* nothing!"

Carl's expression hardened, his face like flint, the muscles in his jaw twitching. "*We can save those that are* left.*"

This is killing him, *I thought. 'Tis killing me too.*

"*We have to assume,*" *Carl continued,* "*that any knowledge Tony has is* compromised. None *of us can go home. One way or another, Tony will be forced to give up every name, every meeting place, every address, every phone number . . .*"

"*Tony not know all.*" *That was Rolf's voice. It was a little fainter than Lorenzo's, but plain to hear.*

"*Yes,*" *Carl replied,* "*but he knows enough. We have to save the ones that're left. Meet us at Tony's house, and we'll see if there's anything we can learn there. I'll call Sergei. He'll be the expert.*"

"*Sergei,*" *Lorenzo said.* "*Si, call Sergei.*"

"*Focus on that, Lorenzo. And* pray.*"

I have offered up many prayers myself, but I cannae shake the feeling, nae, the near *certainty,* that they are all . . .

Please, Father in Heaven! I know that death is nae the ultimate end of life, but death is also nae the worst that Lilith and her minions can inflict on them. Spare them that! In all likelihood, Tony may be the only one to survive . . . and that for only a wee bit. Help him to stay true. But let him give up all *the information! We'll survive . . . with thy help. But help him to stay true!*

The phone rings again.

In-Tae rises from the table. "I'm going to go give them a hand with the search."

Ring.

"Aren't you going to answer that?" he asks as he leaves the room.

With a sigh, I flip it open.

"Aye, Winnie?"

"Moira, thank heaven you answered!"

"Winnie, 'tis nigh three . . ."

"Moira, your house is on fire!"

"My . . . house? On fire?" *What's she saying? Those words should mean something to me . . .*

"What should I do?" Winnie asks.

What's she going on about?

"Do?" *My house is . . .*

"Moira! Aren't you listening? Your house is on *fire*!"

My home! Our home!

"Have ye called nine-one-one?" *I've lived in that house for more than sixty years!*

"Yes! I called them! The fire department's here, but, Moira, I think . . . Well, it's bad."

"Aye, Winnie. Thank ye. Is anyone else's home in danger?"

"I don't think so. I've got a clear view from here."

Aye, lassie, I ken that ye do. Ye've spied on me for decades.

"That's grand," I say, trying to keep my voice calm. "Thank ye, Winnie."

My home's lost! Compared to the loss of Tony, Kathleen, Abby, and Little Tony, 'tis but a wee thing, but I want to just hang my head and weep.

I'm about to hang up when Winnie says, "Moira?"

"Aye?"

"I'm sorry . . . about your flower garden."

My flower garden? "Ach, lassie! Dinnae worry yourself about it."

"But . . . this is the first time in years . . ." Her voice trails off.

Aye, 'tis the first time in years ye have nae dug up my flowers . . . well, ye did dig them up twice in the spring, but ye did nae do it again after I replanted, as ye have done so often in the past.

I can hear the distant sirens and horns over the phone.

"Aye, and they were just starting to bloom too."

"I'm sorry, Moira. It was m . . ."

"I know, Winnie, I know. And all's forgiven."

"I'm sorry."

"I must go now, lassie."

"Moira?"

"Aye?"

"Is this . . . Is this part of that 'war' you told me about? Is that why your house is burning? The war with those . . . *creatures* . . . those *evil* vampires?"

I sigh heavily. "Aye, lassie, more than likely. And we lost . . . some dear friends tonight." Now the tears do spill from my eyes. My voice breaks. "And we'll likely lose more in the days ahead. And, as I told ye, in the end . . . we're *all* going to die. If we *win* this war, all the vampires will be dead, Carl and I as well. But our friends . . . those that were taken this night, and we dinnae know if they are alive or dead or . . . worse . . . They were *mortals*, Winnie, mortals we had sworn to defend. And we failed . . ."

"You're my only friend." It's nae more than a whisper.

I dinnae ken if she *meant* for me to hear it.

But I know 'tis the raw truth.

Over the years, Winnie has driven everyone else away with her bitterness and bile, even her own husband, Heber. In my case, she's made a lifelong career of trying to destroy me, using the ever-youthful Moira MacDonald Morgan as her scapegoat, the source of all her troubles.

That all changed when she was abducted by Müller's man, Bartlett, and used as a pawn in Müller's attempt to destroy Carl and me. Sarah and then I (whom she terms "good vampires") saved her life. In the past month, she has come a long way, healing her body as well as her soul, but it takes time to excise the gall and hatred from your heart when ye've spent decades packing it in there. 'Tis like a toxic plaque in the arteries that nae only restricts the flow of blood; it wears out yer heart as well. But I've seen Winnie make progress since the night we talked in the hospital, the night I told her who and what I was, the night I was finally able to make a breach in that nigh-impenetrable wall she's built around her heart all her adult life.

But real, lasting change? Now that takes a while. We've talked a number of times since that night, and she has poured her heart out to me. I've gone from her nemesis to . . . what? Are we friends? She trusts me, I suppose, and, for Winnie, that's as close to friendship as she's known in many a year.

But now I've simply . . . run out of time.

I'm all she has, apparently, and I'll nae be here soon. One way or the other, I'll be dead. Then what'll become of Winnie? Who will be her friend?

"I'm sorry, Winnie," I say, "I wish . . . I wish there was more I could do, but I cannae return home. 'Tis gone now anyway. None of my friends, none of my vampire friends can return to their homes now. The enemy knows where we live or they soon will." *Tony kept the attendance records and his computer is missing.* "We have nae place to meet. The Sun . . ."

The full impact of my own words hits me like the blow of a war hammer to my skull.

The waking nightmare comes unbidden to my mind. I'm hanging, crucified on Müller's foul cross. I can smell my own flesh and hair burning in the lethal rays of the Sun. On fire! The pain in my memory is bad, but the smell! I'll ne'er be able to get that smell out of my nostrils!

"The Sun'll be up in a few hours," I say in a panic, "and we have nae place to shelter so many from it! We must find a place to hide! Winnie, I have to go!"

I terminate the call abruptly.

"Carl!" I stand and turn to go after him. I can hear him upstairs. *He's searching one of the bedrooms.* "Carl! We have a problem, laddie!"

My phone rings again. I pause and look at the screen. 'Tis Winnie. *I can do nae more for ye, lassie. I've got more immediate problems right now.*

Carl, Lorenzo, Rolf, Sergei, and In-Tae all return to the kitchen.

"What's wrong?" Sergei's the one who speaks, but I can see the same question plainly written on the countenances of the other four.

The phone rings again. I push the button on the side to reject the call.

I face my husband. "Carl! We cannae go home! None of us can!"

"Sweetheart, we *know* this. But the safe house . . ." he says.

"Our home's on fire," I say.

He looks shocked. Then pain twists his face.

"'Tis Lilith's doing, nae doubt."

He opens his arms as if to enfold me and comfort me. "Aw, honey, I'm sorry."

How I want him to hold me right now!

"There's nae time for that!" I shake my head firmly. "D'ye nae ken what this means? Lilith kens where we live! That means Tony's told her everything!"

"But she doesn't know *everything*!" Lorenzo insists. "Tony didn't know everybody's addresses. I don't think he knew of the location of your safe house."

"That'll only delay her," Sergei says, "and not for long. She'll be able to get every name from Tony's computer, and with her resources and contacts, it won't take her long to locate every rental, every hotel room, every real-estate holding. You can't count on her *not* finding out. Her eyes and ears are everywhere."

Ring.

I glance at my phone. 'Tis Winnie again. *Give over, lass! I dinnae have the time!*

"Carl," I say as I reject the call yet again, "we must find a place where we can all shelter. Dawn's coming soon! If what Sergei says is correct, we dare nae use bank cards and the like to purchase hotel rooms or extract money from cash machines."

"That's not a problem," Sergei says. "We can just use Persuasion to get hotel rooms for the night."

"That'd be stealing," Carl says with a shake of his head.

"What?" Sergei laughs once. Disbelief is plain on his face. "You're joking!"

"You're new at this," In-Tae says. "Our oath to Carl can protect us only so long as we keep the commandments of God. If we *willfully* disobey God, the covenant we made with Him could be broken, and then we'd be subject to Lilith again. We have to be *very* careful."

"Is joke, *dah*?" Sergei says. "What? No stealing? No killing mortals; *that* I understand. But what? No lying? No swearing? No women? No sex?"

"Not outside marriage," the Korean replies. "At least, as far as the sex is concerned."

"Do you know how long it's been since I've gone the night without *at least* one woman?" Sergei's hands tremble. "How? How do you just . . . ?" His face has a stricken look.

In-Tae nods knowingly with a sad smile. "Prayer, my friend. *Lots* of prayer. And read the book I gave you. That's one of the reasons you get a senior companion when you join us: to help keep you out of trouble."

"Well, I'm glad *that's* out in the open," Carl says. "Frankly, I was a little worried about you, Sergei. You didn't come to this the same way the rest of the Stake did. Their repentance came *first* and the oath *afterward*. I didn't want to say anything about it . . . I didn't want to suggest it to you . . . Well, I figured it'd be harder for you than most as it is."

Ring.

'Tis Winnie . . . yet again.

"But right now," Carl says, "we have to find a way to survive the night . . . *without* stealing hotel rooms. Maybe the safe house'll be OK . . . for the night . . . but we couldn't get all of us in there. I need *alternatives*, folks, and fast."

Ring.

I suppose she's nae going to give up.

I try to compose myself so that my voice'll nae betray the annoyance I feel. I open my phone and put it to my ear. "Aye, Winnie?"

"Moira?"

"Aye, Winnie?" I repeat.

"You said you need a place to meet and stay safe from the sun, right? How big a place do you need?"

I'm stunned. That's nae what I expected to hear. The men around me look just as dumbfounded as I feel. Especially Carl. He knows Winnie all too well.

"We . . ." I clear my throat. "We need to find shelter for more than seventy people."

"OK. I think I can help," she says.

"How?"

"You can use my dance studio. It should be big enough."

My eyes lock with Carl's. He mouths, "Dance studio?"

"Dance studio?" I echo back to Winnie. "Ye . . . Ye're a . . . *dancer?*"

"What?" She sounds offended. "Are you saying you wouldn't know it to look at me?"

Is she joking? I've known Winnie since she was a teenager, but I never knew her to be a dancer. Once upon a time, she was a pretty thing, but I dinnae remember her ever bein' graceful. And that was two hundred pounds ago.

Hippopotami pirouetting with alligators to the "Dance of the Hours."

That's unkind, lassie!

"Forget about it," she says. "I *did* dance a little ballroom in college, but that was many, many years ago. No, dance was Heber's thing. The studio was his. *I* got it in the divorce. I don't really *do* anything with it. I just hire the teacher, keep the books, and live off the proceeds."

"What about the teacher?" I ask. "The students?"

"The teacher's away for a couple of weeks, touring with her little troupe. The studio should be big enough for your whole group. It even has a couple of showers and one of those instant water heaters so you never run out of hot water. I'm afraid it's only got one toilet, though. That's not much for seventy people."

"Winnie, ye're a lifesaver . . . literally. And dinnae worry about the toilet. Our kind has nae need of one. But the showers would be a blessing!"

"You don't . . . go to the bathroom?"

"Nae once in two and a half centuries."

"Wow." She pauses a tick. "Anyway, the studio basement used to be a Civil Defense shelter in the fifties and sixties. So there's a lot of old cots in the basement. I don't think there's enough for all of you, but . . ."

"It'll be grand, lassie. Thank ye. I'd say this makes us about even."

"Not . . ." Her voice breaks. I hear a choked sob. "Not hardly! Oh, Moira! I'm so, *so* sorry! All those years!"

"Water under the bridge, lassie. Ye've saved many lives this night!"

"But, *not for long!*" The gurgling sound of her voice is horrible to hear. "Oh, what am I going to do? I'll be . . . all alone again!"

"I'm sorry, Winnie. Bishop Adams loves ye too. He'll be there for ye. And dinnae forget that the Savior loves ye. He'll nae abandon ye. When all others have gone, He'll still be there."

She sobs for a moment longer. Then she sniffs long and loud. "You'll need a key."

"Aye, that we will."

"Can you . . . come by the house and get it?" Her voice drops to a whisper. "And say good-bye?"

She sounds like a lost little child.

I look up at Carl, but I know the answer even before he shakes his head.

"More than likely, it's a trap," Sergei whispers. "The destruction of your home could very well be meant to lure you to the area for an ambush. You can't go. You're indispensable."

"*None* of us are 'dispensable!'" Carl hisses.

"Then some are more indispensible than others," the Russian hisses back. "This war is *lost* if either of you dies before you can assassinate Lilith. If I'm going to have to spend my few remaining days without *sex*, I'm going to make da . . . I'm going to make *absolutely certain* you two survive to fulfill your task."

"Moira, are you still there?" Winnie asks.

"Aye, lassie, I'm still here. But, I cannae come by. We think that my house . . . my home was destroyed to draw Carl and me out. We dare nae show our faces in the neighborhood. I'll send someone round shortly to collect the key."

"No, that won't be necessary." She sniffs again. "I'm just being a silly old goose. Laura Adams is here with me tonight. You know: she's here from the Relief Society since I'm not able to get around all that well still. She can meet you at the studio. Here's the address . . ."

◢ ◢ ◢

Saying good-bye to Winnie Morrison, even over the phone, is much harder than I expected. I've spent decades dreadin' the very sound of her voice. But she seems so helpless, so lost. And I feel as if I'm abandoning her. 'Tis unlikely I'll see her again. Nae so long ago, the very thought of ne'er e'er having to lay eyes on her again would have brought a smile to my face . . . 'twould have been a *guilty* smile, to be sure . . . but now, as I close the phone, grief overwhelms me.

I try to choke off a sob, but it escapes my throat. I stumble forward, and Carl catches me in his arms. And all the grief, all the many losses of this night come pouring from me like a storm breaching a levy. The floodwaters devastate and sweep away all in their path.

Tony.
Kathleen.
Abby.
Little Tony.
Sammy, not dead but hurting.
My job.
Our home.
Even the prospect of ne'er seeing Winnie Morrison again.

Somehow, in my loss of control, I'm aware of the soft, retreating footsteps of the others. Only Carl remains with me. He's holding me close, and I'm clingin' to him as if I might drown, were I to let go.

My dearie begins to stroke my hair. My mother used to stroke my hair when I was a wee lass and was sad or frightened. Carl does nae say anything. He simply holds me.

A little tremor runs through his chest.

He's grieving too.

I'm nae alone. Carl's with me. We can face this. Together.

And we'll rid the Earth of Lilith and her thrice-cursed Children.

Chapter 11

Moira

"Moira, what's going on?" Laura Adams's voice sounds as ragged as she looks ... and she has certainly looked better. Normally an attractive woman in her late fifties, Laura's a mess. Her clothes are wrinkled, and her graying hair's untidy. Spending the night fully dressed on a strange couch, only to be awakened by sirens and a fire in a neighbor's house, is nae conducive to getting sufficient beauty sleep. "Winnie sends me here," she says, "tells me you need the key to her studio, and you need it *now*, in the middle of the night, but she won't say *why* it's so blasted urgent! 'It's not my place to say,' she says. So what in the world is going on?"

All of this comes spilling out of Laura's mouth as soon as she pulls up to the curb in front of Winnie's downtown dance studio. She's driving Winnie's car, a late-model compact car (ye'd think 'twould be a wee bit small for Winnie), painted a dark metallic green. There's nae other traffic at this time of night save for a lone blue car that drives by. I bend down, and Laura hands me a key through the open car window.

"Thank ye, lassie. With our home gone ..."

"Your house!" She claps both hands to her face. "Oh, Moira! I'm so sorry! I'm so upset! I'm just not thinking straight! If you need a place to stay, you could stay with us, I'm sure!"

"I appreciate the offer, Laura, but, as ye can plainly see," I gesture toward Rolf, Lorenzo, In-Tae, and Sergei behind me, "there are too many of us to impose on someone at this hour of the night."

"But, Moira, your *home*!"

"I've had my cry already," I say. "We'll be just grand. Dinnae worry yourself about it."

"But your clothes! Your sun-allergy! Those lovely cloaks you always wear! What will you do? What will Carl do without that long coat and the huge Stetson hat he wears?"

The dear, sweet woman! I've known Laura Adams for more than half a century, since she was a wee bairn. I was her teacher in Primary so long ago. Her husband, Jacob, is now our bishop. They've been true friends to me over the years. Bishop Adams knows about Carl and me, of course, but Laura knows only that Carl and I have a mysterious, un-named "medical condition" that masks our true age. She's ne'er once said a word about it. Laura was my escort when I received my endowment and was sealed to my dear husband in the temple.

"To be honest, lassie, he *hated* that cowboy hat. He thought it made him look ridiculous. He just did nae have time to find something better."

And "hated" is putting it mildly. He loathed *that hat. He was always complaining about "the ridiculous Stetson."*

From behind me, I hear Carl whisper (too softly for Laura to hear), "Any sign of someone trailing her?"

"Nothing from the sky," Lorenzo replies just as softly. "Our airborne patrols report no activity over the city at all."

I glance quickly up to catch a glimpse of one of the six members of our bodyguard hovering high above us, keeping watch.

"How the heck did they miss that blasted giant helicopter over Provo?" Carl growls. "For that matter, how did they miss winged vampires flying in to set fire to my house?"

"Moira?" Laura can't hear the urgent discussion behind me, of course. I'll bet she does nae understand why I'm nae answering her. *What did she ask? Ach! 'Twas about the clothes! Normally, I can listen easily and fully follow two or more conversations at once . . . 'tis hard to* nae *listen to conversations going on several rooms away with my hearing, but tonight . . . I suppose, tonight I'm a wee bit frazzled.*

"I dinnae know what we're going to do," I reply. "We may just have to wait out the day in there."

"Oh, that won't do!" she says. "How will you go to work?"

I cannae go to work. Ne'er again. I fear my days as a physician are over. Ach! In a wee bit my life *will be over.*

"It doesn't have to be vampires," Sergei hisses. "Lilith has plenty of mor-tals to do her bidding."

"Yeah," Carl whispers, "you mentioned that. During the battle at Mül-ler's farm, I thought I saw a number of men with M-4 assault rifles under Lilith's pavilion and on board the helicopter."

"That would be the Honor Guard," Sergei says. "Lilith's elite body-guards, every one of them a United States Marine."

"Yeah, you mentioned them when we first met you," Carl whispers. "They're all mortals, right?"

"*Somebody's* got to watch over her and her Court during the day," Sergei replies as if 'twere the most obvious thing in the world.

"If they're evil mortals, how do they keep from being . . . consumed?" Carl whispers.

I turn about to look at Sergei.

Laura makes an exasperated huffing sound.

"I didn't say that they're *evil*," Sergei says. "Our kind . . . well, we aren't much good at resisting temptation, as you know. (Well, maybe *you* don't.) No, if they were evil, they wouldn't survive. An evil mortal *could* be spared or tolerated *if* Lilith were to command it, but she's not one to resist evil blood herself, not in close proximity."

"How then?" In-Tae asks. "Persuasion?"

"Moira?" Laura's voice comes from the car behind me.

"Just a wee moment, lassie," I say, keeping my back to her.

"*Nyet.*" Sergei shakes his head. "Exceptionally strong will and a virtual immunity to Persuasion is an essential qualification for membership in the Honor Guard. As far as *they* know, they're on special assignment from the Pentagon, safeguarding 'invaluable national security assets,' the exact nature of which is above their security clearance. An Honor Guard Marine rarely sees the *inside* of the Court, unless Lilith takes a *fancy* to one of them. If that happens . . . well, a replacement will be sent. It's not that they don't *see* things. The wings are hard to miss. But the Honor Guard is under strict orders to carry out missions for Lilith and obey her commands explicitly and without question."

"Moira?" Laura sounds annoyed.

I turn back to her. "Aye?"

"What's going on?" She nods in the direction of the others behind me. "Who are those men with Carl?"

"They're friends, lassie."

"Are you OK? No, that's silly. Of course, you're not OK. Oh my heck! What can I do to help?"

She looks so flustered, poor lass!

"It's been a stressful night, to be sure," I say.

Carl hisses, "I think I saw a number of these Honor Guard Marines under Lilith's pavilion that day. Wouldn't they have . . . I don't know . . . *questioned* the crucifixions or the battle or the slaughter or the flying vam-pires?"

Sergei chuckles mirthlessly. "Actually, I think they *did*. I wasn't there, of course. I wasn't an Enforcer at the time and wasn't party to that particular excursion, but I heard the Honor Guard was under strict orders not to interfere. I also heard they were slaughtered to a man on the return journey. Perhaps they'd seen too much. Perhaps they rebelled. I don't know. What I *do* know for certain is *none* of them returned, *all* of them had to be replaced, and there were a large number of very big bullet holes that had to be repaired in the helicopter."

Laura places a hand on my arm, drawing my attention back to her. "*Is* there anything? Moira? Anything at all that I can do?"

"Aye?" *I need to pay more attention to her.* "Oh, aye, lassie! That ye can! *Blankets!* 'Twould be as good as cloaks. Blankets and sunscreen. Heavy blankets and heavy-duty sunscreen, the highest SPF ye can find." I reach into one of the pockets of my jeans and pull out the wee coin purse I carry for emergencies. I open it and withdraw several hundred-dollar bills. I press them into her hand.

She looks at the money and there's puzzlement plainly written on her face. "Moira, this is too much! I can get some sunscreen for a few dollars, and we have a couple of spare blankets at the house . . . You *do* only need two, right?"

"Two?"

"For you and Carl, right?"

"Ah, well, ye see, lassie, there are . . ." *Noriko and Juanita are dead!* ". . . seventy-two of us."

"*Seventy . . . two?*" Her eyes are wide. "All with the same skin condition?"

Ach! How am I goin' to explain that?

Her eyes look downward and then go wide. "Moira, w-why are you wearing a . . . a sword? Oh, my! You . . . you've *all* got swords!"

Ach! I've gone daft! How could I forget about the swords? 'Tis twice in one night! We should've hidden them away, but we cannae be without them at night.

"Smell gun!" Rolf hisses.

I spin about to look at him.

"Where?" In-Tae looks wildly about.

"Car!" Rolf nods toward the opposite side of the street. "Evil blood no, but gun!"

I look in the direction he's indicating. A gentle breeze is blowing from that direction. There's that blue car rolling slowly by again, the front windows down. I can see two men seated in the front. I don't *see* any guns, but Rolf's right: I can smell the distinctive scent of the gun oil, solvent, and gunpowder.

"Two times," Rolf says. "Car . . . come two times."

I can clearly see that both men in the vehicle have their faces turned in our direction. One slides open a cell phone.

"*Chort vozmee!*" In an instant, Sergei is airborne, wings outspread, flying at the car. "Honor Guard!" he bellows. "Stand down!"

As Sergei lands in front of the vehicle, the car comes to an abrupt halt amid the stuttering protest of antilock brakes and the squeal of tires. The Russian's wings fold up and disappear. "Marines! Front and center! Report!" His voice has no trace of his customary Russian accent. Instead he sounds much like a proper American Marine Corps drill sergeant.

The two figures seated in the car hesitate a wee tick. Both glance our way and then back at Sergei. The doors of the car begin to open. Both men exit the car. They're dressed in casual civilian attire, but there is nae mistaking those short haircuts.

I'm too startled to do more than gape at the scene, but In-Tae's now in motion. Wingless, he flies across the street toward Sergei. Being the Russian's senior companion, his duty is to be with Sergei at all times to make certain that the new recruit does nae have a lapse. *Such as killing a mortal.*

One Marine visibly starts as In-Tae touches down, landing next to Sergei. In one fluid motion, he drops to one knee behind the open door of the car and barks what sounds like, "Contact! Eleven o'clock!" as he draws a large handgun from a holster at his hip. He fires the weapon twice in rapid succession. Blood sprays from In-Tae's chest. The second Marine also drops and fires twice as Sergei leaps and throws his body between In-Tae and the shooters. Each gunman fires a third shot.

In-Tae collapses like a marionette with the strings cut.

Four blossoms of crimson appear on Sergei's chest and shoulder and neck. *If he'd nae intervened, In-Tae might've taken a couple of rounds to the head!* The vision of Rolf keening inarticulately as he holds the body of Sarah Smythe flashes through my mind.

I leap into the air, but Rolf, Lorenzo, and Carl are there afore me. With a snarl, Rolf rips the gun from the hand of the nearest Marine. Lorenzo disarms the second man. Carl's kneeling on the ground next to In-Tae and Sergei, who're both clawing at their Healing wounds. Carl's protecting them with his body.

Rolf's Marine has drawn a wicked-looking dirk from somewhere, but Rolf relieves him of that weapon as well.

Lorenzo's nae so lucky. His Marine buries his dirk in Lorenzo's chest. *I must get that thing out of his heart!*

I fly quickly toward him, but, before I can get there, the Marine pulls the blade from Lorenzo's chest and draws the long knife to the side, ready to strike again.

He's going to decapitate him!

In that instant, I'm upon the Marine. I snatch the blade from his hand. He quickly moves to punch me with his left hand, but, as fast as he is, he cannae match my vampiric speed. In a trice, I have him facedown on the pavement with my knee in his back and his arms raised painfully behind him.

Rolf has his man in hand, one arm locked tight around the Marine's neck and both of the mortal's wrists pinned against his back. The man's still resisting, however.

"I said, 'Stand down!'" Sergei roars, obviously recovered sufficiently from his wounds. He leaps at Rolf's prisoner, hands reaching in front of him, his fangs extended, wings spread out like an avenging angel of death.

"Stop!" Carl cries.

The Russian freezes in mid air. He snarls with frustration and a murderous rage. "Let me have him!" All trace of the "drill sergeant" voice is gone. He's fully Russian once more.

"Have him?" Carl shakes his head. "For what, Sergei?"

Is Carl more upset that Sergei was about to murder the man or that he, Carl, was forced to give a command? *Most likely 'tis a bit of both.*

"He tried to kill one of us!" Sergei's trembling in his caged fury. "Let me go!"

"When you've calmed down." Carl's voice and face seem tempered as if he's in complete control, but I know my laddie: he's seething with fury. "He was only doing his duty as he saw it. Remember, Sergei: only *evil* blood . . . and then only with *proof* of guilt . . . and even then we don't *kill*. That's the code we have to live by."

"This *mortal zhyvotnoyeh* tried to kill one of *us*!" Sergei growls. "His life is *mine*! He has no right!"

"What *right* do we have to prey upon mortals?" In-Tae says, rising to his feet, still scratching at his chest through the bloody holes in his shirt. "We're not gods who can choose who lives and who dies! We're demons! We deserve death! We're damned! Every last one of us!" He pauses a tick. "Except for Carl, that is . . . and Moira. Our *only* hope for redemption is to follow Jesus Christ. That means we have to *forsake* our old ways. Remember, man? I read to you about the people of Ammon in the Book of Mormon. They buried their weapons. They laid down their *lives*, even refusing to defend their own families, rather than take another life. We need human blood to survive, but we *don't* have to *murder* to get it. We *can't*! Not if we want to have *any* hope of redemption from our sins! And these . . . these are *honorable* men."

Sergei stays frozen in the air, still poised as if to kill, but the tension in his body seems to evaporate. He sighs.

"You can let me go now, Carl."

Carl nods, though Sergei cannae see it. "OK."

The Russian goes limp, draws himself up into an erect posture, and then drops lightly to the ground, his wings vanishing from sight. He stares at the Marine in Rolf's custody. "Marines." His voice is cold as the tomb, but the Russian accent is gone. "Stand down."

"Aye-aye, sir!" the Marine in Rolf's custody says crisply and ceases his futile struggling.

"Aye-aye, sir!" the man beneath me grunts.

"You can release them," Sergei says.

I let go of my man's arms and get off his back.

He climbs painfully to his feet, rotating and working each shoulder to relieve the discomfort caused by my forcing his arms into an unnatural position.

I hope I did nae damage him.

I glance at Rolf and see that he has released his captive as well. The man is now rubbing at his wrists to restore the circulation that Rolf undoubtedly cut off. Rolf's resting his hand on the hilt of his sword . . . *Sarah's broadsword* . . . ready to draw it at the least sign of a threat.

Lorenzo's back on his feet now. His shirt's a bloody mess, but at least he has his head.

"Many thanks, *signora mia*," he says, rubbing at his neck.

I nod at him and give him a wee smile.

"With all due respect, sir," my Marine says, "would somebody mind telling me what in the *Sam Hill* is going on? Why're you consorting with the enemy?"

"Ah, but you see, Marines," Sergei says, "these people are *not* the enemy. They are . . ."

"Muh-Muh-Muh-Moira?" The voice is shaky and quiet, barely a whisper, like someone unable to muster a proper breath. "Muh-Moira?"

Laura! She's seen everything!

I look back at her. She's out of Winnie's car with the door open. One white-knuckled hand's on the door and the other's atop the vehicle. The only thing that seems to be holding her up is her paralyzing terror. Her face is bloodless, her eyes wide. Her lips tremble. "W-what . . . what *are* you? Moira, what's . . . what's going on?" A shudder seizes her body. "Oh my! That *was* you, wasn't it? On the news? On the TV? I . . . I didn't *believe* it! She *looked* like you, but . . ." Her lips work soundlessly. "A-angel? With a sword? The man with the wings! You . . . *killed* him! W-what *are* you?"

Her eyes roll up into her head. Her hand slips from the top of the car.

In an instant, I'm across the street and catching her under the arms as she faints dead away.

Chapter 12

Carl

W e need to get inside, people!" *That's not a command, is it? I wish I'd been able to stop Sergei from killing that Marine* without *commanding him to stop.* "Somebody's probably already reported those gunshots, and every available cop in town will be on their way. We've got three minutes tops." I listen for just a second for the sound of approaching sirens. *Nothing yet, thank Heaven! Would they be coming with sirens blaring?* I point at the Russian. "Sergei, would you *please* get them"—I point at the Marines—"to police their brass, park their car, and follow us inside?" *They're more likely to obey him than me.* "There's a parking garage down the block. And hurry, please?"

He nods. "*Da-da-da.*"

I turn to Sergei's senior comp. "In-Tae?"

"Go with him?" the Korean asks, anticipating my request.

I nod.

"You got it, Cap'n!" He says with a wicked grin.

Why can't they just call me "Carl?"

"Lorenzo and Rolf, park Sister Adams's car for her, if you would. The key should be in the ignition."

Of course, it's in the ignition, Morgan! It's still running! You're wasting time!

Lorenzo nods.

However, Rolf hesitates. "'Police their brass?'"

"It means to pick up the shell casings," I reply.

Rolf still looks confused.

"I'll explain it to him," Lorenzo replies, pulling Rolf by the arm. They hurry off toward Laura's car.

"OK!" I clap my hands twice loudly. "Let's *move* it, folks! *Please!* We're supposed to be *fast!*"

Moira has the door to the studio unlocked already. I catch just a glimpse of her as she carries the limp form of Laura Adams inside.

"What about us, Carl?" The voice comes from above, soft but distinct. Phillipa. One of the bodyguards on watch in the sky. She's got to be shouting to be heard from that altitude.

"*Please*, stay on station for now." I'm not shouting . . . exactly. I don't want to attract any more attention to us here on the ground. *Like a shout would draw any more attention than six gunshots!* "I'll have someone relieve you when the rest of us start arriving."

Did she hear me? Maybe I should call her. Do I even have her number in my . . .

"Sounds good." The reply comes from above. "Carl?"

"Yeah?"

"Sorry we didn't get there in time to help with the fight. By the time I realized the shots were coming from where *you* were . . ."

"Not a problem, folks. But, for now, be on the lookout for anyone else converging on our position from the ground."

"Will do."

"And when our friends approach, make sure you challenge and authenticate *everybody*."

"Yes, sir."

Morgan, you idiot! "I meant, *please* be on the lookout and *please* challenge and authenticate!"

I hear faint chuckles from up above me.

"Will do!"

At least when I'm dead I won't have to use that blasted word *every time I open my mouth!*

They seem to treat it as a joke when I slip up and rob them of their free will. To me . . . it's the ultimate sin. Nobody should have the power to compel obedience in others, to take away their right to choose . . . even if that right has been freely surrendered.

And I have so many who look to me to lead them, to protect them, to keep them alive until we have a chance to kill Lilith and then die. We lost Tony, Kathleen, Abby, and Little Tony tonight. We lost Noriko and Juanita. How many more will we lose before it's all over?

They're in God's hands now. There's nothing more I can do for the dead.

I failed them.

Especially Tony and Kathleen and Abby and Little Tony. (Sharon and Lucy and April and Joseph.)

How many more will I fail? How many more will die because I'm not smart enough, fast enough, good enough to outwit a six-thousand-year-old Queen?

Stow it, Morgan! When this is over, they're all going to die . . . all the vampires at least. You and Moira too. It's in the Prophecy.

Focus on the blasted mission! *Focus on saving the ones you can. Especially the mortals.*

I hear the sound of several people approaching on foot. They're coming from the direction of the parking garage. It should be our people coming this way, but, all the same, I place my hand cautiously around the grip inside the basket hilt of my sword. I don't draw the weapon from its sheath, but having the claymore in my hand is comforting. I'll never be as good as Moira, but I'm no slouch with a blade now.

Rolf is the first to round the corner. He's followed by Lorenzo, the two Marines, Sergei, and In-Tae. The Marines look tense.

No, "tense" is the wrong word. They look . . . lethal.

Their Colt forty-five semiautos are holstered at their right hips and their dirks are sheathed at their left. But, even though their weapons are stowed, these men remind me of vipers ready to strike.

I step forward to join the six of them. As we walk back toward the door of the studio, I whisper ultrasoftly, "Sergei, are our guests OK?"

"The situation's under control," he whispers back. "They still think of me as their superior officer. I've informed them that *you* are *my* commander. They've got questions, but . . ."

"Sir?"

I stop and turn around. It's the Marine that shot In-Tae. His face is hard, like stone roughly chiseled into sharp angles. The rest of the group stops and turns to listen. Both Marines are looking at me intently.

"Yes, Marine?" I say. *We've got to hurry!*

"My apologies, sir. I misread the situation."

Sergei clears his throat. "They had *faulty intel.*" His accent sounds authentically American Midwestern.

I nod. "What's your name, Marine?"

"Sergeant Marcus Ortiz, sir."

I hear a snort. I glance in Rolf's direction. *Is he stifling a laugh? Rolf? Laughing?*

Ortiz points to his fellow Marine and says, "Lance Corporal Hall, sir."

"No harm done, Marines. You can explain once we're safely inside."

Amazingly, his face hardens all the more. "A Marine never explains his mistakes or makes excuses, sir. He apologizes and takes responsibility for his actions."

Great going, Morgan! You've insulted him! "Apology accepted, Marine. We'll debrief you inside." I turn around and walk briskly toward the studio door. "Rolf, you and Lorenzo, as soon as we get inside . . . I want the two of you to activate the calling tree again and get our people here." *That's not an order and I didn't say the dreaded p-word!* "And I want to get the Gallaghers here as well. I think they'll be safer with us. Will you make sure that gets done?"

Lorenzo nods.

"*Si.*"

That wasn't Lorenzo! That was Rolf! The poor guy should be speaking German or, at the very least, English . . . if he could remember it properly.

And he's smiling!

"You've been hanging out with Lorenzo too much, bub!" I punch him lightly on the shoulder.

He looks at me with a quizzical expression for a second. Then his eyes go wide. *He didn't realize he was speaking Italian!* Then he winks. "Aye-aye, Captain Morgan, sir!" His accent is a perfect mimicry of what my dear wife calls my "pilotspeak."

Rolf is the first to the door, and he holds it open for the rest of us. "After you . . ." His face screws up as he appears to be searching for a suitable word.

"Gentlemen," Lorenzo prompts.

Rolf shakes his head. "No. Not the word." He grins wickedly. "After you . . . *ladies* . . . and *sailors*." He looks pointedly at Sergeant Ortiz.

The man gives Rolf a murderous look before locking his eyes forward.

I let the rest of them pass through the door before I whisper softly, "You *do* know that 'sailor' is about the most insulting thing you can call a Marine, don't you?"

The grin on his Aryan face widens. "Aye-aye, Captain Morgan, sir!"

What's got him in such a good mood? "You're evil. You know that, don't you?" It's good to see Rolf smile again. *I wonder what's gotten into him, though.* "Lock the door behind you, *please*."

"Aye-aye, Captain Morgan, sir!"

"OK. Knock it off." I hastily add, "I mean, *please* knock it off!"

Rolf laughs heartily.

I wish I could find something to laugh about tonight.

"Multiple police vehicles approaching at high speed! They're running silent!" That was Phillipa. And, yes, I can hear the cars as well.

Rolf closes the door and locks it behind himself.

Just in time. The last thing we need tonight is to have to deal with police . . . again.

The dance studio looks pretty much as expected. There's a hardwood floor, a wall of mirrors with a handrail in front of it. There's a small office off to the left. I try to picture Winnie Morrison's vast bulk sitting at the little desk in there, but, in all likelihood, she never comes here. The office is probably just for the teacher. There's a single bathroom next to it. At the right end of the room, there's an open door. I can hear sounds of activity coming from there. *That must be the door to the basement.* Which is where we'll all be spending the day.

Sergei, In-Tae, and the Marines are probably already down there. Yes, I can hear footsteps on the stairs.

Lorenzo, however, is hanging back. He watches Rolf as the German passes him on the way to the door. Rolf chuckles to himself. Lorenzo looks at me and mouths, "What's up with him?"

I shrug my shoulders. "No clue!" I mouth back.

I catch up to Lorenzo, and he whispers as softly as he can, "Laughter's better than the silent weeping. I catch him doing that when he thinks nobody can see."

"But after our losses tonight . . . particularly the Lupescus . . ."

Lorenzo's face turns ashen. His shoulders droop. His back bends as if the weight of all his five hundred years has aged him in an instant.

"Oh, man," I say, "I'm an idiot! Lorenzo, I'm so sorry. Your family!"

"I've lost many family members over the centuries. But I haven't been . . . this *close* to any of them since my Mara passed." A tear spills from his eye and down his cheek. "I've seen so much death in my life. All mortals die . . . even those we love. We mourn them and we move on. What else can we do? You're so young. You have so little experience with this. The hard part . . . the really difficult thing . . . is the not *knowing*. Are they dead or are they suffering in the hands of the demon Queen and her minions?"

I have no answers for him.

"And, as you say, Carl, even if they're alive, we don't know where they are. There's nothing, nothing at all we can do for them."

"We can pray."

He nods. "*Si.*" He straightens to his full height. The centuries fall off him like a discarded cloak. "I *can* pray. I will ask God to help them. Either to end their suffering and take them to Himself or to deliver them from the evil."

I put a hand on his shoulder.

He gives me a weak smile. "It's good to see Rolf laugh."

"Yeah," I say. "Good, but *weird.*"

"I'll ask him what's so funny."

"*After* the calling tree." *Is that a command?* I open my mouth to say the dreaded p-word.

Lorenzo wags a finger at me, freezing the word before I can utter it. "Not necessary, *capitano mio.* I feel no compulsion to obey . . . not that I *wouldn't*, mind you. You're barely a fraction of the age of most of those who follow you, but you're a *good* man and a *good* commander. You're doing *fine*. As you are wont to say, 'Don't sweat the small stuff.'"

I sigh. "Thanks."

We head down the stairs to join the others.

"We need to report in, Sarge." Lance Corporal Hall looks stoic but intensely uncomfortable, as if he's sitting rigidly at attention while fighting the urge to scratch a nearly unbearable itch.

Been there. Done that.

If I had to guess, I'd say that Hall isn't as ready as Ortiz to accept the situation. He's a Marine. He'll follow any *lawful* order, but that doesn't mean he'll be happy about it. But honor is *everything* to these guys.

We're sitting on old military-issue camp cots arranged in an irregular circle in the basement of the studio. There are racks and racks of folded cots along the walls, together with old tins of crackers, water, etc. The faded Civil Defense posters are up on the walls in places. It's a wonder Winnie never had all this cleared out.

Laura's lying on a cot, still out cold, at the other end of the huge basement. The cavernous room is broken up only by the square cement columns that support the ceiling above us.

Moira's sitting on the floor beside Laura, checking the woman's pulse. I'm pretty sure Moira's letting Laura rest for a bit. My wife's probably *not* in a hurry to explain to Laura what she just witnessed. Better to let her come out of her faint at her own pace . . . for now.

Moira's most likely using the opportunity to listen in on our conversation over here and to Rolf and Lorenzo as they work through the calling tree. *How does she do that? How does she follow multiple conversations at once?*

Sergeant Ortiz reaches for his cell phone. "Hall's right, sir," he says, looking at me. "We're"—he glances at his watch—"almost three minutes overdue."

Sergei looks dubious. "I'm not sure . . ."

"You have my word, sir," Ortiz says, interrupting, "that I will not . . . compromise the situation." He glances sternly in the lance corporal's direction.

Hall nods curtly.

I nod as well. "Proceed, Marine."

Ortiz pushes a button on his phone. I realize for the first time that it's one of those cell phone/radio combo units that're suitable for instant communications. "Viper, this is Sidewinder."

The radio-phone crackles in response. "Roger, Sidewinder. This is Viper. What's your favorite sport?"

Ortiz stares me right in the eye as he presses the button. "Football. All is well."

"Roger, Sidewinder. Are you en route back?"

"That's a negative at this time. We're going to stay on site and observe a bit longer, but I don't think there's any cause for concern here."

"Roger, Sidewinder. Viper out."

Ortiz puts the phone back in his pocket. "They can track the location of this phone, sir. We'll have to make regular reports or bring them up to speed. Otherwise, they're going to question why we're not en route back to the burn site. We were not informed that Redstar would be in the vicinity."

Redstar? Who the heck is Redstar?

Sergei speaks up quickly. "Sergeant, Lance Corporal, I came out here to infiltrate what I was informed was a unit of hostile paranorms."

So Sergei is "Redstar." That must be his codename with these Marines. And we're the "hostile paranorms."

"And did you, sir?" Ortiz asks, looking at Sergei.

"I was successful, but I quickly realized that we had bad intel. The Wingless are not hostile . . . not to the United States. In fact, I discovered that our intel was deliberately misleading. But, we'll get to that later. Right now, we need to get you debriefed. Tell us about your mission here, Ortiz."

Ortiz glances around the room. "Are all these people Papa-Novembers, sir?"

"Except for the civilian on the rack over there, all of us are paranorms and their clearance in this matter equals or exceeds my own. You may proceed."

Listening to the Russian speak easily in his flawless American accent using military jargon, I can easily imagine what an effective GRU operative he must have been.

Ortiz nods. "Aye, sir." He leans in and speaks softly and distinctly. "Four of us, Hall, Ericson, Kowalski, and myself, were dispatched to Utah. Our orders . . ."

"When were you dispatched?" Sergei interrupts. "How did you get here? All recon ops are supposed to be under my direct control."

"Our orders came from Empress herself."

Sergei nods. "I see."

Empress? That'd be Lilith, I suppose.

"We accompanied Empress and other Papa-Novembers on the MH-47X-ray. We arrived at 0337 Zulu at Hill Air Force Base. There were two cars waiting for us, ready for our use."

"Papa-November" equals "PN" equals "paranorm." By "paranormals" he means us. The MH-47X he's referring to must be Lilith's Chinook helicopter. The "X" means "experimental." In other words, the Chinook has been modified. I've never seen one so big.

"What was your mission?" Sergei prompts.

"We were to proceed to a residence in Salt Lake City and ascertain if the house was occupied. If so, we were to report back to Empress for further instructions. If not, we were to set fire to the unoccupied residence, wait until the house was engulfed, alert the local fire department, and observe. We were to report any sightings of wingless paranorms to Empress. We were to follow any civilian personnel found leaving the scene. Ericson and Kowalski remained at the scene. The Lance Corporal and I followed a green compact sedan to this location. We observed the meeting outside. We were told to be on special lookout for a red-haired woman in particular. We made multiple passes to determine the hair color of the woman we observed. We were about to report that we'd spotted the primary target when you intercepted us and the firefight ensued."

"What were your instructions if you observed the 'primary target'?" I ask.

"If possible, neutralize by putting two in the heart, one in the head, followed quickly by decapitation. As we were briefed, this is the only way to take down a paranorm."

Anger boils up in me. *Keep control, Morgan!* "Let me get this straight." I'm trying to keep my voice even. "You committed an act of arson on a private residence on American soil and you were prepared to assassinate an American citizen?"

"Aye, sir." His voice is calm, steady, matter-of-fact. *He could be reporting on the stock market.* "We were prepared to neutralize a hostile paranorm. We were briefed that friendly paranorms manifest wings and can fly, and that hostile paranorms are wingless. We were briefed to neutralize, on sight, any wingless . . ."

"And when," I interrupt him and growl through clenched teeth, "did it become legal and lawful to employ U.S. military forces against U.S. civilians on U.S. soil without a declaration of martial law, in violation of the Geneva Convention of 1949 and the Fourth and Fifth Amendments to the U.S. Constitution, not to mention the UCMJ?"

"That would be illegal and unlawful, sir."

"And that means you were following an *unlawful order*, Marine. And, by the way, that was my *home* you burned down tonight and that was my *wife* you were prepared to assassinate."

"Aye, sir." He stands and assumes the rigid posture of attention. "I accept responsibility for my actions and am ready to accept the consequences. For the record, sir, Lance Corporal Hall objected to the burning of the house."

"Is this true, Corporal?"

Hall rises to attention as well. He stares straight ahead. "Aye-aye, sir! But I am ready to accept the consequences for my actions, sir!"

The integrity of these men, in the face of what they must believe is certain retribution, kills my anger, deflating it like a punctured balloon. *Was Hall's apparent discomfort due to an internal conflict over his orders?*

"Of course you are," I say. "You're United States Marines, and therefore you are men of honor."

"And for the record, sir," Hall says, "Sergeant Ortiz also objected to the firing of the home."

Neither of them moves.

"At rest," I say.

They relax a little and look at each other and then at me.

"You deserve to know what you've gotten yourselves into," I say. "Take a seat."

They slowly, cautiously sit on the cot again.

"Tell me what you know about your current posting," I say.

Ortiz looks me in the eye. "The Honor Guard is an elite and highly classified unit of Marines assigned to safeguard the paranorms. We report directly to the paranorm codenamed Redstar. We are to follow his orders without question. The same goes for the other paranorms: we are expected to obey their orders. Redstar reports directly to the paranorm codenamed Empress. She reports directly to Major General Brooks at the Pentagon. We are to serve out of uniform to avoid attracting attention. Duty cycles typically last from sunrise to sunset. We are not to ask questions of the paranorms or fraternize with them, and we are not to enter the building, codenamed Night Palace, unless invited."

"And what have you been told about the 'paranorms,' Sergeant?"

"The paranorms are highly classified and essential national security assets, the exact nature of which is beyond my security clearance, sir."

"And what is your clearance level?"

"A security clearance of Top Secret-SCI is required for Honor Guard duty, sir."

That's an extremely high clearance.

"And what," I continue, "have you learned in the course of your duties?"

He hesitates. "Permission to speak freely, sir?"

"Granted."

"I have learned that I don't much care for this posting, nor do I like the people I'm supposed to protect. Redstar treats us with respect, but the rest seem . . . to lack any sense of honor. A Marine from the unit disappeared a couple of months ago and no one seemed to notice . . . officially. I have my suspicions, sir, but I am under orders not to ask questions."

"And what are your suspicions, Sergeant?" I ask.

He looks at Sergei. "Sir, it is my suspicion that the missing Marine was invited inside Night Palace. I have no evidence to support that belief. It's just my gut talking."

"You should trust your gut, Sergeant Ortiz," I say.

"It's true." Sergei nods. "Empress murdered Corporal Reynolds. She has murdered many members of the Honor Guard over the years. In fact, I believe she has murdered or corrupted every single Marine who has ever served her."

Ortiz's jaw twitches. I can hear his teeth grinding against one another.

"You've been lied to, Marines," I say. "It's time for you to learn the true nature of those you've been protecting."

Sergei stands up. "It's also time that you learned the true nature of the man you call 'Redstar.'" His American accent is gone. He's making no attempt to hide his Russian origin. "My name is Sergei Ivanov Tupelev. I was a high-ranking Russian military intelligence officer until about ten years ago. At that time, I became a paranorm. Several months ago, I joined Empress's inner circle. I served her faithfully, and, although I never participated in the murder of an Honor Guard Marine, I, myself, am guilty of many murders. Once, I was a man of honor like yourselves. Now, I'm a serial killer. General Brooks knows who and what I am. You see, Sergeant Ortiz, Corporal Hall, I'm a vampire. That is what the paranorms are. We're vampires. And, with the exception of Carl"—he points to me, but both Marines stare coldly at him—"we're murderers many, many times over. We're trying to atone for our sins and remove the scourge of Empress and all of her Children from the face of the planet. Empress is a six-thousand-year-old vampire, the *first* vampire. She is Lilith, the daughter of Cain, the granddaughter of Adam, and she has been the cause of great evil throughout the history of mankind. General Brooks knows all this. He serves Lilith. He serves her willingly. He has sent many of your brethren to their deaths. In fact, *no* Marine survives Honor Guard duty. They have seen too . . ."

"If you'll pardon me, sir," Ortiz interrupts, his voice like iron, "how do I know this isn't all the biggest load of bullsh . . ."

"Do you doubt the evidence of your own eyes?" the Russian asks. "You have seen me and my friends flying tonight. You've seen your bullets do little more than slow us down. Have you ever seen Empress or one of her Children in the daylight? You, yourself, knew there was something wrong about us. Your 'gut' told you so. You . . ."

"No, sir." Ortiz rises to his feet. "You misunderstand me." He draws his weapon. Slowly. Deliberately. He points the Colt directly at Sergei's left eye. The room is instantly silent except for the sound of breathing, pounding hearts, and sweet blood rushing through mortal veins. "Let me get this straight. You're saying that you're complicit in the death of Reynolds and the corruption of many Marines. How do I know that you're telling me the truth now, Redstar or Sergei or Ivan or whatever the hell your name is? Either you've lied to me all the months I've known you, or you're lying to me now. I don't know which. What I *do* know is, if I fire this weapon, I probably won't survive. Hell, the Lance Corporal was taken down by a *woman*, the same woman we'd been ordered to neutralize. I don't know if this vampire business is a bunch of bull or what. I don't know *what* you are. You're *faster* than us, you're *stronger* than us, and you're pretty damn hard to kill, I'll bet. But, even if a bullet to the head won't *kill* you, I'm pretty damn sure it'd mess you up. And if I'm going to die, I'd rather die on my feet, doing my duty as I see it."

"Listen to me carefully, Sergeant," I say.

"No, Carl," Sergei cuts me off. "I owe this man a debt of honor." He stares at Ortiz intently. "You're correct, Sergeant. A bullet in my brain wouldn't kill me, but it would destroy my memories. It would erase who I am. The man that took you down? They tell me that he took a pair of bullets to the brain. He survived, but he lost all power of speech. He's working hard to relearn, but, even for a vampire, that'll take time. I don't want that or something worse to happen to me, but this man . . ." He points to me. "He's the key. He's a vampire, but he's not a murderer. He is an innocent, *unwilling* vampire, the only one there's ever been. He intends to kill Lilith, and, when he does, the vampires will cease to exist. We'll all die. We're willing to lay down our lives to destroy Lilith and end her long, evil reign. I will *die* for this man, because he's leading me back to Jesus Christ, and Jesus is my only hope for redemption."

"Sarge?" It's Hall. He rises slowly to his feet to join his fellow Marine. "You remember what the Asian said, when Redstar was . . . frozen in the air?"

"Yeah." Ortiz keeps the weapon pointed at Sergei's head. "What about it?"

Hall clears his throat. "He said, 'We're not gods. We don't get to say who lives and who dies.' Isn't that what's been eating at you? The arrogance of the Papa-Novembers? Their lack of honor? These guys could've killed us. Hell, Redstar *wanted* to kill us. Their leader stopped him. I think these guys are the real deal. *Empress* ordered us to burn down a house and murder a woman. These guys . . . I . . . I think we can trust them. Listen to your gut, Sarge!"

Ortiz keeps his eyes locked on Sergei, the gun pointed at his head. "They call you Captain Morgan. Is Morgan your name or is that some kind of joke?"

"Yes, Marine," I reply evenly. "Carl Morgan."

"Captain of what?"

"I *was* a captain in the USAF. I flew B-52s in the First Gulf War. They just call me captain because I'm their leader. I'm going to lead them into battle against Lilith. We're going to take her down. And when we do, we're all going to die. We're going to lay down our lives."

"Why?"

"Because it's the right thing to do, Marine."

"How do you know you're going to die if you neutralize Empress?"

"Because a prophet of God prophesied it, laddie." That was Moira. Her voice carries across the room from behind the Marines. "Six millennia ago, A-dam prophesied that my husband and I would kill Lilith and, when we do, all vampires, including us, will die."

Ortiz doesn't look at her. "You know how nuts that sounds, don't you, ma'am?"

"'Tis God's own truth, laddie."

Ortiz is a statue for a few long seconds. He stares at Sergei and keeps his weapon pointed at Sergei's left eye. *He's a cold one. There's not a bead of sweat on his face, and his pulse is steady. I'm not sure I could stop him from putting a bullet through Sergei's brain.*

Ortiz's jaw unclenches. "Will you let me fight beside you? Reynolds saved my hide in Afghanistan. Twice. I owe him for that. And Empress owes a debt for every Marine she's killed or corrupted."

I suppress a sigh of relief. "You have my word, Marine."

Ortiz's thumb moves and switches the safety back on. He lowers his weapon and puts it back in its holster.

He turns his hard gaze to me. Our eyes lock. "You better be the real deal."

I return his stare. "I try to be."

"Count me in too, sir," Hall says.

I break my stare with Ortiz and look at the young corporal. "Glad to have you aboard, Marine."

◢ ◢ ◢

How're you doing, Laura?" I squat down in front of the cot where the bishop's wife is sipping at water from a paper cup. She's got a woolen blanket draped around her shoulders.

At the other end of the studio basement, Sergei and In-Tae are briefing the Marines.

Why in the world did I let them join us?

Because, Morgan, you're going to need them. And you know it.

"She's grand." Moira's sitting beside Laura. She puts a comforting arm a-round the woman's shoulders. "Ye are, are ye nae, lassie?" Moira looks at me. "She's had a wee bit of a shock. 'Tis a lot to take in."

"You're really two hundred and seventy, Moira?" Laura looks at my wife out of the corner of her eye.

"Aye, that I am, give or take the odd decade."

"And, Carl, you're . . . ?"

I shrug. "Mid-thirties is all."

"Just a wee bairn." Moira winks a gorgeous green eye at me. "Winnie was right after all."

Laura blinks at her. "What do you mean?"

"I was robbin' the cradle!"

Laura chuckles weakly. "And . . . and Jacob . . . *knows?*"

She means Bishop Adams, her husband. I don't think I've ever called him Jacob.

Moira smiles. "Aye, he's known since he was ordained a bishop. They've all known. I had to have . . . a special clearance from the First Presidency to get baptized."

"Some mysterious medical condition!" Laura shakes her head in amaze-ment. "Never looked your true age. You know, Winnie was right about an-other thing."

"Aye?"

"How's any normal woman supposed to compete with you?"

Moira and I exchange a worried look.

"Just teasing you," Laura says. "Well . . . *mostly.*"

Moira wraps her other arm around Laura and gives the older-looking lady a hug.

Laura sniffs softly. "Moira, why . . . why didn't you trust me?"

"Ah, lassie, 'tis more along the lines of why did I nae *burden* ye?"

Laura nods. Then she sighs. It sounds like a weariness as deep as the soul. "I need to get going."

"Back to Winnie?"

"Well, yes, eventually. But, right now, I need to get to the store."

"What for?" I ask.

"Sunscreen," she replies. "Lots and lots of sunscreen. The highest SPF I can find. And blankets. Lots of blankets." She holds up the wad of bills that Moira handed her earlier. Somehow she managed to hold onto them this whole time.

Moira hugs her again. "Ye are a dear."

"Do you feel up to driving?" I ask.

"Not much choice from what Moira tells me. You need to hide out. I'll be fine. Right as rain." She stands up, shedding the blanket.

Moira rises to her feet. "I'll see ye to yer car."

I shake my head. "I'll send Rolf and Lorenzo." I motion to Rolf. He grabs Lorenzo's arm and the two of them head in our direction.

"Aye," Moira sighs, "'tis for the best. In some ways my husband's wise beyond his wee allotment of years." She smiles at me.

Man, she's beautiful!

"Just a 'wee bairn!'" Laura chuckles.

"Laura," I say, pointing at the Italian, "this is Lorenzo Corelli. He's in his early five-hundreds."

Lorenzo bows deeply, takes Laura's hand and kisses it lightly. "I am charmed, *Signora* Adams."

Laura blushes.

"And this is Rolf Oettinger," I say, pointing at the former Nazi. "He's just under a century."

Rolf takes her hand and shakes it.

"I'm not old," he says without even a hint of a smile. "I'm young and handsome."

Laura blushes an even more delicious shade of crimson. "Pleased to meet you both," she manages after a moment.

"If you would follow us, *signora?*" Lorenzo points toward the stairs with his left arm and offers the other to Laura.

She nods and takes the proffered arm.

As the three of them walk away, I look back at our two Marines. Lance Corporal Hall is making another check-in on his radio/phone.

I hope that's still going well. I don't have Moira's talent at following multiple conversations at once.

Our people are starting to arrive. They're beginning to trickle down the stairs in groups of two or three.

I need to get someone to relieve our bodyguards in the air.

Lorenzo told me, once he and Rolf had activated the calling tree, that the entire Stake (what's left of us) should be together again within the next hour or so. I asked him if he'd ever gotten out of Rolf what the German found so blasted funny.

He shrugged his shoulders and said, "All he would say was, 'Ortiz the Marine.' He said to ask you. He said you would know."

"Me?" I said, throwing up my hands. "I have no clue what he's talking about."

Something tickles the back of my mind. For some strange reason I feel like I *should* know what he's talking about, but for the life of me I don't know what it is. *Ortiz the Marine?*

"Carl!" In-Tae motions to me frantically. "Carl! You need to hear this!"

Moira takes my hand, and we hurry over to where the Korean and the Russian are talking with Ortiz and Hall.

"What's up?" I say.

Sergei says, "Ortiz, repeat what you just told me!" His face is split in a wide grin.

Ortiz looks up at me. "Sir, Redstar was telling us that, since he joined up with you, he'd lost contact with Empress, that you don't know where they moved Night Palace to after they bugged out. He tells me that civilians were kidnapped and that they're on board the MH-47X-ray."

"That's right," I say.

Ortiz nods. "I know where they're headed, sir. I was briefed on the new location of Night Palace before we left."

Chapter 13

Carl

O *ne more sunset.*
Twenty-four hours.
Less than that.
That's all we've got left to live.

The last chapter of our lives begins tonight. And then we close the book and leave this existence. Then we go back to the God who made us, to be judged for our works, to rely on the mercy of His Son.

To see Sharon and Lucy and April and Joseph.

And Ben.

I look at the assembled faces of the Stake. Sitting on ancient Civil Defense cots, standing, or leaning against walls and concrete support columns around the basement, they're all looking to me. Most have their hands on the grips or pommels of their swords or other weapons.

Rolf has that spear, the one Moira calls the Spear of Longinus, the spear that Müller used in his horrible crucifixions. Perhaps it's the very spear that pierced the side of Christ. It's the same weapon Rolf used to impale Lilith during the battle at Müller's farm. He's still got Sarah's broadsword belted at his side, but he runs his thumb idly over the edge of the ancient iron spearhead. He cradles the shaft in the crook of his other arm.

Upon hearing the news that we knew where Lilith was headed, where she had taken the Lupescus—Please, Father, let them still be alive! At least *some* of them!—*Rolf had literally flown out the door. Lorenzo had no choice but to follow him. I sent two more of our number to follow the two of them. Lorenzo and the others didn't catch up to Rolf until he was on his way back from Lorenzo's rented house.*

He returned carrying the spear, with the others arriving right behind him. They were all out of breath. To get to Provo and back so quickly, they had to be traveling extremely fast, fast even for us. Too fast to breathe adequately.

Rolf pulls a flat whet stone from a pocket. He spits on it and then begins to sharpen the spearhead, never taking his eyes off me. His stare is intense. The unexplained odd mirth of less than an hour ago has vanished completely.

All the vampires in the room are staring at me, except for Moira. She's standing at my side.

Roses mixed with sunscreen. I love the scent of her!

Our time in this life has come to an end. I'm so glad she's at my side. I don't think I could bear to be parted from her for a second. *I wish . . . how I wish we could have just one more hour alone together . . . or one more chance to visit Ben's grave . . . and the graves of the others, for that matter.*

Sam and Nikki Gallagher are huddled together on a cot at the rear of the basement. They're whispering softly to each other . . . as if whispering would somehow prevent any vampire in the room from hearing them. Their bodyguards are standing behind the cot. Nikki seems to have taken the truth about our . . . condition better than most would, especially under the circumstances. I wonder if someone used Persuasion to calm her. I don't know and, frankly, I don't have *time* to be concerned about it. They can't come with us, where we're going. We'll have to trust to Laura Adams to make arrangements for them until this is all over.

I dispatched two teams of four to Provo. One team to retrieve Sam and Nikki (and to make some kind of temporary arrangement for their cat, even if that meant simply putting out extra food and water) and one team to retrieve the heads and bodies of Noriko and Juanita and provide them with a hasty burial in our little unofficial mountainside cemetery. If we do survive the next twenty-four hours (and if we do, it'll be because we failed or we lost the opportunity to strike), I don't want to leave any bodies for the authorities to puzzle over.

Both teams returned in record time. They understood the urgency of their tasks. They understood how little time remains.

There are four of our sentries in the sky above us, with two more guarding the front door upstairs. Sergei and In-Tae are with the two Marines who're out on what I *hope* won't turn out to be a fruitless mission. The rest of us are here in this room.

This is it. My entire army. It's not much to face Lilith and her potential thousands with. It's like the Stripling Warriors of Helaman facing the Lamanite armies, but the Stripling Warriors all survived.

None of us will survive.

I look into the faces of my friends, my soldiers, as they stare intently back at me. Their expressions are grim. They're immortals facing their own mortality.

And I've seen that look before. Or something very much like it.

Every time we flew a mission over Iraq, my crew and I knew we might not come back. Ground soldiers go into combat and face death for days or weeks or even months at a time before returning to the relative safety of the base. Then they can relax for a bit, enjoy some R and R, and have some time to decompress before going back into the field. But a combat aircrew faces death and then comes back knowing they have to leave the safety of the base and fly out and face death all over again the next day.

And the next.

And the next.

These folks have that look. They know they're at the end of their long lives.

I've given combat mission briefings before. You're supposed to say something inspiring, something motivational. *The mission is vital. We're going to deal the enemy a critical blow. Stay in formation. Deliver your ordinance on time and on target. Within five minutes, within five degrees of heading, within fifty feet of altitude: five by five by five. Then bug out and get back home. Stay sharp. Follow the plan. And God bless the USA.*

I hate giving these kinds of speeches.

Just once, I should've said something more honest. *We're flying deep into enemy territory, and there are going to be a whole lot of people trying desperately to shoot us down. Even if we do everything right, there's a good chance we won't come out of this alive. The jet could break. The weather could suck. The target could be obscured. The air-conditioner is probably gonna fail as we pass ten thousand feet as it has on the last six missions. So it's gonna be a hundred and fifty degrees in the cockpit, and we'll have to fly in full gear plus flak jackets, and, Navs, don't bother asking: no, you can't fly with your headsets on, you gotta wear your helmets the whole time, and you're gonna lose ten pounds in sweat alone, so keep pushing the fluids. And since the blasted air-conditioner's gonna fail again, we'll be flying essentially unpressurized and won't be able to exceed flight level two-five-oh, so we'll be a lot closer to the triple-A and SAMs that Saddam's gonna throw at us. And if, in spite of all that, we manage to hit and blow up the target, we can still get killed on the way out. And, if we make it back to base, we'll write up the crappy air-conditioner again and tell Maintenance to fix it again, and they'll mark it down as CND, "Could Not Duplicate," (and, of course, they can't duplicate the problem since it happens at ten-thousand feet and not on the ground) and clear the jet to fly again tomorrow. Oh, and speaking of tomorrow, get ready to do it all again! Meanwhile the liberal press is gonna swallow, hook, line, and sinker, Baghdad Bob's story that what we blew up was an orphanage and not a chemical weapons dump, and some moron back home's gonna throw red paint on your wife and kids and scream, "No war for oil!" And won't that be nice? Good hunting, gentlemen!*

I clear my throat. "If the intelligence we've received tonight is accurate, and my gut tells me it is, we're going into battle tomorrow night. We're going to face Lilith. We know where she is now . . . or, at least, where she's headed. And there's a good chance we'll get there before she does."

"How's that possible?" That's Ramón, one of the Gallaghers' bodyguards. "She's got quite a head start on us."

"That Chinook helicopter she's riding," I reply, "cruises, when it's not being pushed from inside by vampires, at about a hundred and thirty knots. It has a range of only four hundred miles. They're going to have to refuel twice to reach their destination. From Sergei, we've learned that she won't risk an air refueling, especially in daylight, so that means an additional hour or two at each stop. And, with Sergei compromised, she won't take the normal route home. She won't make the normal fuel stops. That means she'll take even longer. That means they'll be en route for about ten to twelve hours realistically. Maybe more. And when they land, it'll be daylight, or just after sunset. Sergei says she'll take her time, especially at refueling stops, and arrive shortly after nightfall."

"Are you sure we can trust him?" The voice is deep and rich and the accent is very African. M'Benga is leaning against a column, fingering the blade of his falchion, a large sword with a deep curve at the wide tip of the blade. There are a couple of gasps from the Stake in response to what he said, but only a couple. I open my mouth to protest, but M'Benga cuts me off. "We're all thinking it . . . or we *should* be. Everyone has heard about Martha and her treachery. And the Russian—he was an Enforcer. He came to us under false pretenses. Even if he's sincere now, how long will it last? He has spent the last decade or so indulging every whim, every perversion. He's shared the bed of *Lilith. Lilith!* Do you have any idea what that means?"

He doesn't wait for a response. He presses on. "Carl, you have no *concept* of how hard it is to just turn those urges, those desires, those compulsions *off.* Most of us started our repentance with a moment of crisis, but *change, real* change, takes *time.* Sergei's only been *thinking* about changing his life for a handful of *hours.* It doesn't work that way! You *know* it doesn't! You don't get to lay your hand on the top of the TV and say, 'Save me, Jesus!' and that's it! The sex is addictive! The killing is addictive! The *power* is addictive! You've never been through it! You have no idea how hard . . ."

"He's got In-Tae with him," I say.

"All right, but what if Sergei falters?" the big ebony-skinned man counters, taking one step away from the column he's been leaning against. He points his sword at me. "Is In-Tae prepared to slay him? The Russian could betray our location with a single phone call. I've never questioned your leadership before, but it is *too soon* to entrust our lives, our purpose, our *hope* to a man who, until a few hours ago, was bent on destroying us!"

He's got a point.

Those who turned to look at him now turn their faces to me. *They're all thinking the same thing. It's not as if the thought hasn't crossed my mind as well.*

"I hear you, M'Benga," I reply, "and there's wisdom in what you say. Maybe I *am* too trusting. I'm certainly naïve when it comes to the world of vampirism. I've got some years of military experience, but some of you have *centuries* of expertise. I *don't* know what I'm doing half the time. I'm just making it up as I go. And I've made some critical errors in judgment that've cost good people, good *friends*, their lives. Tony and his family, Noriko and Juanita . . ."

Moira grips my hand. I hear her open her mouth to say something, but the African speaks first, cutting her off.

"That wasn't your fault."

"They're still dead," I say. I can see Lorenzo squirming at my words, but I continue. "I screwed up. I should've been more cautious. It's not the first time I've screwed up and cost good people their lives. And it won't be the last. No, scratch that: maybe it *will*. If this works, we've only got one more sunset. We'll never see another . . . not in this life. But, neither will Lilith. The Prophecy says we're all going to die. All of us. I just . . . didn't expect the mortals . . ." There's a lump in my throat the size of a grapefruit. I can't seem to force myself to say anything.

Get control, Morgan!

"Laddie," Moira says.

I squeeze her hand.

Sam Gallagher stares at me with haunted eyes. Nikki clings to him.

"I believe that God is opening doors for us." I clear my throat and try to imbue my voice with a confidence I don't feel. "I feel *strongly* that He sent Sergei to us. He sent the Marines to us. I . . ." And there it is: I feel the confirmation of the Spirit thrill through me. *We're on the right path.* "I feel that we have to . . . see this through."

"But," M'Benga counters, "what if Sergei, In-Tae, and the soldiers aren't successful at . . . whatever it is you've sent them to do?"

"Then . . ." I smile at him sadly. "Then we all get to live a little longer."

That elicits a few chuckles from around the room.

Ironic, gloomy chuckles.

Ramón clears his throat. "So, how are we supposed to get there, wherever *there* is, before Lilith does?"

I point a finger at Ramón. "That's where our Marines come in."

None of the Stake has heard of the Honor Guard, per se, but Andrew, a Master who has visited Lilith's Court on more than one occasion, noted the presence of mortal guards who "carried themselves like soldiers." So, I quickly tell them what I know about the Marines who protect Lilith during the day and about what happened here tonight.

"OK," Ramón says. "That explains how we know where we need to go, but you haven't explained how we're supposed to get there, much less how we're going to get there ahead of the enemy."

I nod. "The Marines have a C-130 tactical transport aircraft and two flight crews on standby at Hill Air Force Base. The C-130 is supposed to fly them back once they're finished here. It cruises at nearly three hundred knots and has a range of more than two thousand miles. Once we launch, we'll be there in less than four hours . . . assuming the other Marines are willing to join us."

"So," Andrew says, "if they *don't* join us, can't we just commandeer the bloody aircraft?"

I laugh. "Even *if* we managed to steal the aircraft without mortal casualties, once we were in the air, NORAD would launch fighters. They'd intercept us and force us to land or, barring that, shoot us down. Besides, who'd we get to fly the aircraft?"

"I thought you were a Yank Air Force pilot once upon a time," Andrew says, nodding in my direction.

A scene pops into my mind from an old cartoon of an ancient man in rags saying, "I . . . was a human being . . . once."

"I was, but I was never rated on turboprops, much less a Hercules."

Andrew cocks an eyebrow. "Pardon me, but would you mind terribly repeating that in the King's English?"

"Ye see what I have to deal with?" Moira quips softly.

That elicits a chuckle or two.

"Sorry," I say, somewhat chagrined. *I get in these military situations, and I don't really account for the fact that the civilians or even the veterans who didn't serve in the last two generations don't understand what the heck I'm talking about. And maybe that's a good thing.* "I flew *jet* aircraft. The C-130 *Hercules* has four turbine-driven propellers. That's a whole different animal. In many ways, it's more complex than flying jets. Plus, each type of aircraft is unique, and just because you know how to fly one type safely, doesn't mean you can fly something completely different without making a smoking hole in the ground. So unless one of you failed to disclose your experience as a one-thirty pilot"—I glance around the room; there are no takers—"that's not an option. We *need* the cooperation of the Honor Guard Marines to pull this off. Besides, we'll be flying in daylight."

That elicits a number of nods.

"And, if we *don't* get the cooperation of the Marines," I continue, "it won't take the enemy long to figure out that Ortiz and Hall are compromised and that the location of Lilith's new hideout is exposed, and that'll be the end of it. We'll lose the window of opportunity. She'll bug out to another location, and we won't have any way to find out where she's . . ."

Lorenzo's phone chimes. *Hopefully that's In-Tae with good news.* Lorenzo flips the phone open and reads a text message. He looks up and there is a terrible intensity to his eyes, a determined set to his jaw. "Success. We take off in one hour."

Ortiz and Hall came through. Sergei and In-Tae too.

There's a collective sigh from the room. Moira squeezes my hand so hard it hurts.

That's it then.

One more sunset.

"Carl!" That's Chen-Han, one of the guards, yelling from upstairs. "You better get up here! Airborne scouts report we've got company!"

Chapter 14

Moira

Multiple vehicles approaching from the north!" Chen-Han's relaying what he's hearing over the phone. The scouts in the air above us are our eyes for now. Most of the Stake has followed Carl and me upstairs into the dance studio. We're clumped around the front door, but we're nae going outside till we know what we'll be facing. On the other hand, I dinnae think anyone wants to be trapped in here. A couple of guards remain in the basement with Sammy and Nikki Gallagher.

"Police vehicles?" Carl asks.

Chen-Han opens his mouth, probably to echo the question, but Phillipa's voice comes over the phone loud enough for every vampire in the room to hear, "I don't think so. Looks like a mismatched bunch of cars, a pickup truck, and a van."

That does nae sound like the police. Could it be the Brotherhood of Tobias? Do they have that many members in the area?

I shudder at the memory of a bullet exploding in my chest.

Carl says, "Are you sure they're headed here?" He shakes his head. "Never mind that. I can hear vehicles pulling up outside."

"One more vehicle approaching from the east," Phillipa says. "Carl, I suggest you hold your position until we see what their intentions are."

Carl nods to himself. "Roger. Wilco."

"Describe the vehicle coming from the east," I say.

"It's a small car . . . green," Phillipa replies. "Sorry. I don't know much a-bout cars. I've never owned one."

"'Twould be Laura, I'd wager," I say with alarm. "She could be heading into danger!" *More dangerous than scores of vampires, lassie?*

I draw my black sword, push between Chen-Han and his companion, Abram, and rush out into the night.

"Moira! No!" Carl cries from behind me.

I ignore him. *Nae more mortals, nae more of my friends shall die this night, nae if I can help it! Especially nae dear, sweet Laura Adams.*

There are indeed a number of vehicles, some stopped at the curb, others pulling up. The street's nearly lined on both sides with cars. Carl joins me at my side, and I can hear the others streaming out behind me, as the first of the vehicle doors opens. I hear the sound of many swords being drawn.

"Protect the Unwilling and the Penitent!"

I dinnae recognize the voice, but others begin to echo the cry.

"The Unwilling and the Penitent!"

"Carl and Moira!"

Instantly, there are scores of bodies forming a barrier around my laddie and me, shielding us from the arriving vehicles. I'm about to take to the air to get a better vantage point, when I hear a number of gasps, a small scream, and an "Oh my heck!"

I recognize that *voice!*

"'Tis all right, everyone!" I cry. "There's nae danger here! They're my friends!"

"Stand down!" Carl orders. "I mean, *please* stand down!" That last was more of a snarl. "And *please* stow your weapons."

Poor lad!

"Let me through!" I say.

Carl motions with his arms, though naebody is looking at him. "*Please* make a hole, people!"

I sheath my blade and begin to push through the sea of protective vampires. They part, reluctantly to be sure, but they part to reveal a very frightened and frazzled gaggle of mortal ladies. Some are huddling together while others remain in their cars. Nary a one of them drives off, though some roll up their windows. I can hear doors being locked. They're dressed in various ways. Some are wearing dressing gowns and slippers. One actually has a curler dangling from her hair. *She must have missed it when she hastily pulled the rest out.* Nary a one of them has even a wee speck of makeup. They must've come in a hurry.

Half the Relief Society must be here!

There's Kathy Fujikawa, the Relief Society president, standing with a bundle in her arms. 'Twas *her* voice I recognized. And she looks terribly frightened.

I run up to her and throw my arms around her, crushing her soft bundle between us. "Kathy! What're ye doing here, lass?" I pat her back. *The poor dear must be frightened out of her wits!*

"I . . . I got a call." I pull back to look in her face. Her eyes are wide, her face bloodless. "Moira, what in the world?"

"Oh my heck!" There's Laura Adams now. She's standing in front of Winnie's green compact car. "She did it!"

"What?" *I'm confused.* "Who? Who did what?"

Laura hurries toward us. "It was Winnie, wasn't it?"

"Winnie?" *What's she on about?*

Kathy nods mutely.

Laura says, "I called Winnie when I was driving off to get the sunscreen and blankets. I didn't want her to worry about me not coming back right away. I told her what I was doing and she . . . I'll be darned if she didn't do it! She said she'd call around and get blankets, coats, gloves, hats, and so on."

"She . . . she said . . ." Kathy can't seem to talk above a whisper. "She said that Moira MacDonald Morgan needed help. She said you needed help *right now* . . . and we had just half an hour to do it."

"It's all right!" Laura says to the other ladies in a reassuring tone. She turns to me and points at the assembled vampires. "It *is* all right, isn't it?"

"Aye, lassie," I reply. "'Tis safe as houses. This is probably the safest place in the city at the moment."

"It's OK!" Laura calls out, turning round again. "You can come out now, but we have to hurry!"

And come out they do. Most come out of their vehicles quickly, but a few hesitate for a tick before emerging more cautiously. They retrieve bags and boxes and bundles from their cars.

"Perhaps," Lorenzo says, "we might want to move this inside."

Carl nods. "Good idea." He raises his voice a notch. "Can we take this inside, people?"

The Stake begins to move toward the door.

Nary a one of the Relief Society sisters follows.

I turn about and take Kathy Fujikawa gently by the arm. "Come along, lassie. There's nae a soul here would harm ye."

She takes a reluctant step with me, hesitates, and then seems to gather her bundle tighter to her chest and, with it, her courage. She steps forward, apparently with more confidence, but I can feel her tremble. "Come on, sisters. The need's urgent and that half hour's slipping away."

And, with that, I hear doors unlock and open. They all come forward, bearing bundles, bags, and boxes. They follow Kathy and me and the Stake vampires into Winnie Morrison's dance studio.

"Moira," Kathy whispers as we enter, "who are these people and . . . why do they have swords and spears? Why do *you* have a sword?"

I sigh. "Ach, lassie, 'tis nae my . . ."

"I'm sorry," she says. "I *promised* Winnie we wouldn't ask questions. *No questions*, she said."

"But, Kathy, ye deserve an ans . . ."

"No! I gave my word." She leans in toward my ear and whispers even softer, "Just *promise* me I haven't led us into . . . danger! Oh dear! I know that sounds so melodramatic."

"Nae, lassie, these people, my friends here, would defend ye with their lives. Ye saw how they moved to protect me and Carl."

She looks at me with an unspoken question in her eyes.

Ach, lassie! Ye've gone and said too much again!

Kathy walks to the mirrored wall and begins to hang the items that comprise her bundle on the handrail. "Over here, ladies." The other sisters begin to do the same. Kathy holds one item back and keeps it folded in one arm. 'Tis a mass of green velvet. "You knew my daughter, Janet, didn't you? Of course you did."

Janet Fujikawa. Aye, of course. I was her Laurel adviser before my current calling as the Sunbeam teacher. She died last year in an auto crash while on her way home from BYU—Idaho for Christmas. So very, very tragic. Such a bonnie, kind, and virtuous lass.

My eyes are suddenly very moist. I smile sadly as I blink back the tears. "Aye. Of course. I loved Janet. Everyone did."

Kathy nods, and tears spill from her eyes. "She thought the world of you, you know. She wanted to be like you. She . . . well, for Christmas last year, the year she . . . Well, I made her this. She never got to wear it, but . . . would you take it? I know she'd . . . want you to have it."

She carefully, lovingly unfolds the green velvet in her arms.

It's a long cloak with a deep hood and a stout lining.

I cannae restrain my own tears as I wrap my arms around Kathy.

She weeps quietly on my shoulder.

"Aye, Kathy. I'd be honored. She was a sweet lass."

"She . . . always admired your pretty cloaks. I made it with a hood, like yours." She pulls back and opens the cloak. She sniffles and then laughs softly as she's forced to wipe her nose on her wrist. "She was about your size." She holds it open.

I turn about, and she places it on my shoulders. I draw it close around me. "'Tis a perfect fit."

"Good," she says and turns to the rail. "I have some of my work gloves . . . you know, for gardening. They're not pretty, but . . ."

I spin around to face her, the cloak swirling about me. "They're perfect." I take the gloves from her hand. "Thank ye, lassie."

Around the room, others of the Stake are being outfitted in various coats, hats, and gloves. Not all the vampires came without protective clothing, but the majority of them were unprepared when they returned from Hunting and got the call to report here. They expected to return home, and now they cannae do so.

Carl stands politely behind Kathy, waiting for her to compose herself. He has nae taken anything for himself.

Kathy takes a deep breath and presses on. "I brought something for Carl too." She looks about. "Where is he?"

"Right behind you, Sister Fujikawa."

Kathy starts. "Oh my heck!" She turns halfway round to look at Carl.

"Sorry." Carl looks genuinely chagrined. "I didn't mean to . . ."

"No, it's all right." Kathy waves dismissively, but her hand trembles slightly. "I'm just jumpy, what with all this waking up in the middle of the night. When you're woken out of a dead sleep, the last voice you want to hear on the phone is Winnie Morrison's."

She gasps, and her hands cover her mouth. "Did I really just say that?"

Carl busts out laughing. 'Tis a grand and hearty laugh.

I try to contain my own, but I cannae help myself.

Kathy looks mortified for a tick, but then she joins in. "I still can't believe it," she manages between chuckles. "Who would've ever thought that Winnie would be bullying people to come to the *aid* of Moira MacDonald Morgan?" She laughs again. "Oh, but that's unkind!"

"Aye, but she's come a long way."

Kathy wipes away tears of mirth. "I suppose she has." She laughs again and then tries to control herself. It takes her a wee moment, but then she says, "It doesn't help my nerves any either, with all these strangers . . . and the *swords*."

Carl opens his mouth to respond, but Kathy throws up her hands and says, "But I'm *not* asking any questions! So *please* don't answer them!"

Carl looks at me with confusion plainly written on his face.

"Winnie made her promise," I hiss. I hope he can catch my words above the din. People are chatting around the room, talking like the aftermath of a church fireside.

Carl mouths, "Oh."

"This is for you, Carl," Kathy says, handing him a coat from the handrail. "My husband, Jerry . . . he's second-generation American, you know . . . is *tall* for a Japanese. He took a shine to your duster when you first moved into the ward. Anyway, I think it'll fit you."

Carl takes the coat and tries it on. It does indeed fit close enough. "Tell Jerry thanks for me," he says.

"And here's a pair of leather work gloves for your hands." She looks up at him. "Do *all* these people have the same sun allergy? Never mind! No questions!" She snaps her fingers suddenly. "I forgot! I've got a hat for you! It's in the car! I'll be right back!"

She hurries toward the door.

Carl hisses to Lorenzo, "Go with her . . . *please!*"

Lorenzo grabs Rolf by the arm, and the two of them follow Kathy out the door. Those two are both wearing donated coats. They're ill fitting, but they'll do. Rolf is sporting a fedora, and Lorenzo a more mundane hat. Those hats could be problematic in the Sun, but they'll provide some protection. Lorenzo and Rolf can pull their long coats up around their faces in a pinch.

I scan around the room. Everyone seems to be covered, more or less. There's a huge poncho and other odd garments. There's nae a single blanket being used, although the dear sisters brought a number of them. Laura Adams is passing out tubes and bottles of SPF 50 sunscreen. She must've cleared out a couple of stores to get so many. *Bless her! Bless them all! And bless Winnie! This would nae have happened but for her.*

Some of the sisters have even brought pies, cakes, and casseroles, most likely leftovers, since they would nae have had time to cook. *Well, of course they'd bring such!* They have nae idea we cannae eat any of it. *Bless them!* Well, the Gallaghers can eat them! And to their credit, nary a one of the vampires has let on. They're accepting the dishes gracefully. There's René Gaston making a grand show of savoring the aroma of a pie . . . as if it did nae make him want to vomit, as the smell of mortal food does.

Gratitude and love for these dear, sweet ladies wells up in my heart and spills out my eyes in fresh tears. "Thank ye! Thank ye all! I'm . . . over-whelmed! I cannae believe . . ." But words fail me.

And then they start to come. In ones or twos they gather round Carl and me.

"All I needed to hear was that Moira Morgan needed help."

"You saved my Jimmy at the hospital. When the other doctors gave him just hours to live, you saved him."

"You helped me through things when my marriage was . . . troubled."

"You inspired me to be modest when I was a Mia Maid."

"You've been my visiting teacher for decades. You never missed a month. Not one month."

"All those nights you sat up reading to me when I was in the hospital. It's like you never slept!"

"I'd be dead if you hadn't helped me when I was drinking. You didn't judge me; you just loved me through it."

"I haven't made my visiting teaching appointment this month. I didn't want to miss you."

"I don't know what's wrong. All I know is you're in trouble. That's all I need to know."

"You saved me *and* my baby when my doctor said it was my life or his."

"When I was sad on Sundays, you always had a smile for me. And it was a *genuine* smile. It lifted my spirits."

"You held me when my Larry died."

"If not for you, I wouldn't be in the Church right now. You visited me for years, even when I wouldn't let you in . . . even when I was so rude and hateful. You brought me back."

"My little Jacob just *loves* his Sunbeam teacher. He woke up when we were scrounging around for coats and such. He drew this picture for you."

"You never gave up on me. Never."

The tears run freely all around. Aye, the hugs do too.

Finally Laura makes her way through the crowd back to Carl and me. She has a huge round box. She turns to Carl. "Jerry wants you to have this as well. It wasn't just your coat he admired."

She opens the box.

And, try as I will, I cannae suppress a giggle.

Out of the corner of my eye, I can see Carl biting his lip. I'll wager he's doing his best to stifle a groan.

"I hope it fits," Kathy says, grinning from ear to ear.

Inside the brightly decorated box is a Stetson hat.

Chapter 15

Carl

"A men!" It's a shout, seventy-five voices raised to signal their agreement and acknowledgement of the group prayer offered by In-Tae. Even with our Seed-enhanced hearing, we have to shout to be heard above the roar made by the C-130's four turboprops. It's not that a vampire can't *hear* someone talking; it's just it's really hard to *understand* what's being said.

When we boarded the aircraft, entering through the lowered cargo door at the tail, we were greeted by the loadmaster. Gunnery Sergeant Douglas was a crusty, older Marine with a hard face that was lined by hard living. He had the mouth of a sailor, one who had long ago elevated profanity to an art form. He handed out a small box to each of us. Moira looked at the package of earplugs dubiously. "Trust me," I said. "You're going to need them."

In-Tae is the only one standing inside the immense cargo bay of the aircraft. *Well, it seems immense to me, especially compared to the crew compartment of the B-52, where standing is possible only on the ladder leading between the upper and lower decks.* The rest of us, including the four Marines, rise from our knees to stand on the deck.

Moira and I are holding hands. I squeeze her hand and release it with a pang that almost breaks my heart. I don't ever want to let go. I want to go on holding her hand forever. But I have to conduct our final mission briefing.

Decorum and all that.

"Please have a seat, folks." They sit in the canvas seats attached to the bulkheads around the fuselage. Their weapons are laid across their laps or held in front of them. Their faces are grim, determined.

Moira sits down behind me. Even with smells of metal, oil, nylon, and fuel, the scent of Moira's hair, her skin, her sunscreen, the scent of *Moira* lingers in my nostrils.

There are a few others who're holding hands. None of them came to us as "couples," but some of them have become close. And they've all received the "lecture." *You're relying on the mercy of Christ. That means you must keep the commandments of Jesus Christ. That means no sex outside of marriage.* So we now have seven married couples. (Eight, including Moira and me.) The others were all married by Bishop Adams, just for time, just for this life, though. No temple clearances for them. There's no time. *No time!* But that Bishop Adams, he's kept a record of every one of them marriages. He has the names of and birthdates of every member of the Stake. He says he'll have the temple work done for them a year after they're . . . after we're *all* gone.

Ah, to heck with decorum!

I look back at my sweet wife and extend my hand. She grants me one of her dazzling, breathtaking smiles. Then she stands, takes my hand, and joins me at my side.

There's a lump in my throat. *How am I going to get through this?*

Focus, Morgan! Focus on the mission! Don't think about the end of it!

I shout, "Here's what we know about Lilith's current home, codename Night Palace. It's a luxury hotel located about twenty-five miles east of the Kansas City Airport. It's called the Chateau Avalon. It's inside wooded acreage near the Kansas Speedway. Her normal home, a well-fortified mansion southwest of the city, was abandoned after the battle at Müller's farm. She's been holed up in the InterContinental Hotel at the Plaza in downtown KC until tonight, when Sergei joined us. She would've ordered the change of location while she was en route to Utah, as soon as she realized her link with Sergei was severed. If he wasn't dead, then any location that he knew about would be compromised. So she ordered her Court to be moved to the Chateau Avalon, a location Sergei wouldn't know about. That probably means the hotel guests and staff are all dead."

"Actually," Sergei interrupts, shouting, "the disappearance of so many at once would draw attention, especially mortals from out of town. And the last thing the Queen . . . I mean, Lilith, wants is to be discovered. She controls the local city, county, and state police forces, but, if there were any guests from out of the local area . . . well, that wouldn't be so easy to cover up. She's improvising, and she doesn't like that. She likes to control things."

"Of course," I reply.

"There would be some cover story," the former spy continues. "Most likely, it'd be a reason the hotel needed to be evacuated and other accommodations found for the displaced guests, something like a gas leak or a bedbug infestation. The staff, on the other hand, may very likely be kept around . . . at least those who can be Persuaded . . . except for the kitchen staff, of course. The other staff would be kept to serve the needs of the Court, making up beds, cleaning up after them, blood, sex, sadistic games. On second thought, the kitchen staff might've been kept around for that purpose alone."

"So there'll be mortals to protect," I say.

He nods. "Most likely. When she originally went into hiding, after the trouble with Günner Müller, she abandoned the Mansion in Overland Park and took over the top three floors of the InterContinental Hotel. She and her Court occupied the top floor and used the two floors just beneath that as a security barrier. When it was decided that I would go out to Utah personally, I proposed, and Lilith agreed, that I be excluded from contingency planning meetings in case I was captured."

"Why? Did she think I'd torture you for information?"

"She has no idea, no idea at all, how you've been able to *turn* any of her followers away from her. There was some speculation that you'd made your *own* Great Covenant with Lucifer, giving you mastery over others of our kind. Nobody who's joined you has ever come back. Some of Müller's people returned to her, but yours haven't."

"Yeah. What happened to them?"

He laughs. It's barely heard above the engines, but it's a mirthless, chilling sound. "They became the most *depraved* of any of our kind I've ever seen, and that's saying something for us. It's funny, you know. They wanted to be Penitents. When that . . . didn't work out, they became fanatics the other way. And ironically, that made them useless to Lilith. They were too *extreme* to be trusted with anything important. They were concerned with nothing but their own urges, that and doing *anything* and *everything* to please Lilith. They were like mad dogs. Useless. No, worse than useless. So the Queen ordered them put down."

Moira squirms at my side. "Did ye personally . . . put them down?"

"Would it matter?" Sergei shakes his head. "Actually, no I did not. I wasn't elevated to Enforcer at that point, but I was there. I watched it. They knelt for their own executions and exposed their necks, not that they could've stopped themselves once Lilith commanded it. They mewled and pleaded for their lives until Lilith commanded them to be silent."

He shakes his head. "But as I said, would it matter if I killed them? I have so many murders on my hands. What difference would a few more make?"

"Aye," Moira shouts. "The Savior said, 'And the last state of that man is worse than the first.' Müller was a false apostle, but those who followed him —they were seeking redemption. When they *voluntarily* returned to Lilith, like the dog to his vomit, they embraced the evil completely, seven times worse than before."

At one time, I would've been amazed at her perfect recall of scripture, but I've come to realize that a photographic memory is par for the course for someone with a Seed-enhanced brain.

"OK," I say. "Back to the mission." *Focus on the mission!* "The Chateau is a small luxury hotel. And, luckily for us, it's a security nightmare. Makes me wonder why Lilith chose it. On the north, east, and south it's nearly surrounded by a large wooded plot. If we come in low, hugging the tree line, they won't see us coming until we're almost on top of the building. We're not going to bother with the doors. We'll go through the windows. There are enough of us to cover almost every window . . . I think. The aerial view Rolf got off the Internet before we left Salt Lake"—Rolf taps the smartphone in his pocket—"doesn't give us many details of the layout."

Rolf takes the phone from his pocket and shows the picture to the group. The vampires can see it well enough, but the Marines won't be able to from that distance.

"Using the photos from the hotel website," I continue, "we've come up with a general plan that'll require some improvisation in the field. You've each been assigned to teams, and each team will be assigned a wall of the building to attack. After this briefing is over, get your individual assignments from Rolf. Those of you that have been designated as team leaders, study the photos on Rolf's phone, and then use your best judgment. There aren't pictures of every wall, so you'll have to make your final assignments in the field."

I see many of the group nodding. I continue, "The plan is to arrive well before dark. That should also be well before the enemy lands. Our C-130 will approach the target from the northeast. The pilot, Major Gillespie, will declare VFR and drop to fifteen hundred feet AGL. That's as low as he can go in FAA-controlled airspace. At that time . . ."

"English please?" M'Benga says.

There are chuckles from the group, though I can barely hear them.

I sigh. *There you go again, Morgan!* "Sorry. Gillespie will clear off from radar ground control and go Visual Flight Rules. That means he'll be navigating on his own by sight. That also means he can drop to as low as fifteen hundred feet Above Ground Level. Then Gunnie Douglas will open the aft cargo door. We'll jump out and fly quickly to the cover of the trees on the northeast of the target. We'll carry the Marines down with us. Don't worry, guys. Compared to a parajump, it'll be a cakewalk!"

Sergei shouts, "In the sunlight?"

I nod.

"How?"

"You have your protective clothing and sunscreen, but we all know that provides protection for only a few minutes at best. And, at the speed we'll be flying to reach the cover of the trees, the slipstream'll expose patches of flesh. So, although that'll be our primary means of defense, we have a backup. Some of you, particularly the newer folks, may not be aware, but Müller discovered that the darkness or shadow we can project to make ourselves blend into darkness can also block the sunlight. It's draining, and you can't keep it up indefinitely, but it'll do till we get to the trees. Once in the trees, we'll need to take turns projecting a shadow large enough to keep the direct sunlight off us."

Sergei laughs and shakes his head. "I heard stories about him, the old fraud! Müller claimed he could challenge God, because he could walk in the light of the Sun! That tricky old charlatan! So that's all it was?"

"In essence, yeah," I say. "He added some embellishments, but that was it. Moira figured it out." I squeeze her hand, and she returns the squeeze. "So . . . once we're secreted in the woods and night's fallen, we'll send the Marines south to keep watch on the front entrance. Once we're certain Lilith's inside the hotel, we'll attack from all sides."

I pause a moment. "Remember, folks, this is a kill mission. Our primary goal is to kill Lilith, not"—I look straight into Lorenzo's eyes—"I repeat, *not* to rescue hostages. Once the primary target is dead, there won't be any vampires left to endanger them. Every night she lives, more mortals die."

"What about collateral damage?" Sergei asks. "Are the mortals expendable if we achieve our goal? What if they're used as human shields? As I recall, you Americans have no stomach for doing what must be done."

I nod. *Trust the Russian spook to ask the really tough questions. But, it IS something we need to cover.* "Avoid mortal casualties. I mean, *please*, avoid mortal casualties." *Argh! Sometimes I really hate that word!* "We are *not* going to put a sword or spear through the heart of a mortal just to get to the vampire behind him. I will not murder innocents just to win a war, even a war as important as this one. I've dropped bombs in combat. I know not all the dead were military combatants. I know some civilians died. But I would refuse an order to bomb a hospital or an orphanage or a church or a shopping mall, and I won't *deliberately* target a mortal. There's a good chance that mortals will be killed in the course of the battle. But, do your *absolute best* to avoid deliberately killing one of them." I grind my teeth. "*Please* do your absolute best to avoid killing mortals."

"What about us?" That was Lance Corporal Hall. He's sitting with the other Honor Guard Marines, Sergeant Ortiz, Corporal Kowalski, and Lieutenant Ericson. "What're we supposed to do once the fighting starts? We can't fly through windows and you'll be inside before we've even been able to break from the cover of the trees."

"I haven't forgotten you," I say. "Your mission is to secure the mortals. You'll be outnumbered and, hopefully"—*Please let the Lupescus be alive*—"hopefully there'll be a lot of mortals to secure. Can you tell the difference between a mortal and a vampire?"

Lieutenant Ericson clears his throat. "The only paranorms we know by sight are Redstar and Empress, but the paranorms, the *vampires*, will be the arrogant sons of bi . . ." He catches himself. The corner of his mouth draws up in a crooked smile, and then he continues, "The vampires'll be the arrogant sons of guns. The civilians'll be the ones crapping their pants. We'll find them, and we'll protect them with our lives, sir." The other three nod in agreement.

Sons of guns. That reminds me of something.

I smile. "Sounds about right. Some of the civilians'll be wearing hotel uniforms. Some, maybe not. We're hoping to find four mortals who were taken hostage. Two are small children, a girl and a little boy. Lorenzo, do you have a picture in your wallet?"

He nods with enthusiasm. "*Sí.* That I do." He digs out his wallet and shows the pictures to the four Marines.

"However," I continue, "I must caution you. Not all vampires are adults."

Moira grips my hand like a vice.

Ben! I miss you, kid!

"Not very likely," Sergei says. "There are none of the Small Ones among the Court."

"All the same," I say, "you need to be warned. Do you understand, Marines?"

"Aye-aye, sir," they answer in unison.

"If we succeed, we, the vampires, are not coming out of this alive. You four will have to take command and take care of the mortals. We won't be able to help you . . . if we succeed."

"Aye-aye, sir," they shout again.

"The rest of you, report to Rolf for your team assignments. Then meet with your team leader and come up with a plan. Blast it all! I mean, *please!*"

◆ ◆ ◆

"Major Gillespie tells me we're about two hours out from the target," I say to Moira as I climb down the ladder from the cockpit. I pull off the ridiculous Stetson I had to wear to shield myself from the sunlight pouring through the many cockpit windows up there. *Why? Why did it have to be a Stetson! I mean, I am grateful to Jerry Fujikawa and all, but why did he have to go all Tokyo-cowboy on me?*

Rolf and Lorenzo are waiting with Moira at the front of the plane, but staying well out of the patch of sunlight. All the windows in the fuselage are covered over with whatever we could find and secured with some duct tape that is most definitely *not* standard military issue.

The loadmaster, Gunnie Douglas, is up in the cockpit. He was the one who supplied the duct tape as soon as he understood why we needed to cover the windows (that is, once he got over the shock of ferrying a plane full of "top secret national security assets" that look like a bunch of civilians in mismatched and poorly fitting coats and hats). Lieutenant Ericson explained that the "assets" were so secret they could "never see the light of day." That was a good one! Douglas then shrugged his shoulders and pulled four huge rolls of duct tape from his OD green crewbag. He came down from time to time to "inspect the load," weaving swear words like a profane tapestry, but, for the most part, he remained in the cockpit with the rest of the flight crew.

Moira takes my hand, and the four of us, Moira, Lorenzo, Rolf, and I, sit on the floor of the cargo bay. Moira rests her head on my shoulder. *Man, she smells good!* I look around the aircraft and watch my troops. During the mission briefing, they were grim and determined. Now, their expressions range from wistful to amused. Not the Marines, of course. They're sitting, talking amongst themselves.

And not Sergei. He looks miserable.

I catch In-Tae's eye and motion him over. He gets up and crosses the deck, stepping around chatting groups, some of them actually laughing.

What are they laughing about? We're on our way to Golgotha and they're laughing?

In-Tae grins. "What's up, o, captain, my captain?"

"I've got two questions: what's everybody, well not *everybody*, but what're folks laughing about, and how's Sergei holding up?"

"Beats me!" he shouts. "I can barely make out the conversation in our group, much less the others."

"Well, your group is laughing the loudest!" I reply.

He laughs heartily again. "That's because Andrew told a joke!"

"A joke? At a time like this?"

"You've been a Mormon all your life, haven't you?"

"Yeah, so what?"

"Well, I was raised Catholic."

There are *Catholics in Korea, but not that many from what I recall.*

"So?" I ask.

"Well, when you're facing the end of your life or the death of a friend, you throw a party."

"A party?"

"Laddie," Moira says, "he means a *wake*."

In-Tae nods. "That's right, bonnie Hielan lassie! It's a party to remember the *good* about life. You sit around and you tell stories about life and the departed and so on. Usually involves huge quantities of alcohol, but we're making do with just telling stories about our own lives . . . just the good parts."

"So, what's up with Sergei?" I ask.

The Korean's expression saddens. "Sergei's new at this, Carl. He was OK as long as he had something to do. Now he's just waiting until we get into action. When he's left to his own thoughts . . . well, that's when the remorse and the withdrawal is the hardest."

"Withdrawal?"

"He's like a junkie. The hardest part is the sex. It's addictive. He's used to having at least one and usually *multiple* women each night. Now, he's on his way to die, and he's trapped in here with all these beautiful women, and there's nothing he can do about it. It's a tough enough thing to lay your sins on the altar of Christ. It's even tougher when you haven't had time to really think about your life, about your sins. He's consumed with regret, especially about his daughter, and tortured by urges that he can no longer satisfy. Itches he can't scratch and acid eating at his heart. He doesn't have time to work out his repentance. He doesn't have time to heal. He's just . . . having a rough time."

Suddenly, he snaps his fingers and grins. "I know what to do!" He reaches to his back pocket and pulls out his well-worn copy of the Book of Mormon. "I'll read to him about Alma the Younger!" With that, he spins around and shouts as he walks, "Hey, Sergei, you old commie spook! I've got something to show you!"

"Unbelievable!" I mutter as I watch In-Tae plop down next to the morose Russian.

"He's a treasure," Moira says. "He was a grand choice for Sergei's senior companion." She kisses my cheek. "Ye did well, laddie!"

"Yeah, In-Tae's a good guy. I like this idea, though, of a wake, of spending our last hours thinking about happier things."

"Aye, 'tis a fine Gaelic tradition." She smiles and, for a moment, she has a faraway look in her eyes as if she's thousands of miles away . . . and a few centuries. Then she blinks and looks at me with those gorgeous green eyes of hers. "What shall we talk of?"

"Well," I say, "first off, something the young L-T Ericson said reminded me of an unfulfilled promise of yours."

She looks shocked. "Aye?" Rolf and Lorenzo glance between Moira and me, intrigued. Then Moira squints her eyes and stares at me intensely. "And how, pray tell, dearie, have I failed to live up to my obligations to ye?"

"Do you remember our wedding night?"

She flushes a luscious crimson. "Aye, laddie, but I dinnae think . . . Surely ye're nae sayin' I was somehow . . . remiss . . . Ach! We should nae be talkin' o' this in front . . ."

I wave my hands defensively in front of me. "You're not going to punch me, are you?"

She glares at me in mock anger.

At least I think she doesn't mean it.

"She broke my jaw the night we met," I say in a conspiratorial shout to Lorenzo and Rolf, "right before she kissed me."

Lorenzo grins widely. Rolf grins too, but I get the impression he didn't follow everything I said.

Through tight lips, Moira shouts, "See that ye give me nae reason to break it again tonight!"

"OK! Peace, sweet lady!" I say, waving my hands again.

She isn't softening her expression one iota.

OK, Morgan! Don't blow it. Don't piss her off when there's so little time left. The joke's funny only if she gets it too.

"Did I say, 'wedding night?'" I shout.

She growls.

"I really meant our wedding *reception!*"

She purses her lips, but her glare doesn't falter. "Aye, laddie. I *do* remember. Now what promise have I nae fulfilled?"

"Did I say, 'promise?' Well, it wasn't exactly a *promise*. You said to remind you to do it, though."

"And did ye remind me?"

"I forgot."

She punches me in the shoulder. It's not hard. *Well, not* very *hard.* And she continues to glare at me.

She punched me, but her left hand remains clasping mine all the while.

"What was it then?" she asks, her tone icy. Then she winks. And her smile is so beautiful.

"At the reception, my friend, Steve Martin, you know, 'Not the famous one . . .'"

"Aye. I remember. 'Not the famous one. Just the *talented* and *good-looking* one.'" She giggles at the memory.

"Yeah. He called me a 'lucky son of a gun.' You told me to remind you to tell me what that expression actually means. I forgot to remind you until now."

Lorenzo snorts.

I guess he gets the joke.

Rolf looks puzzled.

I guess Rolf doesn't get it. He sighs and looks frustrated.

Moira laughs. It's musical, and it lifts my spirits.

Rolf's look of frustration deepens.

"Aye, laddie," Moira says. "The way ye use it today, ye would nae ken that it's actually a terrible insult."

Lorenzo nods, grinning.

"Ye see, laddie, centuries ago, when sailin' vessels would embark on long voyages, sometimes they'd take along a doxie."

"Doxie?" I have no idea what that means.

"A prostitute . . . a whore, if ye will."

"Really? I know a very nice lady who's got that last name. Maybe it's spelled differently, though."

Moira laughs again. "I do hope so! Aye. And I suppose 'tis an older word. By the by, with a different spellin', it can also mean a doctrine of the church as well as a woman of ill repute. Odd that. Ye can be certain that at one time the spellin's were interchangeable. But in those days, a sailin' vessel would take along a doxie (of the female kind). She'd do laundry and such, but, for the most part, she'd hold court, so to speak, in a small tent erected for her at the bow of the ship . . . at the gunnel, or gunwale. When she became pregnant, as she almost always did, the child would be born without her knowin' who the father was for certain. So, the bairn was called the 'son of the gun.'"

"Ah. I see." I chuckle. "I'll never think of that phrase the same way a-gain! And I'd never be able to look at Sister Doxey the same way again! Do you know she's a high school music teacher, and her male students call her 'Foxy Doxey?' That takes on a whole new meaning I'm *sure* they don't in-tend!"

"Actually," Lorenzo says with a smile, "Doxey is an old name from England. It means 'man from the dry ground.'"

"Bloody English!" Moira laughs. "That's so very funny!"

Lorenzo and I share in her laughter, but Rolf shakes his head in disgust.

Poor guy! I wish there was some way to help him. It must be so frustrating to be locked in your own head without adequate means to express your thoughts, even to yourself.

I lay a hand on his knee. "So tell me, Rolf, what was so funny back there at the dance studio? Why were you laughing?"

I remember at the time thinking I should know *what he was laughing about. It was like a memory just out of reach.*

His face brightens a little. "Marine Ortiz," is all he says.

I shake my head. "I don't get it."

His face screws up in frustration again. "Marine Ortiz. He fight in . . . big war. *My* war. He fight . . ." His face brightens. "He fight like Sergei!"

"Your war?" I say. "You mean he, this Marine Ortiz, was in World War II?"

He pauses, uncertain.

"He was a Marine fighting the Nazis? Fighting the Germans? Like . . . you?"

He nods vigorously.

"Nonsense," Lorenzo says. "Your memory must be addled. The Ameri-can Marines didn't fight in the European theatre."

"No!" Rolf says emphatically. "He fight in . . . Europe in big war with my . . . home."

Something clicks in my memory. *That's it!*

"No," I say, "Rolf's right. There *were* some Marines in Europe in WW II. They were mostly working with the OSS. They were commandos and . . . *spies!* Like Sergei!"

Rolf nods and grins.

"And," I continue, picturing an article I once read on the Internet, "there was a Marine Captain Peter Ortiz assigned to the OSS."

Rolf nods and points at me.

That's the one he's talking about! "His exploits were legendary!" I continue. "He liked to frequent the bars and cafés in German-occupied towns where Nazi officers gathered to shoot the breeze. He would go in disguise and gather intelligence from the loose-lipped, tipsy, and often drunk Nazis. And he was one of the most wanted men in occupied Europe."

I smile, recalling the story. "One night he was in a bar, and the German officers were in fine form, cursing the Americans and President Roosevelt. As the story goes, he listened and gathered what information he could, ignoring the insults to his country, his countrymen, and his president. But, when one of the Germans damned the U.S. Marines . . . Well, that was too much for Ortiz. He left the bar, set explosives outside, wired them to a detonator, and then quickly returned to his quarters. Once there, he changed into his full Marine uniform and covered it with a long cape. Then he returned to the bar.

"He walked into the bar, threw back his cape, drew his side arm, and announced in flawless German, 'I'm Captain Peter Ortiz! I'd like to propose a toast! To President Franklin Delano Roosevelt!' He forced the Germans to drink to the health of FDR. Then he said, 'To the USA!' They drank to the USA. Then he said, 'To the United States Marine Corps! Semper Fi!' They drank to the Marine Corps. Then he taught them to sing the Marine Corps Hymn and forced them to sing it at gunpoint. Then he said good-bye and left the bar. Then he blew it up."

I look at Rolf. "Is that right?"

He nods and laughs. He hums a few bars of the Hymn. "'From the Halls of . . .' Yes. Marine Ortiz!"

"I don't get it," I say, perplexed. "What's so funny?"

"Hans was there. I know him. German."

"But, if he was there, he died."

Rolf nods. "Yes. He died. I don't like him. He is stupid man. Ortiz very funny! Make him . . ." He hums a few bars of the Marine Corps Hymn again. Then he makes a sound, imitating an explosion. "Ortiz!" He laughs heartily.

I can't help but laugh with him. Lorenzo and then Moira join in. The laughter swells until tears are streaming down my face.

I shake my head as the laughter subsides. "Rolf, you are one strange guy. But I like you!"

♦ ♦ ♦

The time passes as we tell jokes and funny stories and just reminisce about old friends. However, Rolf becomes more and more frustrated as he tries to follow our conversation, but can't seem to catch much of it.

Suddenly, he growls out loud and shouts, "I no good. Bad soldier. Not understand you. Not follow commands. Not *understand* commands."

Lorenzo places a hand on his friend's shoulder. "You're doing great, Rolf. You learn so quickly. You just need more time!"

Rolf shakes his shoulder, displacing Lorenzo's hand. "No time! No time! I not understand Carl! I make mistake! People die! I not fight good if I not understand Carl!"

He raises both fists in frustration. Then he abruptly freezes. He drops his hands to his thighs and then looks directly, intensely at me.

"Carl. You are God's man. Jesus' man. You give . . . gift . . ." Then he curls his fists in his lap and shakes them in frustration. He opens his mouth and points to his tongue. "You give gift."

"Do ye mean the gift of tongues, laddie?" Moira asks.

He nods. "Fix me. Please."

"Ah, laddie, he cannae give the gift of tongues. That's one of the gifts of the Spirit."

"No!" Rolf's frustration turns to anguish. "No! Carl can fix me. He is God's man. He can. Jesus can!" He grabs my hands suddenly, pulling my right hand out of Moira's grasp. Then he yanks both my hands toward himself and places them on top of his head. "Jesus fix me! I know!"

I look him in the eye. "You want a blessing?"

"Yes. Blessing. I know blessing from Jesus' man fix me."

That's a tall order. But if there's anyone *in our group of Penitents who has faith to be healed, it's Rolf. I hope I have faith enough.* "OK, Rolf."

I stand and reach into my pocket. *It's still there.* I pull out my keychain and its little vial of consecrated olive oil. I walk around and stand behind Rolf. I fall to my knees. I open the vial and place a drop of oil on Rolf's head and gently rub it in there. I recap the vial and replace it in my pocket. Then I place my hands on my friend's head. As I do so, I glance around the cargo bay. Every eye is on us. The engines are still roaring loudly, but, other than that, there's silence amid the cacophony.

I perform the ordinance of anointing. Then I briefly remove my hands from Rolf's head and replace them there. I call him by name, I state the authority by which I'm performing the second half of the ordinance. I then state that I'm doing it in the name of Jesus Christ, and then I wait. I wait for the Spirit to speak. I clear my mind and listen.

I wait for what seems an eternity.

And then it comes. The power of the Holy Ghost flows into me.

"Rolf, you have asked for a gift of healing. Heavenly Father has heard your prayers. He knows you. He loves you. He knows what you would say if you only had the words to say it. He knows your heart. I bless you that your tongue will be loosed and the ears of your understanding will be opened and your language will be restored to you."

I finish the ordinance and say, "Amen."

Then I remove my hands from my friend's head.

Rolf sits there with his head bowed.

He's silent.

There is no sound but the roar of the engines.

I rise to my feet and move to where I can see his face.

Still no sound.

Doubt grips my heart like the cold hand of death.

Tears fall from Rolf's face.

I failed. I didn't have enough faith.

Lorenzo places a hand on Rolf's shoulder. "Rolf?"

Rolf draws a deep breath. Then he raises his face and his hands to heaven.

"Himmlischer Vater! Du hast meine Zunge befreit, aber Wörte können die Dankbarkeit meines Herzens nicht ausdrücken! Vielen, vielen Dank! Ich danke Dir, dass Du mich zur Wahrheit geführt hast! Ich bin sehr dankbar für das Sühnopfer Christi, das meine Seele von der Hölle eingelöst hat! Ich werde Deinen Sohn ewiglich loben! Hilfe mir mit starkem Mut zu kämpfen und ehrenhaftig zu sterben, damit Du mich zu Deinem Königreich aufnimmst! Bitte, vereinige mich mit meiner Sarah wieder! Das bete ich im Namen Jesu Christi. Amen!"

Tears continue to stream from between his tight-closed eyelids. "Thank you, Carl," he says.

I shake my head. "Don't thank *me*. God healed you. I was just . . . the mouthpiece."

I thank thee, Father, for healing him!

He rises to his feet and wraps me in a great bear hug. "I realize that, my Captain, but you are the only one here with the priesthood of God. Thank you for being here . . . and for being worthy. Thank you for helping me find my way."

I look around the cargo bay at the rest of the Stake. There isn't a dry eye. Even the Marines are crying. And two of them barely knew Rolf.

At last he releases me from the hug. Then Moira throws her arms around him. She sobs, "Oh, laddie! 'Tis so good to hear yer voice!"

One by one, each of the Stake vampires comes forward and tearfully hugs Rolf. Ironically, very few words are exchanged.

Last of all, Sergei comes forward. He doesn't hug Rolf, but he extends his hand.

Rolf shakes it warmly.

Then the Russian turns to me. His lips tremble. Tears stain his cheeks. He opens his mouth to speak, but can't seem to force the words out.

"Sergei," I shout. "What is it?"

"Please," he says at last. "Please help me. Give *me* a blessing. Help me to control . . . the urges. Help to me fight back the darkness. I *want* to repent. I *want* . . . to be saved. Saved like young Alma. But it's . . . so hard."

I shake my head. "I can't take the darkness away. Only God can do that. You need to ask Him."

"*Da.* I know. I've been praying . . . for an hour. Help . . . me. Please!"

I look at him. I see the wells of pain in his eyes, deep and bottomless.

"OK," I say. "I can give you a blessing of comfort."

"*Please.*" A glimmer of hope, the faintest spark, is in his sad eyes.

"*Spahseeboh*," he says as I remove my hands from his head. "Thank you. You've given me hope."

"Excuse me, sir!" It's the gruff loadmaster. I don't know how much he saw, but he looks ... different, shaken. "The AC told me to tell you we're approaching the drop zone."

This is it. The end has come.

Sharon, April, Lucy, Joseph, Ben, I'll see you soon!

Chapter 16

Tony

"Wakey, wakey!" Bo, the demon who murdered my son, is shouting at me in his Australian accent. "If I can't bloody Sleep, you won't neither, ya bloody jumbuck!" He doesn't touch me, doesn't shake me to wake me.

I don't think he can.

Before the other vampires, including Lilith, went behind the curtained area of the helicopter to Sleep for the rest of this interminable voyage to hell, Lilith said something to Bo, something I couldn't catch. Then they left him alone with me and Kathleen . . . and the mangled bodies of Abby and Little Tony. I'm pretty sure Lilith gave Bo a command, a direct order not to touch Kathleen and me.

That's why he can't shake me to wake me up.

And I'm not asleep. I just have my eyes closed. I'm exhausted, but there's no way I could sleep. Even with my eyes shut tight, I can't shut out the images, the scene replaying over and over like some lurid waking nightmare.

Abby and Little Tony screaming.

Kathleen pleading for their lives.

Kathleen offering to do anything to save them.

Kathleen forced to make an impossible, horrific choice.

Bo plunging his gleaming fangs into my son's neck.

The life fading from Little Tony's eyes.

Arturo sucking the life from my precious daughter.

The crumpled corpses of my children at my feet.

Kathleen's dead eyes as she blames me for it all.

Lilith whispering in my ear, making my flesh tingle, making my mind race with forbidden, unspeakable thoughts, making my pulse race with desire, even as I watch the deaths of my children and the shattering of my wife's mind.

"Don't ya want ta watch the show, ya bodgy bitzer?"

No! I don't want to watch! Not again!

I can *hear* the rustling, squishing sounds of the "show." In my head, I know it's impossible . . . the noise of the rotors would drown out the sounds

. . . but in my heart, I can hear them.

"Wifey's watchin', ain't ya darlin'? She's not sayin' much, but she can't take her eyes off it."

"Kathleen!" I cry. "Don't watch! Close your eyes!"

"What's that, darlin'?"

If Kathleen's saying anything, I can't hear it.

But the vampire can.

"Yeah, darlin'! These're your babies! Don't they look lovely?" Bo's voice is mocking. "Well, they *did* look lovely! Until ol' Bo got ta play with 'em. Now they're all broken. But I didn't get to play with 'em the way I wanted, so I'll just have ta make 'em play with each other."

I *know* what he's doing. I don't have to watch to picture it in my mind.

It's just dead flesh! It's not them! It's not Abby and Little Tony! They're gone. They're with God now.

Kathleen. I have to save Kathleen. Even if she hates me, even if she never forgives me, even if her mind is gone, I have to find some way to save her.

But how? I couldn't save my children. How can I save Kathleen?

And into my frantic mind comes the story of the prophet Joseph Smith when he was in Richmond Jail. I recall how he listened to the depraved guards as they boasted of murdering Mormon men, women, and children, even infants, and raping Mormon women. I remember how Joseph rose to his feet, bound in irons as he was, and rebuked the guards. His words were so powerful that the guards cowered in fright, causing them to beg his forgiveness and slink away.

Well, I'm no Joseph Smith.

And this is all my fault. I'm the one who . . . who . . . what? What did I do? Am I guiltless? No. I knowingly kept up the chain of emails with Lilith. I'm the one who leaked the information that led her to us. I didn't mean to let anything slip . . . but Carl warned us enough times to be careful what we said, what we wrote, what we posted. If I hadn't kept emailing, if I hadn't been seduced . . . *yeah, Lilith was right: she seduced me . . . if I hadn't been seduced by my thirst for knowledge, Abby and Little Tony would still be alive, their bodies unbroken, and Kathleen's mind would be whole. If not for me . . .*

But I didn't murder my children.

I was stupid. *I didn't listen to Carl. I didn't listen to the Spirit. I was so focused on what I wanted that I endangered my family.*

I was seduced.

That doesn't excuse it. It is *my fault. I am* guilty.

I led the monsters to them. I didn't mean to, but I did.

But I didn't murder my children.

"Want ta join in the fun, darlin'? Too right, ya do! I don't have ta *touch* ya ta unlock your manacles, darlin'. I'll unlock ya and we'll figure a way ta party!"

I didn't murder my children. These monsters did!

I open my eyes.

Bo has dropped the blood-streaked, mangled bodies of my precious little girl and boy to the floor. They're barely recognizable as once having been human. Bo hunches forward, like a hunter stalking prey, his fangs glistening with saliva. On his hands are smears of gore, the blood of my children. Part of me wonders in a detached way how there could be any blood left in the shattered little bodies. The vampire licks the fingers of one hand lasciviously as he advances toward Kathleen. In his other hand, he holds a key. A hideous leer splits his face.

Kathleen leans forward in her manacles, her body as a rag doll. She looks as if, were she not held upright by the restraints, she'd collapse to the floor. Her eyes are hollow, fixed on the crumpled masses of tissue and bones that used to be our children. There are streaks down her face, but no fresh tears. Drool drips from her lips which move as if she's speaking. She seems to be repeating, "My babies," over and over in a litany of loss, grief, and madness.

"Too right, darlin'! You, ol' Bo, and your babies! We're gonna have fun! I can't touch you, but the babies can! And I can touch the babies! We'll make hubby watch, and he won't be able to do nothin' 'cept sit there and be useless."

The words of Joseph Smith in his chains come forcibly to my mind.

I'm no Prophet Joseph, and I can't rise to my feet, but I finally find my voice.

"*Silence*, fiend of the infernal pit! In the name of Jesus Christ I rebuke you and command you to cease! *Leave her alone!*"

The hulking vampire snaps his attention to me. A murderous fire burns in his eyes. He snarls. I can't hear it, but I can see it in the twist of his hideous face, in the baring of his dripping fangs.

"Go!" I bellow. "Leave her alone!"

Bo howls. I *can* hear that, and it's a terrible sound, like the cry of the damned. But there is *rage* in that howl as well, a rage such as I have never imagined. "How *dare* you command me? I am a *god*! You should *worship* me!"

His face is so horrible to behold, his rage so frightening, that I cannot help but shrink back.

But there is anger in me too.

And it is a *righteous* anger.

"Go! In the name of Jesus Christ I command you to go and leave us alone! Go now or God will strike you down where you stand! Go now and live a moment longer!"

Bo throws his head back and howls again.

Then he spins about and stomps off in the direction of the curtain. In a moment, he's gone.

And we're alone.

I know it can't last long.

"Kat! Kat! Come on, Kitty-Kat! Please, honey! Look at me!"

She lifts her head and turns it in my direction. Her eyes are vague, unfocused. Then she squints and looks directly into my eyes. She shakes her head slowly.

"My babies!" It's a scream . . . a condemnation, a curse, a damnation.

"I know, honey! I know! It's just we don't have much time! I'm sorry. I led them to us. I . . ."

"You killed my babies!"

I've never seen hatred in Kathleen's eyes before. Not directed at anyone. Ever. And now raw loathing glares at me from my sweetheart's face, a face twisted in rage and disgust.

Hatred, rage, and disgust. All for me.

"Honey . . . I . . . I didn't . . . I . . . I'm sorry. Forgive me." She probably can't hear me. Probably for the best. There's nothing I can say.

I didn't kill them, but it's my fault they're dead.

My fault.

But, I have to stay alive for Kathleen. If I die, she won't last long.

Father in Heaven! I'm so sorry! My children are dead because of me! Don't . . . Please *don't let Kathleen die because of me! Don't let her suffer any more for my failings . . . my sins. Save her! Take me, but save Kathleen!*

"My babies!"

"Yes, Kat! I know. I . . ."

"Well, isn't that just too sweet? Do you call her 'Pussycat' when you're alone?" The honeyed voice is right in my ear.

I start and snap my head around.

And there she is. Lilith. Beside me.

I didn't hear her approach.

I feel her breath on my ear . . . on my cheek.

Fingertips as soft as feathers trail down my neck.

My flesh tingles at her caress. A burning of desire, of longing, radiates from her fingertips and spreads throughout my body, enveloping me like a warm blanket on a cold winter's day.

Impossible to think clearly.

No other woman could be so beautiful . . . so . . . . consummately female.

"You think of *me* when you're alone with little Pussycat, don't you? You know you do, lover."

Her eyes! So intoxicating!

I need to think! I need to focus! For Kathleen!

So near! I can hardly breathe!

I snap my head forward.

Don't look at her! It's not real! She can't be . . . You can't want . . .

They murdered Abby and Little Tony!

Please, Heavenly Father! Help us! Help me save Kathleen! Help me . . .

Lips as light as the breeze of a butterfly's wings brush my ear.

Help me to resist! Give me strength! ". . . no temptation so great . . ." So great . . .

"It's a lie." My voice is soft, uncertain. I'm sure she can hear it, but even *I'm* not sure I believe me. "*You're* a lie."

Her hand is on my thigh.

"Stop. Don't do this."

She doesn't stop.

"Stop!" *Finally! Some conviction in my voice!*

"Even you know you don't mean that, lover."

"I do! Stop now!"

Her hand freezes. She leaves it there for a moment . . . for an eternity.

"For now," she coos in my ear. "But you *will* beg me. You *will* come to me. In time."

"Adam didn't."

Suddenly her hand is gone.

I feel shame burning in my cheeks as I mourn her hand's absence.

"I was young and not fully ripe in my powers." Her voice has a hard edge to it, venom mixed with honey. "I wouldn't fail now were the old fool not dust beyond the Flood. You *will* come to me, if for no other reason than to save your plain little wife."

"You have no intention of sparing her."

"I said I would. You have my word."

"Your word means nothing. My children are dead."

"*My babies!*" Kathleen screams.

Lilith puts her lips to my ear again. "My word is law." There is more honey than venom, but the venom is still there like a bitter aftertaste.

She doesn't like to be questioned . . . challenged.

"Bo! Attend me!"

The monster emerges from behind the curtain. He's hesitant in his movements, like a dog expecting a beating after soiling the carpet. But he comes. He stops a pace away from her, his head bowed submissively.

He's trembling!

This is the same man who seemed so powerful, so unstoppable just minutes ago?

"Yes, my Queen?"

"You abandoned your post. You woke me from my Sleep with the blood of the mortal spawn on your hands. Is this not so?"

"Yes, my Queen." His head remains bowed and his trembling turns to quaking.

"Did I not command you to watch over our guests and not touch them?"

"Yes, my Queen."

"And how is it, Bo, my love, my dearest Child, Son of my heart, husband, that you could possibly disobey or fail to carry out the least of my commands?" All hint of venom is gone. Her voice is pure sweetness. Irresistible. "How is this possible, beloved?"

"'E *commanded* me!" It's a whine! Bo, the implacable demon is whining like a petulant child! "I couldn' 'elp m'self! Wha' was I supposed ta do? I never felt such . . . *power!* I couldn' stop m'self! 'Ave mercy, my Queen! 'Asn't ol' Bo always done right by ya? I serve ya, my Queen! I serve only you! I love only . . ."

"Power, dear, sweet Bo? *Power?* There is no power greater than me! You know that, darling."

Bo says something, but I can't hear it above the rotors.

"Speak up, Bo! So our guests can hear."

"Yes, my Queen! You 'ave all power!"

"But, dearest husband, your failure might convince our guests otherwise." She purses her lips as if in thought. "Yes. A demonstration, I think. You have failed me, Bo. You know the price of failure, my dearest love."

The massive vampire prostrates himself on the floor. "No, my Queen! 'Ave mercy!"

Bo's Queen rises from her seat beside me and kneels down beside Bo's head. She extends a hand and runs her fingers through his hair. She looks as if she's petting a dog. "Bo, Bo, Bo," she says, "did I say that *you* would have to pay the price of your failure? Would that be fair? *Of course*, it would. That would be *justice*. It would be what you *deserve*. But you know how I *despise* justice. I'd rather exact the price from someone else entirely."

She rises to her feet and moves a pace or two away. Bo remains prostrated, but he lifts his face to watch her. Tears glisten on his cheeks. Lilith turns and faces me. Then she kneels again. Tilting her head back, she raises her hands as if in supplication. She claps her hands twice and shouts *"Shenah Mishphatu Phosferno!"*

I think I know what that means!

And I pray I'm wrong.

But I know I'm not.

Bo props himself up on his elbows. His expression alternates between eager anticipation and dread.

He knows what's coming. Or, rather, *who.*

So do I.

Lilith claps her hands six times more and cries, *"Shenah Adenoi Helel!"* Then she prostrates herself, her face to the floor, her arms extended, her hands turned up.

Nothing happens. Bo's expression becomes one of worry.

Maybe I was wrong. The words, though . . . I thought I recognized them. But maybe . . . just maybe I was wrong.

Let me be wrong!

Seconds tick away. Lilith remains prostrate, waiting.

Suddenly there's a bright light in the space between the two vampires. Inside the light, there's a shape, vaguely manlike. The light *seems* intense and I *feel* as if I shouldn't be able to look at it, that I *should* need to avert or cover my eyes, but . . . I can stare right at it.

"HERE AM I!" The voice is loud and terrible, frightening, like the roar of a storm.

"So we can all see, Fallen One." Lilith says. I look over at her and see that she has risen to her feet. Her posture is no longer deferential. In fact, she looks completely indifferent. She waves dismissively. "You can dispense with the 'angel of light' facade. I'm no longer the naïf, the abused young helpmeet and mother who worshipped you as a god six millennia hence."

The light fades and vanishes, leaving in its place a man dressed in a perfectly tailored white suit with a golden tie and highly polished black shoes. His features are perfect, ageless, the epitome of masculine beauty. His hair is black. His eyes are dark brown and piercing. He locks eyes with me, and I feel naked, completely exposed, as if he can see into my very soul.

He can't, Tony! "There is none save God that knowest thy thoughts and the intents of thy heart." *Lucifer cannot see into your soul!*

"Why have you summoned me?" His voice is petulant. The terrible roar is gone. He looks . . . *contrite.*

"My reasons are my own," Lilith says, "and I am under no obligation to answer you. Is that not so?"

He stares at her in silence.

"I asked you a question, you unborn, bodiless serpent." Lilith's voice is calm, though loud enough to be heard above the helicopter's rotors.

Lucifer bows his head submissively. "Yes."

"Yes?" Her voice, though still calm, has an undercurrent with menace.

His lips move in answer, but I can't hear him.

"Louder, worm!" Lilith shouts. "So my guests can hear!"

He looks up and stares at her, his eyes blazing with loathing. "Yes, *Mistress!*"

"Avert your eyes, Helel."

The Devil lowers his head. "Yes, Mistress."

Lilith nods approvingly and turns her gaze to me. "You see, lover, the order of things." She begins to walk languidly toward me, her hips swaying. "You see who is the Queen here, and who the vassal."

"Why do you bow to me and perform the Summoning in the ancient manner?" Satan asks. "To mock me? I who made you what you are, who gave you life eternal, who made you a goddess?"

Lilith laughs. It is a high, musical, utterly *female* laugh. It's not mocking; she seems genuinely amused. "Oh, Morning-Son! You can still divert me! After all these thousands of years!" She laughs again. "Oh, my! I haven't laughed like that in . . . well, at least half a century!" She purses her lips in a small smile, her lips luscious, full, and red as blood. "Very well. For making me laugh, I will indulge you."

Still looking at Lucifer, she places a hand on my cheek. My flesh burns at her touch.

I'm looking at Satan himself, and still my thoughts race to forbidden places.

"And"—her fingers trail down my neck—"it could be *educational* for my latest conquest. He lusts for knowledge. He sold his family, his children, for knowledge. He was seduced with tidbits of ancient history."

She blows lightly into my ear. I cannot stop my body from trembling.

"Didn't you, lover?"

I clench my jaw. *Resist her. She's like* him. *A cheat. A lie. 'No temptation so great . . .'* *She's* not *the consummate woman!*

She takes her hand from my neck.

I struggle to ignore the sense of loss and longing I feel at the absence of her touch.

She sashays a few steps in the direction of the man in the white suit. "Lord Lucifer, *you* set the conditions of our Covenant. *You* set forth the forms of the Summoning. *I* honor my portion of our agreement. *I* perform the ritual of Summoning as you required and *you* come to me as you are bound to do. *I* seduce and corrupt the innocent. *I* send the unrepentant to the judgment of Father. *I* feast on blood and draw strength."

Without turning back to me, she says, "You see, lover, Lucifer was not happy with the bargain he made with my father, Qayin. Oh, my father murdered his brother, Hevel." Now she glances back at me. "I'm sorry. I'll use the modern forms. That way Pussycat can understand . . . that is, if she can understand *anything* at this point, poor dear." She turns back to face Lucifer. "*Cain* murdered *Abel* and *Lucifer* made Cain Master Mahan. And my father spread the Covenant and corrupted others, but then he became a vagabond, an outcast. He was of no further use to Lucifer. He became worthless as a tool."

The man in white glares at her for a second then lowers his eyes again.

"Lucifer was *inexperienced* back then. He could never know mortality. He hadn't learned how to possess a mortal body even for short periods yet. My father gave him great knowledge. But once Cain's usefulness was spent, Lucifer sought *another* tool. One that could *endure* and bring more souls under his sway for all eternity. So he found me. Only this time, he did things *differently*. With my father, Lucifer promised to serve him in the world to come. With me, he promised to serve me in *this* life, and he made me immortal so I could continue my work forever. He promised to lend me strength, power."

She grins widely, wickedly. "In short, he made a colossal *error*. He made me the *Mistress*. Now he comes at *my* call, so long as I follow the ancient forms and keep my end of the bargain. Now he gives me strength, so long as I consume the blood of the children of Adam. And as long as I live and consume blood, his strength is *mine*."

Lucifer's head snaps up, and he looks at her.

And there's *fear* in his eyes.

The Devil *fears Lilith.*

"Which, Fallen One, brings me to the reason why I Summoned you."

The fear in Lucifer's eyes turns to terror.

"No!" He shakes his head violently from side to side. "Not me! It doesn't have to be *me*! The Host. Draw from *them*! Not from *me*!" His voice is pleading.

What are they talking about? What can she possibly do to him?

Lilith turns so I can see her face in profile. She points to Bo. "My Son has failed me. I require that a price be paid for that failure, but, at the moment, I would rather punish *you* in his place. And this has the *added* benefit of displaying my *true* power to my latest mortal lover. You see, Helel, I think Tony may still have *hope*. I think he still *hopes* that Father will save him. I want to show him just how vain that hope is. And the truth is that I *enjoy* what I get from our . . . relationship."

Satan drops to his knees and extends his hands. "Please! My Host! You can have them all! All their strength! It doesn't have to come from me! *Not from me!*"

Lilith turns to face me. Her eyes lock with mine. "Have you ever wondered, lover, how my Children and I can survive on so little blood, what the *true* source of our power is?"

Sam Gallagher's words last night . . . *Was that just last night?* . . . flash through my head: *". . . a quart of human blood doesn't contain enough calories to account for even one day's worth of normal activity, much less vampiric activity. Scientifically, it makes no sense! . . . that means the energy has to come from some other source!"*

"MY BABIES!" Kathleen screams. Her eyes are filled with the fires of madness. Spittle flies from her chapped lips.

Lilith starts visibly. Even the Devil stares at my raving wife.

Then a smile spreads across Lilith's face. "Yes, I am in a *magnanimous* mood. I had intended to allow your husband to fulfill my needs, but you will do nicely." Her fangs extend. She licks her lips. "Yes, Pussycat. You'll do nicely. Two birds and all that."

"L-l-leave her alone!" I can barely speak.

The Queen of the Vampires turns her face to me. Even with her fangs extended she looks sensuous. She runs a pink tongue across her blood red lips. Suddenly I find it hard to breathe. "You *want* me, lover? You *crave* my touch? You want to know the ecstasy of letting me drink your blood?"

Heaven help me, but I do! At the moment I want nothing more than for her to touch me again, to take my blood!

"But, of course, you do. Your Penitent friends have Fed from you many times, I'll warrant."

"N-n-never," I manage to choke out.

Astonishment is plain on her face. "*Never?* Inconceivable." Then she regains her composure. "It is of no consequence. You will beg for me soon enough. But right now I intend to keep the promise I made to you." She licks her lips suggestively. "I'm going to Heal your little wife."

"Please," I plead. "L-l-leave her alone."

"What, lover? Aren't you going to command me as you did with poor Bo?" Her smile is mocking, but still breathtaking. "You *know* you won't because you want me too badly and you *want* me to Heal her mind. And, most of all, you *lust* for the knowledge, the mystery, that only I can give you."

Then, swift as a striking snake, Lilith pounces on Kathleen and locks her lips on my wife's neck.

"My babies!" Kathleen cries feebly and then her eyes roll up into her head and her lips gape, quivering. A look of sheer joy fills her . . .

A scream of agony fills the air in the helicopter. It is impossibly loud and long and piercing. Lucifer writhes on the floor. He shrieks again and again and again, clutching at his face, pulling at his hair, gnashing his teeth.

Lilith holds her lips on Kathleen's neck for a moment longer, and then she breaks contact and licks the wound made by her fangs. She rises off the floor, her white wings unfurled and beating. Her back arches and her arms fling wide. "*Yes!*" she screams in a paroxysm of ecstasy. "*More! Fill me with it!*"

Lucifer continues to scream and writhe. "NO!" he cries. "Enough! No more!" His screams become inarticulate.

"Yes!" Lilith cries. "All of it! Till I can hold no more! MORE!"

Bo, still on his knees, laughs maniacally.

Lilith is causing Lucifer pain? "Drawing strength . . ." from Lucifer? Only at the moment she's drawing strength from him alone . . . *and not from the "Host" of his minions?*

"Tony?" *It's Kathleen!* "My babies! My babies! They killed my babies! Tony!"

Lilith alights on the floor, and her wings fold up and disappear. Lucifer continues to roll on the floor, and he appears to be trembling, but he no longer seems to be in agony.

"Tony! Where are my babies?" She looks at me, and her eyes are lucid, but confused.

"They're dead, sweetheart." I don't know how long this will last. "I'm sorry. It's all my fault."

"Your fault?" She looks around and, locking her eyes on the broken bodies of our children, she screams.

"Don't look at them, Kat! Focus on me!"

She closes her eyes. She turns her face to me and opens her eyes slowly. "Your fault?"

"I led them to us. I didn't mean to, but I did."

"Yes, Pussycat," Lilith says. "Your husband, the father of your children, led me to you. He *sold* you to me, you and your babies. He sold you to me so he could know me better, more *intimately*. Do you remember?"

"Yes, I remember." She turns her gaze on Bo. "*You!* You killed my son! You made me *choose!*"

"Yes, and you *did* choose, didn't you, Pussycat." Lilith shakes her head in feigned sadness. "You chose your little girl over your helpless little boy. And you didn't save either one. Poor Pussycat! You *failed* at everything. You failed as a mother, as a wife. You poor, pathetic, wretched creature! It drove you mad, quite literally mad. But now I've Healed you. Now your mind is clear. Now you can recollect your abject failure with perfect clarity."

Kathleen sobs.

"May I go now?" Lucifer has risen to his feet. He straightens his tie, but he looks unsteady. He smoothes his hair with trembling fingers. "Have you exacted your price?"

Lilith turns to face the Devil. "*Most* of it, Helel. And, as satisfying as that was . . . I still don't tolerate failure. You may go."

Lucifer locks eyes with me. I have that feeling again that he can see into my soul. "Deliver me," he says. "I'll give you *anything*. Knowledge beyond your wildest imaginings."

And then he's gone. There's no ceremony. He simply vanishes from sight.

But, before he vanished, there was something in his eye. Something I can't quite put a name to.

I suddenly become aware that Bo is groveling again. "No, my Queen! 'Ave mercy!"

"You failed me, my Son, my husband."

"You said you would spare me!"

"I lied."

"NO!" Bo crawls forward, reaching for her feet.

"Don't touch me." Lilith's voice is calm, but the command it contains is unmistakable.

Bo stops moving forward, stops reaching toward her, but he grovels still.

"Do you love me, Bo?" Lilith coos.

"You know I do!"

"Do you *ache* for my touch?"

"Yes, my Queen!"

"Then show me how much you love me."

"Anything!"

"Get up."

Bo rises quickly to his feet.

"Go to the hatch." She points to a door on the opposite wall.

Bo rushes over to the door.

"Open it."

Bo opens the hatch. It folds down, and light streams in from outside. Direct sunlight. Bo steps quickly back from the light.

The noise of the rotors and the rush of the air are suddenly even louder.

Lilith shouts, "Bo, dearest Bo, the bodies of these children . . ." She points to the crumpled corpses on the floor. "They don't look very pretty. And they are beginning to smell. Will you dispose of them for me?"

"Me?" Bo looks terrified. "But the light!"

"Their presence offends me, dearest. And they seem to be distressing our guests."

"It'll *burn* me!"

"Then I suggest you be quick."

"Yes, my Queen! Thank you, my Queen! I can be quick! Quick as lightning!" He scrambles forward to scoop up the remains of my children, one in each arm. Their broken bodies twist and flop in unnatural ways. Bo turns to run toward the door, carefully avoiding the patch of sunlight.

Kathleen chokes out, "My babies!"

"Bo-o!" Lilith calls.

He stops in mid stride and the mutilated corpses flop about like broken puppets.

"You forgot their clothes. I don't want the constant reminder of them lying around."

"Yes, my Queen! No worries! Too right, ya are." He transfers Little Tony from one arm to the other and drapes his body over Abby's. Their mangled little faces are pressed together as if they're kissing. Their arms dangle down and hang in a manner that should be anatomically impossible.

Bo begins picking bits of clothing from the floor. The items are scattered about, and he rushes to gather every one. When he has collected them all, he heads toward the hatch again, staying as far away from the broad swath of light.

"Oh, Bo, dear heart!"

He spins around, dropping a soiled pair of boy's pants to the floor. He stoops to pick it up. The little heads slam into the metal deck. "Yes, my Queen?" He looks like an eager puppy, ready to play.

"I think the children deserve a proper funeral, don't you?"

He blinks at her. "I don't understand."

"I think they deserve a proper funeral. You can't exactly bury them, can you?"

Bo laughs nervously. "No. I can't bury 'em."

"Are we over water?" Lilith shouts.

"Nah! No water."

"Then a pyre is the only solution."

Bo blinks stupidly.

"They will have to be burned, Bo!" Lilith smiles sweetly. "Fly them to the Sun, my love!"

"NO!" Bo screams even as his wings appear and he flies out the hatch and into the sunlight. The murderer of my son bursts instantly into flame as he disappears from sight.

Chapter 17

Moira

One helluva ride!" Sergeant Ortiz and the other Marines are supposed to be getting some "rack time" (as my husband puts it), but they've spent the hours since we flew out of the back of the airplane talking excitedly about their adventures with the vampires. Nae that I blame them in the slightest. Even though 'tis day and I should be exhausted after the events of the past twenty-four hours, I would nae waste a moment of my last few hours on Earth. I wish with all my heart that Carl and I could be alone together one last time. But 'tis nae to be.

The time is precious to me, as Mr. Dickens wrote.

"Couldn't see a da ... a ... a blasted thing!" Ortiz continues. "I mean, I've jumped out of airplanes before ... we all have. I've jumped at night. I've jumped through the soup! But you could always see *something*! Stars, the ground, once you got through the soup ... *something*! But not like that! And the lady that carried me down! I guess she could see out of this black cloud thing they do. But I can't. And she's so *small* ... at least compared to me! Lifted me like I was a baby in her arms! Pretty little thing, too! Gorgeous! Yeah, yeah! I know she's married and could rip me in half with her bare hands ... I mean, she took me down easy enough! You should have seen it, L-T! Fast as a bullet! I never saw her coming!"

"Ortiz," Lieutenant Ericson says, "I cannot say that I am the *least* bit surprised that a *girl* took you down!"

There is some good-natured laughter from all four of the Marines.

"You do *realize* she can probably hear you, hear every word you just said." That was Lance Corporal Hall.

"You got that right!" Ericson agrees.

Ortiz swears softly. Then, louder, he says, "Sorry, Mrs. Morgan!"

I cannae suppress a wee smile, though 'tis a weary smile to be sure. I try to tune out the chatter of the Marines. I have to maintain my concentration for 'tis my turn to project our protection. Keeping the cloud of darkness around the lot of us, even huddled as we are, for ten minutes at a stretch is very tiring. The trees provide a great deal of shade, but the sun breaks through in small but frequent patches in deadly shafts of light. So maintaining a large patch of darkness is a necessity. Carl tried to insist on taking my turn as well as his own, but I would nae have it. I dinnae want any special treatment, nae even as the wife of the "Captain" (as everyone seems to insist on calling him). And I dinnae want to tire my laddie out any more than is necessary. We're going to need all our strength to face the battle to come. *We'll rest when we're dead,* as the old saw goes. *And that right soon.*

Beside me, Carl squeezes my hand. "Let me finish for you!" he whispers. "I know you're exhausted, and I need you at your best."

"None of that, laddie! My time's almost up." *Our time's almost up!* "See, there's Collin approaching."

Carl nods. "Yeah, he's next on the duty roster. Hold on just a bit longer, my love."

"Dinnae fret yerself, laddie."

However, when Collin taps me on the shoulder and says, "I got it now, love," I gladly release the darkness and breath a huge sigh of relief.

Carl wipes the sweat from my brow with a cool hand. Then he kisses my forehead lightly. "Up for a walk?"

"Aye, laddie." He extends a hand and helps me to my feet. "Ye lead. I'll follow."

The weariness falls from my shoulders like a discarded cloak. Carl takes my hand in his, and we intertwine our fingers.

Though even our eyes cannae see far in this projected cloud of darkness, we can see well enough to pick our way between the closely huddled clusters of vampires. We'll nae venture outside the cloud and we cannae hope for even a wee bit of privacy (since any vampire nearby would hear the slightest whisper), but it feels grand to be "strolling" with my dearie for one last time.

"Carl?" That's Sergei. I hear the sound of a cell phone snapping shut at our left. A man rises to his feet barely a pace away. We halt, and he takes a step closer. I can barely make out his features clearly enough to put Sergei's face with his voice. "I have a report."

We haven't spoken with the Russian since we landed in the woods outside the chateau, but when we left him, he was kneeling in prayer.

"What's up?" Carl asks.

"I just received word from the mortal head of the Brotherhood of Tobias. Before we left Utah, I sent him a message to have the Brotherhood watch the skies for a large black helicopter and any activity by 'winged demons.' He just reported a sighting from a member in western Kansas. What was remarkable was that he reported what looked like a missile being fired *from* the helicopter."

"It's armed?" Carl sounds astonished.

Perhaps this type of helicopter does nae normally carry weapons.

Sergei shakes his head. "No, it's not armed. Lilith would never risk an armed engagement in daylight."

"Then what?"

"My guess would be that it was an execution. She ordered someone to fly out into the light and commit suicide."

"Who?" I ask.

"Only the remaining eleven Enforcers would be with her, since she sent the Honor Guard out on a mission. So it would have to have been one of them. The Queen does not tolerate failure."

"Failure?" Carl asks. "Failure at what?"

"Who knows? Perhaps something went wrong with the mortals."

"Ow!" Carl cries as he shakes the hand I'm holding.

I ease my death grip on it. "Sorry, laddie! But the Lupescus!"

"There's nothing we can do!" I can hear Carl grinding his teeth.

"I'm sorry, Moira," Sergei whispers, "but there's very little chance they're all alive. Tony might be. He's the valuable one. But, to control him, assuming Lilith hasn't already taken him to her bed, you only need one living hostage."

"Then Kathleen or one of my little grandchildren is already dead."

I did nae notice Lorenzo's approach.

"Possibly all three or all four of them," Sergei replies, his voice grim. "That is the type of failure for which I could easily see Lilith executing one of the Twelve . . . I mean, the *eleven*."

"Lorenzo!" I choke down a sob of anguish.

He wipes tears from his eyes. "They're with God. Perhaps there'll be one left to save."

"Remember the primary objective . . . if you will," Carl says.

"Never forgotten, *signori*. If we, our kind, are all dead, they'll no longer be in danger. You need not worry about me. I won't fail you. I'll gladly sacrifice myself to save my family."

Carl releases my hand and throws his arms around Lorenzo. "You're a good man, Lorenzo. I'm proud to fight with you at my side."

Lorenzo pats Carl's back. "*Si*. I must pray."

Sergei coughs discreetly. We turn our attention back to him. "Given the time of the report, I'd say that we should see them arrive within the hour."

"They'll land here?" Carl asks.

The Russian shrugs. "Why not? They'll fly without lights and there'll be little chance of their being observed. And Lilith will be anxious to raise two more men to her inner circle with the loss of myself and at least one other." He bows his head for a tick and then cocks it to the side. "I wonder who it was. Larry? He's stupid enough. Patrick? Bo? It might've been Bo. There's this game he likes to play with his prey . . ."

Carl raises a hand, stopping him. "Is this *valuable* intelligence?"

Sergei purses his lips and then shakes his head. "Most likely not."

Carl nods. "I really don't need details of how depraved they can be. Just pray that some of the mortals are alive. I mean, *please* pray."

Sergei says, "I have been praying without ceasing ... that is, until my phone rang."

"*Please* keep me apprised of any new reports. And *please* spread the word: we're to observe complete silence once the Sun sets. We don't want any awakening vampires hearing us."

Sergei nods. "Yes, sir."

"Excuse me, Captain Morgan, sir!" The voice comes from the direction of the Marines. I think that's Lance Corporal Hall. "I know you can hear me, sir. Do you have a minute?"

Carl looks at me questioningly.

I nod in the direction of the Marines. "Aye."

He offers his arm, and I take it. We walk carefully in the direction of the mortals, weaving our way between the immortals.

Immortals! We're an hour or two from death!

"Yes, Lance Corporal?" Carl halts us a couple of paces from the Marines.

"Is that you, Captain?" Hall looks about blindly. "I can't see a thing in this soup!"

"It's me. What's on your mind, Marine?"

"Pardon me for asking, sir." Hall looks in our general direction. "But . . . well, you know ... if all goes as planned ... I may not get a chance to ask ..."

"'Tis all right, laddie." I smile at him and then chide myself for a fool since the mortal cannae see my face. "Ask yer question."

"Uh, OK. Hi, Mrs. Morgan! I hope our ... comments earlier didn't offend, ma'am!"

"Ye're fine, laddie! Nae offense meant, I'll wager, and none taken. What woman of nigh three centuries would nae wish to hear that she can still turn a head or two?"

He laughs . . . a wee bit nervously, to be sure. "Three centuries! Wow!"

"Give or take a few decades," I reply.

"Your question, Marine?" There's some annoyance in my laddie's voice.

Dinnae fret, laddie! My heart is yours! Now and for all eternity!

"Aye-aye, sir! Um ... that thing you did aboard the aircraft, sir? When you ... made it so that that one guy could talk again? The German guy, sir?"

"Rolf." Carl's tone softens. "Yes?"

"Rolf! Aye, sir! Uh ... was that a ... a *vampire* thing ... or a *Mormon* thing?"

Carl laughs.

'Tis good to hear him laugh!

"Definitely a 'Mormon thing,' son!"

"That was amazing, sir!"

"It was none of my doing, Marine. I'm just the agent. Rolf had the faith. God did the healing. I just spoke the words."

"But, sir, the German . . . he said that you were the only one who could do it."

"I was the only one aboard who held the priesthood of God. Moira and I are the only members of the Church in our little group. I'm the only priesthood bearer. So, you could say that I was the only one who could perform the *ordinance*, but Heavenly Father has the power. In fact, every worthy adult male member of the LDS Church has the same authority."

He looks puzzled.

"You got access to a computer, son?" I ask.

"Aye, sir. At home."

"When you get back, got to mormon.org. You'll get your questions answered there, and you can even arrange for two young missionaries to come visit you, if you like."

"I'd like that, sir." He puts up a hand to stop us from going, even though we made nae motion to leave. *Poor lad cannae see a thing!* "W-w-would you . . . pray with me, sir? Actually, would you pray with the four of us? I . . . I never felt *anything* like that . . . like I felt aboard the Hercules . . . never in my life. None of us have. We've been talking about it."

"Please, sir." That was Ericson. The other two echo the sentiment.

It's funny to think of these battle-hardened soldiers asking a vampire to pray with them. But, as the old saw goes, "There are no atheists in foxholes."

Carl smiles. "Sure, Marine. I'd be delighted to. Take a knee, men."

Carl and I kneel down. Hall drops carefully to his knees, and the other three get up on theirs.

"Would it be OK," Carl asks, "if Moira says the prayer?"

"That'd be great, sir," Ericson says, nodding in our general direction.

"Aye, sir," the other three say in unison.

I bow my head and begin, "Dear Father in Heaven, we are so very grateful to be given a chance to serve Thee . . ."

Nae sooner do we finish the prayer than I feel the rush of strength and power that accompanies the extinguishing of the last deadly rays of the Sun. I hear a collective gasp from the assembled Stake.

Carl tosses aside the hated Stetson hat.

We'll nae live to see another sunrise. I lay aside my bonnie green cloak.

The Marines open their eyes and gaze about, shielding their eyes with their hands. The half-light of the gloaming's too strong for eyes that've seen nary a thing save blackness for hours.

Carl points to his team leaders and gives a prearranged hand signal. *We're being silent now, silent as stones in a kirkyard.* The teams form up and begin to move to their assigned locations. The Marines head to the south to take up a position in sight of the front door of the hotel.

Once the Marines signal that "Empress" and company are inside the chateau and the Honor Guard Marines have been dismissed for the evening and are safely out of the way, Carl will send a text to all team leaders with a specific time to begin the assault. The attack time will be a few minutes after the messages are sent to insure that all team leaders have time to receive them. The watches of the team leaders have been synchronized to Carl's watch.

Now there's naught that we can do but wait ... wait for the last moments of our earthly lives.

◢ ◢ ◢

An hour passes, and there's still nae sign of that beastly black thing. Sergeant Ortiz has long since sent a message that the Honor Guard's safely away.

Has Lilith somehow learned of our plan? Has this all been for naught?

There! Against the nigh-black sky! Like a great black dragon, it comes! A black shadow. The enemy comes and with her, the end of our lives. I can just see the helicopter between gaps in the trees. It's low, just above the horizon.

Carl squeezes my hand. Then he pulls me to himself and we share a quick, but sweet kiss. *How I love this man!* Then our attention is turned back to the approaching aircraft.

Will they fly out of the helicopter while it's still aloft and risk being seen flying? Or will they risk the spectacle of landing in the parkin' lot? We'll have to wait to find out.

As the black craft approaches, it becomes plain to me that 'twill be landing nearby. Soon it disappears from sight.

The Marines are our eyes now.

We wait.

I glance at the faces of the vampires in our team. They're hard, determined.

They seem to say, *We will fight and die with honor. May God show us mercy.*

I can hear the helicopter flying away.

They're here.

Carl's phone lights up. He flips it open and reads the text: "E + 10 PN. 2 civs. 0 children."

Lilith and ten other vampires. Two mortals. No children. The wee ones are dead! The poor wee bairns! At least their suffering is over. Poor Kathleen! Poor Tony!

Poor Lorenzo!

A second message arrives: "All secure."

Lilith and her party are inside.

Carl quickly sends the signal text: "Five before the hour."

I look at the time on his phone. 'Tis nine minutes before the hour now. We have just minutes left before we die.

Carl turns his watch to his face. We wait as the final minutes tick away. When there are only twelve seconds left, Carl lowers his arm and counts down the remaining seconds silently.

I watch his lips move.

Ten.

Carl releases my hand for the last time, and I feel a terrible pang of loss.

Nine.

The entire team stands.

Eight.

All of us draw our swords and other weapons.

Seven.

I have my ebony blade of truth.

Six.

Carl has his basket-hilted claymore and his dirk.

Five.

Carl smiles at me with that lopsided grin of his, and my knees threaten to give way.

Four.

I smile back.

Three.

"I love you," he mouths.

Two.

"I love ye too," I mouth back.

One.

We leap into the air.

Chapter 18

Carl

*P*lease! Please! Please! Please! Please!
*Preface every blasted command with a "*Please!*" Leave your people room to think and act for themselves!*

I point the tips of both the dirk and the sword straight at my assigned window. We have someone for every window and every external door with a few people to spare. Consequently, Moira's going to follow me in.

At the last moment, I shut my eyes.

I feel the impact with the glass and hear it explode. There are multiple similar explosions occurring all around me.

My eyes snap open.

We're in the spacious lobby of the hotel. There's a registration desk, a large, wide staircase, elevators, and a couple of doors leading elsewhere. The lobby's deserted, except for three men, each wearing a sword at his hip. *They're standing guard.* I fly straight at the nearest one.

I have my dirk in his heart before he can draw his blade. My sword takes his head off.

I hear women screaming and men cursing.

Moira has dispatched her man.

Sergei has his sword through the heart of the third vampire, holding it there. The dying vampire's face is frozen in shock. For an instant, I wonder if the man is more shocked by the sword in his heart or by the sight of *Sergei* fighting against his former Queen.

Our troops are flying as much as possible. Being wingless makes it easy to tell friend from foe. And we can move faster in the air.

"Tally ho!" That was Rolf shouting. He's on the top floor. *And he has found Lilith!* "She's coming your way, Captain!"

"*Please* cover the exits people! *Please* don't let her escape! *Please* drive her downstairs! And, if you get a shot at her, *please* take it!"

"Protect the Queen!" I hear that repeated a number of times. The voices are coming from above.

"Defend me!" That was Lilith. "Kill them all!"

A man comes flying at me, wings beating hard, from what must be the kitchen. He's armed with a long kitchen knife. As he flies past Phillipa, she takes off the man's knife-hand and then his head. The corpse hits the floor and slides to a stop at my feet as the head rolls across the floor.

I nod my thanks to Phillipa, and she flies off in the direction from which my assailant came.

Moments later, she returns with a dozen or so of our troops. In-Tae and Sergei emerge from another door with two more of our number. "Ground floor's secure!" In-Tae says. "Twenty-two mortals in the kitchen."

The front door flies open, and two men enter at a run, each with side arms raised in one hand and a dirk in the other. They're followed immediately by two more.

Here come the Marines! They must've started running at the door before we started into the air. They're running into a building filled with vampires, armed only with a pistol and a knife. They know what they're facing and they know it's a virtual suicide mission. And still they come.

That's true courage.

Quickly dashing unbidden tears from my eyes, I point my sword in the direction of the kitchen. "Marines, secure the hostages!"

"Aye-aye, sir!" four voices cry together. Lieutenant Ericson leads the way as they run past me toward the kitchen.

Phillipa points behind her. "There's a basement, but I don't hear or smell anyone down there."

"Take a team of six and do a sweep to be sure." *Blast it, Morgan!* "I mean, *please* take a team and do a sweep!"

She nods and begins barking orders to her team.

"Carl!" *Rolf again.* "Incoming! They got past us!"

I can hear the sounds of combat coming from up the staircase. And the sounds are getting louder.

A mass of bodies come flying down the stairs. Solid-looking, but ephemeral wings pass through each other and through other bodies. None of the enemy seems to have swords, but many of them have improvised clubs. They're protecting her with their bodies and with chair and table legs. Some of them are missing arms.

All are covered in blood.

As they careen toward me, I catch a glimpse of two faces I recognize: Tony's and Lilith's. *Where's Kathleen?*

Phillipa and her team come streaming from the kitchen door. *She wouldn't have been able to come back if I'd made it an* order.

In-Tae and the others meet the enemy head on. Moira and I fly toward them, but one man detaches from the rest and flies at Moira. She impales him on her sword just as . . .

Something slams into me hard.

I hit the floor, and my head hits something, and I can't see. Everything's flashing colors and lights.

I'm flat on my back, and there is a crushing weight on me.

Can't breathe!

I feel pain in my left cheek.

I don't seem to have my sword anymore. My left arm is pinned to my chest, but I've still got my dirk.

I shove upward with my left arm, and suddenly I'm free.

My vision clears enough to see my opponent as he flies back at me. He has only stumps for arms. His fangs are bared and his mouth is red with blood.

My blood.

My cheek itches as the Seed begins to repair it.

I'm still on my back, but I manage to swing the dirk at his neck. And then he's on me again. His teeth snap at me once, and then the severed head rolls away, jaws still snapping furiously.

"Laddie!" Moira cries as she pulls me to my feet. "Ye're all right?"

I nod.

Collin's right behind Moira. He's got my sword in his free hand. "Cap'n!" He tosses it to me, and I snatch it from the air.

I quickly scan the lobby. There are bodies everywhere. None I recognize. The sounds of combat come from the direction of the kitchen and from below us. Lorenzo and Rolf are leading a stream of our people, heading toward the basement.

I look at Moira. "Lilith?"

"Below," she says. "Forced their way down there."

Without a word, Collin, Moira, and I glide to join the flying column of Stake vampires flowing into the basement. As we pass through the kitchen and into the basement door, I spot two of our Marines, Ortiz and Hall. I don't see the hostages. *They must have gotten them out.*

"Captain!" Hall shouts.

"Hostages secure?" I ask.

"Aye, sir, but . . ."

"Later, Marine!" I follow the gaggle of vampires flying slowly . . . *too slowly!* . . . ahead of me into the door leading to the basement. *It's a bottleneck! Only one can fit through the door at a time!*

"Captain!" Hall cries again, but I'm not listening.

Lilith's down here and I have to stop her! Nothing else matters!

Then I'm through the door. The space opens up. The whole basement seems to be a huge open area held up by columns and lit by fluorescent lights. Could be a meeting room or an empty storage room. A service elevator, the stairs, the columns, and nothing else. Except for a mass of bodies.

The battle's raging here. I can't see Tony or Lilith . . . *Where's Kathleen?* . . . but they have to be in the center of that jumble of people. They're all protecting Lilith.

The enemy's being hewn down by our forces, but still they fight on. When they raise one of their clubs, the arm's hacked off. Missing arms and legs in some cases, they protect their Queen, even if it's only with their teeth or their bodies.

The mass seems to be moving slowly but persistently toward one corner of the huge basement room. *Why? There's no door there, no escape. Is there a weapons cache?*

With a roar like a charging bear, one huge vampire, with arms and legs still intact, breaks free of the wall of bodies and launches himself at M'Benga. He rips M'Benga's sword from his hand and beheads him. He slashes at In-Tae and severs the Korean's sword-hand.

Then he turns on Sergei.

The Russian has his back to the attacker. He seems fixated on something. *Sergei doesn't see him coming! I can't get there in time! If I yell, Sergei will look at me! There's nothing I can do!*

"*Ah-ni!*" In-Tae screams at the attacker. Sergei turns his head to look, brings up his blade to stop the blow, but he's too slow. In-Tae throws his body between the attacker's sword and Sergei. The blow catches In-Tae in the neck and passes through. The head falls to the floor.

"*Traitor!*" the attacker bellows as he lifts his weapon to strike at Sergei again.

Sergei roars and hacks off the man's sword arm. Then he slashes across his opponent's abdomen. A third blow takes off the vampire's head.

Sergei falls to his knees. He scoops up In-Tae's head. "Why?" Sergei howls at the dying head while decapitating yet another one of the enemy. "You were a *good* man! *I* deserved to die! Me! Why?"

"Watch yerself, laddie!"

I spin around and see a black blade protruding from the chest of another vampire. Suddenly the blade disappears and the vampire drops to his knees. I see Moira behind him. She delivers the killing stroke to the man's neck. She nods grimly at me and turns her attention back to the enemy.

We stand side by side, ready to attack.

"Hold them here, my Children!" *That's Lilith's voice! Coming from the mass of bodies!* "Let none escape! I love you all! You have served your Queen well!"

The mass of enemy vampires in the corner seems to explode toward us in a final desperate assault. They throw themselves on the blades of my soldiers, knocking the front line to the ground.

"Protect Carl and Moira!" Rolf cries as he flies up to the ceiling, avoiding the onslaught. Stake vampires throw themselves in front of the enemy to shield Moira and me.

Up near the ceiling, Rolf suddenly draws back and hurtles his spear at the corner. "For Sarah!" he cries.

I hear a scream. *"Thakhati peni, sporanot caperno!"* Lilith again. I can't see her, but Rolf must have hit her.

Suddenly the spear comes flying back, striking Rolf straight through the chest. He falls to the floor and I lose sight of him.

I fly to the ceiling to try to get to Lilith. Moira's at my side. In the space that moments ago had been occupied by Lilith's people, there's only a rectangular hole in the floor, leading down to blackness. *A trapdoor!* The cover slams shut.

"She's bolted!" Moira cries. "Down a tunnel!"

It was an escape route!

I land beside it, searching for a handle of some kind, but I can't find one. *Idiot, Morgan! Tactile telekinesis!* I simply put a hand on the trapdoor and imagine myself pulling it open.

It comes up easily.

Suddenly the floor beneath my feet jumps. I'm knocked on my back as dirt and gravel spray out of the hole. Then the floor beneath me crumbles.

A hand grabs hold of my arm and I'm lifted into the air. I glance up and see Moira holding me as she hovers near the ceiling.

Lilith must've rigged the tunnel to explode after she fled!

"Captain Morgan!"

I twist my head around to see Sergeant Ortiz at the top of the basement stairs. Hall's behind him.

"We have to get out!" Ortiz shouts. "This whole place is rigged to blow!"

If she rigged the tunnel . . .

"Get out!" I cry. "Out the door NOW!"

As one, the Stake vampires turn and fly at the door. But only one at a time can fly through. *It's a trap. We're all going to die down here! We failed! Lilith escaped! I failed!*

Below us, the soldiers of Lilith latch on to any of my people they can reach. They latch on with their teeth, with their hands, if they still have them. They pin them to the floor with their bodies.

She commanded them to hold us here!

I look at the door. Most of us are still in the basement! They can't escape! *I failed them all!*

"Is there nae way out then?" Moira's still holding my arm. "That's it? We're doomed?"

The words of Colonel Daggett flash through my mind. *First, you fly the airplane!*

Think, Morgan! Find a way out!

I pull my arm free of Moira's hand and hover on my own power.

Rolf, apparently recovered and holding his bloodied spear, rises to hover beside us. "We're trapped! The door's too small!"

The door's too small.

So make a bigger door!

"This way!" I shout.

I fly straight at the wall to the right side of the door where my people are flying through too slowly. I hit the wall at full speed and smash through. Moira and Rolf follow me through the wall, creating a larger opening.

"Through the wall!" I cry, shouting from the kitchen through the gaping hole. "Get out now!"

The wall explodes toward us, knocking us to the floor. The Stake begins to fly out en masse. But I can't move. I'm covered with debris. I'm pinned!

Moira! Where's Moira?

"Laddie!"

She's somewhere to my left. I can't see her because of the rush of bodies flying out of the basement of the doomed hotel.

"Get Moira out of here!" I manage to choke out.

"Laddie!" she screams, but the sound is fading. *Someone got her out!*

A pair of strong hands grasps me under my shoulders.

"I've got you, sir!"

Hall!

He begins to pull at me.

"Leave me, Marine! That's an order!"

"Never leave a man behind!" he cries as he pulls harder.

An explosion rocks the building.

Hall pulls me free.

Idiot, Morgan! Tactile telekinesis! You could have pulled yourself free!

Another bomb goes off. Another. Another.

I grab Hall's shirt in one hand and pull him to my chest. I fly through a storm of debris, shielding the Marine as best I can with my body.

The shock of another blast hits me directly. The air's crushed from my lungs.

Blackness envelopes me.

Chapter 19

Carl

L addie!"
Moira's calling me.
"Carl! Where are ye?"
"Carl!" Other voices. Others are calling me.
Where am I?
"*Carl!*" Moira sounds frantic. "*Laddie!*"
There was an explosion. The hotel . . . collapsed. Hall . . . tried to save me.
I can't see anything.
Mouth . . . full of dust.
I cough.
My chest! Pain in my chest! Lungs won't work right. Can't get air! And the itch! The Seed's trying to fix something . . . and it can't.
Heavy weight on me . . . all over me.
"*LADDIE!*"
I open my mouth. *So dry.* "H-h-h . . ." I can't make my mouth work. I can't . . . answer her.
I cough again. The pain in my chest is . . . The itch is . . . *So hard to think.*
Whenever I breathe, there's a bubbling . . . like sucking the last bit of soda through a straw.
That can't be good.
"There's somebody over here! I heard a cough!"
Lorenzo. He's found me.
"It's a Marine!"
No. Not me. Lorenzo found someone else.
That's OK. Maybe it's Hall. Maybe Hall survived.
"Who?" I try to speak, but my throat is suddenly full of blood and all I can do is choke and gurgle.
"It's Hall!" *Lorenzo again.*
"Is he alive?" *I think that was Andrew.*
"No. His torso's crushed. He's gone."

"Then, 'twas nae he that coughed! There's someone else alive in there! Carl! Speak to me, laddie!"

Hall's dead. Sacrificed himself for me. I could've pulled myself free . . . if I'd been thinking clearly. But he stayed . . . or came back . . . for me. He knew the hotel was rigged to blow, but he came back anyway. "Never leave a man behind," he said.

"H-h-h . . ." I try to call out. Then I choke on my own blood and cough again.

Pain!

Itch!

"I definitely heard someone cough over here!"

I should be able to get out . . . to fly out.

Just need to concentrate . . .

The pain!

The itch!

No air!

I think maybe I'm drowning . . . in my own blood.

"I've got someone!" *Lorenzo?*

Points of light start to form before my closed eyes. *They are closed, aren't they?* I feel like I'm floating . . . or sinking.

Time to flip on the O2 switch. You're going hypoxic, Morgan.

"Over here!"

Suddenly the weight is off my legs . . . off my chest.

I should be able breathe better, right? I still hear that bubbling sound again. *Soda through a straw.* Only, it's softer now . . . slower. *No, it's stopped.*

"*Aiuto!* Help me! He's dying!"

Pressure on my face . . . gone. Should be able to see. Still black.

"*CARL!*"

Moira's screaming. Why's she screaming? Did I do something wrong?

There's another ripping pain in my chest, but it's . . . distant . . . like it's happening to somebody else.

The itch. I can feel that.

I'm floating now. I'm sure of it.

"Carl! Oh, my poor, poor dearie! Dinnae leave me! Carl!"

She's upset. I did something . . . something . . . bad. People died. My fault . . .

"Father in Heaven! Save him! Please save my Carl! Take me! Take me in his stead! Dinnae take him from me! Dinnae let him die! *Please*, Father!"

Moira's voice fades.

Lights dance in front of my eyes. The lights dance closer and closer together until they join up as a single spot of light. The spot's getting brighter. It's taking shape.

A familiar shape.

A face.

I know that face. A face I haven't seen in a long time.

The face of love.

Sharon.

I'd forgotten how blue her eyes are.

She smiles. "Hi, sweetie. I miss you. I love you so much!"

"Sharon?" *I can speak now. The pain's gone. So's the itch.* "How? Am I dead?"

"Pretty much. And we don't have much time. I have a message for you. Your task isn't done. You have to go back. The Lord is pleased with you. Remember . . ."

"But people're dead! Good *people!* I was *stupid.* I commanded *them and they died. If they'd been able to think and act for themselves, they might've gotten out. At least* more of them might've gotten out."

"Honey, you were always *too hard on yourself. If the Lord is pleased, then you must* be doing just fine."

"Sharon . . . the night you died . . . I'm sorry. If I hadn't been late . . ."

"You mean if I hadn't gotten angry and taken one of my 'walks?' That wasn't your fault either, sweetie."

"How are the kids?"

Her smile widens. How I love that smile!

"They're just fine. They miss you. Don't worry about us, though. We're in good hands. We'll see you soon enough. I love you."

"I love you too, sweetheart. I miss you. Uh . . . Sharon? I . . . uh . . . I got married again."

"I know. She's wonderful! Don't worry, sweetie. I like Moira." *Her smile suddenly seems sad.* "You have to go now. Remember Moira's sword. The truth is your greatest weapon. We're watching over you. He's *watching over you. You're never alone. Fight the good* fight and then come home to me."

Her face is swallowed in light. Then light fades quickly to blackness.

I try to call out her name, but I can't. I can't because . . .

. . . something's covering my mouth, forcing air into my lungs. I feel a huge impact on my chest. Another. And another.

"He's gone, Moira." *Lorenzo's voice, broken, like he's crying.* "We're too late. We . . . failed."

Another blow to my chest. "Fight, blast ye, Carl!" Another. "Fight! *Breathe!*"

A mouth covers mine again, creating a seal around it. Air's forced into my lungs once more, filling them.

I cough violently.

The seal around my mouth is broken.

The pain's gone. The itch is gone.

I'm *breathing.*

My head's still fuzzy, but it's clearing.

My eyes open, and I see Moira's face. It's filthy, and there are tear streaks cutting rivulets through the grime. Her bedraggled red hair hangs down around her face, framing it in shadow. She looks as if she's been through hell and back.

And she's so beautiful.

"Laddie!"

"Hi, gorgeous." That's all I can manage. I'm about to say more, but her lips lock onto mine . . . and I can't say anything else.

Chapter 20

Carl

"How many did we lose?" I'm sitting on the ground twenty yards or so from the blast zone. Moira's got one arm around my shoulders. Andrew's sitting nearby, his sword lying across his lap. Moira's black sword . . . *Remember Moira's sword* . . . lies next to mine on the ground beside her. The dirk's probably lost in the rubble. I see signs of some frenzied activity coming from the wreckage of the hotel, but I don't see anyone else over there. I smell the aftermath of the explosions: charred flesh, blood, dust, smoke, burning wood. There's an odd scent that I *should* be able to identify, but what it is eludes me at the moment.

"How many did we lose?" *I know I heard Lorenzo's voice earlier, when I was under the rubble, but he's nowhere to be seen now. Is he searching the blast zone for survivors?*

Andrew lowers his head. I glance at Moira and see fresh tears spill from her eyes.

"It would be easier, perhaps . . ." Andrew swallows hard. "It would be easier, perhaps," he continues in his flawless British accent, "to . . . tally the survivors."

"Out with it, laddie!" Moira says. "Tell him the butcher's bill."

"Sergei and Rolf . . ." He hesitates.

"We lost Sergei and Rolf?" I ask, horrified.

He shakes his head. "No, Captain. They survived."

I sigh audibly. "OK. Sergei and Rolf are . . . ?" I prompt.

"They're searching for survivors. At least Rolf is. Sergei . . . he's searching for something else."

"Forget about that, man! *Who's left?*"

He looks me directly in the eye. "You, me, Moira, Sergei, Rolf, and Lorenzo, plus the Marine, Ericson. And the mortals from the hotel."

The air around me suddenly seems as heavy as a mountain. I can't quite catch my breath. "That's . . . *all?*"

"Unless Rolf or Sergei manages to find other survivors."

Moira lays a hand on my thigh. "When we were searchin' for ye, we did nae hear any other signs o' life. 'Tis nae certain, what with the shiftin' o' the rubble, but 'twould seem unlikely anyone else survived."

"But I *ordered* them out!"

"Yeah, Carl." Andrew nods. "And we *did* obey you. Every last one of us. But as soon as we were out, the very *instant* we crossed the threshold, to a man—or a woman—we turned about and came back for you and Moira. Without the two of you, this is all for nothing."

"It *was* all for nothing!" I snap. "We didn't get her!"

"Maybe not," Sergei says as he flies toward us, "but she's going to be virtually undefended." He lands and holds up the mangled remains of something that once upon a time might have been electronic. His expression's one of grim triumph. "Because she left *this* behind!" He waves the broken thing in his hand. "With this I can prevent her from getting reinforcements! But I have to act quickly! With your permission, Carl?"

I'm still reeling from the enormity of the death toll. "What're you talking about?"

"*This* is her laptop! Lilith's computer! The hard drive's intact. I'll have to find another machine to connect it to since the rest of it's worthless . . ."

"How . . ." *I'm not following him.* "How did you find it in all that . . ." I wave helplessly at the rubble.

He smiles, but his eyes remain hard. "She prefers a window facing toward the First Place, as she calls it, Adam's country. From here, that's roughly on the northeast side. And you *know* she'd only occupy the penthouse. So I knew the general area to look in." He grins wide, stretching his lips across his teeth. "And I *found* it!"

"I don't understand. How're you going to prevent reinforcements . . . ?"

"The phone number of every single Master is on here! Oh, she'll be sending out the *Call*, as soon as she collects herself. And they'll *want* to come. In fact, it'll drive them *crazy*, but I'll telephone each one. (They're all required to carry a cell phone.) I'll *order* them to stay *where they are*, to keep their Cults with them, to not come here under any circumstances, and to destroy their cell phones and not use any electronic communications whatsoever! They won't be able to receive any messages from Lilith to the contrary! I'll order them to *ignore* Lilith's Call!"

I stare at him blankly.

"I'm still an *Enforcer*! My orders to the Children supersede all others except for Lilith's herself! And if she can't communicate with them, other than the psychic Call . . ."

"That could *work*!" Andrew claps his hands. "And it *will* drive them bloody bonkers! The Call's impossible to ignore, but it's vague, nonspecific. You just feel compelled to come. If you have a direct, spoken command, with specific instructions . . . it'd be like a maddening itch you can't scratch because your hands are tied down! Fabulous idea, Sergei! You probably won't get them all, but you should take a huge slice of whatever Lilith could've mustered. But the sooner you get started, the better!"

"What do you think, Carl?" Sergei looks at me so expectantly, so hopefully. "Please! I need to do something "—his voice breaks—"something to atone . . . for In-Tae . . . for my friend."

"That wasn't your fault," I say as Sergei looks down at the ground. "Look at me, please!" He looks me in the eye. "In-Tae knew what he was doing. He sacrificed himself for *you*. He *believed* in you. Make his sacrifice mean something . . . please. Go do what you have to . . . please. *Please* take Andrew with you."

I glance at Andrew. He nods.

As Andrew stands to go, I say, "You're both very new at this, although Andrew's been on the path of repentance a lot longer than you, Sergei. One piece of advice: stay away from anyone or anything that might tempt you to return to your old ways. That's advice, not an order."

"You don't have to tell me that," Sergei says, his lined eyes grim. "When I saw *her* last night, I almost . . . I really *was* in love with her, you know. I guess I still am." He turns to Andrew and extends a hand. "I'd appreciate the company . . . and the support."

Andrew takes his hand. "England and Russia. Allies again." He shakes Sergei's hand vigorously.

"Godspeed, laddies," Moira says.

Andrew and Sergei take to the air and head off to the north leaving Moira and me alone under the stars.

We sit that way in silence, her arm around me, her other hand on my thigh. I place my hand atop hers, and she grips it in return.

They're dead. All dead. So many. I can't get my mind around it. How many died because of me not using that blasted word?

I can see Rolf now. He's climbing down slowly from the rubble. Once he reaches the ground, he stands still a moment. Then his shoulders droop, and his head bows. The fires burning in the debris behind him cast his face in night shadow. He's still holding his spear, and Sarah's sword is sheathed at his side. The spear is pointed at the ground. He looks utterly defeated. He begins to walk slowly toward us.

Moira looks at him and then squeezes my hand. "I know what ye're thinkin', dearie," she whispers. "Ye should take yer own advice: make their sacrifice meanin'ful. And dinnae blame yerself. Ye had nae way of knowin' 'twas a trap."

"It wasn't a trap," I whisper back. And in the instant I say it, I know it's true. "She wired the place to blow, just in case, but she didn't expect us to be here, at least not so soon."

"How d'ye know?"

"Because, other than the three in the lobby, they weren't *armed*. We caught her off guard. We lost most of our troops, but she lost *all* of hers. At least she lost all her inner circle, all her Court. And, if Sergei's right . . . and if he can pull it off, she might not have much support . . . at least not from the Cults, that is."

Rolf slows as he approaches. Then he stops and sits at my feet. He says nothing.

"Ye did yer best, laddie," Moira says softly.

"I should do more, but . . ." Rolf's voice trails off. "I can't hear any breathing . . . any hearts beating. There are no more survivors." He points at me. "You were the only one we pulled from the rubble alive."

The nearly stagnant air begins to stir. There's that scent again: charred flesh, blood (always blood), dust, smoke, burning wood, and . . .

"We need to move!" I say, jumping to my feet, pulling Moira up with me. Rolf scrambles to his feet as well. We leap up and fly away from the ruins of the hotel. A massive explosion shatters the night behind us. A wall of air slams us to the ground, knocking the air from my lungs.

I turn over and watch as a huge fireball rises into the sky. The three of us stare at the flaming ruins, trying to force our lungs to pull in oxygen.

A flaming mass plummets to the ground nearby with a sickening wet splat. *Vampire flesh. It must be. Extremely flammable.* The mass, about the size of a basketball, continues to burn bright and hot. I smell burning flesh. *I wonder who that was. Mario? M'Benga? One of Lilith's people?* It'll most likely continue to burn until it's completely consumed. Seed-infused flesh tends to do that. *There'll only be a charred spot to show that a human being, albeit a vampire, was ever here.*

When my breathing eases a bit, I glance at Rolf, still gasping on the ground, his face illuminated by the blaze. "Didn't you smell . . . the gas? You were . . . right on top of it!"

"Yes . . . but I . . . had to be . . . sure . . . we got everyone."

I nod. I can understand. "Still stupid."

He nods. "Yep. That's me."

"Where's Lorenzo? You said Ericson made it out too."

Moira answers, "They're with the hostages."

"Did we lose any of them? The hostages, I mean?"

Rolf shakes his head. "No, I think they got them all out before . . ."

"Tony was with Lilith," I say. "She took him."

"Aye, laddie," Moira says, "I saw that."

"Carl! Moira! Rolf?" Lorenzo drops from the air and lands beside Rolf. He kneels down and begins to probe Rolf's body with his hands, but Rolf brushes his hands aside. "Are you all right? Where are Sergei and the Breton?"

"We're OK," I say. "Sergei and Andrew are off on a mission." He looks at me questioningly. "I'll explain later. How's Ericson? How're the hostages doing?"

Lorenzo shakes his head. "Ericson is not so good. He's very upset, as I'm sure you understand, about his fellow soldiers, the dead Marines. The hostages, for the most part will be OK. I used Persuasion to convince them this was all a hallucination induced by a gas leak. Kathleen, now, she's . . ."

"Kathleen?" Moira cries. "She's alive?"

"*Si*, but the *bambini* . . . they're dead." For the first time I notice the tear streaks on Lorenzo's face. *Poor guy!*

"Take me to her!" Moira's all business now.

Lorenzo rises to his feet. "Yes, of course. Follow me."

Chapter 21

Moira

Moira! She took Tony!" Kathleen throws herself into my arms. Her great sobs shake her whole frame. The other mortals, the hostages from the hotel, look on, like confused and frightened sheep.

I hold Kathleen tight and I gently try to still her quaking. "I know, lassie. I know. But he was alive when last I saw him. And she'll nae harm him, nae so long as she needs him for a hostage."

"My babies!" She wails. "They're . . . They're . . ." Her legs buckle, and now I'm holding her up.

"I know, lassie. I know. I'm sorry. I'm so sorry we did nae protect ye better. We did nae comprehend the danger . . . how close . . ." I cannae suppress my own sobs.

We stand like that for a long time. Kathleen slowly stills her crying and straightens her legs under herself, supporting her own weight again.

I slowly become aware of a conversation taking place a distance away. It sounds as if it's been going on for some time.

". . . went back inside." *'Tis that Marine, Ericson. I've ne'er caught his Christian name. I dinnae think I caught any of the Christian names of those brave Marines.* "Kowalski's the EOD, you know, the Explosive Ordinance Disposal expert. I mean, he *was* . . . He noticed signs of explosives, and after we got the hostages out, he went back inside to disarm the bombs. Ortiz went to help him. Hall . . . he went to warn you. That guy would run into a burning building to . . ." His voice cracks. "Uh, yeah, anyway I think that's why the whole building didn't come down right away. Kowalski must've disabled some of them. Without him, nobody would've gotten out. I was on my way back in, after getting hostages to a safe distance, when one of you guys . . . It happened so fast . . . I didn't see who . . . one of you guys flew me out of there . . . just before the whole thing blew."

He pauses and sets his jaw in determined fashion. "I should've died with my men."

"Stow that talk, Marine."

That's my laddie.

"It doesn't help," Carl says. "*I* led us into this."

Aye, and that's my laddie too, blaming himself.

"It's my responsibility," he continues. "Hall . . . died trying to save me. He said, 'Never leave a man behind.' He was a good man. I'm honored to have known him, him and Ortiz and Kowalski. I'm honored to know *you*, Marine."

I hear someone clear his throat. "What's the plan, Captain?" Ericson asks.

"We're still working on it, but we need to bug out of here. We're lucky we haven't seen police or firefighters yet. They can't be long in coming. We're sort of isolated here, but we're not *that* isolated. Lorenzo, you sure the Persuasion'll hold?"

"Yes. Lilith would've had those that couldn't be Persuaded disposed of or consumed before her arrival. As you saw, her Court was already here."

"OK. Find one of them with a working cell phone. Have him or her give us fifteen minutes and then call nine-one-one, assuming the fire department isn't here by then. I mean, *please*, do all that . . . what I just said."

Kathleen's body heaves with a huge sob. I stroke her hair and try to focus on the conversation.

"I can see some cars still intact in the parking lot," Lorenzo says. "Why not let those who *can* drive home?"

"Bad idea, Captain," says the Marine. "It's not safe to be near the blast site. There could be more explosions."

"You're right, Lieutenant." Carl replies. "Lorenzo, will you get them taken care of?"

"Yes."

Carl looks at Rolf. "Rolf? Will you *please* give him a hand?"

"Sure, Carl," he replies.

Carl says, "Good. Now we need to find a place to hole up, to regroup."

"About that, Captain . . .," Ericson says. "Why not use the previous Night Palace, the Hotel at the Plaza? The top three floors should still be unoccupied. I seriously doubt she'll go back, and if we don't go in by the front door, nobody will know we're there."

After a moment of silence, Carl says, "Sounds like a plan. Ericson, how many of your fellow Honor Guard Marines do you think you can trust?"

"I trust all of them with my life, sir."

"You know what I mean."

"Aye-aye, sir. I'll feel out Lieutenant Todd. He's the CO."

"Get on it."

"Aye-aye, sir." He pauses a tick. "Sir, General Brooks . . . he needs to *pay* for what he's done. He betrayed his fellow Marines. He betrayed the honor and ideals of the Corps."

"One thing at a time, Lieutenant. The primary objective is still to take down Lilith. After that, you can deal with Brooks. Understood?"

"Aye-aye, sir."

Kathleen has ceased her trembling.

I let go of her, and the two of us sit on the grass under the trees. Lorenzo's following Carl's instructions concerning the hotel people. Carl and Ericson continue their conversation, but I try to ignore them; Kathleen needs my attention.

She sits with her head bowed. "Can you save him?"

I know who 'him' is.

"We're going to try, lassie. She'll keep him alive. He's nae use to her dead."

She nods her head. "It was Tony. He led them to us. It was him on the computer. He was emailing her." Her voice is dead, nigh emotionless. She lifts her face and looks me in the eye. Her face is dirty, streaked with tears, but there are nae tears in her eyes now.

So that's how Lilith found us! Tony was the leak.

"Kathleen-lassie, surely ye dinnae think he did so *deliberately*?"

She laughs. It's a hysterical, frightening sound, all the more disturbing after the dead tone. "No! Of course not! But he did it! He did what he always does! Obsesses over some obscure bit of ancient history! He couldn't *resist* chatting with someone who's been around for six *thousand* years! No, not e-ven if that someone is a *murdering, monstrous, WHORE! My babies are dead!* And she's got him!" She pauses a tick. "Maybe he should just stay with her!"

"Ye cannae mean that!"

"Oh, can't I? My children are dead! And he led the monsters right to us!"

"He was stupid, Kathleen," Carl says, startling Kathleen and me. He's standing beside me. I did nae notice his approach.

"*Stupid?*" Kathleen hisses at him.

Carl nods. "Yes, stupid." He kneels down and stares her in her venom-filled eyes. "Stupid, but not evil. Kathleen, *I* was stupid. I led sixty-nine good people to their deaths tonight. Two more died at your home last night. They were protecting you and your family on *my* orders. I ended up becoming a *vampire* because I was stupid, because I was in the wrong place, hanging out with the wrong people."

"But he *knew* she was a monster! He did it anyway! *My babies are DEAD!*"

Carl's expression is firm. He's nae backing down. "My wife and children died because I stayed late at work one night. At least, that's what I told my-self. And it *is* true. If I hadn't been there that night, my wife and children would still be *alive*. I was working on a video game. 'Dark Mage Three.' You ever heard of it? Of course not. It didn't do all that well. Definitely *not* a classic in spite of all the effort, all the late nights and weekends our team put into it. And my wife, Sharon, and my children, April and Lucy and Joseph and our unborn child, they died because I was working on that *stupid* game instead of being with them. *But I didn't kill them!* Some punk, high on drugs and driving a stolen car, ran them down. *He's* the monster. *He's* the killer. Not me."

He shakes his head. "Tony was stupid. That's all. Everybody makes mistakes. People back out of a driveway without looking and run over the neighbor's kid or their own child. That's stupid, not evil."

Carl reaches out and places a hand on her knee. "Kathleen, Tony . . ."

Kathleen's face suddenly twists in horror. She begins to breathe rapidly. *She's going to hyperventilate!* Suddenly, she stops breathing for a moment. Her mouth opens and a pitiful wail escapes it. "He . . . made . . . me . . . *choose.*"

"What's that, lassie?"

She looks at me, and her eyes are filled with more pain than any mortal should have to bear. "Bo . . . that vampire who murdered Little Tony . . . he made me *choose.* He said he'd spare one of them . . . if I chose one of them to . . . to die. I'd have done *anything* to save them! Anything! I didn't *want* to choose! He *made* me! And when I did . . . when I did . . ."

Ach, nae! I cannae imagine . . .

"He killed them both anyway," Carl finishes.

She looks at him. "I chose . . . my little boy. I chose him to die. He looked at me the whole time. The last thing he saw was his mommy . . . *killing* him. He . . . he said, 'I love you, Mommy.' And then he died. And then . . . another one . . . he murdered Abby."

I cannae but stare at her in mute horror.

"You didn't kill them," Carl says. "Those *monsters* did. Nobody else. Tony is not to blame. And neither are *you.*"

Kathleen begins to sob again.

I lean forward and throw my arms around her again. After a moment, she puts her arms around me as well.

And together we weep.

"Why can't we have the lights on?" Kathleen's voice is shrill with panic. She's squeezin' my hand in a painful grip as we sit together on the edge of the hotel bed. We're in a room on the middle of three floors of a downtown Kansas City hotel that, until recently, was occupied by Lilith's Court. 'Tis black as the Pit, but the small red LED of the smoke detector casts enough light so my eyes can see Kathleen's face well enough. And she looks terrified. "It's so dark! I'm scared!"

"Hush now, lassie," I say as I stroke her hair with the hand that she's nae crushing. "None of that. We cannae have the light on and risk anyone finding us here. 'Tis unlikely they'd be looking for us in this place, mind ye. But, to be sure, we'll keep the lights off and keep our *voices down*."

"But we're *not* safe! They could be outside the window! They come when you're sleeping!" Her eyes move frantically, casting blindly about, searching the blackness of the room. She squeezes my hand even tighter.

I cannae suppress a hiss of pain.

She jumps. "What? Do you hear something?"

"Nae, lass. Ye're crushing my hand." I shake my injured hand, still gripped in hers, gently.

Kathleen eases her hold just a wee bit. "I'm sorry. I'm just so scared!"

"We'd hear them if they were outside, granddaughter," Lorenzo says from over by the heavily curtained window. "We have very sensitive hearing. I'll stand guard by the window. Rolf will guard the door. Sergei and Andrew are in the next room."

Rolf nods, though Kathleen cannae see it. "We'll keep you safe," he says. "I promise."

"Aye, safe as houses," I say.

"Rolf?" Kathleen looks stunned. "Is that you? You . . . You can *talk*?"

Rolf laughs softly. "Yes. It's a miracle. Carl healed me . . . or rather Carl used the priesthood to heal me."

"That's . . . That's wonderful," she says, but her voice is flat. She sounds weary down to her bones.

I can sympathize with ye there, lassie! I cannae remember when I last Slept. And I'm famished. I need to Feed.

And so does Carl.

I stroke her hair again. "Now lie down, lassie. Rest."

She releases my hand and gropes frantically for me in the dark. Her hands find my shoulders, and she throws her arms around me. "You're not leaving, are you?"

"Aye, lassie, I must."

"No!"

"Carl and I must go. We are . . . sorely in need of sustenance. We must Hunt evil men. But we'll nae be gone long. Lorenzo and Rolf will be here to protect ye."

She shakes her head violently against my shoulder. "No! Don't go! I'm scared!" She's quaking, the poor lass.

I sigh. *I dinnae want to do this.* "Come with me." I stand and Kathleen stands awkwardly as well, still clinging to me. I gently but insistently pry her loose, though I take her hands in mine. "This way, lassie. Mind yer step now."

Walking backward, I lead her to the bathroom, open the door, and usher her inside. I release one of her hands, though she protests with a wordless cry. Then I switch on the light.

Ach! 'Tis so bright!

Kathleen squints, shading her eyes with her free hand. I swiftly grasp the back of her head and force her to look at me. As soon as we make eye contact, I say in the commanding tone of Persuasion, "Sleep."

Her eyes roll up into her head, and her knees crumple. I catch her before she can fall to the floor. Scooping her up into my arms, I switch off the light. I open the door and carry her out of the bathroom and to the bed. By the time I tuck her in, she's already snoring gently. She must have been completely exhausted by her ordeal.

From the next room, I can hear Sergei. He's making quick, terse phone calls. Each is essentially the same:

"This is Sergei Ivanov Tupelev. You recognize my voice, *da*?"

"Yes, my lord."

"You are the Master?"

"Yes, my lord."

"Listen carefully and obey. Stay in your city. If you have already departed your city, return to it immediately and remain there. Take no mortal life. Seduce no innocent. Convert no one. Ignore the Call of Lilith. Do not accept any message from Lilith by any means ever again. Do not attempt to contact her or get a message to her by any means ever again. Command your Cult and all Children of Lilith you might encounter to do the same."

"But, my lord! The Call!"

"You will obey?"

"Yes, my lord. But . . ."

There is a brief pause, and then I hear the voice of Andrew reading the next phone number.

This cycle has repeated dozens of times since Sergei and Andrew rejoined us. When Carl called him, Sergei's phone was dying. Carl told him where to meet us. Sergei was stunned by the choice of Lilith's "home in exile," but he conceded 'twas a clever choice.

Sergei had purchased a laptop and something he called an "adaptor" to connect the recovered hard drive from Lilith's damaged computer to the new laptop. He was nae concerned about using his credit card. "She knows I'm alive, and she knows I'm here," he said. He's been calling nonstop since they rejoined us with Andrew feeding him each number, starting with the closest Cults and moving outward geographically. "She doesn't have a cell phone of her own," Sergei explained. "Others make the calls for her, but she'll increase the urgency of her Master's Call to an unbearable pitch. However, if I get everyone, all three hundred and fifty-two Cults, she'll have no vampires to come to her aid."

"She'll be defenseless?" Carl asked.

"Hardly. She has many mortal allies. She'll be in touch with them soon, but she's not used to doing any of this herself. My fellow Enforcers and I handled or delegated the running of her empire. It won't take her long to start calling for help, though. I can't do anything about the mortal allies. The ones I know personally would've probably all been contacted, informed that I'm compromised. But I can stop the immortals. I need to get started. I have to stay ahead of the Sun around the world. I have to contact them while it's night where they are."

As I exit the room, Rolf says, "Good Hunting." I wearily smile my thanks at him and close the door behind myself.

My dearie's standing in the doorway of the adjoining room, watching Sergei and Andrew, and waiting for me. He turns and begins to close the door.

Sergei, just finishing another call and without looking up from his plugged-in and charging cell phone, says, "You won't have to go far. The Mafia is very active here in the Plaza." Then he lifts the phone to his ear and says, "This is Sergei Ivanov Tupelev. You recognize my voice, *da*?"

Carl closes the door.

"She's asleep," I say.

"I heard. Ericson's snoring on the bed in there. He was beat." He points at the room he just left.

"Aye, I can hear the poor lad."

"How long will Kathleen be out?"

"As long as need be. The Persuasion was broken the instant she passed out, of course. But she's exhausted, and she should sleep awhile. When her REM cycle starts, she may be awakened by bad dreams." I turn my head and look at Sergei and Andrew's room. "I could hear some of what they've been doing. Have they missed anyone? Have any Cults slipped through the cracks yet?"

"None so far. I think Sergei was right. She's let others do her day-to-day, I mean, night-to-night operations for so long, she won't be able to start calling right away. We know she can use the Internet, but Sergei says he's never seen her use a phone."

"Aye, if she's like most queens I've known through the centuries, she does very little for herself, and her empire is managed by her trusted subordinates."

Carl sighs. "At least Sergei's occupied. I think he's really struggling with his feelings about Lilith. I think seeing her was tough on him."

"Aye, laddie. He loves her and hates her at the same time. His heart's warring with his head."

Suddenly, Carl puts a hand to his head and sways on his feet.

"Laddie?"

"I'm running on fumes. I need to Feed."

"Aye, well, your body's been through an extended period of critical injury and sustained, Healing—Healing that was constantly thwarted by the debris inside and on top of you. Ye're in need of nourishment. I'm famished as well."

He takes my hand. "Shall we?"

◆ ◆ ◆

We exit the hotel as we came, through a service door on the roof. I broke the lock with my sword when we arrived. I felt awful about the damage until I learned later, from Sergei, that Lilith owns, through one corporation or another, both this hotel and probably the one that was destroyed earlier this evening.

Once on the roof, we take to the sky, relishing the cool evening air as it rushes past our faces. The night is overcast, so there are nae stars nor Moon to be seen. But 'tis a small thing. We're alive for one more night. And I'm alone with my dearie. 'Tis nae the intimacy I crave, but perhaps that'll come later . . . after we've Fed.

Carl lets go of my hand and points twice to his left and behind him with two fingers. *Take up the Number Two position.*

I slide into place three feet to his left and three feet back from him. I scan the black sky for "bandits." Then I let my senses expand, feeling about, even from this altitude, for the presence of evil. We'll nae be able to *smell* evil blood from up here, but we can *feel* its presence, if we're trying.

We fly that way for a few seconds in silence, slowly making a circle around the area. Carl, flying in a prone position ("superhero style" as he calls it), rocks to the left and to the right. *Cross over to the other side.* I slide down and back and then move over to his right side. Then I slide back up into position on his right. I scan the sky from that side and see nothing amiss.

"Sorry about the dirk," Carl says.

That dirk belonged to my father. It'd been in my family for centuries. If it survived, 'twill be in the smoking rubble of the other hotel.

"'Tis of nae consequence, laddie. I'd rather lose the dirk than lose ye."

"Still, I'm sorry I lost it."

"Dinnae bother yerself about it."

"At least we found Donald's sword."

"At least we found *ye*. I can live without the claymore and the dirk. I cannae abide the thought of living without ye. I saw that the young Marine Lieutenant found yer hat."

Carl growls.

I cannae suppress a wee smile. "I think it looks good on ye. But ye'll need a new coat, nae to mention yer shirt bein' in tatters and all blood . . ."

And there 'tis.

Evil.

Carl stiffens. He senses it too.

He points twice with one finger up and to the right. *Go "tactical."* I slide up and away about a hundred yards or so from him. *We're going to be moving fast, and we need room to maneuver.*

Carl tilts his body head down, at a steep angle, and dives.

I follow.

The closer we get to the ground, the stronger the pull of the evil blood becomes. There are a number of sources. This area fairly screams violence to my senses. Carl alters course abruptly to the left.

Ah! There 'tis! The irresistible savor of evil blood, sweet and pungent!

My fangs extend, and my mouth waters.

Carl pulls up abruptly and scans the skies and then the ground. I follow suit. 'Twould appear that 'tis safe for us to descend.

I can see two men standing in an ill-lit alley behind a restaurant. Italian food, by the nauseating scents arising from it. Italian food's very popular, but to me all mortal food is revolting. Nae, amid the putrescence of marinara and Alfredo sauce comes the delicious scent of two men who've done great evil in their lives. One man lights a cigarette as he faces the dark end of the alley. His companion glances toward the other end, the exit to the street.

We stop a few hundred feet in the air and watch, drool spilling from our mouths. We watch and we wait for *proof* of their intent to do violence.

What could they be plotting together? My only knowledge of the Mafia comes from the movies. These two *look* the part: trench coats, gloves, scent of gun oil and spent powder. *And* they're speaking Italian.

My own Italian's nominal, and these men are certain to be using an Americanized dialect. To be sure, there's a definite Midwestern twang mixed with the lilt of Italian. I dinnae understand what they're saying. The conversation sounds casual, though. They could be discussing murder or a recipe for clam sauce; I cannae tell. I do wish they'd get on with it. My thirst is nigh unbearable! And the familiar rage burns in me like a wildfire!

The second man, the one without the cigarette, glances at the alley exit once more as he steps closer to his companion. In a move too swift and smooth to be unpracticed, he pulls something thin and long from a pocket and wraps it around the other man's neck. He pulls hard.

In an instant, Carl and I both rocket toward them.

Too slow!

Blood, sweet blood, sprays from the victim's neck. His head tilts at an unnatural angle.

He's been garroted!

Carl swoops down upon the killer from behind and latches onto the man's neck. I land in front of the dying man, who has fallen to the ground. There's naught I can do for him. His neck is nearly severed. The sweet blood is wasted as it pools on the ground.

Wrath at the murderer consumes me, making me tremble. 'Tis all I can do to keep it contained as I wait while my husband Feeds. Finally, Carl releases the killer and shoves him toward me.

I sink my dripping fangs into the man's foul neck and life floods into my mouth. I drink ravenously. With great effort, I pull my lips from his neck before his exsanguination can become fatal. I lick the two wounds on his neck to seal them, briefly tasting once more the nectar of corruption.

I hold the man at arm's length. He looks at me with wretched desire.

"Please," he says weakly. "More!"

"Who are ye?"

"Leo. Please. *Please!*" His breathing's labored.

So long as he's under the influence of the Seed, there's nae need to Persuade him . . . yet.

I glance at the corpse on the ground. "Why did ye murder him?"

"Mario had no honor. He offended the Family."

"Ye're Mafia?" *How silly that sounds!*

His breathing eases a wee bit. The euphoria of the Seed in his blood is evaporating. He struggles feebly to break my hold on him. "Hey!" he says, panting. "What gives, lady!" Suddenly he looks angry. "You ain't supposed to do this! What about the treaty? Ain't we got a deal with you guys?"

Carl comes around to face the gangster. "Deal? What deal?"

He looks confused. "You know. The Covenant. Come on! We got a deal! You guys are in *big* trouble!" Confusion gives way to suspicion. "Wait a minute! Ain't you with the Queen? I mean, if you ain't with the Queen, are you like a rival family movin' in on her or somethin'? The Don's not gonna like this! And *she* ain't gonna like it neither!"

I stare into the mobster's eyes. "Explain yerself, rat!" I command. "Tell me about this Covenant!"

All the fight, what wee resistance there was, drains out of him like the squandered blood of his victim. "The Covenant's been in place since the days of the DiGiovannis, almost a hun'red years . . ."

Chapter 22

Carl

. . . by any means ever again. Command your Cult and all Children of Lilith you might encounter to do the same."

Sergei's winding up yet another call as Moira and I reenter the hotel room.

"*C'est impossible!*" The voice on the phone is notably French. *Does he understand Sergei?*

"You will obey? And answer me in English."

"Yes, I will obey, my lord, but . . ."

Sergei pushes a button on his phone. He looks beat. He turns to Andrew and looks expectantly. The faces of both vampires are illuminated by the ghostly light of the laptop that Andrew's using and by the glow of Sergei's phone.

Andrew shakes his head. "We've got thirty-two minutes before sunset for the next one. Take a breather, mate."

The Russian sets the phone down on the desk in the hotel room and leans back in his chair. He rubs the side of his head. "The phone was burning my ear."

Andrew laughs. "The ruddy thing's been charging the whole time, mate."

"Shush!" Moira whispers. She nods in the direction of Ericson asleep on one of the beds. "Ye'll wake the poor lad."

Ericson snores steadily, undisturbed.

Andrew winks at her. "I don't think there's any danger of that. The soldier bloke hasn't stirred since Carl told him to 'get some rack time.'"

"Kathleen's sleeping like a stone too." Rolf's voice comes softly from the next room.

"Aye," Moira says. "I can hear her."

"OK," I say, "now that we've established that the mortals're asleep and that you two have a short break, Sergei, I want you to tell me about Lilith's Covenant with the Kansas City Crime Family."

Sergei nods. "I take it you found one of them to Feed you."

"Yeah, we did. But, first, let's take a moment and say a prayer for our fallen friends . . . and for Abby and Little Tony Lupescu." I look at the door in the wall between us and the next room. There's a matching door on the other side, leading into the room with Lorenzo, Rolf, and Kathleen. Moira unlocks the door on our side. A moment later, Rolf unlocks the door from their side. He enters and kneels on the floor. Lorenzo kneels in the doorway. *He's not going to leave Kathleen for even a second.*

Andrew slides off his chair and onto the floor. Sergei does the same.

I'm suddenly aware that Ericson's no longer snoring. *So much for letting him sleep!*

He rubs his eyes and looks at us. "We're praying?" Instantly, he's off the bed and on his knees.

Moira and I kneel together. It's a little cramped in this room with the seven of us, but it's strangely comforting to be this close. We haven't had a chance to mourn our comrades, and there's not a lot of time for it now, but we, all that remain of the Vampire Stake, plus one Marine who lost all his men . . . *We* need this. The rest've gone back to see a loving and merciful Father.

We still have a monster to kill.

"Sergei?" I say.

He looks puzzled. *"Da?"*

"Would you be the one to pray?"

His eyes widen. *"Yah?"*

Does that mean, "Yes?" No, that'd be German.

"Me?" he asks.

"Yeah," I say. "I'm not sure why, but the Spirit's prompting me to have you be the mouthpiece."

He looks terrified. "I . . . I don't know how."

"Ach!" Moira says. "Laddie, I saw ye prayin'. We've all seen ye prayin' for hours at a time."

"Not in English. And I don't know how to pray . . . in your fashion . . . your *Mormon* fashion."

"Nothing to it," Rolf says. "Just talk to God, to Heavenly Father. Tell him what's in your heart. And remember to finish by saying that we're praying in Jesus' name. Say, 'Amen.' That's it."

Sergei swallows hard. "I don't know if He will hear me."

Moira smiles kindly in the ghostly light. "Oh, aye. He hears ye, laddie. Why have ye been prayin' if ye dinnae believe He'll hear ye?"

A tear spills from his eye. "Because . . . I *want* to believe. I *want* to believe there's hope for me . . . hope that I'll see my wife, my Lara, and my Mashenka again . . . and that . . . Mashenka will forgive me. I want to be forgiven like . . . like Alma."

"Go ahead," I say. "I'm positive it's *your* turn to pray."

He nods and bows his head.

And all is silent save for Kathleen's gentle snoring and the noise of the city outside.

At last Sergei opens his mouth and draws a deep breath. "Heavenly Father. We lost many good people tonight . . . and . . . last night as well. They were like me . . . only better. In-Tae was better. They gave their lives to cleanse this world of the *evil* that is Lilith. And we failed to stop her. She escaped. And we're very sorry for that. And we're sorry for all the lives we've taken, corrupted, and destroyed. We're sorry. But . . . you *forgave* Alma. He destroyed many, many souls. And you *forgave* him. I've done far, far worse. We *all* have . . . except for Carl the Unwilling. Forgive us all. *Please*, forgive us. And . . . help us to be strong. Help *me* to be strong. I love her, God. I do. I *desire* her. And, when I saw her tonight . . . I . . . hesitated. And my friend, my loyal friend, In-Tae, gave his life to save me. He died because I lusted after a woman who's destroyed countless lives, corrupted many souls. Forgive me."

He pauses for a few seconds. "And please," his voice breaks, "welcome home and forgive our friends. We pray for the dead, those who died to rid the world of Lilith. We pray for Kim In-Tae, for Thomas, for M'Benga, for . . ."

He does really well. He remembers about fifty names or so. Rolf quietly prompts him with the rest.

"And lastly we pray for those brave mortals, those United States Marines who gave their lives that others might live. We pray for Sergeant Michael Ortiz, Corporal Peter Kowalski, and Lance Corporal Malachi Hall. They were brave men who lived and died with honor. And, In-Tae showed me in that Book of Mormon that my Mashenka is saved in your kingdom. So, we do not pray for the two children who were murdered." I hear Lorenzo choke off a sob. "They are with You in heaven. But, please, comfort their mother. Ease her pain. And help us to save their father. Don't let Lilith corrupt him. He has suffered enough."

He pauses again and then says, "We pray in Jesus' name. Amen."

Our voices echo his. "Amen."

I look up. The laptop screen has gone dark. The only light in the room comes from the smoke detector, the battery light on the laptop, and a dim trickle of light leaking through from the curtained window. But there's enough light for me to see that we're all weeping, even Ericson.

The Marine rises to his feet. He takes the two steps that separate him from Sergei. The Russian rises and faces him with tears streaming down his face.

Ericson clears his throat. "Redstar, I . . ." He swallows hard. He opens his mouth, but can't seem to give voice to his feelings.

Sergei says, "Forgive me," his voice thick with emotion. "I deceived you. Your men are dead because of me and my kind."

The Marine stares into the former GRU agent's face. "My men are dead because they had courage, because they were Marines and people's lives were in danger. I mourn them, but they died well." Ericson extends his hand.

Sergei hesitates a moment and then takes the offered hand and shakes it vigorously.

Silently, Lorenzo and Rolf withdraw, closing both doors behind them.

Reluctant to interrupt this wonderful moment, I need to make sure we don't miss our window of opportunity. I point at the laptop. "How much time, Andrew?"

He stands up quickly and seizes the mouse, moving it around. The screen comes back to life. "About seven minutes."

"OK," I say, "Sergei, tell me about the KC Crime Family and Lilith's connection with it."

Sergei sits in his chair at the desk, and Ericson returns to the bed and sits on the edge. "What'd you do with . . . ? How many were there?"

"Two," I reply. "That is, until one murdered the other. We Fed, but we couldn't stay and fully question the one that remained, because the police showed up."

Andrew looks shocked. Ericson's expression is hard, the look of a man who's seen death too many times.

Sergei simply nods. "It's the same in some large cities. The local Cult and the organized crime family learn to coexist."

"How can that be?" Moira asks. "How can they . . ."

"How can the vampires resist the evil blood?" he asks.

"Aye."

"By working through a third party. Lawyers for the most part. It wasn't my area, but I know Lilith's lawyers would meet with the mob lawyers and arrange things."

Lilith has lawyers?

"What sort of things?" I ask.

"The deal or covenant. The name varies from city to city. The Cult or, in this case, the Court would ensure the authorities looked the other way through Persuasion or seduction. In exchange, the mob provided certain services."

"What services?" I ask.

"Deliveries."

Seeing the question on my face, he says, "Food." Judging by his expression, he could be discussing groceries.

"You mean people," I say.

"Yes. Your Cult, I mean the Cult in Utah was very small. Only four Children, yes?"

I nod. *Ben!*

"If the Cult is large . . . The *Court* was quite large. If the Cult is large, it is difficult to keep enough Novitiates to supply the needs of the Cult. And, if there are too many unexplained murders or disappearances in a given area, it draws unwanted attention. So mortal allies are used to supply . . . people."

"Müller used at least one serial killer to supply his disciples with blood," Moira says. "I used to wonder how his henchman Bartlett was able to meet with him and not kill him. Now I realize Bartlett was simply under orders not to kill him."

"In the case of the Court here in Kansas City," Sergei says, "the crime family simply uses drivers who don't know what they are delivering."

The door between the two rooms opens, and Rolf pokes his head in. "Oh, they know," he says, a scowl on his face. "They lie to themselves and say they don't know, but they do. The people who lived near Auschwitz knew what was going on, though they denied it later. Trust me. They know."

"But where do they get them?" I ask.

"The homeless," Andrew says, "vagrants, the mentally ill, and, on occasion, those who run afoul of the mob."

"Yes," Sergei says. "That is true in many such arrangements. Here, it's a bit different. Here the crime family is used mainly to make deliveries from the Farm."

"The *Farm*, did ye say?" Moira looks horrified.

My mind conjures up terrible visions of Müller's pig farm, where he kept human beings as "livestock." For a time, the "cattle" included Winnie Morrison.

Sergei nods. "It's every bit as bad as it sounds. In fact, it's worse. I wasn't . . ."

"Sorry to interrupt," Andrew says, "but time's up, mate. We need to get on with gumming up the works."

Sergei picks up his phone, but looks at me. "I have to get back to calling the Masters, but if you want to check it out"—he grabs a hotel memo pad and pen, and scribbles quickly—"here are the directions we used to provide for delivery drivers." He pulls off a sheet and hands it to me. "The actual entrance is through vault 17C. You shouldn't have any trouble." He pulls his wallet from his back pocket and fishes out a thick card. It's a passcard with no photo or writing on it. "This should grant you access. Once inside, follow your nose. I . . ." He hesitates. "I am deeply ashamed of what you will find there."

Andrew begins to read a number to him. Sergei dials.

Ericson checks his watch and says, "I've got a few more hours before I can call the CO to see if I can recruit him to our side. Mind if I catch a bit more rack time?"

"Go for it, Lieutenant," I say.

He stretches out on the bed again.

Rolf retreats back into the room with Kathleen and Lorenzo, closing the adjoining door behind him.

"You are the Master?" Sergei asks into the phone.

Moira opens the door of the room. I nod and follow her out into the hall.

Once the door's closed, she extends a hand to me. I take her hand in mine. So warm. So soft.

So strong!

She's pulling me urgently down the corridor. Her pace is insistent.

"Where are we going?" I ask.

"Up a floor. The Farm'll wait half an hour, laddie."

"But . . ."

"Ye're nae goin' to argue with me, are ye?" She stops and gives a look with those gorgeous green eyes, a look that saps all resistance away.

"No, milady," I say, grinning stupidly. I hurriedly stuff the directions and passcard into my pocket. "I am yours to command!"

At least for the next thirty minutes.

Chapter 23

Moira

The Farm is located in a vast cave, or so 'twould seem. I had nae idea Kansas City had such a gigantic *underground* industrial complex. I've ne'er imagined such a place.

Sergei's directions led us to a massive subterranean facility called "Sub-Tropolis," which, according to the huge sign at the entrance, is the world's largest underground business center. Once upon a time, 'twas a limestone mine carved from the banks of the Missouri River. Now 'tis a thriving community of businesses, ranging from cold storage to manufacturing to data services. The nigh-constant temperature makes it ideal for many such purposes and inexpensive to operate. The high ceiling is supported by huge, square limestone columns, five feet on a side. We see huge semis moving, maneuvering, and passing each other between the columns on a paved floor! In stark contrast to the limestone, there are finished walls, doors, signs, and windows to mark the offices of the various companies. Some of the areas are unused. Perhaps they are spare storage space or perhaps unused or overflow warehouses.

We got more than a few curious looks as we walked down the brightly lit tunnels. Before we left the hotel, we showered quickly so our faces and hair would nae longer be streaked with blood, soot, and grime. We kept our swords under coat and cloak, so they'd nae attract attention. But nothing could hide the dried blood on our clothes, nor the great rips and holes in Carl's shirt and duster.

At one point, we were approached by a security guard driving a large black pickup, but once he scanned the pass card Sergei had provided, the guard offered us a ride to the door of the appropriate warehouse. In fact, he was unusually deferential.

When we climbed in and out of the truck, 'twas impossible to fully conceal the swords. If the guard noticed them, he held his peace.

He must've thought we were Mafia . . . or perhaps something worse.

After delivering us to our destination, he bade us an enthusiastic good-night and drove away.

Carl and I entered the warehouse and drew our swords.

And here we stand, the pair of us, inside a dimly lit chamber before a door labeled "17C." The door itself is wide enough to drive a pickup through (or perhaps a forklift). In the warehouse, there are rows and rows of wooden pallets, laden with tall stacks of boxes. I cannae hear nor smell anything to indicate the presence of mortal or immortal within the warehouse. All I *can* hear are ventilation fans and the sound of vehicles moving outside the chamber. Still, in this place, with its subdued lighting, my imagination conjures up a vampire lurking behind every limestone column and every pallet of boxes.

Carl holds his claymore in his right hand and the pass card in his left. As soon as he swipes the card through the card reader by the door, the light on the reader changes from red to green, and I hear a click. Carl pulls the handle on the door, and it opens onto a passage. Inside the passage, fluorescent lights flicker on. A thick, black cable runs along the ceiling. *'Tis most likely providing the power for the lights.*

Unlike the rest of SubTropolis, the walls of this passage seem much more rough hewn. To be sure, the rest of the walls and columns are anything but smooth, but these walls seem as if they've been hacked haphazardly (perhaps with swords). In any case, the passage is wide enough for two or three to walk abreast.

The passage slopes down but does nae continue in a straight line. I cannae see where it leads or how far. Carl pockets the pass card and then points to himself. He holds one finger up. Then he points at me with two fingers. He's saying that he's taking "point." I'm to follow. I shake my head. In the air, he's in his element, but when it comes to sword fighting, I'm the better of us.

He hesitates a tick and then nods. He points down the passage with his sword, makes a wee bow, and mouths, *Ladies first.* I wink at him, and he smiles, but as I pass him and take the lead, I see his expression harden. *We're going into danger again, and he's frustrated at the thought of nae being able to protect me.*

We follow the passageway for a few hundred paces or so. The lights overhead are so spotty that we go for long stretches in near darkness. To our eyes, the light's sufficient, of course, but a mortal would be groping in the blackness. The air smells stale, and I cannae detect any ventilation. Perhaps the only movement of the air occurs when the door is opened. There's nae scent to indicate that anyone uses the passage regularly, but there is evidence of at least occasional travel. I see footprints made by bare feet on the limestone floor. There are scratches on the walls and tracks on the floor made by something long and flat. And there are chips and splinters of wood, pine by the scent. And bits of straw. *Hay? For feeding animals?*

As we round a curve, the tunnel comes to an abrupt end. The cable running along the ceiling disappears into the rock above us. The way is blocked by a massive rectangle of limestone. 'Tis as if a door has been cut from the wall. Perhaps that's precisely what it is, though I cannae discover a hinge. In the right side, however, I see an indentation between the "door" and the wall. The gap's wide enough to put my hand into, and when I do, I feel another indentation. 'Tis most definitely a crude handle carved into the stone. Looking at the floor, I can see the arc where the door has been pulled open many, many times. The floor is worn smooth there.

'Tis a stone door without a hinge—a door only a vampire could open. A door to prevent mortals from escaping.

I'm about to pull it open, but Carl lays a hand on my shoulder. I look back at him, and he shakes his head. He motions me away from the door. He points at my sword and then at me. He points at the door and then at himself.

I nod in understanding. I step back and hold my sword at the ready.

Carl puts his free hand into the indentation, braces his feet, and pulls. The great stone swings slowly out, making a horrible grinding noise. Carl grimaces at the din as he pulls.

'Tis sure to alert any of our kind who might be on the other side.

Carl has the door open just wide enough that we may slip through one at a time. *We dinnae know what we'll find on the other side . . . or rather, who. And if we must escape this way, 'twill be more defensible if the door is open only partway.*

I slip through the opening, my ebony blade held in front. Beyond the door is a vast cavern, a natural limestone cave complete with stalactites and stalagmites and the sound of dripping water.

I can hear Carl enter through the door behind me. He steps to my side, his claymore up.

The cave is dark and dank, but nae devoid of light. I can see numerous points of artificial illumination in the distance. The electric cable runs along the wall and disappears into the blackness beyond.

The nigh-motionless air does nae smell as stale as it did in the passage, so there must be some natural ventilation. There's also the scent and sound of moving water. 'Tis difficult to judge distances in this light, but I'd guess the cavern extends for a mile or two, perhaps more.

What I cannae detect is the scent or sound of *people*. People would be the only "foodstuff" a vampire farm would produce. *How horrible to apply that term to children of God!* There's the faintest odor of dried blood, but I cannae smell *living* people. However, this place *does* smell like a farm. I can detect the odors of animal waste, hay, and tilled earth. *Perhaps those scents are masking the aroma of humans and human blood.* And, although I dinnae see them, I can hear the bleating of sheep.

Off to our right, there are several large wooden crates. *These* smell of human occupancy. I take a moment to examine the closest one. The bottom's worn, probably from being pushed up the tunnel, the crate laden with human cargo. And there are bits of straw near some of them. Perhaps the same crates that carry people up the tunnel are used to transport hay for animals.

Carl taps my shoulder again, and I turn round. He points at the door near the handle. *Dried blood!* I see streaks and smears of long-dried reddish-brown. 'Twould seem that long ago the inmates of this dark place sought to claw open the door.

The scene reminds me of a horrific autopsy I once performed. Nigh a century ago, I examined the corpse of a victim of premature burial. She was a wee lass, less than twelve, mistakenly buried alive. The poor creature had worn her fingers quite literally to the bone as she tried to claw her way out of her coffin. She died of heart failure before she could suffocate. I imagined her scratching at the wooden casket, screaming in horror in the blackness, growing weaker and weaker as the air grew stale, as her heart beat frantically until it finally burst.

Carl taps me again, urgently this time. I wheel about, sword at the ready. I see nothing, but I can hear the sound of footsteps, slow at first and then fast, and then they stop. *Someone's trying to approach without being seen.* And there's the sound of a heart beating, blood rushing, of air being pulled into human lungs. Two hearts. I can hear two hearts.

Human blood.

The perfume of human blood finally reaches my nostrils. And the pungent odor of unwashed human flesh. *Perhaps 'tis human flesh that's* ne'er *been washed.* And the odor of . . . *Is that wool?*

Carl points almost directly in front of us. I look in the indicated direction, but I see nothing save a few stalagmites. I stare, but I see no movement . . .

A face! Or rather part of a pale face peeking around the side of a large natural pillar of limestone. I see a pair of eyes peering cautiously at us. A second pair of eyes appears on the other side of the stalagmite.

I start to advance toward the two lurkers. I expect them to bolt and run away, but, to my surprise, they both emerge from either side of the stone.

Two slight figures step around the column and stop, apparently waiting for us. They hid from us but a moment ago, but now they show nae fear at all. They appear to be a lad and lass in their early teens. Their skin is at once pale and slightly brown. An unnatural shade of brown. *Aye, down here in the absence of sunlight, the paleness is to be expected. These poor creatures are being raised with insufficient vitamin D, unless, perhaps, they're getting what they need from milk. I hear water. Are there fish in that water? They* could *get the necessary vitamin D from fish. They dinnae seem to have rickets.* The children are dressed in rough tunics made of what appears to be sheepskin. And they're wearing crude leather boots on their feet. They dinnae seem well fed, but they dinnae seem malnourished either. And the lass . . . Aye, the lass is very pregnant. *She cannae be more than thirteen!* The lad does nae have the slightest scrap of beard on his chin. Both of them have long, curly brown hair. And dark brown eyes . . . almost black.

They say nary a word as we approach them with our swords held before us. They simply stare at us. The expressions on their faces are eager.

When we're about a dozen yards or so away, the children both drop to their knees and prostrate themselves on the floor of the cavern. Then, as one, they stand upright again. Nae. They're nae quite upright: their heads are tilted to the side. They open their arms as if to invite an embrace. *Like children expecting a hug when mother and father come home.* They stare at us both with . . . Aye, 'tis longing I see in their eyes.

They expect us to Feed.

I think I may be sick.

Fighting down my sudden urge to vomit up Mafia blood, I say, "Dinnae be frightened. We'll nae harm ye."

But they dinnae appear frightened at all. They simply stare mutely at us, their arms wide and their necks bent.

I sheath my sword. Carl keeps his blade ready. I close the distance between myself and the children. I stop in front of the lass. She tries to wrap her arms around me, but I gently push them down. She offers nae resistance, but keeps her head tilted. I reach up and gently pull her head upright.

"What's yer name, lassie?" I ask, my voice soft and gentle.

She stares at me, confusion plain on her face, but she says nothing.

"What's yer name?" I repeat.

She remains mute.

"Why doesn't she speak?" Carl asks from behind me.

"'Cause they don't talk less'n Ol' Shep tells 'em to!" The voice is shouted from a distance. And I hear the sound of beating wings!

I jump back from the lass and draw my sword. *Daft fool! If I'd but kept my tongue . . .*

In the middle of the vast space between the ceiling and the floor of the cavern, I can see a winged figure flying swiftly toward us. I cannae tell if the approaching vampire is male or female, but that voice sounded male. I dinnae see a sword or any other weapon. The hands appear empty.

The two mortals glance behind them and then prostrate themselves on the cavern floor. The lass is lying on her back, while the lad stretches out on his belly.

"Greetings, my lord and lady!" cries the voice. "Welcome to the Farm!"

Definitely a male voice, though highly pitched.

The man appears misshapen somehow, but from this angle, I cannae say how. "Y'all can put your weapons away. Y'all won't need 'em here. The cattle ain't no danger to ya. They don't dare harm the gods! And y'all ain't got nothing to fear from Ol' Shep."

The odd figure slows and swoops up to a vertical posture. With the lights behind him, he's little more than a winged silhouette to my eyes, but I can see immediately that he's deformed. I've ne'er seen nor heard of a malformed vampire. This man's a living catalogue of congenital deformities. His spine's curved and his back humped, indicative of severe scoliosis. His arms and legs are dramatically disproportionate. And he's quite short in stature, at least in proportion to his wingspan. I even catch a brief glimpse of extensive webbing between his fingers, a severe case of syndactylism

What would motivate another vampire to Convert such a pitiable creature?

After Carl was Converted, the Seed healed the chest scars he received while in the Air Force. But this man's condition . . . or, perhaps, *conditions* must be genetic and congenital. The Seed'll nae make a vampire beautiful. It'll repair physical damage, but it cannae correct genetic anomalies.

The misshapen figure alights on the ground behind the lad and lass, who remain lying on the cavern floor. The unduly large wings of the vampire fold up and disappear. He cannae be more than three and a half feet tall. With the disproportionate shape of his body, I would diagnose achondroplasia as well. I can see the vampire more clearly now. His skin's pale, but nae so much as to indicate albinism. His face is malformed and lopsided, and his upper lip is cleft. *Perhaps add Van Der Woude syndrome to the list?* He smiles and raises a hand in greeting. The interdigital webbing is plainly visible now with his hand backlit by a distant electric light.

The dwarf bows at the waist, at least as much as his curved spine will allow. "Ol' Shep's yours to command, great ones!" He straightens to the extent he can. "What can Ol' Shep get for you, sir? For you, ma'am? What's your pleasure? A girl? A boy? Both? Ol' Shep's got one thousand, two hundred, three score, and eleven head to choose from! I got everything from newborns to youths to adults, all chosen for their beauty. I got prime breeding stock for you, sir. Not all of 'em are with child, mind, and we need to keep replenishing the herd!"

Unbidden, my brain conjures up the image of a ghoulish midget carnival barker, calling one and all to sample the pleasures, oddities, and freaks of the midway. Any pity I may have felt for this fiendish dwarf is borne away by the tide of my rising gorge. It takes all my will to keep from vomiting up the Mafioso's blood as it roils in my stomach.

Carl says nothing, and we both keep our swords ready.

The twisted vampire seems unconcerned. "Perhaps y'all'd like to take your case in my guest quarters? We got a dozen guest chambers, carved out of the cave walls, where y'all can rest unmolested by the livestock, or you can indulge in whatever pleasures y'all can imagine in privacy. I got fresh clothes. The Farm can even offer y'all a hot bath, with your choice of cattle to bathe you. Would y'all prefer one chamber or two?"

As this revolting creature hawks his "wares," the two mortals remain as they are, unmoving, waiting to be used.

"How many other guests do you have at the moment?" Carl asks.

He's assessing the number of enemies we might have to deal with. Always thinking militarily—that's my laddie.

Shep smiles, showing a mouth, full of crooked teeth. "Ah, my lord, y'all wouldn't want Ol' Shep to be talking out of turn about *you*, would ya? I never betray a guest's confidence, no siree!"

"How many?" Carl repeats.

The creature shakes his head and smiles obsequiously. "My lord, y'all know I can't do that."

"Answer the question," Carl demands.

"None," the dwarf says. He frowns. "Now, I shouldn't-a done that! Why'd y'all wanna go and make me do such a thing?"

"Do what?" I ask.

"Y'all made me talk about other guests, only there ain't none right now, but I ain't supposed to do that." He's wringing his hands.

"Why?" I ask.

"The Queen, she told me not to talk about other guests."

"So, why'd you answer?" Carl asks.

"Because y'all told me to!" He takes his hair in two misshapen fists and pulls large sections of it out. The hair begins to grow back rapidly out of his torn, but Healing scalp. "How'm I supposed to do both? Keep everybody's secrets *and* obey everyone's orders? Can't do both, can I? No, sir. Can't. I'm a beast. The Queen says so. 'Shep, you're a beast,' she says, 'not fit to live.' Well, she's right, ain't she? My own daddy wanted to drown me in the river when I was a baby, but my mamma, no, she wouldn't hear of it. Course, *she* didn't keep me around neither, did she? Gave me to Mammy to look after, didn't she?"

The dwarf looks at us suddenly, terror in his wide eyes. He falls to his knees and extends his webbed hands toward us, pleading. "Don't tell her majesty what I done! Please! My lord! My lady! Don't tell her what Ol' Shep done! Y'all can see I didn't have no choice! No choice! No, sir!"

He's such a wretched sight, for a wee moment I almost pity him again, but kneeling as he is between the two mortals, the lass with her pregnant belly protruding, I cannae think of this *shepherd* of human beings as anything but a monster.

"Get up," I say, and nae too kindly. "Get away from them."

Instantly, the hideous dwarf jerks awkwardly to his feet. He limps back a few paces.

"Stop right there," Carl commands.

Shep halts and turns around.

I point at the dwarf. "Laddie, ye mind this *creature* while I check out these two."

Carl nods.

I rush over and kneel beside the lass. I listen and probe and examine her. Her heartbeat is strong, her lungs are clear. The bairn's heartbeat is fine as well. She must be thirty-five or thirty-six weeks along. Very pale, but that would go along with spending her entire lifetime down here.

Now I can hear the approach of many feet. I look up briefly and I see scores of these poor mortal wretches are walking toward us. They're all pale and clad in sheepskin like the poor children at my feet. There are women and children, but few men.

Carl advances toward Shep, his sword pointed at the vile shepherd.

"My lord!" the monster cries. "Y'all don't want to hurt Ol' Shep, do ya? I'm your man! I have to obey your every command. I can't hurt any guest. The Queen commands it. I'm at the bottom of the dung heap, I am. The lowest of the low. I'm not fit to lick your boots, my lord. Don't hurt Ol' Shep. Ol' Shep wouldn't harm a soul! Not a soul!"

"Nae a soul?" I cry. "The lass is too young by far to be bearing a child!"

"She's thirteen!" the monstrous shepherd yells from behind Carl. "More'n old enough to bear. I have to breed 'em young to keep up with the demands of the court and still keep some available for those who prefer the taste of them as *ain't* with child."

"With her hips," I snap, "she'd nae be able to deliver."

"Well, then I cut 'em out! No sense in losing the calf as well as the cow!"

"And ye'd leave her to bleed out?"

"Of course not! Ya think I'm a fool? I consume her before she can do that. I don't waste nothing down here! Especially not a pretty li'l thing like her."

I want so very badly to tear that creature limb from limb!
Keep yer head, lassie.

I look the lass in the eye. "What's yer name, lassie?"

She looks away and says nothing.

"She ain't a-gonna answer," Shep says, peeking around Carl. "They don't know how to speak."

"They're mute?" I ask.

"No! They ain't *allowed* to talk, but I catch 'em doing their own gabble sometimes. I can't understand it, no ma'am, but they does it just the same. They don't understand me real well, but they understand enough to come, sit, kneel, lie down, and such. I ain't never heard any of 'em say more'n a word or two in English, least not in several generations. Sometimes they say, 'No,' but that catches 'em a beating."

I look at the lass again. "What's yer name, dearie. Dinnae be scared. I'll nae hurt ye. Ye can speak."

She says nothing and continues to avoid my gaze. A crowd of sheepskin-clad mortals has gathered, hundreds strong. I see curiosity on their faces, but nae sign of fear.

"Tell her she can speak," Carl says. His voice is hard, deadly.

"Go ahead, cow," the dwarf says in a loud voice. "Speak to her!"

The lass says nothing.

"She ain't a-gonna talk to ya," Shep says. "She's just a cow, something to play with and to Feed from. She don't even understand what I said."

I take the lass's head in both my hands, and force her to look at me. "What's yer name?"

The throng of mortals closes in around us, like a herd of curious sheep.

"She ain't got a name!" the dwarf says.

The lass keeps trying to move her eyes to avoid mine, but I'm persistent.

"What's yer name?" I repeat.

At last, her eyes lock with mine. Her mouth opens. "Mimi."

"Mimi?" I repeat. "Is that your name?"

"Mimi gonosay ahfeeyo." She turns her head to the side and pats her neck. "Mimi gonosay ahfeeyo. Ahfeeyo."

"What's she saying?" Carl asks.

"How would I know?" the dwarf replies. "Ol' Shep don't understand that cow talk."

The throng presses closer staring curiously.

"Ahfeeyo," the lass repeats, stroking her neck.

"I dinnae understand ye, dearie."

She points into her mouth. "Ahfeeyo." She pats her neck again.

The lad pats his neck as well. "Ahfeeyo," he says.

"Ach!" I cry in disgust as understanding dawns. "She wants me to Feed."

"They like it," Shep says. "They love when Ol' Shep Feeds. Makes 'em feel good. Fixes what ails 'em. If they're a-hurting, they come to the good shepherd to fix 'em up."

"Vile monster!" My head snaps up, and I snarl at the horrid creature. "Ye're a parasite, living off these poor souls! There's one Good Shepherd, and that's Jesus Christ. Ye're nae but a foul leech! Did ye impregnate this lass too?"

"Could be, of course, my lady! Why do ya think I accepted the Queen's offer? No woman would have Ol' Shep, not even the slaves on daddy's plantation, not that daddy would've allowed it. Lilith came along and offered me all the women I want so long as I keep her and her court in food, so long as I keep the Farm. I even got to take my pick of the pretty darkies on daddy's plantation."

Shep squawks as Carl lifts the dwarf up, holding him by his shirt. "'Their beauty!' You said they were chosen for their beauty! What do you do with the ones that *aren't* beautiful, the ones you spawn?"

"My lord! Let Ol' Shep be! Why're y'all doing this?"

"Answer me!" Carl snaps.

"I consume them! What else? If a calf is born all malformed or showing any signs of being Ol' Shep's brood, I kill it. I gotta cull the herd! If the signs show up a little later, like, say, if'n their back's all bent or their legs and arms don't grow right . . ."

"You *murder* your own children?" Carl cries.

"Of course, I do! Can't let 'em grow up, can I? What use would they be? Gotta keep the herd pure. As long as I keep the herd strong, I got all I need down here. I got all the blood I want. I got all the *women* I want. They *worship* me! I'm a *god* to them! I got my own kingdom! My own plantation! All I want! All I need!"

Carl raises his sword.

Is he going to execute this monster?

"Laddie!" I cry.

I hear a collective gasp from the crowd around us. They look terrified.

Are they afraid for themselves . . . or for their monstrous keeper?

"Why?" Shep wails. "Why you wanna kill Ol' Shep? I'm just doing what I'm supposed to do, what I was *commanded* to do!"

With a snarl, Carl drops the monster to the cave floor.

Instantly, Shep is groveling on the ground in front of Carl. "Thank you, my gracious lord!"

Is he trying to kiss Carl's feet?

Carl steps back quickly. "Stop that!" His face is a mask of revulsion as he stares down at the creature.

The mortal wretches are pressing close. So close. There won't be room to move soon. The smell of unwashed bodies and dirty sheepskin is overwhelming. *Is the entire population here?*

Shep continues to grovel, wringing his webbed hands. "Thank you, my lord! Thank you! Shep is a worm! How have I failed you, my lord? I don't understand. What'd I do?"

I feel hands brush my back, my shoulders, my hair.

"You sick, perverted abomination!" Carl cries. "You rape girls, and you murder your own children!"

"My lord," the dwarf whines, still groveling, "ya know all this! If y'all're here, if y'all have a key, that means y'all was sent by the Queen. She must've told y'all what it's like here."

"Lilith didn't send us," I say.

Still at Carl's feet, the dwarf asks, "Y'all ain't guests?"

"Nae," I reply.

I see Carl's head snap in my direction, but 'tis too late.

Nae lifting his head from where he crouches, Shep shouts a single word. "Kill!"

With a wordless scream, the mob falls upon us.

Chapter 24

Carl

One of the mob impales herself on my sword. Right through the heart! *She was pregnant!*

Other bodies slam into me. I'm knocked to the ground. Hands claw at me. Teeth sink into my arm.

Somehow I manage to hold onto my sword.

So many of them!

Fly! Get out of here! Get to Moira!

Up, out of the mass of bodies.

Even as I lift free, I feel claws grab hold of my arms, my legs, my coat. I shake and twist my way out, but one of them, a small boy of no more than ten, still clings to my coat.

I'm now fifty feet above the mob. I don't dare shake the boy off. If he falls from this height . . .

Moira!

I spin about to find her. *There she is!* She's airborne, carrying the girl she was examining earlier.

I lurch upward.

The boy! Falling!

I dive and catch him by his sheepskin tunic before he can hit the mob below. I pull him close and climb back to safety, joining Moira and her charge in the air.

I grit my teeth, expecting an attack, but the boy simply clings to me.

Not like fighting off Müller's Penitent slaves. These people aren't reaching frantically for me. They're not trying to get to me at any cost. Now that they can't reach me, they're just staring. Some are pointing, but nobody's saying anything.

"You OK?" I ask Moira, keeping my eyes on the crowd below. *There must be hundreds of them!*

"Aye, laddie, I'm grand."

"Where's Shep?" I glance around quickly, but don't see the monster. *Could he be hidden inside the mob?*

"Check your six," she says. "He's runnin' away, the coward."

I turn around and look. *There he is!* "Tally. Eleven o'clock high." Shep's bugging out, flying up toward the roof of the cave.

"I think 'tis safe to put these two down," Moira says, nodding in the direction of the girl in her arms.

I just killed one of them! She threw herself on my sword!

Moira points at the crowd below. "The rest of them dinnae seem interested in tearin' us apart . . . anymore."

"OK, but let me try first."

Moira gives me a stern look. "Laddie . . ."

I know that tone! "Hey, it's not sword fighting. Just hold back, please? And watch where Shep goes."

She purses her lips and then nods. She turns her face toward Shep, and her look hardens.

Holding the boy to my chest, I drop cautiously toward the throng of mortals below. The kid doesn't seem frightened at all. He just keeps his head cocked to the side and stares at me. *He's exposing his neck!*

"I'm not Feeding from you, kid," I say.

The boy says nothing.

The crowd stares up at me as I descend, but they don't seem to be aggressive. I rotate my body to a horizontal attitude and lower the boy toward the people. I keep my sword ready, but I hold it at my shoulder away from the crowd. I hope that looks nonthreatening.

Blood from the girl I killed drips down on my hand. *You didn't kill her, Morgan! She did it herself! Focus. Fly the airplane!*

Several hands reach up from below to take the child from me. I release the boy as they take his weight. OK, he's safe. I fly up toward Moira, who's staring fixedly at a point in the distance.

"Take her," she says. "I've got my eye on the spot where I last saw that vile shepherd. He disappeared into a hole in the upper wall. Most likely 'tis his chamber or one of the 'guest rooms.'"

I stick my sword in my belt and take the girl in my arms. "I got her."

Moira lets go, and the girl puts her arms around my neck. She cocks her head to the side, exposing her throat. I carry her down to the waiting arms of people below. They take the girl, and I climb to rejoin Moira.

Hovering beside her, I draw my sword again. "Ready?"

"Aye," she says, pointing her black sword at about eleven o'clock high. "Follow me."

I join up on her Number Two. As we fly away from the crowd below, I feel a wave of relief that makes me shudder. I'm glad to be putting some distance between us and them. Their blood smells delicious, but their unwashed bodies and bad breath make me want to gag. *It reminds me of one Halloween when my daughter April ate so much candy that she threw up. Sweet and sickening at the same time.*

And their faces! Their expressions!

"Doesn't it creep you out," I say, "the way they just stare at us, never smiling or frowning or showing any emotion at all?"

"Aye. They've been treated as cattle all their lives. They've known nae human kindness nor love for generations. Nobody's taught them."

But don't they have some human instinct? Don't they have the light of Christ?

Noting the speed we're flying at, I ask, "Aren't we going a bit slow?"

"I'm afraid I'll lose sight of where we're headed if we go any faster. I dare nae so much as glance away or blink."

"Roger."

She does accelerate a little bit, though.

I scan the blackness for bogeys, but don't see any. I don't think Shep was lying when he said there weren't any other 'guests' here. I don't think he *could* lie, not so long as he thought we were sent by Lilith and not so long as I ordered him to answer. I look below and see more people joining the others. There's a dark lake below us. I see sheep munching at bales of hay. Off in the distance under bright lights, I can see rows and rows of straight lines of green.

Crops?

"Seems they grow crops here to feed themselves," I say. "How did they do that before they had electricity down here?"

Keeping her eyes fixed ahead, Moira shrugs her shoulders. "Without a source of light, they could nae grow anything down here. There's just a trace of the scent of old smoke, so there *was* some light before. They could've made candles from sheep tallow, but that would nae have been enough to grow crops. Shep must've had soil brought in to grow what they're doin' now. Prior to that, they must've been livin' on just the sheep and the fish and whatever supplies were brought in. I'd wager there was another entrance before SubTropolis was created, though. The air in here gets circulated from somewhere. Now, laddie, I *do* need to focus on our destination, if ye dinnae wish me to lose my bearin's."

"Roger that."

We fly in silence for a moment.

"Can ye hear that, laddie?"

I listen and . . . something just on the edge of hearing . . .

Shep's voice!

"Affirmative," I answer.

"Who's he talkin' to? Himself? I dinnae hear anyone else."

She speeds up. I hold position on her left and strain to make out Shep's words.

". . . smell like Children, but they ain't got no wings, your majesty." A pause. "The man's got brown hair. The woman red . . . yes, my Queen."

Where is he? Up ahead, certainly. I don't see anything . . .

"At once, my Queen!" Shep's voice says.

A bright light, in the shape of a rectangle—*A door?*—appears directly a-head, high on the cavern wall. Moira halts, floating, her sword ready. I pull up beside her.

"Well, come on!" Shep cries, his grotesque form now silhouetted in the light. He motions with one webbed hand. "The Queen wants to speak to y'all. Carl, is it? Flying without wings! How do y'all do that? Quite a trick. Anyway, the Queen's waiting."

Lilith's here? No, at this distance we'd be able to smell or hear the presence of another vampire.

As we hesitate, hovering, Shep says, "Come on in. I won't hurt y'all. I ain't even got a weapon, no sirree. Ain't allowed to."

He's gotta be kidding! "You just tried to kill us!"

The hideous creature chuckles. "Ol' Shep just does as he's told. I meant no harm, my lord." He smiles wide, his harelip exposing a mouth, full of crooked teeth. But his smile falters, and he begins wringing his hands. "The Queen says she wants to talk to y'all. I've got one of them telephone things in my chamber. She's waiting."

"Careful, laddie," Moira says. "'Tis another trap."

"Of course it is," I say. "But she hasn't had time to set this one up prop-erly. She's improvising."

"Carl!" Moira doesn't look at me—she wouldn't take her eyes off the midget for a second—but her tone carries all the alarm she can't convey with her face.

"I don't think we're in immediate danger," I say.

"No, sir!" The monster beams again. "That you ain't."

Moira points the tip of her ebony blade at the midget's black heart. "I dinnae believe him! How can ye trust this vile, murderous creature?"

"I don't." I point to Shep with my free hand. "Will the cord stretch?"

The monster blinks. "The cord? The wire? Y'all mean . . . out here?"

I nod.

"I . . . I dunno." Shep cocks his lopsided head to the right. "Let me see." He waggles a webbed finger toward the ceiling. "Ol' Shep'll be right back, my lord."

Shep disappears, and the door—*of course, it's a door*—closes. No light at all escapes around the edges. The chamber is effectively hidden. If you didn't know where to look, you'd never see this opening in the canted limestone wall.

After a moment, the door opens again, and Shep emerges, wings un-furling, to hover outside. He's holding an old-fashioned pink handset. It's attached to a long, twisted pink cord.

"I think it'll reach." He begins to fly toward me. "Y'all're goin' to have to come a bit closer though."

"Halt right there!" Moira cries.

Shep stops in midair.

"We'll come to you," I say.

Moira and I advance slowly. As we get close, Shep extends the handset toward me.

Moira places the edge of her blade against Shep's throat. The midget doesn't even flinch. With her other hand, Moira takes him by his long, greasy hair. "Move a muscle and I'll take yer head off yer shoulders. D'ye understand me?"

Shep glances down at her sword. "That's a purtty one! I ain't never seen . . ."

Moira snarls. "D'ye understand?"

"Of course I understand!" He looks annoyed. "I'm ugly, not stupid."

I take the phone from Shep's outstretched hand. My fingers briefly touch his webbed ones. I can't suppress a shudder of revulsion. *How can Moira stand to touch his filthy hair?*

"May I put my hand down now, my lady?" Shep asks, his voice all Southern charm again.

"Slowly," she says.

"Much obliged, my lady." He smiles that hideous grin again. "Much obliged."

I put the phone to my ear and move back a couple of feet, as far as the cord will stretch. *I need to leave Moira room to move.* "What do you want?"

"Manners." It's that honeyed voice. "You are speaking to your Queen, my Son."

For a moment, I can't answer. I *want* to obey her, to beg her forgiveness for my impertinence.

I'd forgotten the effect her voice has.

"What do you want?" I repeat.

"Your head on a pike, Carl. Or you in my bed. Either would do. Your little wife stripped and . . ."

I grind my teeth so hard I think they'll break. "Yeah. Right. Now get to it. What do you want?"

"As I was saying . . ."

"Listen, lady—and that term doesn't apply to you in any way—you called this parley. Now tell me what you want or stop wasting my time."

"Oh, Carl, simply to be allowed to speak with me is the greatest honor of your immortal life."

"This is pointless. Either tell me what you want or I'm done. You don't think I know you're stalling so you can send your people after us? You've got ten seconds."

"Very well. Since you mentioned it, I have no *people*. You killed them all."

"*You* killed them. You blew up the place." *Shut up, Morgan and let her talk!*

"Yes, I did." *She's purring!* "And I imagine I took a number of your *people* along with them. Pity I failed to get you or your wife with the rest. That would have solved my problem. Ah, well. Next time!"

I feel as if an icy hand is wrapped around my guts and twisting. *Sixty-nine people dead!* "You're stalling."

"As you wish. You have something I want. I have something you want. I propose a hostage exchange."

She's got Tony, but . . . "Hostage? I have no hostage."

"I want my husband back. You have Sergei Ivanov Tupelev. You're holding him prisoner."

I actually laugh out loud. "You've got to be joking! Sergei is free now. Free of *you*. He joined us of his own free will."

Now she laughs. It's a beautiful, melodious, quintessentially female laugh. "Oh, Carl, Carl, Carl! How delightful! You actually *believe* that! Do you truly believe that *anyone* who has sealed himself to *me* would leave of their own accord? One of my Twelve? Oh, that's perfect! And, even if he did, do you think Sergei could resist me once he saw me again, once he heard my voice? He *loves* me. Perhaps he's a little confused at the moment, but he'll come back. Just offer him the chance. You'll see."

Unfortunately, she may be closer to the truth than not. Sergei said he's still in love with her. But I suspect she has another motive, another need. She has to suspect that Sergei is behind her inability to contact her Cult Masters. Sergei's the key to getting her people back.

"What's the matter?" I ask. "Lonely? Feeling abandoned?"

"What's the matter?" Her honeyed voice is mocking. "Unsure of yourself, of your hold on him? Go ahead: offer him the chance to return to me. He'll take it."

"And if he does?"

I hear a soft sharp intake of breath coming from Moira. *I hope Lilith didn't hear that. I'll have to assume she did.*

"I'll return Tony to you," she says.

"Unspoiled? Pure?"

"If he can resist me for so long . . ."

"Unspoiled and pure or it's no go."

"I suppose. Very well then. Agreed."

"When and where?" I ask.

"I don't suppose you have Sergei with you, do you? Shepherd said you and Moira came alone."

"Sergei's safe."

"Why don't we meet tomorrow night at midnight at the Farm?"

"On your territory with no escape routes? Not on your life, lady! We'll do the exchange someplace public."

"Where do you propose?"

"Someplace where there'll be a lot of people."

"Very well. The Sprint Center. Midnight. It's a basketball arena. There's a concert there tomorrow night. Will that do?"

"Agreed."

"You'll come alone? Just you and Sergei?"

"Not a chance. I'll be there with bodyguards."

"But *I* will have only Tony to protect me."

"Don't insult my intelligence. I know you have allies. You won't be alone. We'll meet on the concert stage. Midnight."

"But . . ."

"Be there with Tony, unspoiled and pure." I raise my sword and sever the phone wire. I crush the handset and let the shards drop into the darkness below.

Crap! Why didn't I ask to speak to Tony? How do I know he's still alive? Of course, she'd be stupid to kill him. He's her best bargaining chip.

"Now why'd y'all wanna go and do that?" Shep is obviously distressed. "I'm gonna be in big trouble now. How'm I supposed to communicate with . . ."

"Listen to me," I snarl. "You have two choices. You can take an oath to leave this place and never return, to take blood only from the truly evil, to never corrupt another innocent, and to never take another life. Do that, and I'll let you live. Refuse and I'll take your head off myself."

"Not even the cattle?"

"Especially not these poor souls here."

"They ain't got souls! They're just animals! The original stock was all runaway slaves."

Moira hisses. "They're more human than ye are, ye vile, monstrous murderer of yer own children. Ye dinnae deserve to live!"

His face twists in anger. "Who do y'all think you are to judge me! If I'm a monster, I was *born* to it! It's not my fault!"

Moira shakes him by the hair. "Ye had a choice. Ye chose to do this, to become a vampire! Ye chose to rape and murder yer own kin!"

"Like y'all didn't! Y'all chose just like I did!"

"I didn't," I say, my voice cold and quiet. "I didn't choose. I was Unwilling."

The midget's eyes go wide. "No! I can't believe it! The Unwilling?"

I nod.

"Aye," Moira says. "And I'm the Penitent. The Curse is come upon ye."

"But that means . . ."

"Yes," I say. "It means we're here to kill your Queen and put an end to all this."

"But we'll all die!"

"That's right," I reply. "But you'll live a little longer if you swear the oath. Which is it going to be?"

"I'll swear your damned oath!" he snarls.

Moira whispers, "Go on."

He looks wildly about.

Is he hoping for rescue?

We're wasting time!

"In the name of Lilith," he says, "Queen of Vampires, Mother of Night, Consort of Lucifer, I swear that I, Shepherd Leslie Reginald Lee, will leave this place . . ."

"The Farm," I prompt.

"I remember! I will leave the Farm, never to return. I swear to take no blood except evil blood. I swear to harm no innocent, corrupt no innocent, to never take another life."

He licks his malformed lips. "There. Are y'all happy now?"

I nod. "Go."

Moira cries out in surprise as the midget pulls out of her grasp and flies away.

Shep looks as shocked as she does.

He turns toward us, but keeps flying in the direction of the entrance to the cave. "Can't I even take my things?"

"What?" *What's he talking about?*

"His oath," Moira says. "The Seed is forcin' him to fulfill his oath."

"Wow!" I say. "It worked!"

"Ye can say that again, laddie!"

From the distance, Shep cries. "Damn you! I'll see y'all in Hell! Y'all got no right to take my things! And my cattle! Y'all got no right!"

His voice cuts off. *He must've entered the tunnel.*

I let out a relieved sigh.

"Ye're nae seriously considerin' givin' Sergei back to Lilith, are ye?"

"Not for a New York minute."

"Nae even tempted?"

"No way. I won't trade one life for another . . . unless it's my own."

"So what are ye plannin'?"

"I don't know for sure. In the immortal words of Professor Jones, 'I'm . . .'"

". . . makin' it up as ye go?"

"Yep."

"I love ye, Carl Morgan." She sheathes her sword and gives me a big kiss.

"And I love you too, but we've got a more immediate problem."

She points at the crowd in the distance. "Aye, these poor wretches."

"What in the world are we going to do with them?"

Chapter 25

Carl

The stench of these people is unbelievable. And they're pressing so close! At least they're not trying to murder us this time.

Where's the girl I killed? I don't see her body anywhere, but I can smell her blood.

Innocent blood. On my sword.

Maybe they have some place where they dispose of the bodies. If so, there could be thousands of bodies in there.

Images flood my mind, images of the charnel pit in Michael's secret tunnel. And smells. Hundreds of bodies, the victims of the Cult in Salt Lake City. Rats everywhere, feasting on the corpses. Rats were chewing on me, their sharp teeth biting, tearing, their claws scratching . . .

I shudder violently at the memory.

As Moira and I try to make our way through the crowd, some of the people cock their heads to the side, exposing their necks. Others are touching us, pawing at us. I can't tell if it's simple curiosity or *worship*. Whatever the motivation, it's making me seriously uncomfortable.

There are so many of them!

I hold tight to Moira's hand. I don't want to lose her in the press of bodies. I squeeze her hand, and she glances my way. She looks as weirded out as I feel.

I say, "What do we do with twelve hundred and seventy-one . . ." My voice breaks. "Make that twelve hundred and seventy . . ."

"Laddie, that was nae yer fault!"

My fault or not, she's just as dead!

Focus on the problem at hand, Morgan! "What do we do with twelve hundred and seventy refugees who don't speak English, who speak a language nobody else understands, who know nothing about how to behave around other people . . ."

Someone grabs my butt. I let out a yell as I try to pull away. ". . . who have *no* sense of personal boundaries!"

"'Refugees.'" Moira brushes a groping hand away from her chest. "Aye, 'tis as good a word as any, laddie. An apt comparison. Like Cambodian boat people arrivin' on the coast of . . . *Ach, now! Stop that!*"

The crowd backs off a little. They seem cowed—*Such an awful word!*—frightened by the tone of Moira's voice.

At least now we've got breathing room.

"We can't leave them here," I say. "Not even for the day."

"Aye, Lilith knows we're here. We cannae stay and we cannae leave any of these poor wretches at her mercy."

"I'm more worried about the Mafia. Did you see the way that security guard was so friendly, the way he treated us once he saw our key card?"

"Aye, he did everything but bow to us. I'm certain he saw our swords and the blood on our clothing. He either thought we were Mafia or . . . something worse. The Covenant would prevent one of Lilith's people from revealing the *precise* nature of vampires, but that does nae mean the guard and others like him have nae dealt with 'guests' of the Farm before. There's much they could guess about the nature of Lilith's people. The mobster in the alley—he seemed to ken what we were."

I eye the mass of people around us. They're closing in on us again.

"That guard has to know something *funny* is going on in Vault 17C," I say. "That means others know. They see the trucks making deliveries of hay, food, maybe sheep. They see the trucks ferrying the victims to and from the vault. We know the Mafia's been making those deliveries. They know what's in here."

"Aye, and they could . . . *Please! Back away! Ach! Give us some space!*"

The crowd pulls away a little, and Moira draws closer to me.

We could fly, but it's awfully difficult to connect with them from above. I just wish they didn't seem to insist on connecting with us so physically.

"The bottom line," I say, "is we have to get them out of here and to someplace secure. We have to find someone to watch over them, keep them safe." I glance at my watch. "And we really don't have much time to do it, not before sunrise."

"Aye, and someone to educate them, teach them to speak English, teach them how to be *human* and nae cattle."

"So where can they go and who'll take care of them? We have to move them tonight, even if it's only to a temporary location."

"Where? I dinnae know where. What about the Church? We could get the Relief Society involved."

"In the middle of the night?" I ask.

"They came out to help us in Utah last night."

"Yeah, bullied and pushed into it by Winnie Morrison. But we don't know who to call out here."

"Ye could call Bishop Adams back in Salt Lake. He could call that bishop's hotline thing he told us about, and they'd know who to contact out here."

"Fair enough," I say. "The Relief Society can help feed and clothe and care for them, which would be a massive job by itself, but we need someone to guard them *tonight*. We need somebody to contain them and keep them safe. They can't be walking around in the open. They'd be in danger and vulnerable and . . ." A hand slides up my chest. "*Cut it out!* And they don't know how to behave!"

"Lieutenant Ericson," Moira says.

I nod. "We'll call in the Marines! I'd bet Ericson has enough connections. They could relocate all of them to Richards-Gebaur Air Base."

"That'd work, laddie, but nae tonight. There's nae time."

"Yeah. We need to find somewhere close, and it needs to be tonight."

"Why nae here?"

"Here? No good. Both the mob and Lilith know about . . ."

"Nae, ye ninny! Nae here in this *cave*, but here in this *place*, this Sub-Tropolis! As we drove through the tunnels, I saw a number of unused warehouses. Even the warehouse we came through, the one with vault 17C and the tunnel, 'twas large enough to house them till the Marines or the Relief Society can arrange transportation to a better facility. What d'ye think?"

"Well not *that* warehouse, of course."

"Of course."

"But I think you're right."

"Of course I am, laddie. I'm always right. And best ye remember that!"

"Secret of a happy marriage, I always say!" I grin impishly. "Rule Number One: Moira is always right. Rule Number Two: if Moira is ever wrong, wait until she figures it out herself!"

"Ooh, laddie! Ye're walkin' a dangerous road, ye are!" She smiles. *Dazzling!* Then her face twists in disgust as hands brush against her. "*Ach! Stop that!* We're here to help ye! D'ye nae understand? We dinnae want yer blood and we dinnae want yer bodies! We want to save ye."

"Will ye save our souls from Hell?"

Who said that? The voice came from behind us.

I turn around, toward the sound of the voice. Moira turns as well. The crowd isn't looking at us anymore. Almost as one, the mortals turn toward the voice also.

"Who said that?" Moira calls. "Show yerself!"

"Notoshdae. Daehelyo. Lemeebai." *That's the same voice, but now I can't understand the words.*

The crowd parts like the Red Sea in that old Charlton Heston movie. About twenty yards inside the space created in the throng, I can see a woman, one of the few adults I've noticed here, clad in skins, like all the others. She doesn't look any different from the rest.

A young boy, around six or seven years old, is holding her hand. The child doesn't seem to be afraid of us either. He stares at us with curiosity. He tugs on her hand and looks up at her. "Are they the angels, mother?"

"Who are ye?" Moira asks again.

"I am Esther," the woman replies. "Art thou and thy companion angels sent from the Lord?"

"We're not angels in the sense you mean," I say. "But we do want to help you. We need to get you out of this place."

Esther raises a hand above her head. "Ye *are* the angels my mother said God would send to deliver us from the bottomless pit." Then she falls to her knees. The boy drops to his knees too. Esther bends forward. "O, Lord! Thou hast delivered us, thy people, from our enemies, from the Devil and his angels! Blessed be the name of the Lord! Blessed be the messengers who come in the name of the Lord! Blessed be . . ."

"Ye speak English," Moira says, interrupting, "ye and yer son. Do any of the rest of ye speak English?"

The woman lifts her head and looks at Moira. She remains on her knees, but she straightens up. The boy, never having prostrated himself, remains upright. He looks at his mother.

Esther says, "I speak the words of God's book. I learned them from my mother, and she from her father, and he from his father, and he from his mother. And so it was from the beginning, from the day when we were cast into Hell. I am the keeper of the holy book, as my son, Daniel, will be if I am consumed. We have prayed for deliverance, and God hath sent you to redeem our souls from Hell."

I wish she'd just answer the question. "Do any of the others speak English?" I ask. I look around at the others. "Do any of you speak English?"

There's no answer.

"Blessed one," Esther says.

"Don't call me that!" I say, a bit too sharply.

Esther recoils as if slapped.

"Look," I say, walking toward her, "I'm sorry. I don't mean to be rude. It's just that we're running out of time." I pull out my cell phone and check the time. Sunrise is less than three hours away! "We have to get you out of here. Does anybody else speak English?"

Esther shakes her head. "The keepers of the holy book remain hidden from the demons. The demons may know us, they may take our blood, they may plant their seed in us, but they must never know of the keepers of the holy book. We must hide the holy book from them. We must hide the keepers from them. The keepers pray to God, for the people know not how."

I sigh in exasperation. "I'll take that as a no. But you can speak to the rest of them, right?"

"I speak the tongue of the people."

"Good," I say. "Tell the people to gather all their things."

"Things? What is 'things?'"

"Laddie," Moira says, "I think ye must limit yerself to words she understands."

"You mean words from the Bible, right?"

"Aye."

"Fair enough." I point at Esther. "Gather your flocks and your herds. Gather water. Do you have . . . bottles or skins or . . . vessels for water?"

She nods.

"OK," I say. "Gather your grain, your clothes, your . . . Gather anything else . . . thou mayest possess. And be quick. We need to depart before the . . . before the demons return. Do you . . . Dost thou understand?"

She nods. "Thou wilt lead the people from this place? Thou wilt open the gate of Hell and lead us to the light?"

"Something like that, but you need to hurry."

"'Hurry?'"

"Be swift. Make haste." Moira says. "Go. Gather thy possessions. We must go."

Esther rises to her feet. The boy, Daniel, joins her. "Gehyoships!" She cries. "Gehyofoos! Wegosna! Gehyowaddainnaposs. Wegosna! Wegosna! Heryo! Heryo! Wegosna! Wegosannokomsbak."

Like a flock of—*Oh, boy! Bad analogy!*—The crowd turns, almost as one, and begins to make their way quickly down toward the expanse of the cave, toward the sheep bleating in the distance, toward the water.

Esther's face splits in a huge smile. Her eyes are bright. "I must go to the place where the book is hidden! I must gather the book! Praise to the Lord! In Him is all praise! Blessed are they who come in the name of the Lord!"

Taking the boy by the hand, she turns and follows the crowd. She's not exactly skipping—*Does she even know how to skip?*—but there's definitely a spring to her step.

In less than a minute, Moira and I are standing alone in the forest of stalagmites, watching the entire population of this horrible place hurry off into the twilight below. Now they're shouting in their incomprehensible dialect.

At least it's incomprehensible to me.

"OK," I say. "That's got them moving. Since they're bringing their sheep, they'll have food for a little bit."

"Aye," she says, pointing off in the distance. "Seems they've got pots or vessels for carrying water."

I look where she's pointing. Yep, there's a lake in this place . . . and a stream flowing into one end of it. I can see people, mostly girls, filling jugs at the stream.

I nod. "So food and water, at least for tonight and tomorrow. That's good. But we can't just march them out of here without knowing *exactly* where we're going."

"Aye, ye can go and figure out that part. I'll watch over them and get them to the door. I want to talk to that Esther again, find out more about these . . . people." Her lovely face twists in frustration. "Ach! We cannae keep callin' them . . . 'them' and 'these people!' We must find somethin' else to call them."

"Yeah. I know what you mean. You think on that while I'm gone. Time's flying and dawn won't wait. We have to get them settled and be gone before that."

"Go, laddie. I'll see to things in here."

I kiss her quickly and leap into the air, flying for the limestone door. The slab of limestone, with its gruesome reminders of an escape attempt long ago, still stands ajar. I'll need to open it all the way before we try to lead these people out, but that can wait till I come back this way.

I zoom through the door and into the tunnel, lit by its spotty fluorescent lights. I have to slow way down. *Won't do to knock myself silly against the sides or ceiling!* The tunnel's about eight feet tall, so I continue to fly a foot or so off the ground.

Now I can make sense of the smooth floor with its wood chips and bits of hay. I can picture Shep pushing wooden crates filled with sheep and hay going one way and human cargo going the other.

The thought of that sick, twisted monster and what he's done in this place makes me want to puke.

The face of the girl I killed fills my vision like the specters of all the mistakes I've made, all the lives lost tonight because I wasn't smart enough or fast enough to prevent it.

It wasn't my fault she died; that was Shep's doing. But she's still dead, and the baby inside her is dead too. Not my fault, maybe, but it was still my sword she died on.

Because I didn't react fast enough.

And my friends who died tonight . . . That wasn't my fault either . . . not exactly, but I still led them to their deaths. We didn't even take out the target! The fact is, I'm not the best person to lead in this war. I'm no ground commander! I don't know *squat* about land tactics. I didn't kill the folks who followed me, but I still led them to . . .

Focus, Morgan! Focus on the objective! Stop wallowing in . . .

Someone's in the tunnel!

"I'm tellin' ya, I *heard* somethin'!" *I don't recognize the voice.*

I stop and hover. I can't see anyone, but I can hear them distinctly. From the sound of things, whoever it is could be close, maybe just past the slight curve of the passage, or he could be at the other end of the passage. It's hard to tell distances in here.

The air's so still. I don't smell anyone.

"Stop bein' such an old woman, Renny!" *Another voice.* "I'm tellin' ya, you're just spooked 'cause you're dealin' with *her* people. They ain't here! Even the Creeper's gone. The guard said he saw 'im bookin' it out the front gate. Flyin'! Wings 'n all! I thought they was supposed to stay outta sight, not go flyin' around where everybody and their dog can see."

"I ain't never heard of the Creeper leavin' the warehouse," the first voice says. "Usually he just comes to that door up there and handles the deliveries. At least that's what I heard."

"You done the delivery?" Renny asks.

"Yeah. I done it once. Freaked me out, I tell ya, like nobody's business. Even bein' told up front what the Creeper looks like and what the shipment is . . . I don't like this job. The Creeper, he came and looked at me like he wanted to kill me. I ain't never seen nobody so angry. Not even Carlo when he . . . You know. An' it was just *me*. The Creeper didn't look at the *driver* that way. I could tell: he wanted to kill *me*."

"Yeah," Renny says. "I heard about that. They ain't supposed to come near us 'cause they *do* wanna kill us. I don't know why they do. They can't, though, or at least the Creeper can't, 'cause *she* orders 'em not to. An' that's why we send the drivers. But once in a while, one of the Family has to go. So you got stuck with it, huh?"

"Yeah. Lucky me. Lucky Joey. The Creeper was bad enough, but those *people*, ya know, the cargo? They smell! Like they don't never take a bath or nothin'."

"Even if they *did* take a bath, their clothes would still stink. They don't wear nothin' but those damn sheepskins, I hear."

"Well, it don't make no matter what they wears," Joey says. "From now on, it ain't our problem. Once we blow this tunnel, ain't nobody gonna know what's on the other side of it."

They're going to blow the tunnel. They're going to get rid of the evidence.

Still hovering, I start moving silently up the tunnel toward the voices.

"I didn't even know the boss had this stuff in the warehouse," Renny says. "He musta knowed he might have to get rid of the evidence someday. Did you know about this stuff?"

"Yeah, I knew," Joey replies.

"You knew? How come I didn't know?"

"'Cause the boss, he don't trust you like he do me. All I know is I get a call in the middle of the damn night, sayin', 'Joseph, go do this thing. Take care of this problem for me. Oh, and, Joseph, do it right now. You got thirty minutes.'"

"And here we are," Renny says.

"And here we are," Joey echoes.

"So, we about done now?"

"Just about. All I gotta do is run a few more wires and set the timer for say . . . ten minutes and we'll clear out."

"Ten minutes? Can't ya make it twenty, Joey? Give us time to get away safe? Ten'll barely give us enough time to get outta SubTropolis. Maybe not that. What if the rest of the place goes? We could be like trapped . . . or killed . . . or somethin'. An' even if we get away, I don't wanna be the last guy seen leavin' this place just before it blows. We'll be on the security cameras!"

"The Family *owns* the cameras, ya moron!"

"What about the guards?"

"The Family owns the guards too. You know that! You're jumpin' at your own shadow."

"What's that?" Renny cries.

They can't have heard me. I'm barely breathing!

"What's what?" Joey asks. "I don't hear nothin'!"

I hold my breath. There's no way they could've heard me!

"I don't know, Joey. I swear it feels like someone's walkin' on my grave. I think there's somebody in here."

"Hey!" Joey shouts. "Is somebody down there? One of you bloodsuckers?"

For a moment there's silence except for the sound of their breathing and their pounding hearts.

"See, Renny?" Joey says. "There ain't nobody there." His voice sounds calm, but the thundering of two hearts, one of which has to be his, tells a different story. Joey's scared too.

Finally the scent reaches me.

I'm nearly overwhelmed with the sweet perfume of evil blood. They must be a ways up the tunnel still, for me not to have smelled it before.

But I smell it now. My fangs extend, and my mouth fills with saliva. And the old rage, the primal anger boils up, threatening to overflow.

Kill them! Drain them! Rip them limb from limb! Murderers! Monsters! Kill!

Get control, Morgan!

They've got guns. And in this space, no matter how fast I move, they can't miss.

You don't want a bullet in the brain like Rolf got. Think, Morgan! Focus!

I've got to save those people in the cave. I can't do that if I get shot, or they manage to blow up the tunnel.

Stupid! I should have been prepared for the smell. They're murderers.

I should have been prepared.

Ignoring the rage—*Kill them!*—I make my way up the tunnel. I should be almost there.

How close am I?

Close enough to smell the gun oil. And the C4.

"You're right, Renny." Joey says. "I'm just jumpin' at nothing. Nothin' at all."

The voice sounds calm, but their hearts sound like they're about to burst out of their chests. *Who're they trying to fool? Themselves or whoever they think might be coming up the corridor?*

They've got to be . . .

They're right in front of me. Two men. Maybe ten feet away.

I can see a dozen bricks of C4 stuck to the walls and ceiling, each impaled with two blasting caps, with wires running to a timer.

But it's not the explosives that have my attention. It's what the men are holding: one holds a gold crucifix, and the other, a large black gun pointed straight at my face.

Chapter 26

Carl

W e don't want no trouble." Joey's voice, coming from a man wearing a trench coat, T-shirt, and jeans. He's the one with the cross.

The other trench-coated guy—the one with the big, black gun—is Renny, then. His hand's shaking. I don't think I've ever seen a handgun so huge. Maybe if I rush him . . . No. A man that spooked could have an itchy trigger finger. And his hands are trembling.

Don't these guys have a treaty with Lilith?

"What about the Covenant?" I ask. *Was that the word the thug used tonight? Or was it "treaty?"*

Kill them! Kill! Murderers!

Focus, Morgan!

I swallow a mouthful of saliva and try very hard *not* to attack them.

"Yeah, yeah, yeah," Renny says, waving the huge pistol in a quaking hand. "The Covenant. That's the thing, ain't it? I figure, if we blow this tunnel, that's kinda breaking it, right? Your queen, she ain't gonna be happy, that's for sure. So it's best if ya don't rat us out to her."

Kill!

"Quit talkin' and shoot, man!" Joey cries, brandishing the cross in a hand quaking so hard I'm surprised he can hold on to it. "Why you always gotta talk before you whack someone?"

"'Cause I just gotta," Renny says. "I can't just shoot someone without 'em knowin' why. It goes against my nature."

"Aim for the face an' just do it!" Joey looks frantic, terrified, his eyes as big as saucers. "He's like the Creeper! He's gonna kill us an' turn us into one o' them!"

Before I came into view, they must've been *pretending* to be calm in order to put me off my guard, to lure me in, to make a mistake.

It worked.

Struggling to keep the molten rage out of my voice, I say, "That gun won't kill me. You know that."

"Yeah, I know." Renny shakes the gun at me.

Something about the barrel looks odd.

Kill! Kill!

Renny points the gun right at my face. "You think I'm stupid? I seen Buffy. Only I ain't got no crossbow. I got somethin' better! It won't kill ya, but it'll put ya outta commission."

I've got no room to maneuver.

Kill them!

He's aiming at my face. Maybe I can duck, if I'm really fast.

His hand abruptly ceases its trembling.

Renny pulls the trigger.

I drop to the floor of the tunnel.

Something hits me between the eyes. My face feels wet. Am I bleeding? No. It's just . . .

"Water?" *A squirt gun? It's painted like a bigger-than-life semiautomatic.* "You shot me with *water*?"

"Why ain't he burnin'?" Joey cries.

"That damn priest!" Renny fires multiple small jets of liquid at me. "I watched him bless it myself!"

I laugh.

And even to *my* ears, the sound of my laughter is creepy, echoing, seeming to fill the tunnel. Evil. The mirth of a monster gloating over its prey.

Drain their worthless lives! They're killers!

I rise from the floor to hover there, laughing low in my throat, licking my fangs.

Joey goes white as a shroud, and a thin stream of yellow runs from his trembling pant leg, down the tunnel toward me. The mobster falls to his knees, now wielding the crucifix before him with both hands.

Renny keeps on firing holy water at me. As I continue my eerie laughter, all the blood drains from Renny's face. He drops the oddly realistic, but over-sized squirt gun with its too-small barrel to the tunnel floor and reaches inside his coat.

Gun oil! He's going for his real gun!

In an instant, I close the gap between us. I snatch the pistol from his hand as he pulls it from inside his coat. I crush the weapon in one hand and fling it away. Taking a handful of his gelled hair in my fist, I pull his head to the side. I plunge my fangs into his neck and sweet corruption fills my eager mouth.

Kill him! Drain him!

No. I may need him.

For what? Kill him!

I need him to . . . Do what?

So sweet!

Report. Yes, that's it. I need him to report back that he succeeded. *Sweet evil!*

I need to buy time to get the people . . .

Kill him! Tear his head from his neck!

. . . to get the people in the cave to a safe place. Or, at least, a *safer* place.

I pull my lips away from Renny's throat. Blood continues to spurt from one of the wounds, hitting me in the face.

Such a waste!

I must have nicked the jugular.

I clamp my lips down, sealing off the jet of blood, and lick the wound until the Seed closes it, greedily gulping the blood that spurts in the meantime.

Dropping Renny to the tunnel floor, I hear him moan in ecstasy. He wants me to take more, of course. He's definitely not going anywhere.

I turn my attention to Joey.

He could've gotten his own gun, but instead he's still kneeling holding the crucifix before him with both hands, trying to ward off the demon.

Stupid, Morgan! You can't afford to be careless. Too many lives at stake.

In addition to wetting his pants, Joey's soiled himself.

As soon as my eyes lock on his eyes, he screams. It's a high-pitched sound that would do a soprano proud.

Soprano? Like that gangster show I never watched? I chuckle again.

I'm enjoying this too much.

Joey is breathing rapidly, like a rabbit caught in a snare. He'll hyperventilate and pass out at this rate. His lips are working. He's mumbling something. ". . . kill me. Please don't kill me. Please. I'm sorry. I'm so sorry. Don't turn me into one o' you. I'm sorry. I'm sorry. So sorry."

I chuckle. "You've wet yourself, Joey. And you've crapped your pants. Now *you* stink. You stink worse than those poor souls in the cave. But you know what doesn't stink, Joey? Do you?"

Joey shakes his head almost imperceptibly, whimpering like a frightening dog.

I smile, exposing my fangs. Drool mixed with blood spills from my mouth. "Your *blood*, Joey. It smells so *sweet*."

The mobster screams again as I plunge my fangs into his neck. *Careful about the jugular this time, Morgan!* I force myself not to take too much. *Leave some for Moira!*

Joey's screams turn to moans of pleasure.

Reluctantly, I unlatch from his neck and lick the wound to seal it.

Joey's hands are on my shoulders, holding me close. He moans. "More."

"More," Renny echoes from behind me.

As I look back to check on Renny, my eyes sweep across the wires.

The bomb! A quick glance at the timer reveals a digital readout counting down.

Twenty seconds.
Nineteen.
Eighteen.

I tear myself free of Joey's embrace and dive at the timer. Ripping the wires from it, I toss the timer up the tunnel and away. *Is that enough?* I don't know much about explosives, but even I know that C4 won't blow without the blasting caps. I yank all the pins from the bricks of plastique and toss them, wires and all, up the tunnel after the timer.

Now, I turn back to Joey and grab his head by the hair. Turning his face toward the explosives, I say, "Is that it? Did I disarm it?"

He blinks stupidly.

"Is it disarmed?" I roar, shaking him by the shoulders.

"Yeah," he replies. "Can't go off now."

I turn his head back to face me and fix him with my stare. "Gather all the bomb stuff up and put it away," I command. In my mind, I feel the all-too-familiar click, assuring me the Persuasion is working. *I truly hate doing this, even with a murderer like Joey.* "Then call your boss and convince him you successfully blew the tunnel. Make him believe you. You *did* blow the tunnel, right?"

"Yes," he says, his voice eager, "I blew it, all right. Blew it to kingdom come!"

"Go and tell him that," I continue, "and then surrender to the police. Confess all your crimes. And tell them everything you know about the Family. *Everything.* Tell them about this place. Do you understand?"

"Yeah. Yeah. Tell them everything."

"Make them believe you."

"They already do," he says. "They already know everything."

I'm stunned. "The *cops*? The cops know everything?"

"Yeah. Not all of 'em, but a lot are on the take."

"Are there any *honest* cops?"

"Yeah, some."

"Find one and tell him everything."

"Yes."

"OK," I say. *How deep does Lilith's control go in this town?* "Go. Now."

Joey climbs to his feet. He begins pulling C4 bricks from the walls and stuffing them into a nylon gym bag.

I hadn't noticed the bag before.

The sooner he gets that stuff and his reeking pants out of here, the better.

And his blood.

I rub my eyes. My fingers come away bloody. My face is still covered in Renny's blood, apparently.

Licking the sweet scarlet from my fingers, I turn my attention back to Renny.

He hasn't moved, but he doesn't have the vacant look that accompanies Seed-induced euphoria anymore. He stares at me as I wipe more blood from my face with my hand and lick it with exaggerated relish.

He says, "I'm gonna turn into one of you now?"

I chuckle and smile wickedly.

Joey, stinking of human waste and having retrieved all the bomb components, is walking rapidly up the tunnel.

I call after him, "Joey!"

He turns and looks at me. "Yes, sir?"

Our eyes lock again. "I told you to put that stuff away," I say. "On second thought, after you talk to your boss and convince him you blew the tunnel, turn those explosives over to that honest cop you're going to find. Will you obey?"

"Yes. I'll obey."

"Go."

He turns and continues quickly toward the tunnel exit.

Now back to Renny.

His face is pale, and now he looks as terrified as Joey did before I Fed from him. "How long before I turn into one of you?"

I wipe my face once more and lick the smear of Renny's blood from my hand. I force my fangs to retract. "You're worried about becoming a vampire? You're already a bloodsucking leech, as far as I'm concerned. You're a murderer. How many people have you killed?"

"Don't know what you're talkin' about." He has the air of a practiced and skilled liar. "I ain't never . . ."

I fix him with my stare and demand, "How many?"

"I killed seven people. First, I killed Osaka, the Jap grocer down on . . ."

"That's enough. I don't need to know the details. Save it for the police. When I'm done with you, you *will* go to the police, find an *honest* cop, meaning one *not* on the take, and confess everything to him. You got that?"

He nods. "Yes."

"You will obey?"

"Yes. I'll obey."

"Good. Now come with me."

🌢 🌢 🌢

"Done so soon?" It's the same guard who drove us to the warehouse, the same warehouse which acts as a front for the Farm. He's sitting in his truck, leaning out the driver's window, beaming at me. "I didn't expect to see you folks again till tomorrow night at least!"

He doesn't *smell* evil. I'd have noticed it before. No, he's no murderer, but he knows something.

He nods at Renny. "Hey, Mr. De Marco."

Renny says nothing. He's not under my direct control at the moment. He just looks . . . lost.

The guard looks at Renny with obvious concern. "What's with you, Mr. De Marco? You feeling OK? You look like you seen a ghost." He chuckles, but there's an uncomfortable edge to his voice. He glances furtively in my direction.

"He's OK," I say. "Just a little under the weather. Nothing a little rest and some good food won't cure."

The guard looks back at me and grins wide, showing yellowed teeth with metal fillings, but his big smile looks strained, and it doesn't extend to his eyes. He also pulls back and straightens up in his seat. "I hope you had a good time, sir. Your lady friend? She staying behind?" He glances quickly at my sword. One hand drops from the steering wheel and out of sight. I can't be sure from this angle, but I'd bet money, were I a betting man, that he's putting a hand on his side arm.

I'm not bothering to conceal my sword this time, though I'm sure he saw it earlier, when he gave Moira and me a ride.

"She'll be along shortly," I reply. "Give us a lift?"

"Sure!" He laughs nervously.

I nudge Renny in the right direction, and he lurches forward. We walk around behind the security truck. I listen carefully for any sudden increase in the speed of the engine. I note that the guard places both hands on the wheel again.

And, yes, he's wearing a side arm.

Once we reach the passenger side, I open the door and slide into the middle. This time I make no pretense of hiding the claymore, especially since I have to hold it between my legs. I look at Renny. "Get in." The gangster slides in beside me.

The guard laughs nervously and smiles again. "The front gate?"

I shake my head. "Show me your largest empty warehouse."

"That'd be the entire Ninety complex over on Hushpuckney Road. Almost three-hundred seventy-five thousand square feet of interconnected warehouses." He puts the truck in gear and we drive off. "It's got rail service too."

I guess it makes sense that all the roadways in this place are named, but it still seems weird to think of street names underground. I guess you have to navigate somehow down here.

"Does it have water?" I ask. "The warehouse, I mean. Does it have bathroom facilities?"

"It's a warehouse! It's got sprinklers, lights, walls, and columns. Always lots of columns. And not much else."

Well, I didn't expect it to be ideal. So sanitation *will* be a problem.

"You need Porta-Potties for some reason?" the guard asks, as if reading my mind. "You going to be leasing a warehouse?"

"Something like that," I mutter.

"Well, we can have Porta-Potties and a water buffalo or two . . . you know, like a mobile water tank . . . brought in, if you want. We bring them in all the time for construction crews. One just finished up over on . . ."

"Yes, that'd be fine," I say. "Can you get them there tonight?"

"Tonight?" He laughs nervously. "That'd take some doing. And I'm just security. That'd take management and . . ."

"Can it be done tonight?"

He glances at Renny. The gangster sits, not speaking, looking pale like a . . . like a man who just lost a quart of blood.

"Mr. De Marco?" Beads of sweat (that have no correlation to the temperature in the truck) appear on the guard's forehead.

Renny says nothing.

The guard looks at me. Then he looks straight ahead as he turns the truck left. The sign says "Hushpuckney Road."

If Moira were here, she'd ask him his name and be gentle and diplomatic. She'd try to set him at ease and charm him.

I'm not Moira.

"Can it be done?" I ask again, more forcefully this time.

He stops the truck in front of double-truck loading bay labeled "90-26." Ahead, I can see a set of railroad tracks crossing Hushpuckney Road.

He puts the transmission into "Park" and turns his head and shoulders partway toward me. He looks at Renny again and then at my sword.

I couldn't do much with the sword in the cab of this truck, but it's not like I'm not dangerous without it.

He puts both hands up in a warding gesture and glances around nervously, not meeting my eyes. "Look. I know I'm supposed to show you every courtesy, since you've got the *card* . . ." *The passkey?* ". . . let you do pretty much whatever you want . . . but I can't do what you ask without attracting *attention*, you know? The Hunts . . . You know, the people who own this place? They don't know about . . . the *arrangement* we got with the Family . . . with Mr. De Marco, you know? They don't know about what goes on in that ware-house. Only security knows and . . . Mr. Dailey in management. I'd have to wake him up and . . ."

"Renny," I say, nudging the mobster next to me, but not taking my eyes off the guard, "tell this man to help us."

Renny turns his face toward the guard. "Orlando, give him whatever he needs." His voice is flat, lifeless. "Whatever he needs."

This isn't Persuasion. Why's he acting like that? Does he still think he's going to turn into a vampire?

I nudge Renny again. "Tell him he doesn't want to make me angry."

"Trust me, Orlando," the gangster says, his tone devoid of inflection of any kind, "you don't want to piss him off."

All the color drains from the guard's face. "Yessir!" He looks at me, really looks at me, for the first time. "Right away, sir! Anything you say! Not a problem! Not a problem at all! You can count on me!" He smiles wide, but his eyes are filled with fear. "You know," he says, never breaking his terrified rictus smile, "I got a kid—a little boy."

"There are children in that cave," I say, making no attempt to hide the loathing I feel. "But you know that, don't you?"

He hesitates and then nods slightly, still maintaining a forced smile.

"And maybe," I say, giving him a hardened look, "someday you'll be able to look your son in the eye and tell him that *tonight* was the night you started to do the right thing."

His ghastly smile falters.

"Now, call your Mr. Dailey," I say. "Wake him up. Make the arrangements." I grin. It's not a pleasant smile. I don't think, judging by Orlando's expression, that my smile could scare him any more, even if I were showing my fangs. "I suggest you hurry. You don't have much time."

He begins to scramble out of the truck.

Make that I don't have much time.

Dawn is coming.

Chapter 27

Moira

D aniel, tell them to stop here and wait." I look at the boy, one of only two people in this entire population who understands English. "Canst thou do that, laddie? Ach! Canst thou do that, *lad*?"

The bright-eyed child with the curly brown hair looks up at me and nods enthusiastically. "Yea, I can do that." He releases my hand and turns, facing back down the tunnel. "Stobyo! Stehna!" His voice is bonnie and clear with just a wee hint of a childlike nasal quality.

The column of people, standing two abreast, had already stopped—they halted when I did—but I'm worried they may bunch up. Aye, they are bunching up, but nae excessively . . . yet. The column stretches out of sight, around a curve. The odor's nigh overwhelming, especially here in the confines of the tunnel. The heat of the bodies of the people and the sheep causes the stench to travel up the shaft, assaulting my nostrils. In fact, I nearly missed the dried, but recent trail of urine winding its way down the passage.

And, amid the stench, the sweet scent of evil human blood.

"Keep the people here, Daniel." I say to the boy, as he beams up at me. I speak slowly, choosing my words carefully, nae because I think the boy slow witted, rather because I have to stick to biblical terms. "I am going to go on for a short distance. I shall return . . ." I search my mind for a word he'll understand. "I shall return anon." *That word's only used twice that I can recall. Will he know it?*

He nods and smiles, turning back to face the column of people and animals.

Now to the matter at hand, lassie.

Someone's been here.

I'm pretty sure whoever was here is now gone. The trail of dried urine *could* mean that someone merely relieved himself, but given the scent of blood . . . that could mean he encountered Carl or *Carl* encountered *him.* 'Tis nae uncommon for prey to lose control when confronted by one of our kind.

I wish my laddie would return. He's been gone longer than I thought

he'd be. Far longer. It's been over two hours. And our phones dinnae func-
tion in this hellish place.

He has to be all right! He has to be!

I nearly lost him once tonight. 'Tis almost more than I can bear, being
separated from him now.

*Father, I ken that we're going to die—and that right soon—but please, Heavenly
Father, let us die together!*

Neither of the prophecies say anything about being together when the
end comes. *Let it be together!*

I need to investigate quickly, make certain 'tis safe to continue, and then
get these people moving again.

Besides, even with the help of the lad here and Esther, his mother, who's
at the end of the line . . . even with their help, herding all these people and
their sheep is a massive undertaking. We have to move quickly, but I'm terrified of the possibility of a stampede in this confined space.

I continue up the tunnel, following my nose. My ebony sword of truth is
in my hand, gleaming in the light of the fluorescent tubes above.

There! A spray of dried blood on the wall and floor . . . and a bloody par-
tial shoeprint. More footprints going up the tunnel. Whoever made these
traveled under his own power. Carl was here, I'd wager. He encountered one
or more evil mortals. Blood was spilt—mortal blood. There's nae spoor of
vampire blood.

A crumpled handgun lies nearby, as does a golden crucifix and . . .
What's that? A child's squirt gun?

If I'm reading the signs aright, Carl was nae wounded—*I thank thee, Father, for that!*—and he encountered one or more mortals who were *expecting* to
encounter vampires, but did nae ken how to truly protect themselves.

A squirt gun, though? Why a squirt gun?

How I wish I could talk to Carl! What can have kept him?

Dawn is coming! We're running out of time!

I dinnae wish to be trapped in this subterranean Hades all day.

"Daniel?" I call back down to the laddie. "Canst thou hear me?"

There's nae reply save the bleating of the sheep and roar of twelve hundred voices speaking in hushed tones.

Of course, he cannae hear me over that din.

I fly down the tunnel until I can see the laddie and the head of the pro-
cession of the people of Esther. *"The Tribe of Esther."* Carl asked me to come
up with a name for them. Esther seemed pleased. She simply calls them "the
people."

"Come hither, lad," I say, motioning him to proceed. "Get them going!"

He smiles. "Wegoouna!" The troop begins to move again, with little Daniel at their head. He looks like a wee general leading an army . . . an army
composed mostly of girls and pregnant women. That illusion is shattered as

he begins to caper and dance about as he goes. "Wegosna!" he shouts again. That cry is echoed and passed away down the tunnel. Even the sheep seem to take up the shout as their bleating intensifies.

A wee Moses leading the children of Israel.

'Tis just as when we began this exodus out of the cave and into the tunnel. I dinnae know how much the Tribe understands, but I tried to explain our plan to Esther: to move to a temporary shelter for the day, and then move to another place outside afterward. She in turn tried to explain it to them. From the brevity of her explanation, I wondered if she simply didn't bother to translate everything or if she lacked vocabulary in the degenerate tongue of the cave. After listening to their speech, so often whispered (I can only assume out of habitual fear of punishment), I began to ken wee bits of it here and there. It seemed to my ears to be simply a corrupted form of the dialect of black slaves.

As the Tribe gathered their few possessions, I learned what I could from Esther. The Tribe are all descendants of runaway slaves . . . bred with vampires, of course. According to the tales handed down to Esther from her ancestors, Shep lured them to this place.

"He said it was a road to freedom," Esther told me. "He said he was the Kondukka. He said he would take our fathers and mothers on the unnagro rayro to the promised land. He spake falsely. He led our fathers and mothers into the pit."

I pondered this for a wee tick, trying to divine her meaning, and then it dawned on me. "You mean Shep said he was a conductor on the underground railroad?*"*

Esther simply shrugged.

Aye, I thought, he did lead them "underground."

My contempt for that monstrous fiend was nigh unbearable. He was like Michael Beaumont to the tenth degree.

And to think I once, for one brief moment, felt pity for the horrid creature!

Trusting Daniel to lead the Tribe up the tunnel, I turn about and fly on ahead. I should be getting near the door, near the exit into the warehouse, the door marked "Vault 17C."

Ach! The air in here is so stagnant. There's nary a whiff of circulation! Before long, I'll have people passing out from lack of oxygen.

I'll speed on ahead and open the door . . .

And suddenly the air changes. 'Tis sweeter, purer up ahead.

Someone has opened the door!

Carl!

I rush ahead to meet him, grinning like a daft fool!

And fly nearly right into the first of three men, spaced about ten yards apart, walking in a low crouch. They're all armed with wicked-looking automatic rifles.

For a moment, I hover there, frozen, as the barrels of all three weapons zero in on my heart.

There's nowhere to run, no way to escape.

How can I protect the people behind me? They'll be slaughtered!

Still pointing his weapon (complete with grenade launcher) right at my heart, the foremost man says, "Moira Morgan?"

What?

"Moira Morgan?" he repeats.

"Aye," I say, realizing I had forgotten to breathe.

"Stand down!" He shouts, lowering his rifle.

"Stand down!" The cry is repeated by each man in turn. I hear five distinct voices in addition to the foremost man.

At least six of them.

All three rifles are pointed at the floor of the tunnel, away from me. I can see another man, similarly armed, coming into view from farther up the passage.

The foremost man now rises to his full height. "Lieutenant Todd, ma'am. You're husband sent me."

I blink at him stupidly. "Ye're . . . the Marine? Lieutenant Todd, the Marine? Lieutenant Ericson's . . ."

"Aye, ma'am." He nods once. "Ericson's CO."

I breathe a huge sigh of relief and let my feet settle to the tunnel floor.

Carl's OK. "Am I ever glad to see ye, lads!"

"We're here to escort you and your . . . charges to another warehouse, but we need to get moving."

"Aye, that we do," I say, "but there's nae room for ye to do aught but lead the way out."

He nods, "Aye-aye, ma'am. We'll secure the outer warehouse and await you there." Turning around, he calls out, "Clear the tunnel! Spinelli, on point!"

The other Marines turn about and retreat up the passage, moving quickly in that crouching, ready posture, their weapons pointing the way.

Todd, however, hangs back, remaining in sight.

He and I wait, as I watch the other Marines pass around a bend and out of sight.

Ere long, Daniel and the Tribe catch up to us. Nary a one of them seem to take any particular notice of the heavily armed Marine.

Todd takes in the sight of the sheepskin-clad people, only a twitch of his nose betraying any reaction. Then he turns and proceeds up the tunnel, crouching with his rifle sweeping back and forth.

As he marches along beside me, Daniel beams at me. *I wonder how often he's been used to satiate the lusts of one of Lilith's Children? How he reminds me of my wee Ben!*

♦ ♦ ♦

As I exit the tunnel door, I count twenty Marines. They're armed to the teeth with automatic rifles, side arms, grenade launchers, grenades, and dirks.

Lieutenant Todd is closest to the door of Vault 17C. He nods at me and says, "The warehouse is secure, ma'am." Glancing over his shoulder, he calls out, "Polazhynets! Front and center!"

A tall Marine with broad cheekbones and intense eyes trots up. From the name and the facial structure, I'd say he's of Slavic extraction. He does nae salute (probably because none of these men are wearing military uniforms), but his manner is that of the consummate soldier. "Aye-aye, sir!"

I glance behind me. The Tribe and their sheep, with Daniel at their head, begin to pour out of the tunnel, like floodwaters from a drainpipe.

"Sergeant," Todd says, addressing the tall Marine, "corral these people and their animals. Be courteous, but firm. Once you have them contained, get moving back to the nine-zero warehouse complex. Understood?"

"Aye-aye, sir!"

"Dismissed."

"Aye-aye, sir!"

"Uh, Sergeant?" I say, but the tall man does nae respond to me. So I say to Todd, "Lieutenant?"

"Polazhynets!" Todd barks. "Belay!"

The intense Marine turns back.

Daniel, looking about him in wide-eyed wonder and, aye, perhaps terror, spies me and runs to my side. He puts his little hand in mine, but continues to gaze frantically around him.

"Sergeant," I say, turning to Polazhynets, "these people, all save two, cannae speak English." I point at Daniel, who seems to be trying to hide behind my leg and sheathed sword. "This laddie here speaks it . . . well e-nough, at least. He can translate for ye. His mother also speaks English, but she's at the rear of the column. Ye could use them to translate for ye."

The big Marine glances at Todd, who nods. "Aye-aye, ma'am," Pola-zhynets says.

I kneel down and pull the laddie around in front of me. "Daniel, the people are filled with fear. These men will aid thee. Thou must go with them. And thou, art thou unafraid?"

He nods curtly. "I am unafraid." His wide eyes, big as teacups, tell a different story.

"Good lad," I say. "Daniel, this is Sergeant Polazhynets. He is here to lead thee to a place where thou wilt wait, and then thou wilt be taken to another place of safety."

"I desire to remain with thee," he says.

"Aye, lad. I know thou desirest to remain with me. But thou must go with him. He will lead thee and thy people. He is in need of thine aid."

"Mine aid?"

"Aye. Thou must speak to the people, as Aaron did for Moses. Wouldst thou do this? They are afraid. Be thou of good courage, and aid him."

He nods.

I stand and, taking Daniel by the hand, lead him to the tall Marine. "Sergeant, take his hand."

Polazhynets, wrinkling his nose, stares at the laddie's wee hand warily.

"Go on, sergeant," I say to the tall man. "He'll nae bite ye. I might, but the lad will nae."

He looks up at me dubiously.

"'Tis a joke, laddie."

Polazhynets takes Daniel's hand. He nods, his jaw set in a hard line.

"And, Sergeant!" I say as the pair of them start to move toward the giant mass of humanity and sheep. "He only understands *biblical* English. I'd advise ye to limit yerself to that. Can ye manage it?"

He grimaces slightly. Then he nods. The two of them continue on. Polazhynets barks orders to the other Marines and then speaks, more softly, but stiffly to the lad. Daniel relays his instructions to the crowd.

The Marines, moving quickly, contain the burgeoning Tribe. They remind me of border collies trotting back and forth, barking, insisting, and nipping as they herd sheep. Border collies with rifles, grenades, and dirks.

Todd steps up beside me, and we watch as the tunnel continues to disgorge people and sheep from the bowels of the earth. Ere long, Esther emerges from the tunnel, and the stream of humanity ceases. She looks about frantically.

She's looking for her son.

"Esther!" I shout. She continues to look around. She cries out, "Daniel!" but cannae make herself heard above the din. I lift into the air.

One of the Marines gasps audibly, but then turns back to his business. Todd, who has remained close by me, shouts, "Mrs. Morgan!"

I ignore him.

I fly in Esther's direction. When she spies me, she cries, "My son! Where is my son?"

I get closer to her and shout, "Thy son is here. He is safe."

As I fly over the crowd, many hands reach up toward me, but I stay out of reach.

What do they think I am? Angel? Devil? Master? Shep taught these people to worship him and the other Children of Lilith as gods. I suppose that's how they see me: as something to be worshipped. They're trying to touch the divine. It makes me intensely uncomfortable, to say the least.

As I get directly above Esther, I reach down, grasp her arm, and lift her into the air with me.

In moments, she is reunited with her son. They've been separated for less than an hour, but to look at them, hugging each other frantically, 'twould seem to have been an eternity.

And very soon, that'll be me and my Ben. I dinnae want to die, but that'll be a joyous reunion!

Truth to tell, I've seen precious little affection among the Tribe. Aye, there's women with babes in arms and a few children being led by the hand, but most of the wee ones run about with nary an adult to take any notice. I dinnae see a single couple, nary a man and woman or a boy and girl holding hands.

They've been abused and corrupted from their youth. I've seen nae evidence that fam-ilies—a father, a mother, and children—exist among them.

"That's all of them!" Todd barks.

"Move out!" Polazhynets' voice is clear, even above the din.

And aided with commands translated by Esther and her son, move out they do. The Marines trot around the Tribe, reminding me again of border collies, with Polazhynets, Esther, and Daniel at their head.

Todd, however, remains at my side as I walk quickly outside the moving circle established by the other Marines. The lieutenant sweeps his weapon back and forth as he scans the area ahead and behind us. He points the rifle at the Tribe as often as nae.

"Would ye mind aiming that thing away from those poor wretches?" I say. "They've been through enough."

"I have two primary objectives here, ma'am." His sweeping pattern does nae change one bit. "And protecting these people comes second. Captain Morgan said to safeguard you at all costs. That coincides with my assignment here: to guard the paranorms."

"Ye do know what we 'paranorms,' as ye put it, are . . ."

"Vampires. I know that now. Ericson briefed me."

"And ye know that the woman you know as 'Empress' is . . ."

"Evil incarnate. Aye, ma'am. She murdered Marines."

"And ye know that my husband and I are . . ." This time I pause, waiting for him to finish my sentence. He does nae disappoint me.

"You're the real deal. The good guys. I trust Ericson."

"Ye trusted that general of yers . . . that General Brooks."

His expression hardens. "The general will be called to account. He has betrayed his fellow Marines and the ideals of the Corps."

"But ye trust Ericson?"

"Aye, ma'am. And even if I had reason to question his word, you and the Captain are . . . different. You *feel* different. In my gut, I know you're worth protecting, worth laying down my life for. I trust my gut."

I stop where I am.

Instantly, Todd is at my side again. "What is it?"

"Ye're sweet," I say. I kiss him lightly on the cheek. "Thank ye, laddie."

He blinks for a moment, and a bit of delicious crimson colors his cheeks. 'Twould seem I've broken through his composure.

Then his expression hardens again. "We'd better get moving. We're falling behind."

"Aye, laddie. I agree. But I have nae intention of *following* this troop out of here."

Noting that his finger is on the side of his weapon, nae on the trigger, and that the rifle is pointed away from the Tribe, I fly behind him at vampiric speed. I place a hand under each of his arms, lift him into the air.

To his credit, he barely lets out a yelp. Quickly, I fly to the front of the group, carrying Todd below me. When we're about ten feet or so in front of the mass of people and animals and very near the warehouse exit, I set him down and then land beside him.

"Do a guy a favor next time and warn me, OK?" he growls.

"What'd be the fun in that?"

He grunts. Under his breath, he mutters, "And I'm supposed to protect her?"

I draw my sword. "Lead on, Lieutenant!"

♦ ♦ ♦

We hit a bottleneck at the warehouse exit. It takes a while to herd everyone through to the underground street outside. As soon as everyone's out of the warehouse, we start down the roadway. The confines of the street itself help to keep people and animals moving at a good rate.

Ahead, a semi rumbles past on a cross street.

Although some of the Tribe are a wee bit startled, I'm surprised to see that nobody seems particularly frightened by the huge and noisy machine. *I suppose most or all of them have, at one time or another, been transported aboard motorized vehicles such as that. They've been ferried to and from Lilith's foul court, there to be used and returned to the Farm.*

I hear another vehicle approaching from the same street. 'Tis a much smaller truck this time.

Instead of continuing past the intersection, though, it slows and comes into view as it rounds the corner. 'Tis a black security truck like the one Carl and I rode in earlier. I dinnae recognize the guard driving it. 'Tis nae the same man we encountered when we first arrived at SubTropolis.

Beside me, Todd drops into his ready crouching walk. He's nae aiming the rifle (which he calls an "M-4") and its grenade launcher at the approaching vehicle, but I have the distinct impression that he's ready to aim and fire in a fraction of a second.

The truck angles over to the right and stops at the side of the road.

Lieutenant Todd raises a hand over his head, and I hear shouts of "Halt!" and "Stobyo!" and the bleating of a thousand sheep as the Tribe slows, but does nae quite stop. The Marine Lieutenant quickly positions himself between me and the truck.

The vehicle door opens, and a uniformed guard steps out. His hand is nae on his holstered side arm, but 'tis nae far from it all the same. In his other hand, he's holding a video camera. He looks directly at me, points the camera, and nods. He begins to slowly, cautiously walk in our direction. His lips are moving, but even with my Seed-enhanced hearing, I cannae make out what he's saying over the noise of the Tribe.

But in my heart, I know what he is. He's one of that daft Brotherhood of Tobias. He's found his "redheaded she-demon."

"Halt right there!" Todd calls.

The guard stops where he is. He makes nae move for his weapon, but he continues to point the camera in my direction.

"Dr. Moira Morgan?" he yells.

Aye, my worst fears are confirmed. He's one of those fanatics; he knows who I am.

"Dr. Moira Morgan?" he shouts again.

I cannae see his eyes.

Keeping my eyes glued to his weapon, I nod.

"I'm a Brother of Tobias!"

"Aye!" I reply. "What d'ye want of me?"

"Thank heaven I've found you!" he cries.

He falls to his knees and lays the camera down.

'Tis nae what I expected.

Todd does nae relax, but neither does he raise his weapon.

The guard bows himself to the floor. "We didn't know it was you! We didn't know *you* were the angel of God! *You* slew the demon! Forgive us!"

Chapter 28

Moira

How may I serve you, blessed lady?" The guard remains prostrate on the floor. He's about twenty yards away.

Lieutenant Todd keeps his body between me and the guard, protecting me.

Behind us, the Tribe has finally ground to a halt, though they're far from quiet.

I dinnae know what to say to the prostrate guard. I expected him to try to shoot me, just as that lunatic Holdtenschmidt did at the hospital. *Was that only last night?* Instead the man's nigh worshipping me.

"Have him surrender his weapon, ma'am." Lieutenant Todd's words startle me from my thoughts.

"His weapon?" I nod, though Todd does nae see it. "Oh, aye." Raising my voice, I shout, "I'd feel more comfortable if ye'd relinquish your firearm."

The prostrate man stiffens. Then he lifts his head. "Why . . . Why would an angel of God fear an earthly weapon?"

Careful now, lassie! Ye're dealing with a fanatic! "I'm nae afraid for myself." I'm trying to keep my voice calm despite having to yell. "I fear for the safety of these innocents behind me. They're nae immortal as I am." *Dinnae overplay yer hand!* "I dinnae want anyone to be injured by imprudent gunfire."

He straightens up to a kneeling posture.

The Marine Lieutenant, his weapon pointed at the guard, shouts in a commanding voice, "Be advised, sir, that I am authorized to use deadly force. If you make a sudden or threatening move, you *will* be killed!"

"Why would an angel fear a gun?" the guard asks again, apparently oblivious to his peril.

"Stand down!" Todd orders.

"Dinnae shoot him, Lieutenant," I say. "I can handle this."

"Slowly unfasten your gun belt," Todd orders, "and leave it on the ground!"

The guard does nae comply. Instead he begins to rise to his feet.

Nae! Ye daft fool!

"Stay down!" the Marine orders. "I *will* fire!"

Even if I do manage to stop Todd from killing him, I've nae doubt that other Marines will also shoot.

I must diffuse this. "Lieutenant, I'm fast enough to disarm him before he can fire." *Truth be told, I'm nae certain of that.* "I dinnae want anyone being hurt. Let me deal with this."

The Marine does nae move a muscle. "My orders . . ."

"If ye fire, Lieutenant, or if any of yer men fire, I'll be between ye and this man here before the bullets hit." *That's nae true, lassie. Though a fair number of bullets'd hit ye before they stopped firing.*

"I believe you'll try, ma'am. I know you're fast, but . . ."

In an instant, I move between him and the guard.

Todd curses under his breath.

"I'll deal with him," I say just loud enough for Todd to hear.

"Why does an angel of the Lord need an armed escort?" the fanatic cries. I notice for the first time that the strap across the top of his weapon is un-snapped.

In a heartbeat, I close the distance between myself and the guard and snatch the man's side arm from its holster. I fling it away.

He stares at me, wide-eyed, fear and wonder striving for mastery in his face.

Grasping the front of his shirt near the neck, I hoist him off his feet. Dangling at the end of my arm, he's nae threat to anyone.

"I dinnae need an escort," I say. "I dinnae fear yer weapon." I shake my head from side to side. "And I'm nae an angel."

He grabs my forearm in both hands. He's a large man, and his hands easily encircle my arm. But he does nae kick or fight back. "What are you?"

"I am one of those ye seek to destroy, but I'm fighting on the side of the angels, fighting against my own kind. I seek to slay their Queen. Will ye help me?"

"You . . . You're a . . . demon?"

"Aye, but a repentant one."

"But . . . you don't have wings. You slew the winged one, the winged demon. Then Brother Holdtenschmidt tried to kill you and . . . Thank God he failed! After that, Father Superior, the head of our order, he realized we must have erred. Brother Holdtenschmidt tried to kill you, and you *still* saved his life. We realized that . . . that we were hunting the wrong . . ."

Out of the corner of my eye, I can see Lieutenant Todd approaching. I glance quickly in his direction. He has retrieved the guard's discarded weapon.

I look back at the man suspended above me. "What's yer name?"

"Dewey . . . Dewey Sparks." He grips my forearm tighter and wriggles a wee bit. "C-c-can you put me down?"

"Are ye willing to help me, Mr. Sparks? Help me to destroy the demons?"

He nods vigorously. "Oh, yes! Forgive me! Of course, I'll help you."

I lower him to the ground. "There's nothing to forgive."

He straightens his crumpled shirt and tucks it back in. "You're a demon, you say, but you're . . . on the side of the angels?"

"God works in mysterious ways, laddie."

Todd, standing a couple of yards to my right, says, "We need to get moving. The natives are getting restless, and the first deuces could be here any time."

Deuces? What the devil are deuces?

"Mr. Sparks," I say, "I dinnae have time to explain it all to ye just now." I point behind me. "These people here are the *food* supply for the demons. We must get them to safety. The armed escort, as ye put it, is for *their* protection, nae mine."

Todd grinds his teeth. "Ma'am . . ."

"Aye, lieutenant, I know. I think Mr. Sparks here can help us."

The guard nods vigorously again. "How may I serve?"

Someone screams behind me.

I whirl about. *Someone's hurt?*

Nae. 'Tis nae but a wee toddler, a girl, who's gotten away from her mother, away from the mass of the Tribe.

Todd curses under his breath.

In a flash, I run to the wee bairn and scoop her up in my arms.

The lassie squeals in delight. 'Tis a grand game to her.

I smile at her, and she smiles back. *How I ache for a bairn of my own! But such cannae ever be.* She has dimples, pretty brown eyes—like my Ben's—and a mop of curly brown hair. Aye, she's a bonnie wee thing.

'Tis nae difficult to identify the mother. She's the young woman struggling to get past the Marine who's blocking her path.

I deliver the bairn to her mother and turn about, dashing tears from my eyes.

Todd's standing right in front of me. "You OK, ma'am?" Doubtless he's keeping his eyes locked on Sparks, who has remained where we left him.

I smile at Todd, but 'tis a wistful smile, to be sure. "I'm grand, laddie." I wipe away another tear. "I just wish . . . I'm grand."

"Seriously, ma'am," he says, obviously getting back to business, "I don't need another man, and my unit's a tight-knit group."

"Dinnae worry, lieutenant. He's nae coming with us. I have something else in mind for our Mr. Sparks."

◆ ◆ ◆

The Marines begin to funnel the Tribe and their animals into the door of a warehouse. The image of border collies comes to my mind again, this time herding sheep into a sheepcote.

I still have nae seen hide nor hair of my laddie. And even if Carl happens to be nearby, I'd nae be able to hear him above the din of the Tribe.

Lieutenant Todd stays with me, of course, as the mass of sheepskin-clad people and their animals slowly pass inside. Todd gestures a "come-hither" to Polazhynets, who's overseeing the herding of the Tribe. The tall Marine sergeant trots over.

"It's your detail, sergeant," Todd says. "Get them secured and cover all the exits. I'm going to locate Captain Morgan. He's gotta be somewhere in this . . . mess."

"Over by the loading docks, sir," the Slavic-looking Marine says, tipping his head to the right.

The lieutenant nods and opens his mouth to speak, but I'm already moving in the direction the sergeant indicated.

I can hear Todd swear an oath. He sounds frustrated, and I'm sorry for that, but I've been separated from my dearie long enough. Let Todd follow as best he can.

Just beyond a slight curve of the street, I find a pair of raised loading docks, suitable for semis.

And there's Carl.

He's alive. We have a wee bit longer together in this world.

Carl seems to be having a less-than-friendly discussion with a frazzled-looking, balding man who, by the look of things, was awakened nae so long ago. The balding man does nae look at all pleased.

There's also a man, an *evil* man, sitting dejectedly on the floor next to Carl. This must be the man Carl encountered in the tunnel. Carl must have Fed. The man's just pale enough. He has nae wet himself, though, so there must have been one other as well. His blood calls to me, begging me to take it, but I force the call to the back of my mind, and focus my attention on my laddie.

Carl's eyes drift in my direction. Our eyes lock, and he smiles briefly, but turns his attention back to the discussion with the balding man. *He*, the man, does nae smell evil.

". . . assure you that neither I nor Mr. Hunt knows anything about these people!" the man says. "And Hunt Industries will not be held liable for . . ."

"How much are you being paid to look the other way, Mr. Dailey?" Carl's voice is low, laden with menace.

"How?" Dailey splutters. "What? How dare you? I had no knowledge . . . And I categorically deny . . ."

Carl growls. "You categorically deny what, Mr. Dailey?"

I dinnae think this Mr. Dailey has any concept of his peril.

Nae that Carl would hurt him.

Carl's reluctant to use Persuasion, I'm sure, or there'd likely be *nae argument occurring here.*

Dailey straightens himself and looks as if he's "putting on his dignity," as we used to say. "I categorically deny any knowledge of smuggling in this facility. And I categorically deny ever receiving any m . . ."

"Smuggling?" Carl looks as if he cannae believe his ears. "*Smuggling?* We're talking about human trafficking. We're talking about sexual slavery. We're talking about child rape. We're talking *murder*, Mr. Dailey."

The blood drains from the balding man's face. "Murder? Child r . . . I had no idea!"

"If you took one penny or turned a blind eye to any of this, that makes *you*"—Carl jabs Dailey with a finger—"an accessory. Your best chance is to do everything in your power to help these people . . . starting . . . right . . . *now*." Carl punctuates each word with an accusatory jab to the manager's chest.

Dailey's mouth works, but nae sound escapes it.

"Well, Dailey?" Carl whispers.

Still the man says nothing.

"Mr. Dailey," I say, and both of them turn their eyes to me. Dailey's are wide with panic and fear. "As we speak here, video evidence of what has gone on in this place, what has taken place under yer very nose and apparently with nae wee cooperation on yer part, is being posted on the Internet." *Thanks to Sparks and that daft Brotherhood.* "Soon 'twill be all over the news. The world will know about these poor, wretched souls. Would it nae be prudent, do ye think, to be expending all yer energy to right this wrong, by the time the press arrives?"

Dailey glances from Carl to me and back again. "Do I have a choice?"

Carl nods. "You always have a choice."

"Choose *wisely*," I say.

The man's shoulders slump. He suddenly looks to have aged a decade. "Whatever you need."

"Am I to understand, sir," Lieutenant Todd says, and now our eyes turn in his direction, "that you are *voluntarily surrendering* the use of this facility?"

Dailey looks lost, confused. "Surrendering?"

Todd enunciates, "Are you volunteering this facility as a staging ground for the evacuation of these refugees?"

"Y-yes." Dailey nods.

"Are you the manager of this facility and are you authorized to do this?" Todd sounds so formal.

I suppose he's trying to establish the legality *of what we're doing. Carl spoke truly when he said that honor is everything to these Marines.*

I can hear another truck approaching. Or is that two? More?

Dailey straightens up a wee bit. "I'm the general manager here. Whatever cooperation I can provide, whatever resources are under my control . . . Whatever it takes."

The lieutenant nods, apparently satisfied. "Good thing, because it looks like your security's already let my deuces through." He points to a small convoy of three military trucks on the other side of the mass of people and animals now being funneled into the warehouse.

"Deuces?" I mouth to Carl.

"Two-and-a-half-ton trucks," he whispers. "Deuces."

A dozen more Marines jump out of the back of the truck. These men are in combat fatigues, colored in the hues of the desert. And they're all heavily armed.

Why are Todd's men in civilian clothes and these men wearing uniforms?

"Todd!" a Marine shouts from the back of one of the trucks . . . one of the *deuces*. I can see the officer's insignia on his cap. I believe that's the emblem of a major or lieutenant colonel. Carl would know the difference. I cannae tell. In any case, 'tis certain he outranks Lieutenant Todd.

Todd waves and shouts, "Over here, sir!"

The newcomer (who's armed with only a side arm and a dirk) jumps from the back of the truck and attempts to make his way through the thronging members of the Tribe. The glimpses I can catch of his face clearly show him wrinkling his nose and grimacing. A pair of uniformed Marines attempts to follow him, but apparently finding it difficult, encumbered as they are with their heavier weapons. "Make a hole, people! Make a hole!" one of them cries as he holds his rifle above his head. The crowd does nae heed him nor do they seem to understand. Soon the hapless Marines, including the officer, are shouting, "Stop that!" and, "Watch your hands!" and the like.

Aye, they've got their work cut out for them, herding and watching over these people. I should nae envy them, but I'd rather endure their plight than have to face our prophesied death.

I look at my dear husband. We're going to die, but now we're together again. Well, as together as we can be in the midst of all this bedlam.

At least ye had one last moment together before ye came here. Be grateful for that, lassie.

"Sitrep!" the uniformed officer shouts as soon as he emerges from the tumultuous sea of humanity.

Todd remains by my side, but he turns toward his superior. "Best estimate: we've got twelve hundred souls, two thousand sheep."

"Twelve hundred and seventy," I say just loud enough for him to hear.

"Close enough for government work," Todd mutters.

"Nae, laddie," I say, my tone a bit sharper, perhaps, than it should be, "twelve hundred and *seventy*. Every last one of them counts. Every wee bairn matters."

He nods. "My apologies, ma'am."

"Ach! Ye meant nae harm, laddie. I did nae mean to snap."

Todd shakes his head. "But you're right. They're people, not animals. They deserve better."

The uniformed officer strides up to us. The other two Marines, having broken free from the Tribe, run to catch up. "I know the numbers, lieutenant," the officer says. "Your men?"

"Three casualties, sir," Todd replies. His expression's grim, but his tone all business. "Ortiz, Kowalski, and Hall are MIA, presumed KIA. Ericson's acting liaison to the Papa-Novembers offsite."

The face of the other officer betrays nae emotion. "Ericson lost his squad?"

"Aye, sir," Todd replies. "Ericson would've died too, if he hadn't been forcibly evacked by a Papa-November. There were massive casualties among the Papa-Novembers as well."

"The exact nature of these Papa-Novembers you're still unable to reveal?"

"Aye, sir."

"Thought as much," the officer replies. "I called General Brooks to confirm your authority to commandeer my men and equipment. Woke him up, just like you did me. And I take great pleasure in informing you, Marine, that the good general was not a happy camper."

"Sir!" Todd's composure evaporates in a look of alarm. "Colonel, I have reason to believe the general is . . ."

"Compromised?" the colonel interrupts him. "Acting under duress? Maybe a traitor to the Corps?"

Todd stands there with mouth agape.

"Now, before you get your panties all in a bunch, Todd," the colonel continues, "I contacted NCIS after the last 'sudden mass transfer' of the entire Honor Guard detachment to damned-if-anyone-knows-where." His face hardens. "General Brooks has been under investigation, Marine. Are you aware that every single member of your unit, present company excluded *so far*, has vanished without a trace?"

Todd's expression is grim. "Aye, sir. I was informed only tonight."

"Well, Todd, I'll use every resource at my disposal to help here. But, I'm gonna need you to tell me what the hell is going on. Brooks isn't telling me squat, and I'm sticking my neck out here."

"Sir, I . . ."

"I'm not asking you to betray your oath, Marine, or reveal classified information, but you *will* be questioned by NCIS, and I can assure you that *they* have sufficient clearance, and I *will* be sitting in on that debriefing. At least tell me who these *refugees* are."

"Sir, I regret to inform you that my orders do not allow me to . . ."

"Colonel?" I say, smiling widely. I glance at the name tag sewn on his camouflage tunic. "Colonel Evans?"

"Ma'am?" he says turning to me.

"Moira Morgan," I say extending my hand.

He shakes it. "Lieutenant Colonel Tyrone Evans. I assume you're one of the Papa-Novembers?"

"That I am, Colonel," I say, fingering the basket hilt of the black sword at my side. "Let me make this easy on you and the lieutenant. I'm a vampire. My husband"—I point at Carl who's still conversing, albeit less combatively, with Mr. Dailey—"and I are both vampires. But we're the good guys. We're going to destroy the Queen of the vampires and end her six-thousand-year reign on Earth, thereby destroying all vampires, ourselves included. These poor wretches ye see here have been kept and bred as a renewable food supply. They've lived underground in a cave attached to this very facility. Their ancestors were imprisoned there before the Civil War. We're rescuing them. And ye're very sweet to be helping out."

Evans stares at me in shock and, aye, horror.

I turn to a stunned Lieutenant Todd. "I believe that covers the long and the short of it, laddie. Ye've nothing more to reveal. Now ye've delivered me safe and sound to my husband. And I thank ye heartily. My husband and I must be off. We must rejoin the others of our kind who are fighting on the side of the angels, and we must fly before the Sun turns us to ash."

I turn to go, but Todd manages to break through his shock to say, "But, ma'am, if you go, we have no . . . we have no authority to protect these people."

Now, 'tis my turn to look shocked. "Ye cannae be serious!"

"As a heart attack, ma'am." He gives a decisive nod. "My orders allow me to use deadly force to protect the paranorms. It is illegal for a Marine to use deadly force in what is essentially a civilian law-enforcement issue. I've got no right to protect and defend and detain these people on U.S. soil. If you or your husband stays, we can protect you *and* them along with you. But once you go, before we can get them transferred to a military reservation, they're free to go where they will, and I cannot use force to protect them."

"But we cannae stay here! The Sun'll be rising soon!"

"Ma'am, I'm authorized to protect *you* as a vital national security asset, not them."

"But yer authorization came from a corrupt source."

"I'm authorized to protect you," he reiterates, "not them."

"Vampires?" Evans says. "The Papa-Novembers are . . . *vampires?*"

The two Marines on either side of him exchange dubious looks.

"Aye, vampires," I say. I open my mouth and my fangs extend. "Convinced, laddie?"

The colonel visibly starts and puts a hand on his holstered side arm. Both his guards point their weapons at me.

"Stand down," Todd says.

I force my fangs to retract, and the two Marines hesitantly point their rifles down again.

"*This* is the 'national security asset' you're ordered to protect?" Evans points at me, but glances between me and the lieutenant. His hand has nae left his pistol.

"Aye, sir," Todd replies. "Actually, we *were* guarding the murdering bitch vampire Queen. These two and a couple of others are trying to take her down. She's had Brooks under her control apparently . . ."

"National security assets?" Evans interrupts. He takes his hand off his weapon and jabs a thumb in the direction of the Tribe. "And these poor devils are their *food* supply?"

"Aye, sir," Todd replies. "The food supply for the Queen and her . . . people. Though not for Mrs. Morgan and her group."

The colonel nods. "That makes them supplies in *support* of your assets."

"Laddie," I say, anger rising, "dinnae refer to them that way. They're *people*, nae vittles."

Todd chuckles. "No, ma'am. You're right, of course, but that *definition* means I have authority to *guard* them, detain them, and, if necessary, use deadly force to defend them!"

"Ye mean . . . Carl and I can go and leave ye to it?" *The logic of the military mind! I cannae follow it. But as long as 'tis sufficient to . . .*

"Aye, ma'am," Todd says. "But I want your *word*, ma'am, that we'll be there to fight alongside you tomorrow night."

"You have it, Marine!" *'Tis Carl!* He's evidently finished with Mr. Dailey. "It'll be an honor to have you there. Empress won't know you're coming to the party."

"But, laddie," I say, "she may at that. Colonel Evans here telephoned General Brooks."

Carl frowns and then extends his hand. "Colonel."

Evans looks at Carl's hand and then stares hard at his face. "You a vampire too?"

Carl and I exchange a quick glance. "I've revealed what we are to Colonel Evans. 'Twas to expedite communications, as ye'd say, since Lieutenant Todd still felt bound to secrecy."

"O . . . K," Carl says. "That's what I am: a vampire. Carl Morgan, Captain, USAF-retired." Carl's still extending his hand.

Evans continues to stare hard at Carl's face. "I consider myself to be a good judge of character. I'm having a tough time reading you and your wife. I feel an *urge* to just take you at your word. Is that something . . . supernatural?"

"Yeah," Carl replies. "Sort of. The fact is I could probably compel you to help us, but I really hate doing that. It makes me . . . uncomfortable."

Evans still has made nae move to take Carl's hand. "So you could manipulate us into helping you?"

"Probably, but I won't."

Evans nods his head in my direction. "Could she do it?"

Carl nods. "Yes, sir."

Evans shakes his head slightly. "Well, she hasn't, least as far as I can tell. My gut says to trust you." He takes Carl's hand and shakes it firmly. "Tyrone Evans."

"Time's running short, Colonel," Carl says. "My wife and I need to rejoin our friends before the Sun rises."

"What?" Evans laughs mirthlessly. "Do you turn to dust?"

"Nae, we burst into flame," I say.

"I'll have Todd brief me then," Evans says.

Todd grimaces. "Actually, sir, I just learned the exact nature of the Papa-Novembers tonight."

"Figures," Evans says. "Anyway, I apologize for tipping Brooks off. He's under investigation by NCIS." He turns to me. "That's the Naval Criminal Investigation Service. Looking back, it was probably a boneheaded move. I was pissed at being dragged from my beauty sleep. But that's no excuse. And as we say in the Corps, excuses are like a ..." He glances at me. "My apologies, ma'am."

I give him a quizzical look. *What was that about?*

"Well," Carl says, "Brooks is another wild card we'll have to watch out for."

Evans nods. "We'll coordinate through Lieutenant Ericson. I assume he's with your group?"

"Yes, he is." Carl replies. "And that arrangement works for me."

"Is Ericson in any danger?" Evans asks.

Carl laughs grimly. "Colonel, we're at war with a six-thousand-year-old vampire Queen. I know Moira and I and the other two good-guy vampires with us aren't going to come out of this alive, even if we win. *Especially* if we win. Ericson knows what he's getting into. This war has already cost the lives of three good Marines. So"—Carl shakes his head—"I can't vouch for his safety."

"Death in combat is one thing." The colonel nods in Carl's direction. "I meant, is he in any danger from *you*? I mean, you might be the 'good guys,' but you're still bloodsucking vampires, aren't you?" He shakes his head and mutters, "I can't believe I'm talking with two vampires, straight out of a Bela Lugosi movie."

"Colonel," I say, "I have nae killed a mortal in more than two and a half centuries." He looks at me, a raising of his eyebrows and a sudden quickening of his pulse—his delicious blood—the only betrayal of his shock at my words. "And my husband has nae ever taken a life, save in combat."

Evans takes a deep breath. "I'm going to help you, and I'm going to fight beside you, 'cause my gut's telling me to trust you, but if I'm going to act on faith, *somebody* who knows *something* better survive this war of yours in order to answer my questions, or I'm going to die one very frustrated Marine!"

He turns to Todd and says, "Lieutenant, I expect to be told where and when to place my men. And no arguments. I'm willing to go out of uniform, if that suits you and your orders. *You* make the call on deployment—this is your op—but I'm coming along for the ride with all that can be spared from this baby-sitting detail."

And with that, he turns on his heel and bellows, "All right, Marines! Let's get 'em loaded up and move 'em out! I want the first batch loaded and gone in five minutes. I don't want to be at this all night!"

And the chaos begins.

And I thought 'twas bedlam before!

Marines are shouting, and sheep are bleating, and the low roar of the Tribe changes in pitch as Evans and his men begin splitting off part of the Tribe and loading them into the back of the olive drab, canvas-covered trucks. The people are hard enough to load, with many of them being pregnant, or mere lads and lasses. But the sheep! They have to be chased, gathered and then hefted into the truck beds. In the end, uniformed Marines are consigned to do most of the lifting.

Perhaps the next time, they can back the trucks up to the loading docks, but 'tis nae practical with half the Tribe still in the subterranean street.

Meanwhile, Polazhynets and his men continue to herd the bulk of the Tribe into the warehouse. Lieutenant Todd takes his leave of Carl and me, and supervises the Marines in civilian garb as they labor to move the Tribe to the relative safety of temporary confinement.

"Do not forsake us!"

I spin around to see Esther, broken free from the Tribe and the Marines guarding them. She throws herself at my feet and grasps me by the knees. Daniel's close behind her. "Why dost thou forsake us?"

"We are nae forsaking you," I say. "These men . . . men of arms will deliver you to another place of safety. There you will be fed and clothed and taught so that you might be truly free."

"But they desire to feed us to the great iron beasts!" Her face is filled with horror, her voice pleading. "The beasts take us ever to the house of pleasure and feeding, to the temple of the demons. Many return and many do not."

The "beasts?" Does she mean the trucks? The deuces? "Do ye mean . . . Dost thou speak of the . . . wagons? The chariots?"

Tears spill from her eyes. "Yes, blessed one. The chariots of iron!"

I pull her to her feet and give her my best comforting smile. "Nae, Esther. The chariots will take you to a place of safety. You will be safe from the demons. These men of arms will protect you. Have no fear."

"Dost thou swear that we will be safe?"

"Yea, child. As safe as we can make you."

Sergeant Polazhynets is there behind her. "I'm sorry, ma'am. She was too quick."

"Aye, laddie. 'Tis fine." I look at Esther and at Daniel. "Suffer yourselves to be led by these men. They will bring you to safety and freedom. Have faith."

She dashes away her tears. "I will have faith in thee."

"Nae, lady," I reply. "Have faith in God alone."

"He sent thee to us."

"Yea, I believe He did. Now, go with these good men."

"Wilt thou visit us again?" Daniel asks, looking at me with moist eyes.

"Nay, child. God has called me to another place. God be with thee." Now I'm wiping away tears. "God be with thee."

With urging from the tall Marine, Esther and the boy turn and go. But they look back in my direction a few times.

"I can feel it!" The voice comes from behind Carl. 'Tis the man with the evil blood. He's still sitting on the floor. "I'm changing! I'm turning into a bloodsucker!"

What's this?

Carl rolls his eyes and raises his eyebrows in exasperation. "I've told him enough times, but he's just not buying it. Hi, by the way." He gives me a quick kiss.

"Laddie . . ." *Ach! The evil blood's so close. 'Tis difficult to keep my head!* "Why on Earth did ye nae Persuade him and send him on his way to the police?"

"That's what I was planning to do, at least as soon as he connected me to the people who run this place. But now, I'm worried about what the Mafia might . . . what role they might play when we . . . when we meet with Lilith tonight. I think Renny here could be of some use to us. I'm just not sure how."

"What were they doing in the tunnel? I assume 'twas more than one of them."

"Two. They were going to blow the tunnel and seal the people in. Erase the evidence of the mob's involvement. Did you ever come up with a name for them?"

"Aye. I've been calling them 'the Tribe of Esther,' at least in my own noggin."

Carl looks dubious and then nods. "'The Tribe of Esther'? I guess that works. Not terribly original, though." He grins that lopsided grin of his.

'Tis a wicked, mocking grin.

"Aye, and ye're such a wordsmith, laddie!" I say. "I'm surprised ye did nae invent some incomprehensible military acronym!"

His grin widens. "How about T-O-E?"

"Toe?"

"Tribe Of Esther," he says, feigning innocence.

"I'll show ye *toes*, laddie. Five of them! On your backside!"

"You *could* do that, but I've got a better idea," he says, taking me in his arms and kissing me tenderly.

"Seriously!" the evil man, Renny, moans. "I can feel it happening! I'm so hungry. I need to drink blood, don't I? Oh, man! Just kill me! Kill me, quick! Please don't let me become one of you! But, if I die . . . I still turn into a vampire, right? I am so screwed!"

"We want the Mafia out of the picture, do we nae?" I whisper to Carl.

"Ideally, yeah." He smiles. *Ah, that lopsided grin of his! It makes my knees go weak!* "OK, pretty lady, what do you have in mind?"

I reach down and grasp the lapels of Renny's trench coat in my fist. Lifting him in the air, I look into his terrified eyes. I dinnae use Persuasion, for I want him to act of his own free will, but I do want his undivided attention. "Ye wish to avoid becoming a vampire, ye murderous thug? Do ye?"

He looks so terribly frightened, but he does nae even try to escape. "Yes! Anything!" He's weeping. "I'll do anything!"

"Aye, then. This is what ye must do . . ."

Chapter 29

Tony

The howl of rage and frustration seems to reverberate through the farmhouse, the huge wooden frame shaking like an outhouse caught in a tornado. At least that's what it feels like. Logically, I'm pretty sure even *Lilith* can't make the whole house tremble, but it seems as if the place could disintegrate around us in the maelstrom of her fury.

As her scream fades, so does the shaking of the house.

She began making phone call after phone call once we arrived here (that is, after murdering the older couple who lived here and drinking their blood). But every single time, every single call (other than the one she made to arrange for some other number to be forwarded here), *nobody* answers. And with each successive failure, her fury mounts. At first the calls were ten digits, making them domestic calls. But for hours now, they've been eleven digits, maybe more. So she's been calling overseas. And still nobody answers.

The only break in this pattern was when the phone actually rang and she got to speak to someone on the other end, someone with whom she had no patience. Gone was all pretense at seduction, at civility. She spoke with blatant scorn and loathing. She spoke softly so that I couldn't catch anything of what was said, until she abruptly growled, "Now, worm!" Then there was silence for a period.

Then she was all honeyed sweetness and seduction and condescension again—the beloved Queen gently chiding one of her loyal subjects. And I could hear her well enough to catch the gist of her side of the conversation.

She was talking to Carl!

That meant that Carl had survived the explosion at the hotel! I wondered if anyone else made it out. Moira had to be alive. She had to! The two of them had to live to fulfill the Prophecy! They had to live long enough to kill this monster, this demon in the shape of a woman!

Were they able to get Kathleen out? Was she still alive? Did I dare hope for a second that Kathleen was safe? Free and safe?

". . . Sergei Ivanov Tupelev." She was talking about Sergei.

They were negotiating a prisoner exchange! Sergei for me. For a brief moment, a moment I was deeply ashamed of, I hoped Carl would agree, but then I realized I wanted to keep Sergei away from Lilith, to give him a chance at repentance.

Me? I wasn't worth saving.

But with that moment came a glimmer of hope. If they were negotiating for Sergei, others might have survived.

I was stunned when I realized that Carl had actually agreed *to the exchange.*

Why?

And still no one answers.

No.

Wait.

Lilith's face lights up as she holds the old black handset to her ear.

Somebody answered.

"Yoh-boh-seh-yoh! Joo-een-un iss-oh?" A pause. *Asian language of some kind.* "Chohn-hwah-roh jab-ah!" Another pause. "Bah-lee! Bah . . ."

Another scream of fury.

I'm *sure* the house shakes this time. It can't be my imagination. A chunk of plaster falls from the ceiling and crashes onto the corpse of the old man in the living room. I can see the two bodies from the kitchen. Some plaster falls onto my head and some into my lap, but I can't move to avoid it. My wrists, bound by twisted rods of wrought-iron that used to be the poker and shovel from the fireplace, are secured to the arms of an old wooden chair. My feet are free, but even if I tried to stand up with the chair on my back, I couldn't move quickly enough to escape.

Lilith slams the phone onto the cradle of the simple, old-fashioned telephone. Shards of plastic and scraps of metal fly as the phone explodes in countless pieces. The sturdy, wooden counter top cracks.

"Ma chosek peni ha-maim!"

I have no idea what that means, but I'm sure it's Adamic, the First Tongue, as she calls it. With a pang of guilt and self-loathing, I realize I was tempted for a moment to ask her to translate.

Seeming to calm herself, Lilith carefully unplugs the phone cord from the wall above the kitchen counter. She scoops the remains of the shattered device onto the floor and walks into the living room. Her blood red gown, dirtied and wrinkled from our flight through the tunnel and through the air, sways as she walks. I can't seem to stop my eyes from following her. Even now, with her anger barely in check, she seems to glide and sway in a manner meant to draw the eye. The way her luscious black hair bounces as she . . .

My children are dead, and maybe Kathleen too, and I'm still unable to take my eyes off this creature?

Pathetic!

She kicks the corpse of the old woman aside rather than walk around her. Even that callous move reminds me of the grace of a dancer.

Now she's out of sight.

And I feel a pang of loss.

In a moment, though, she returns with another telephone, as black and old-fashioned as the one she destroyed. She plugs it in and sets it down on the cracked counter top, and sparing me a brief glance where our eyes lock, she smiles. "Miss me, lover?"

And she's transformed. Beautiful as she is when she isn't looking at me, now she's female beauty beyond compare. She's Kathleen and Lilith and every glamorous movie star, every pretty teacher I ever drooled over as a kid, all rolled into one irresistible package. However, Miss Harden, my first grade teacher, my first crush, never looked so voluptuous, so blatantly sexual. I can't tell or remember if Lilith's eyes are brown or blue or green or black or if her hair is brown or blonde or black or red. Sometimes, even the luscious color of her skin is hard to pin down—creamy pink, honey brown, or . . .

She lifts the receiver of the phone and turns her attention away from me. Her smile's gone too.

And the spell is broken.

Black. Her hair's black. I remember now. And her eyes are brown.

Kathleen's hair. What color is Kathleen's hair? Her eyes? How could I . . . ?

Calm down, Tony. Think. You're an academic. You're supposed to be good with your mind. Just calm down.

Blue. Kat's eyes. They're blue. Blue like sapphires. And Kat's hair is blonde.

Lilith's just clouding your mind. *She's like The Shadow, "able to cloud men's minds."*

Actually, that might not be too far from the truth. When she looks me in the eye, her effect is overwhelming. When she looks away, when her attention isn't on me, I can think a little more clearly. Only, it isn't just when she's looking at me. When she's close, when her breath touches my skin, when her fingers caress my face . . . just the smell of her is . . . intoxicating. Even from here, with my mortal sense of smell, her scent is almost impossible to ignore.

Why doesn't her breath smell like blood? Why does it smell so sweet? Sam would know. I hope he's OK. He was so upset when I talked to him. How long ago was that? Just two nights? Less than thirty-six hours? It seems like forever.

It *was* forever. When I went to bed two nights ago, Abby and Little Tony were still alive. Two nights ago, Kat was still . . .

Heavenly Father! Watch over Kathleen! Please! Oh, please! I don't know if she's alive. But if she is, please watch over her!

I struggle against the twisted iron which binds my wrists, but it's no use. There's no give at all.

"Careful, lover." Lilith isn't looking my way, but I'm sure she can hear my efforts. She's listening after having dialed yet another number. What a memory she must have! Hundreds of phone numbers without looking anything up! "You wouldn't want to start bleeding. I've Fed well tonight, but I wouldn't be averse to dessert." She grimaces briefly—another failure—and hangs up the handset. "And once I get the Seed inside you, all your pathetic resistance will be gone." She lifts the handset again and begins to dial. "And I want you to give yourself to me *freely*." She turns her head and smiles at me, taking my breath away. "And you *will*, lover." She licks her luscious lips. "It is inevitable. No one can resist me. All fall to me in the end."

"All except Adam." My voice is barely a whisper.

She laughs. It is musical and disarming.

I played this card once before. It's not working this time.

She shakes her head, and her hair shimmers in the light of the kitchen bulbs. "You're no Adam, lover."

It's hard to breathe. . . . *no temptation so great . . .*

She purses her full red lips. "You're simply a man who has nothing left to live for . . . except *me*."

"And . . ." My voice falters. *She's all the way across the room, but her presence, her scent, her eyes . . .* "And you're a Queen with no subjects."

She frowns. It was a guess. A good guess apparently.

"What's the matter?" I'm trying to project confidence, but I can't carry it off. My voice sounds weak, even in my own ears. "Did I hit a nerve?"

She says nothing.

"You've been calling for hours," I say, "but you can't reach anyone. You're calling . . . whom? Your Cults around the world? You're cut off from your subjects, aren't you? And your Call, your psychic link with your Masters?" As she continues to frown, I'm able to force a little strength into my voice. "They aren't heeding your Call, are they?"

Her frown deepens, and her eyes . . . her lovely eyes—they're brown . . . Her eyes harden.

I manage a weak smile. "You're cut off. A Queen with no resources, with no followers. You're the Queen of nothing." *Maybe if I provoke her . . . she'll kill me. Then she won't be able to exchange me for Sergei. Maybe that'll save him.*

She smiles now, but her eyes remain flint. "I'm not just the Queen of the vampires, lover. I'm the Queen of the whole Earth. I have other subjects."

She turns back to the phone and dials a new number. A domestic number. She waits as it rings.

She smiles. Someone must've answered.

"Lieutenant? This is Empress. I'm ever so sorry for waking you, lieutenant, but I've had to relocate Night Palace yet again. I'm afraid you're going to have to send some of your handsome men immediately to my new location." She pauses. "Let me give you the new . . ." Her jaw drops. "What's that sound? Are those . . . . *sheep?*"

She slams the phone down again. "*Benim ha-Eli!*"

She dials another number, her face twisted in rage. "Brooks!" she snarls into the receiver. "Your pathetic, useless men have been turned again! If you ever wish to spend another night in my bed, you'll have to provide me with more reliable . . ." Fury is replaced by shock. "Who is this? Where's General Brooks? Put General Brooks on the phone!" A pause. "What do you mean, 'Detained'?"

She hangs up. "Taken my pretty Marines, have you, Carl? Well, I have other arrows in my quiver."

She dials again.

◆ ◆ ◆

A cornered tigress.

Cornered and extremely dangerous.

She paces the floor, dialing number after number, having fruitless conversation after fruitless conversation. I can't tell who she's talking to with every exchange, but I can identify some of them—the highway patrol, the FBI, a couple of governors, a mayor or two. All of them apparently—in spite of threats, both to body and reputation, and denial of privileges—all of them refuse to help.

After calling someone who sounds like a reporter of some kind, she stalks into the living room, kicks aside a corpse, and turns on a television. I can see the TV well enough, between her stomping back and forth in front of it. It's a cable news channel. I can't hear what's being said, but they're running a shaky video. It shows a large crowd of people and . . . *Are those sheep? Sheep? What's the significance of the sheep?* The crowd's walking down a wide tunnel. They're being led, escorted perhaps, by heavily armed men and a woman . . . with red hair and a sword!

That's Moira! She's alive! Carl and Moira are both alive!

I thank Thee, Heavenly Father, for that! Please let Kathleen be alive too!

The caption at the bottom of the screen says, "MYSTERIOUS COLONY FOUND IN KANSAS CITY CAVE." The image freezes and zooms in on Moira's face. Then the screen splits, and a black-and-white image appears on the left side. It's Moira from the footage of her battle with Müller at the Conference Center. The caption at the bottom now reads, "'BATTLING ANGEL' OF SALT LAKE CITY?" Eventually this pair of images is relegated to the upper right corner of the screen, and that display alternates with the video of Moira leading the crowd of people and sheep, all while a series of talking heads are shown on the left. The news ticker now reads, "Colony may have been underground since 1800s"

I have no idea what those people on TV are saying, but Lilith seems very upset by it. She keeps muttering. I can't catch a word of what she says, but it's obvious she's furious and . . . worried. She stops her pacing and hugs herself. She lets loose another primal scream. The farmhouse shakes again. There's no mistaking it this time. She *is* shaking the house.

Her fury is terrifying. If I could get free, I'd be cowering under the table.

She raises a fist to heaven and bellows, "You haven't got me yet, old man! I'm not finished! I'll go into hiding if I have to! I'll find other allies, other slaves! I still have the Light-Bearer! *He* still serves me. I can wait your prophesied ones out. I'll hunt them down and destroy them from the shadows. I can wait. Her *face* is all over the news. She cannot hide! They'll find her. They'll hunt her down, and then where will your precious Curse be? It'll be over, Father! Null and void! Broken! I will *win*. And when I return, it'll be in *all* my glory. I'll reign with horror and blood and majesty, and I'll destroy your impotent priesthood. I know where they are now! I'll slaughter them all and drink their blood! I'll seduce your precious chief apostle. He'll . . ."

She stops abruptly and collects herself.

She drops to her knees. She tilts her head back and raises her hands. She claps twice and shouts "*Shenah Mishphatu Phosferno!*"

Not again.

Lilith claps her hands six times and cries, "*Shenah Adenoi Helel!*" She lies on the floor, face-down with her arms extended, her hands turned up.

Once again, the light appears with a man-shape inside it. But this time, as the light dissipates, Lucifer makes no attempt at projecting majesty. Instead his demeanor is wary, almost cringing. "What do you want of me?" he says.

Now that the ritual is over, Lilith rises to her feet. There's no pretense at mocking subservience.

She's the dominant one here. "Find me the closest of my Children and bring him to me. There must be *one* nearby."

"What makes you think I can do that?" Lucifer's *whining*. "I'm not the omniscient one."

"Do not attempt to dissemble, Fallen One. The Host is everywhere. My army is denied me for the moment. Sergei Ivanov Tupelev is at the heart of it, I'm sure. Once I have him back, he'll reverse whatever command he has given. But for now, you and your Host of minions will be my eyes and ears. Find me the nearest Child and send him to me. Or her. It matters not. And when you've done that, find me the Unwilling and the Penitent. I want to know where they are. I want to know how many they have. You will bring me constant reports. *You* and no other, Serpent. I know you understand me, so go and obey."

The Devil stands still a moment, straightening his gold tie and then smoothing his hair.

"Now!" Lilith roars.

Satan bows his head and says, "Yes, Mistress."

He glances at me, and our eyes lock. I get the distinct impression that he's pleading with me again. *Deliver me.*

And he's gone.

Lilith stomps over to the phone and dials another number. Someone answers, and she commands, "Get me the Don. Now. Tell him it's the Queen. Drag him out of his bed." There's a short pause. "He's up? Well, then get him on the phone, worm!"

A long pause.

She smiles. "Johnny, I have need of your ..." A pause. Lilith looks confused. "What? What do you mean? The Covenant? I haven't broken the Covenant! What're you talking about?" Another pause. "That was not me or my ... No, it was not, I tell you!" Another pause. "The news? Johnny, I *own* the news ... Too much? Are you afraid? I'll teach you fear, little man! I will slaughter your whole wretched Family! I'll drink your blood after I slaughter your wife, your children, and your mistresses in front of your eyes! I'll ..."

She stops her tirade and stares at the phone, disbelief and shock plain on her face. "*Mishphatu Phosferno sher lif!*" She slams the phone down again. Her face screws up in fury. *She's going to bring the whole house down around us this time.*

There's a knock at the door.

Lilith stops and blinks in the direction of the sound.

The knock is repeated.

Lilith sniffs the air. Her lovely face twists in disgust and loathing, but that expression is quickly replaced with a beatific smile.

Like turning on a light switch.

Instantly, she's gone, moving out of my sight, probably in the direction of the door. I can hear it open.

"My Queen." I hear a voice. It's odd. Something's wrong with it, as if the speaker has some kind of speech impediment.

"My Son," Lilith says. "You've come to me."

"Forgive me, my Queen! I had no choice! I've failed you."

"It matters not, my Son. So many have failed me this night. At least you are here. At least you have not abandoned me."

"I left my post! I left my charges! They're all lost to me!" Whoever it is, he's wailing, lisping, and spluttering like a hysterical child. "Forgive me!"

"All is forgiven, my Child. You are the first to reach me."

She enters my field of vision, walking toward me from the living room, stepping gracefully over the corpse of the old farmwife.

Behind her is a monster, a demon of the Pit.

The newcomer is a nightmarish gargoyle of a dwarf. He has a huge hump on his back and he's bent low, as if he can't straighten up. His deformed face has a very prominent cleft in its upper lip. One eye's bigger than the other. His fingers are webbed. One arm's longer than the other, and one leg is much shorter. He walks with a pronounced limp.

Is he a vampire? Lilith called him "Son," but how can he be so hideous? So revolting? Wouldn't the Seed cure all his deformities?

"Shepherd," Lilith says turning back toward the monster, "how did you manage to find me?"

The creature drops to the floor and grovels at her feet. "Have mercy on Ol' Shep, my Queen! I was banished from the Farm, from my lovely cattle! Traitors, my Queen! Traitors among the Children!"

She makes no move to stop him from his sycophantic mewling. "I understand, Shepherd. It's my own fault, really, making you the lowest of the low, forcing you to obey all my other Children. It . . . handicapped you." She smiles as if she's amused at her own little joke. "So how did you find me, Child?"

"I've been looking for you ever since I was banished. I went to the Palace, but it was gone, destroyed. I've been searching here, in the First Place. I knew you would be here, my Queen."

The 'First Place?' Does that mean what I think it means?

"Such a clever boy, you are, Shepherd. Of course you'd search for me in this place."

"Yes, my Queen!" The monster looks up at her, like a puppy pleased with his master's praise. "I knew you'd return to the place where it all began."

"But how did you find me here, in this house?"

"Lord Lucifer came to me. He pointed the way."

Lilith's smile is tight. She doesn't look pleased. It seems this creature was not what she wanted Lucifer to send to her. She sent Satan out to find the nearest vampire, and he did.

"Well, that devious worm," she says through tight lips. "He found *you*. I suppose I shall just have to *thank* him later, won't I?"

"My Queen?" Shepherd looks perplexed. "You are displeased?"

"Well, Shepherd, let's just say you were not my first choice."

He's groveling again. "Of course not, your Majesty. Ol' Shep's a worm!"

"Yes, my Son, you are the lowest of the low, but for now, you are my entire army."

"My Queen?"

Lilith places a hand to her forehead, as if she's about to faint. "Yes, Shepherd. You are the only one of my Children who has not abandoned me." She drops the hand to her breast. "All the rest were murdered tonight, all my Inner Circle were murdered by the traitors who banished you. How many of them were there, my Son?"

"Two. A man and a woman."

"A woman with red hair?"

"Yes, my Queen."

"The man had brown hair?"

"Yes, my Queen."

"They are the Unwilling and the Penitent of the Curse. They have come to kill me. They have come to destroy us all."

"They . . . they *bested* you?" Shepherd stares at his Queen, his disproportionate eyes wide with disbelief.

"Me? No, foolish Child! They did not *best* me! They slew my foolish Children, my foolish Enforcers who could not protect their Queen, their Mother. My husbands failed me, Shepherd. They're all dead."

You blew them up yourself, you murderous demon! How can she . . . ? Stupid question, Tony! She's Lilith.

"All dead?" the deformed dwarf says, horror-struck. "The entire Court?"

"No, not the entire Court. I sent most of *them* away myself when I went into exile. But they might as well be dead. I have no way to reach them at the moment."

The dwarf's face brightens in a hideous cleft smile. "But, my Queen, Ol' Shep knows how to reach 'em!"

"What do you mean?"

"Ol' Shep's kept meticulous records of the comings and goings of my guests. I always record their names and telephone numbers, in case there's any problems I might need to report, any *abuses*. If'n you recall, I tried to call you once about that time when . . ."

Lilith grabs him by the shoulders and lifts him from the floor. "And you have these numbers?"

"Of course, my Queen!" He taps his temple. "Ol' Shep's got a mind like a steel 'possum trap! I remember 'em all. All two hundred and seven of the Court who've visited my Farm over the last decade or so."

Lilith smiles. It's a smile that is at once beautiful and malicious. "Shepherd, dear one, for this you shall be my Chief Enforcer, First in the Court, and my First Husband."

"Oh, my Queen!" The creature's expression is pure rapture. He's still being held aloft by Lilith, but he wriggles in delight. "I live to serve you! I love you!"

"Of course you do, Shepherd, but first we must summon the Court and rebuild my army!"

She drops him to the floor. I hear a sound like a bone crunching, and the dwarf screams in pain. He grasps at his ankle, fumbles with it in his webbed hands, and straightens it.

Lilith is back at the phone now. She smiles at me.

My breath catches in my throat. Lilith, Kathleen, the epitome of desire and lust and beauty.

It's all a cheat, Tony. She's a monster. Abby and Little Tony are dead. Maybe Kathleen too.

"Give me the first name and number," she says. "Start with the men."

Shepherd, his ankle obviously healed, limps over to her and says, "Yes, my Queen . . . my *love*."

With her back to the dwarf, she rolls her eyes. "The name and number?"

He smiles with a joy that makes me think of someone in a paroxysm of religious ecstasy. "Steven McCray, eight-one-six . . ."

◆ ◆ ◆

I've kept count. She's able to contact one-hundred and thirty-seven vampires, one-hundred and eight of them male. Twelve are coming here with all due haste. She gave them an address, but I couldn't hear it. She covered the mouthpiece and spoke softly when she said that part.

She probably didn't want me to hear. The remainder of her Court were ordered to be at the Sprint Center, the place for the prisoner exchange—the place for the ambush—shortly after sunset. She wants twelve bodyguards here, but this place won't shelter the rest.

The twelve are en route and will be here before sunrise. They're coming here, to the First Place. I know where we are, at least the general area.

I need to find some way to warn Carl and Moira. I don't know how many survived, but even if it were everybody (and I don't think many could've made it out of that battle alive), they'd still be outnumbered two to one. Carl and Moira don't know what they're walking into. They don't stand a chance. Maybe, just maybe, if it's only two to one, they might . . .

The living room glows with light. It's bright, and I feel as if I should have to look away, but I don't. It's a false glory after all, isn't it?

Lucifer has returned.

And Lilith didn't even perform the ritual. It's hard to believe, but Satan really is Lilith's lapdog. The Covenant he made with Lilith *binds* him.

Deliver me.

He stands there in his white suit with its gold tie and black shoes. He bows to Lilith and says, "There are six of the rebels. My angels report five men and one woman, the Unwilling, the Penitent, and four others. They're on the move, so I cannot predict where they *will* be, but I do know they'll be at the arena tomorrow night at midnight. They plan to arrive only half an hour early to avoid provoking a conflict that might result in mortal casualties. Is that sufficient?"

Lilith replaces the handset on the phone cradle. She and the dwarf were trying again to contact the members of the Court who did not answer before.

It's not like she needs more than a hundred and thirty-seven vampires, plus the dwarf and her, to ambush five. And you can't count Sergei if he's a prisoner to exchange.

Did Sergei turn back to Lilith's side after all?

Lilith is gathering her army. My friends don't stand a chance. I have to warn them somehow!

Lilith nods to the Devil. "You may go for now. Keep me informed. Do not fail me, Fallen One, or I shall spend the next century conjuring you and drawing only from you. Do you understand me, Serpent?"

"I do, my Queen." Once again Lucifer glances at me. His words at our first meeting echo in my mind. *Deliver me.*

And with that, he is gone.

Lilith turns to Shepherd. "And now, my First Husband, kneel before me and receive your reward."

Shepherd, his face a study in rapture, awkwardly kneels at her feet. He looks up at her with longing and lust. His tongue, like a dog's, lolls at the side of his mouth.

Lilith smiles at him. "Bow your head, Shepherd."

He bows his head.

She lays both her hands on his misshapen head. It looks like an ordination.

Perhaps that's precisely what it is.

"Shepherd Leslie Reginald Lee," she begins, "in the name of Lucifer, I ordain thee Disciple of Lilith, Enforcer, Chief Enforcer, and First Husband. Thou art bound to me as my consort till the end of thy nights. And I confer upon thee all the rights and honors and privileges that go with this office. Thou art blood of my blood, heart of my heart, flesh of my flesh."

Twelve. She ordered twelve men to join her here.

"Rise, Shepherd," Lilith says, "and kiss thy bride." She removes her hands from his head. One hand she places on his shoulder at the base of his neck. The other she places under his chin.

Twelve. Not eleven.

And she only keeps twelve.

The hideous, malformed creature shambles to his feet. His transport of joy is complete.

One hand still on his shoulder and one below his chin, Lilith gazes down into his eyes. She smiles. "And now thy reward."

In one smooth motion, she rips Shepherd's head from his neck.

The body crumples to the floor (just like Little Tony and Abby). Blood spurts from the neck in a pulsing geyser.

Lilith holds the head in both hands now and raises it to her lips. Shepherd's lips work soundlessly as he tries to scream.

"Farewell, First Husband," Lilith says. She kisses the writhing lips.

She tosses the head in my direction. It lands on the floor, rolls, and stops. The eyes stare at me and the hideous lips mouth unintelligible words. The lips slow their gruesome motion and then stop. The eyes glaze over in death.

Chapter 30

Carl

bsolutely not." I shake my head vehemently at Sergei. "No way." *I can't believe my ears.*

In the darkness of the hotel room, lit only by the glow from Sergei's laptop, the Russian looks at me intently. "Are you saying I have no choice? Because, that didn't *feel* like a command, and yet you're saying I cannot pretend to rejoin Lilith. I *am* a spy, after all."

I rub my temples in frustration. "No, of course not. I'm not going to force you to . . ."

"Good. Because I *am* willing to lay down my life to save Tony Lupescu. I deserve death many, many times over for my crimes. *He* does not."

"'Tis nae yer *life* we're talkin' about." Moira says. "'Tis yer immortal *soul*. We're all goin' to die. But death is nae the end of eternity. 'Tis but the beginnin'."

"You can't go back to her, mate," Andrew says, "not even for a second. You know that. And if you don't, you're a fool."

"It'd be like an alcoholic walking into a bar," I say. "Stupid beyond belief."

"But I know what she is now," Sergei replies. "My oath to you, the blessing you gave me, my new faith in Jesus Christ—these things will protect me."

I shake my head again. "Not if you willingly go back to her, even if it *is* just with the intention of gathering intelligence. You're not strong enough to resist her. I've never been bound to her, never been in love with her, and even *I* find it difficult to resist her. I *want* to do as she asks. I *want* to please her." I glance over at Moira and squeeze her hand. "Sorry, but it's true."

Moira gives my hand a reassuring squeeze.

Does she really understand what I meant by that? I hope so, because the last thing I want to do is hurt her, especially with less than a day left to live.

I keep thinking that, and the Lord keeps sparing us a little while longer . . . a few of us, at least. So many lives lost tonight. But how many more last-nights-on-Earth can I take?

"Sergei," I say, trying to make my voice as gentle as I can, "are you *sure* this isn't about wanting to see her, to be with her one last time?"

The Russian looks at me, opens his mouth, and then shuts it. He looks away and turns to the curtained hotel room window. He's quiet for a moment. The only sounds are the distant noise of the city, the heartbeats and breathing of Sergei, Moira, Andrew, and me in this room, and Rolf, Lorenzo, and Kathleen in the next room. And Kathleen's gentle snoring.

And Ericson. The Marine, armed only with a handgun, stands guard outside in the hallway. I can hear his heart and breath as well.

"I don't know," Sergei says at last, still staring at the curtain. "I *do* love her. I know she's . . . not genuine. And I know she doesn't love me. I don't think she's capable of loving anyone. But I *do* love her. I *do* want to be with her. It's *painful* to be parted from her. I know . . . I know what's right, what I have to do, but . . . I want her so very, very badly."

He parts the curtains ever so slightly and gazes out at the brightening sky. "And I guess . . . therein lies the truth does it not? You're right. I can't go back, not even for a second. Even *seeing* her, even being in the same place with her . . . will be difficult enough."

Releasing the curtain, he turns to face me with a heavy sigh. "I'll do as you ask, my Captain. I'll play my part, and go no further. May God forgive me for my weakness."

Moira releases my hand and walks around the bed to place a hand on his shoulder. "Laddie, confessing yer weakness allows God to . . ."

He brushes her hand violently away from his shoulder. "*Nyet!* Don't touch me!"

Moira pulls her hand to her chest, but doesn't back away. Shock and hurt are plain on her face.

The door between us and Kathleen's room opens, and Rolf with his spear, followed closely by Lorenzo with his sword drawn, enters the room and looks about, ready to fight.

I raise a hand, and they halt.

"Sergei," I say. "Are you . . . ?"

The Russian groans. "I'm sorry." He looks at Moira with a pained expression. Then he bows his head.

Moira begins to reach out to him again. She hesitates, her hand halfway to his shoulder. Then she drops her hand to her side. "What's the matter, laddie? Have I done ought to offend ye?"

"It's not your fault," Sergei says. He looks up at her again. His expression . . . *Is that guilt I see?* "During the fight at the Chateau, there was a moment, a brief moment, when I locked eyes with Lilith. It was only for an instant, but . . ." He stares intently at Moira. "What do you see when you look at Lilith? Has she ever looked you in the eye?"

Moira looks confused. "I . . . I've only seen her clearly the once, and there was nae time in the heat of the battle."

"I honestly don't know how she affects women," he says. "I know how she affects men, how she affects me." He hesitates. *Definitely guilt.* "When she looks me in the eye, she transforms. She appears to be every woman I've ever loved, every woman I've ever truly desired. And I can't tell if it is each woman individually or all of them at once." He pauses again. "When I saw her tonight, she looked . . . like *you.*"

What? What's he saying?

I hear Moira gasp.

Moira?

He means Moira.

"I'm sorry," Sergei says. "It's been so long since I've had to control any of my . . . baser urges. And you are so . . ." He looks away again. He opens the curtain slightly again, but draws back as a ray of sunlight peeks through. "Forgive me."

Moira smiles wistfully. "Ach, laddie, forgive ye for what?"

Sergei looks back at her. Guilt gives way to confusion.

Moira's smile broadens. "All ye've done is pay me a sincere compliment."

Sergei laughs softly and cocks his head at me. "You're a lucky man, Carl."

I'm a blessed man is what I am.

How does Moira do that? She seems to make everything better.

"You got that right," Andrew says with a grin.

Rolf and Lorenzo both smile widely.

I make a loud coughing noise. "OK, gentlemen, if you're all through ogling my wife, let's go over the plan."

◆ ◆ ◆

"The bottom line is we don't know how many people she's going to have with her," I say with a huge sigh. *I've Fed well enough, but I need Sleep. No chance for that. And I'm not giving up a minute of my remaining time with Moira.* "We don't know what allies she'll be able to bring. And we can be darn sure she's not coming alone."

Moira looks at Sergei. "How many Masters did ye miss in all your calling last night?"

"Now I'm insulted," Sergei says, sitting up straight on the bed. We're all sitting on the edge of one of the two beds facing toward the middle of the room . . . all of us, except for Lorenzo who remains standing in the doorway between our room and Kathleen's. She's still fast asleep, poor thing. "You gave me a task to do and I did it. Nothing more need be said."

"You mean you got them all?" I ask. "*All?*"

"Of course," he replies stiffly. "They are required to keep the lines of communication open at all times, most especially since the Breaking. Now, of course, those lines are severed."

"She does nae have *anyone?*" Moira asks. "When she spoke to Carl over the phone, she told him that she had only Tony to 'protect her,' but surely she'd nae agree to a meeting all by herself. She cannae be so arrogant and so sure of her powers as to risk an ambush."

"I didn't say she'd have no one," Sergei says. "She just won't have anyone from the Cults. But there's still the Court."

"Weren't they all killed at the Chateau?" Rolf asks.

Sergei laughs mirthlessly. "Not hardly. Most were left to fend for themselves once the Queen went into hiding, but they're still around."

"How many are we talking about?" I ask.

Sergei shrugs. "About two hundred, but she has no good way to contact them."

"What do you mean?" I ask.

"She knows how to contact her Masters. She knows them all and she knows their phone numbers, but that is of no consequence: they've been cut off from her. The members of her Court? They're mostly beneath her notice. I doubt very much she'd know how to contact any of them. They were the responsibility of Horst. He handled the Court."

"That sounds better," I say, "if she can't contact them."

"That's not to say she won't have any of them," Sergei says, shaking his head. "Her Call will be going out. Even though they're not Masters, the Call's so strong they'll be seeking her out, wherever she is, especially if she's in the area."

"And where is she, pray tell?" Moira says.

Sergei shrugs. "I have no idea. She owns property all over the metro area, but I know all those locations, or most of them. She won't risk going to any of those. She'll be someplace I know nothing about."

"OK," I say, "so she *may* have some vampires with her."

"Yes," Sergei replies, "she may, but there are other allies to worry about. The National Guard perhaps. The police certainly. The Crime Family perhaps."

I grin. "Maybe not the Crime Family. Moira and I met up with a couple of thugs who were planning on blowing the tunnel to the Farm. Now that we're done with them, one, at least, is doing his best to convince the Mafia bosses that Lilith has broken the Covenant."

Sergei looks impressed. "Who? Did you get a name?"

"Renny," I say. "Renny De Marco."

"Renny?" Sergei now looks astonished and impressed. "Renaldo De Marco is the nephew of the Don! Johnny Joe Sorrentino'll listen to Renny. I think we can probably count them out of the fight, at least for now." He laughs. "Well done!"

"We're not out of the woods, though," I say. "Lilith picked the place and time. Long enough to set an ambush. But the odds are, most of them'll be mortals, although mortal enemies . . . I want to avoid mortal casualties."

"Then," Rolf says, "I say we beat her to the punch. We get there before she does."

"How?" Lorenzo asks. "We don't have any way to get there before night-fall."

"Do ye think Colonel Evans might be able to spare one of those deuces?" Moira asks.

"Too conspicuous," Rolf says.

"'Deuces?'" Lorenzo asks.

"Military trucks," Rolf explains.

Andrew snaps his fingers. "A stretch limo! The hotel could arrange for one. We could cover up, and with those tinted windows . . ."

I nod. "Good idea. Would you like to go downstairs and arrange for one ASAP?"

"My pleasure." He rises to his feet. "I'll be back in two shakes."

"Well," I say, as Andrew closes the door behind himself, "with the Marines on our side, the odds should be in our favor. Let's hope . . . No. Let's *pray* we succeed this time."

"Aye," Moira says with a sigh, "let's pray that we succeed." She throws up her hands. "After all, who wants to live forever?"

"'Once more into the breach, dear friends, once more,'" Lorenzo says.

"Laddie, I have a question." Moira squeezes my hand.

"What's that, my love?"

"'Tis a wee thing, really, but something Colonel Evans said, or rather *started* to say. It's been bothering me. I'm curious. Something about excuses being like . . . I dinnae know what he was going to say. Then he apologized."

I laugh softly. "I think I'll let the good lieutenant field this one." I rise and walk to the door. I open it, revealing Lieutenant Ericson, standing there, on guard. "Lieutenant?"

"Aye, sir?" the man says. He doesn't look at us, just keeps turning his head back and forth, scanning the hallway.

I don't even try to suppress a smile. *We could use a laugh or at least a chuckle.* "Hey, my wife wants to know something. What's that saying you Marines have? 'Excuses are like . . .' How does it go?"

Ericson turns and looks at Moira. "Excuses are like a . . ." His cheeks flush a delicious shade of crimson. "Uh . . . Excuses are like . . . like . . . a certain bodily orifice: everyone's got one and they all stink."

Moira giggles. *It's so sweet to hear her laugh!*

Sergei grins too.

The Marine's cheeks redden even more. "Will that be all, sir?"

"Sure thing, lieutenant."

He resumes scanning the hallway.

I close the door and rejoin my wife.

"That was . . . nae nice, laddie," she says, giving me a pretend scowl.

"Made you laugh, though," I say with a grin.

Her scowl melts away, and she favors me with a heart-stopping smile.

Andrew bursts into the room. "You're never going to believe it!"

"What?" we ask all at once.

"What you did!" he cries. "At the Farm! What you did." He laughs. "It's all over the *bloody* news!"

He steps quickly to the TV and turns it on. "The limo will be ready in the hour, by the by." After a moment and some soft cursing as he tries to find a news channel, he steps away from the flat-panel TV in triumph. "Voila!"

On the screen is Moira and the Marines leading the Tribe of Esther through the tunnels of SubTropolis. We all watch and listen in rapt fascination as the anchorman describes, ". . . the scene early this morning as a previously unknown colony of more than a thousand people . . ."

"Twelve hundred and *seventy*," Moira hisses.

". . . were discovered living in a cave underneath the industrial complex known as SubTropolis and the Worlds of Fun and Oceans of Fun amusement parks in Kansas City, Missouri. Details are sketchy at this hour, but early reports are that these people, or rather they and their ancestors, have been living there for more than a century. How they got there is still unknown at this time. They're currently being relocated to Richards-Gebaur Air Base, south of Kansas City. The Red Cross . . ."

The report continues like that for a few minutes, providing few details that we don't already know, but it's still fascinating to see this all coming to light.

". . . asked Mr. Charles Dailey, General Manager of SubTropolis, for comment."

Dailey's now on the screen, looking more rumpled than he did when Moira and I left him. He's got a microphone thrust in his face. "Hunt Industries is doing all we can to assist these poor people to find a home. The Hunt family has pledged more than a million dollars . . ."

Soon Dailey is replaced by a man in a business suit. "I can assure you that the governor has no knowledge . . ."

The press secretary is replaced by another man in a three-piece suit. "Mr. Sorrentino is an honest businessman. To suggest that he is somehow involved in human trafficking is absurd and libelous. However, out of the goodness of his heart, he has pledged two million dollars to help . . ."

Now a man in a police uniform is shown. "I have no comment at this time except to say that the city is cooperating to the fullest . . ."

And so it continues with everyone disavowing knowledge, while at the same time pledging support. Moira and I exchange several glances, and she squeezes my hand so hard, I'm sure I'd have bruises if I were mortal.

Moira, however, is grinning from ear to ear.

The footage of the Tribe is shown again. Moira's walking at the front of the mass of people and sheep. The image zooms in on her face and freezes.

Her grin disappears, and she squeezes my hand *hard*.

The announcer says, "I want you to take a good look at this woman. Now compare her face to this image taken last year." Moira's picture moves to the right side of the screen and the black-and-white image of her face from the Conference Center security film is shown. "They appear to be one and the same. The image on the left is from the video we showed you earlier this week of the so-called 'Battling Angels of Salt Lake City.' The woman on the right appears to be carrying the same sword shown in the video on the left. If you have any information regarding whereabouts, please contact Fox News at the number shown on your screen."

A third image appears between the first two. It looks like an ID photo. "Our Fox News affiliate in Salt Lake City has reported that this woman has been identified as Dr. Moira MacDonald Morgan. She's a trauma surgeon at LDS Hospital in Salt Lake City. Attempts to contact Dr. Morgan at LDS Hospital or at her home have so far been fruitless. We have unconfirmed reports that the home of Dr. Morgan was destroyed in a fire two nights ago. At this time, the whereabouts of Dr. Morgan or her husband, Carl Morgan, are unknown, although this footage would indicate she's currently in Kansas City."

Now they're showing *my* photo alongside Moira's.

Moira sighs. "Well, the truth was bound to come out. 'Tis nae as if we'd e'er be able to return to Utah. We dinnae plan to live out the night, do we?"

At the back of my mind, I feel an itching, like something I'm supposed to remember.

The newsman continues, ". . . neighbors paint a picture of a virtual saint."

Of all the people I might expect to see on the news, Winnie Morrison would not be among them. But there she is, sitting in her wheelchair, in what I assume is her front doorway. She's waving at the microphones, batting at them in anger. "Moira Morgan is the nicest, sweetest woman I've ever known. She's a hero, and you better just leave her alone! She saved my life. She's saved so many lives. And she never asks for anything for herself! Now just go away and leave her be!"

And there's Bishop Adams on the screen. "Moira MacDonald . . . I mean Moira Morgan is a wonderful woman whom we've had the privilege to know for years. We just love her . . . her and her husband, Carl. And we hope and pray they're safe."

"Yep," I say, "the cat's out of the bag."

"Aye, the truth will out," Moira says.

"The truth!" Lorenzo shakes his head. "Ha! They have no idea."

You can't handle the truth!

Something clicks in my mind, like a key turning in a lock. *Remember Moira's sword. The truth is your greatest weapon.* Sharon's words from earlier tonight.

While I was dead.

"The truth," I whisper.

"What's that, laddie?" Moira asks.

"The truth." I tap the hilt of her sword. "The truth is our greatest weapon."

Moira turns her face from the TV and looks at me with those gorgeous green eyes. "What are ye saying?"

"We need to give them the truth. Call the news. Call them and offer them an interview. Tell them to meet you at the Sprint Center. Promise them the story of the century. Tell them that they'll want to have *lots* of cameras. We're going to bring Lilith's empire down. Expose everything. Drag it into the light. We'll give the media her database."

Moira closes her eyes and purses her lips, obviously considering. She nods. "Aye, but won't that scare her off, put her into hiding? Then we'll ne'er be able to find her."

"So, we'll grant the interview and make them agree to hold it until after she gets there. She's not going to slaughter people in front of the cameras. There's no way she can cover that up, especially if it's live. Even if she survives, even if we fail, it'll take her a long time to rebuild everything . . . and people will know what to look for!"

"People are sheep," Rolf says. "I know that's a terrible thing to say, especially coming from an ex-Nazi, but it's true. They'll be lulled back to sleep. You know that."

"Maybe so," Lorenzo says, "but I've watched the American experiment from its inception. It took only one tenth of your people to start the Revolution and free an entire nation. Enough people will wake up *if* they know the truth. I'm with Carl on this one."

"Very well," Moira says. She smiles at me, but it's a smile that's at once sad and brave. She pulls out her phone and dials the number on the bottom of the TV screen. It takes a few tries, but eventually I hear it ring.

Someone answers. "Thank you for contacting the tip hotline. Do you have information about Dr. Moira Morgan or the 'Lost Colony'?"

"Hello," Moira says and she glances at me and exhales sharply. She sits up straight. "This is Moira Morgan. I understand ye'd like to speak with me."

Chapter 31

Carl

"Just kill me now!" Lorenzo shouts. Even with him shouting, it's not easy to understand him over the deafening racket of the concert. "I've spent my entire life, centuries, savoring great music. I've seen and heard Mozart and Salieri, Beethoven and Handel. In person! I love John Williams and Danny Elfman! But I can't *believe* I'm spending my last night on Earth listening to *rap!*"

At least he didn't call it "rap music."

He shakes his head in disgust. "In all my five centuries, this is the most foul, perverse, vile, degrading, and obscene dreck to which I've ever been forced to listen. Hell must be filled with such torture."

"You think that's obscene?" I yell back. "You should see the ticket prices! I can't believe anyone would pay a *dime* to listen to this violent, misogynistic crap, much less pay hundreds of dollars in some cases!"

He growls. "It's been four hundred years since I wanted to commit murder. But right now, every molecule of my body cries out for me to fly down and tear that ersatz artist's vocal cords out of his neck in vengeance for this brutal rape of music."

The six of us are perched around the top of the gigantic central scoreboard suspended high above the floor of the Sprint Center arena. I look at Lorenzo, and a homicidal rage blazes in his eyes. The knuckles of his hand are white as he grips the hilt of his sword. He looks as if he's ready to draw the weapon and . . .

Not that he'd actually *murder* the gold-laden, jewel-rich, talent-free sociopath chanting filth as he struts on the stage below. Lorenzo just needs somewhere to direct all the anger and anxiety and guilt that are eating at his guts like a cancer.

The anxiety, guilt . . . and the scent of evil blood.

It's hard to be in a crowd this size and *not* have someone truly evil in it. But we have to ignore it. We can't respond. We can't seek out and devour the consummate sweetness of evil. There's too much at stake. Does this kind of "music" attract evil? Some of the lyrics certainly encourage it. That idiot on the stage isn't evil, but one of his songs glorified a rape. Several glorified murder.

And of course, there's the 'minor' point that we're here to kill Lilith and die.

Another "last night on Earth." And, as strange as it sounds, I pray it'll truly *be* the last. I pray that we'll finally win, that no more innocents will suffer or be corrupted by Lilith and her Children. Not if I can help it.

But as bad as all this is, I'm pretty sure the music and the evil blood are not what're really gnawing at Lorenzo.

"I'm worried about Tony too." I don't shout it, but he's looking at me. He knows what I said.

He bows his head and says something I don't quite catch.

I mouth, "What?"

"It should be me, not Sergei. I should be the one. Tony's *my* grandson, *my* family."

"You know it has to be Sergei. And rescuing Tony cannot be our primary objective."

He nods. "My head keeps telling me so. My heart is not listening." Lorenzo folds his arms across his chest. For a moment his fangs extend, and then they retract. "It would still bring me great pleasure to rip out the throat of that *maiale* down there."

I don't know what *maiale* means, but I'll bet it's not a term of endearment. Sometimes being in such a multinational group of vampires reminds me of when I taught Korean at the Missionary Training Center. I was surrounded by missionaries and instructors throwing around words in many languages.

"Ach! Ye'd be doing the world a great kindness," Moira shouts. "To be sure, drivel such as this can fuel the evil I smell in the crowd."

Moira read my mind.

She's next to me, holding my hand. There's a desperation and ferocity to her grip that is at once painful and comforting.

Lorenzo's on my left. From up here, we can see the entire arena. All, that is, except the center of the floor below. Lieutenant Todd has that covered. He and four squads of Marines are positioned in the tunnel entrances at floor level. Colonel Evans and fifty more Marines are positioned at upper entrances to the arena, two at each entrance. There's also a roving squad of four Marines patrolling the boxes and suites on the third level. That makes eighty-eight. They're all out of uniform. And they're all heavily armed. M-4 rifles, side arms, dirks, and grenades.

It took a fair amount of Persuasion to get the cooperation of arena security, but we're here and we're ready.

Well, as ready as we're going to be.

"In a way," I shout, "it's a blessing that it *is* a rap concert!" That earns me dirty looks from Lorenzo and Sergei. "People in this crowd seem to think the weapons are just part of the show! Just atmosphere, you know?"

Andrew laughs at this. "I kinda like this music. It reminds me of my mum, the things she used to say to me as a kid." The five of us turn our heads in his direction. He grins sheepishly. "It was a dysfunctional family, all right? I was one screwed-up tyke! I mean, no wonder I grew up and chose to become a bloody, murdering vampire!"

"Music like this is used to desensitize people and to normalize evil," Rolf shouts. "I've seen it before."

I bet you have. "Hitler used opera as a . . . ."

"No," Rolf cries. "I was referring to American rock and roll!" He looks completely serious.

"Well, maybe . . ."

My earpiece suddenly crackles to life. "Pirate? This is Mariner. Do you have a tally on Empress?" Colonel Evans is calling me on the tactical radio. And his voice is loud in my ear. It was Lieutenant Todd's idea to use baseball team mascots for codenames. But I'd bet money he wanted to call me "Pirate" because I'm "Captain Morgan."

I thumb the switch on my throat mike. "No joy, Mariner." I switch the mike off again. I reach down to the small radio clipped to my belt and turn the volume down yet again. I've been turning it down by degrees ever since the concert started, thinking I wouldn't be able to hear it above the racket blasting from the arena sound system.

Obviously I was wrong.

"Roger that," Evans replies. "Brave? Mariner. Sitrep!"

Evans is letting Todd "run the op," but he's still the senior officer on site. It'll be his butt in a sling if, and most likely when, *this goes south.*

"This is Brave," Todd answers. "Nothing yet. All squads report!"

"Cub One. Ready."

"Cub Two. Ready."

"Cub Three. Ready."

And so it goes. Each of the "Cubs" reports "ready." All the way down to Cub Three-Zero. There are four squads of six and twenty-eight squads of two. Todd's squad of six is codenamed "Brave" and Evans and the single Marine with him are "Mariner" (of course).

"White Sox. Nothing to report." That's the roving team patrolling the box-seat level.

This process has been repeating every fifteen minutes or so since we positioned ourselves.

Well, we didn't expect Lilith to make an appearance before the planned meeting on the stage. And that's just as well. The concert should be over soon, and the crowd will be gone. Less chance of mortal casualties that way.

Arena Security has instructions to clear the arena afterward, rather than allowing the expected drug dealing to proceed. Then Security is supposed to bug out themselves. The only mortals left in this place should be those we invited and the ones Lilith brings with her. Even the clean-up crew won't be here till the morning.

But we're in place and we're waiting and watching.

The hour of our death approaches.

Midnight. It's eleven now, and the concert does seem to be rising to its crescendo, to its end.

To our end.

I squeeze Moira's hand again.

She grimaces. "'Twas the hardest ... aye, well, *one* of the hardest things I've e'er done."

I glance at her. "You mean the interview?" We haven't spoken of it, not much at least, since it took place here at the arena around noon, but I imagine it's been on her mind.

She nods.

I laugh. "It was no picnic for me either."

"Telling, for all the world to see and hear, *everything* I've kept secret these centuries. I felt so ... exposed. So naked. I haven't felt that way since ... since I was mortal." *When she was beaten and gang-raped by British soldiers and left to die.* "Are ye certain, laddie, that they'll wait to broadcast it until after ..."

". . . until after we're dead? I think so. I hope so. Especially after what we promised them *if* they waited. I think they'll hold off."

I couldn't let her face the interview alone. I know she's capable and extremely brave, but she's my wife, darn it! I want to protect her! Besides, they wanted to talk to me too. So we showed them everything. The fangs. The wings. All of it. One of the cameramen fainted dead away. Split his head open when he fell. Moira, exercising incredible restraint and control, Healed the man using the Seed in her saliva. The reporter, a man named Matthew, manned the dropped camera and taped the whole thing.

"It'll be worth their while," I say.

The crowd below roars.

The concert's over! Finally! I begin to offer a silent prayer of gratitude, but it becomes obvious that the "artist" is going to perform an encore.

"Kill me now," Lorenzo says again.

I'm pretty sure there's no rap in Heaven.

Please let there be no rap in Heaven!

♦ ♦ ♦

"Cub Three-Zero. Ready."

It's quarter to midnight. The audience is gone.

Looking down on the now empty stadium, I'm astonished at the amount of garbage left behind by the rap aficionados. Does this kind of music inspire . . . ?

Silence on the radio.

Somebody didn't report in.

"White Sox, this is Brave." Todd's prompting the roving squad to report in.

Silence.

"White Sox, report!" That was Colonel Evans.

"Mariner, White Sox," comes the reply at last. "One of the boxes is still occupied. Suite three-zero-seven. We're gonna check it out."

"Roger, White Sox. Standing by."

As one, five vampires draw swords. Rolf has his spear at the ready.

"This is White Sox. Negative on the target. Just a party running late."

I let out a sigh. I must've been holding my breath.

I probably wasn't alone in doing that.

One time, the video game company I work for rented a huge box at a Utah Jazz exhibition game. We stayed and partied for a while after the game was over. There were video games and food . . .

"White Sox, Brave. Are you sure?"

"Affirmative. No female present. Only males."

. . . and caterers, mostly women.

My gut twists. Something's not right.

I thumb my throat mike switch. "White Sox, Pirate!"

Silence.

"So you've taken my Honor Guard, have you Carl?" That honeyed voice, distorted by the radio. "That was rude. They were mine."

"White Sox!" That sounds like Todd.

"Don't bother," Lilith says. "You sent four of my pretty soldier boys after little me. But they move so slowly. I'm sorry to say they didn't stand a chance. Still they were delicious. Thank you for sending me such a pretty meal."

"Cub two-eight, two-niner, three-zero!" Evans commands. "Converge on . . ."

"Oh, don't be silly," Lilith says. "Don't waste any more of that marvelous Marine Corps blood. We'll come to you."

I thumb the switch. "This is Pirate. Hold your positions. Go ahead and let her come to us."

"You're calling yourself 'Pirate,' Carl? How darling, prosaic, and utterly appropriate, given the circumstances! You *are* a kidnapper and a thief. Very well, then. We're on our way. Bring my husband. *Empress* over and out."

From high box seats at the end of the arena, opposite the stage, seven winged figures emerge. One woman and six men. Make that seven men—one of the men is carrying Tony under one arm. That's Lilith in the middle. All the male vampires have swords. Lilith appears to be unarmed.

Not that she needs a weapon of steel.

Obviously she was able to contact some of her Court.

Still, seven to six, plus the Marines on our side. I like those odds.

However, she seems confident. Does she disregard the Marines entirely? Is she that arrogant, that confident?

Possibly.

And maybe she has a few more vampires held in reserve, out of sight. As far as the Marines are concerned, she has the advantage of the air.

As far as I can see, Lilith isn't wearing or holding the throat mike she used to speak to us. I thumb the switch on mine. "This is Pirate. Stick to the plan."

As they pass through the space below us, I hear an odd noise. Somebody's singing. *Singing?*

Lilith and her guards alight on the now abandoned stage. They turn about, the men taking defensive positions around their Queen. One of the guards, a tall, massive brute, sets Tony on his feet and holds a sword to Tony's throat.

Tony's lips are moving. He's the one singing. From here he looks . . . off somehow. Has he lost it? Who could blame him, after what he's been through? Poor guy. Nothing Kathleen told us led me to believe he'd gone insane. But maybe he's been driven over the edge.

"Come to me, my prodigal Son," Lilith says. It's not loud enough for the Marines to hear, but audible to our ears. "Come to me, my dear husband."

Even from here, her power is incredible. I feel that urge to obey her, to please her. I note the red, floor-length dress that hugs and accentuates every curve.

Switching my mike on, I say, "This is Pirate. Going hot-mike. Pirate is moving out."

Moira and I lift into the air. The other four join us. Moira and Rolf are on my right. Sergei, Andrew, and Lorenzo are on my left. Our weapons are at the ready.

As we drift slowly down to the stage, Tony continues to sing quietly, his head lolling back and forth. The vampire who holds Tony's arms, restraining him, looks irritated. He shakes Tony roughly. Tony pauses briefly, but then quickly resumes his singing.

I don't recognize the tune. I'm no singer, not like Moira. But I recognize the words. *Sort of.*

"Behold, a royal legion, with banner, sword, and shield."

He repeats this opening line over and over. Even as a pathetic singer, I know this hymn. It was one of the few I used to sing with gusto (if out of tune) when I was a teenager, dreaming of becoming an Air Force pilot. But the tune's not right.

Tony looks awful. Well, he's been through hell.

We descend slowly, watching for any sign of ambush.

I know it's coming. Lilith must have something planned. I think we've taken the Mafia out of the equation for now. Possibly the police as well. The Marines are with *us*. She's got a half dozen vampires that I can see. So we're pretty evenly matched there. What else is waiting for us? She's confident. She wouldn't be doing this if she didn't have some plan. What could it be? Get Sergei and escape? Take back control of her Cults with Sergei's help? Is that all there is to this?

No way.

Still singing the same tune, Tony changes the words to "Pigs is pigs is pigs is pigs is pigs is pigs is pi-igs."

Now he changes tune completely. "Slowly, slowly, they sank into the sea. To the very bottom they sank into the sea."

I recognize that one. It's from some old Disney movie, not a cartoon. Lilith's eyes catch mine for a moment. I'm suddenly reminded of Annette Funicello.

There's something off about the words Tony's singing.

Now it's back to "Pigs is pigs . . ."

As we land on the stage, about fifteen paces away from Lilith's group, I say, "We agreed to 'unspoiled and pure.' What's wrong with him?"

Lilith shrugs. "It's nothing the Seed can't cure. But you insisted unspoiled, so I haven't Fed from him. He's uninjured . . . physically. This bizarre behavior began only after he watched us kill my pretty Marines. I think it was too much for his fragile mortal mind."

"Kathleen's safe," Moira says.

Tony's singing pauses for a second.

Moira got through to him.

He starts singing again. "Slowly, slowly, they sank . . ."

Lilith looks at Tony. "Do you hear that, lover? Kitty-Kat's alive . . . and well, I assume?" She turns back to Moira looking for confirmation.

Out of the corner of my eye, I see Moira nod.

Lilith claps her hands in delight. "You see, lover? Your little wife is alive!" She smiles sweetly.

My breath catches.

"Now," she continues, her voice dripping honey, "when you're at last reunited with her, she can spit in your face!"

"Behold, a royal legion . . ."

Lilith's smile falters slightly. "Silence him, James."

The big vampire claps a hand over Tony's mouth. Tony continues to hum, alternating between the two tunes.

Lilith's gaze returns to us and her flawless smile makes her face breathtaking. Moira. Sharon. Annette Funicello. She is *woman*. The essence of every . . .

Focus, Morgan!

"Andrew!" Lilith's lips purse in a disappointed pout. I feel as if I'd do anything to erase that look of disappointment, anything to please . . .

"Not *you*, my love!" She's not talking to me. She's talking to Andrew. "Consort! How could you betray your Queen? I *love* you, Andrew!"

"I . . ." Andrew chokes.

"Sergei!" Such a lovely smile. "You've come back to me! Beloved husband." She extends her arms. "Come to me, my love!"

Sergei sheathes his sword. He takes a halting step forward.

Lilith smiles, a look of supreme triumph, like the cat who has convinced the canary to approach.

"Please hold up, Sergei," I say. The Russian stops, looking uncertain, confused.

I can't lose him now. I need to distract her, shake her confidence.

And I've got just the thing. "Wave to the cameras, Lilith."

She blinks. "What?"

It's easier to breathe.

I grin. "You're on the national news, Queenie. Actually, your face is going out by satellite to the world!"

Her jaw drops. "The . . . the Great Secret! You can't . . ."

"I was never bound to keep your Great Secret," I say. I point at her with my sword, relishing the look of horror on her face. "Whole world, allow me to introduce Lilith, Queen of the vampires. She looks pretty good for six thousand years old, doesn't she?" I raise my sword and make a sweeping gesture above my head. "Lilith, the whole world."

I smile broadly and point at the Jumbotrons high above us. "Your secret's out." Lilith's face is displayed larger than life. Her shocked expression is priceless.

Her hands go to her face as if to cover it.

"Too late to hide your face, lady," I say. "Your lovely mug is probably all over the Internet by now. And you can't alter your face with plastic surgery or cut your hair or even change the color. Might I suggest a wig? Maybe a red, white, and blue afro. Take a good look, folks. This is the face of evil."

I glance at one of the broadcast booths above. "Did you catch all that, Matthew?"

In the booth, the reporter gives me a big thumbs-up.

I wink at Lilith. "Great directional microphones they have in this place, huh?"

Lilith's vampire guards look around in confusion and—*Yes!*—fear.

The vampire Queen's face is twisted in fury. "You *dare* defy me? You will suffer as no one has ever suffered in all the world! I will see to that. I'll kill your whore of a wife in front of you and then I'll . . ."

Tony's humming is louder. More desperate. Is he crazy, or is he faking? If so, why?

"So," I say, "you still want Sergei?"

Her look of fury hardens into a scowl. "Release my husband."

"Release Tony," I say. "Release Tony, or Sergei stays with me, and you'll never hear from your precious Cults again."

Sergei looks at me. He's no longer confused.

He's still with us.

Lilith turns her head toward the vampire holding Tony and nods.

Tony's free. He sings, "Behold a royal legion . . ." He takes a step forward.

I flick my sword in Lilith's direction. "Sergei."

The Russian begins to walk toward Lilith.

With just a few steps more, they'll meet in the middle.

Tony sings louder. He puts emphasis on the word "legion."

It's not "legion." It's "army." A royal army. Pigs sinking, drowning in the sea. My name is *Legion* for we are many!

Tony's not crazy!

"She's got an army!" I shout. "Now!"

Instantly, Sergei's airborne, scooping Tony up, wheeling about, and flying low to the ground toward an exit tunnel. And Sergei will *stay* low. If we succeed and kill Lilith, I don't want Tony to die in a free fall from altitude.

Godspeed, my friends.

"Kill them!" Lilith screams.

Winged vampires are everywhere, flying down from above us. There must be a hundred of them! More!

Gunfire erupts as Marines fire on the enemy.

I leap into the air, sword before me. Straight for Lilith. Kill her and this ends.

Moira and the others follow my lead.

Lilith's bodyguard surges forward. Six to five. But they're attacking, not protecting Lilith.

She ordered them to kill us.

The big vampire, James, comes at me. I parry his blow and swing my sword for his neck. He doesn't even try to defend himself. I take off his head. The other bodyguards fall quickly to my friends. Lorenzo takes a blade to the gut, but he's still moving, Healing.

They were commanded to kill, not to fight. They can't defend themselves until they've fulfilled Lilith's command.

Where's Lilith?

"Protect your Queen!" she screams from above us.

She has realized her mistake.

Winged vampires swarm to shield her with their bodies. But that's a mistake too. It only clusters them around her, making a bigger target.

Vampires fall from the air, their wings vanishing, as the Marines shoot them down.

"All floor squads, engage and decapitate!" Todd orders through the radio. "Upper squads, cover us! Mariner, keep them off our backs!"

The Marines in the tunnels come at a run, firing into the air as they go. In moments, they're engaging vampires on the floor, firing weapons and then beheading the fallen vampires with their dirks. They know they have to move quickly before the vampires have a chance to Heal.

The vampires don't appear to be fighting back. They keep trying to get airborne to protect the Queen, and the Marines keep shooting them down. Some manage to get airborne again and fly back to shield Lilith. Then they get shot down again.

No free will.

We're winning.

Lilith's screaming orders, but I can't understand her, and I doubt her troops can either.

We don't dare fly up into the air to assist. We'll get caught in the cross-fire.

But there's something we *can* do.

"*Please,*" I shout as I leap from the stage, "help the Marines!" A vampire is just rising to his feet, his shirt red with his own blood. I behead him.

Moira and the others follow my lead.

We dispatch two or three vampires each as more rain from above, landing in twisted shapes on the arena floor. Lilith's numbers are dwindling.

The mass of winged vampires encircling Lilith dives for an exit. A mistake. Many more fall to the Marines as the huge target gets closer to the shooters. The vampire mob pulls back toward the center.

I behead another vampire and move to intercept yet another falling from the air. Moira, Lorenzo, Rolf, and Andrew are spread out across the floor, killing as they go. Rolf wields that spear of his like an extra-long blade, first thrusting through a chest and then hewing through a neck.

Lilith's vanishing army makes another dive toward an exit, this time one of the floor tunnels. They're driven back yet again.

And there's more butcher's work for us.

Whatever her vast experience may be as a "ruler from shadows," Lilith doesn't seem to have much, if any, combat experience. She's a pisspoor field commander. She doesn't let her people think or act for themselves. It's just "Kill!" or "Protect!" with nothing in between. And she's put herself into a kill zone. Self-preservation seems . . .

There's a sword sticking out of my chest.

"Forgive me," a voice says behind me.

Pain!

The sword withdraws, and the itch of the Seed is worse than the pain as it begins to reform my heart.

Can't think.

Getting stabbed in the heart really sucks.

I fall to my knees. My sword drops from my hand.

Useless.

Defenseless.

As the itch fades and my head begins to clear, I hear Moira screaming my name.

"Stay back, or I'll take off his head." It's the same voice.

A voice I know.

Fingers entangle themselves in my hair. My head is yanked back, and I look up into the tear-filled, bloodshot eyes of Sergei.

Chapter 32

Moira

"Why?" Carl asks, Sergei's sword to his throat.

A trickle of blood from where Sergei has cut my laddie's neck pools atop Carl's throat microphone. There's a slight tremor to the traitor's sword hand.

Carl's kneeling on the floor amid the ruin of scattered, broken, headless bodies, and shattered chairs. Sergei stands behind him.

Two more of Lilith's vampires fall from above.

We leave them to the Marines.

Carl and Sergei are nae but twenty yards from me, but I dare nae move any closer.

Lorenzo's another ten yards farther on the other side. "Where's my grandson, traitor?"

"The mortal's alive," Sergei says, his expression hard.

He lifts his head and shouts into the din of gunfire, vampires screaming, and bodies crashing, "The mortal, Lupescu, is safe, my Queen! He's in your box upstairs, Persuaded, and awaiting your return!" He looks at Lorenzo and barks, "Stay where you are, Lorenzo!" He glances behind himself and barks, "That's close enough, Andrew! Move out here where I can see you. Now!"

Andrew circles quickly until he stands next to me.

"Why?" Carl asks again.

"Because I love her." Sergei's voice is soft, quavering. "In spite of everything, I love her. Seeing her tonight . . ."

"No," Carl interrupts him. "I meant, why haven't you killed me already? Why didn't you kill Tony? You've had chances to do both."

Sergei visibly starts. A fresh stream of blood runs down my husband's neck.

I feel so helpless!

Carl winces. "You don't know, do you? If you've truly returned to her, turned your back on Christ, you'd have murdered me and Tony already."

"Shut up, Carl," Sergei snarls. "Order the mortals to cease fire!"

"So, was it yer plan all along to betray us?" I ask.

A vampire falls nearly on top of me, crumpled and bleeding.

I lop off his head.

Sergei makes nae move to stop me.

He's breathing heavily. "No. For a while, I really believed. Maybe I still do . . . a little. But what does that matter now?"

"You haven't killed me, and you didn't murder Tony," Carl says. "You haven't because, deep down, you're fighting it. If you were back under Lilith's control, you'd be carrying out her orders. You'd . . ." Carl grunts in pain, and fresh blood runs down his neck. "You'd be *bound* to kill me."

"Because I'm still bound to *you*, aren't I?" Sergei says. "Why don't *you* just order me to stop? One command from you, and I'd drop my sword. I'd kill myself if you told me to."

"Is that what you want?" Carl asks. "Me to make it easy so you won't have to choose? So you won't have to choose between the woman you love and the God who loves you?"

"Command me, damn you!" Sergei cries.

Aye, command him!

"No." Carl's voice is calm.

"Why not?" Sergei sounds as if he's pleading with Carl.

"Because, if I do that, I'll take away your choice. If I do that, I'm no better than Lilith. I won't do it."

"I *HAVE* NO CHOICE!" Sergei howls. "I gave it up when I murdered my Maschenka!"

"You always have a choice," Carl says, his voice soft and steady.

"Did you have a choice when you were Converted, *Unwilling*?" Sergei spits out the word like an epithet.

Bleeding afresh, Carl grimaces. "I didn't choose the hand I was dealt, but I chose what to do with it."

"Stand down, Redstar!" Lieutenant Ericson has a rifle pointed at Sergei. "Stand down, or I'll blow your head off!"

"Go ahead, Marine! Fire!" Sergei shouts.

Aye, fire!

"No!" Carl says, holding his hand up to the Marine. "Stand down, Marine. Sergei has to choose."

Ericson doesn't move. He's still sighting down the barrel of his weapon at Sergei. "If we lose you, sir, we lose the war. You're the one mentioned in the prophecy."

Sergei laughs bitterly. "What about that, Carl? Are you willing to give up your life, your mission, your *calling*, in a futile attempt to save one damned soul?"

"Always." 'Tis barely a whisper. "Stand down, Marine," Carl says a wee bit louder. "Please."

Ericson continues to point his weapon at Sergei.

"Please, Marine," Carl says. "Let him choose."

Ericson lowers his rifle, but he continues to glare at Sergei.

"It's too late," Sergei whispers, his blade trembling against Carl's throat, drawing fresh blood. "There's no going back, you said."

"All you did was stumble, brother," Carl says. "I stumble every day. It's never too late." He brings his hands up slowly and wraps his fingers around Sergei's blade. "You always have a choice."

Slowly, carefully, Carl pushes Sergei's blade away from his neck.

Sergei does nae resist him. He bows his head.

Carl stands up slowly. He turns and puts his arms around Sergei.

With gunfire blazing all around us, vampires raining down, Carl embraces the man who, but seconds before, held a sword to his throat.

A great sob shakes Sergei's body. His sword arm hangs at his side, the blade still wet with Carl's blood. A scarlet drop falls from the sword tip like a bloody tear.

"Now," Carl says, pushing gently away, "*please* take Lorenzo and get Tony. Please get him clear and then rejoin us. And please stay low to the ground, just in case . . ."

Sergei wipes away tears. "Of course. Fly low, just in case you win, and we all drop out of the sky?"

Lorenzo grips Sergei's arm. His knuckles are white. "Take me to my grandson!"

Sergei's airborne in an instant, flying low and heading for a tunnel. Lorenzo's hot on his heels.

"Well done, laddie," I say as I spin about searching for more of Lilith's soldiers to dispatch.

There are several nearby. The four of us spread out and recommence our butchering.

Perhaps I should feel pity for these slaves of Lilith. Aye, pity them I do, but I'll nae give them the opportunity to rejoin her.

The vampire before me scrambles on broken, Healing legs, struggling to get upright. His wings appear just as I take his head. The ephemeral wings vanish, and both body and head fall to the floor.

"Captain!" Ericson points upward. "Empress is bugging out!"

I lift my eyes and see that Lilith's small army's been reduced to but a wee fraction of its former strength. I'd estimate nae more than a dozen remain to her. They're forcing their way through a storm of bullets toward the upper level. Three more fall before they fly into the box. Yet again, Lilith has sacrificed almost all her protectors in her desperate escape.

Marines scramble up the stairs to dispatch downed vampires.

"All Marines, Pirate," Carl says. "Take out the fallen. We'll pursue Empress."

The sudden absence of gunfire is deafening. *There's nae anything to shoot at.*

A burst of gunfire breaks that silence. There's another burst. *'Tis simply Marines preventing vampires from rising before they can be killed.*

"Roger, Pirate. We'll mop up here." I can hear Todd's response through Carl's earphone quite clearly. "Godspeed, Pirate."

Carl leaps into the air, pursuing the fleeing vampires. Rolf, Andrew, and I follow.

"It was an honor, Marines," Carl says. "Pirate out."

We fly up, pursuing the enemy to the highest level of the stadium. Carl slows as we approach the box. I pull up beside him on his right flank. *"His right wing," as he'd call it.* Rolf stops and hovers on my right and Andrew on Carl's left.

There are a few rows of seats and, above that, the glass walls and door to the suite beyond. The room's dark, but my eyes can easily see 'tis deserted, save for the bodies of four Marines like broken dolls lying strewn on the floor. I cannae see Tony. And there's nae hide nor hair of Lorenzo or Sergei. *I hope they got here before Lilith. I hope they got Tony to safety.*

I hope Sergei has nae had yet another change of mind.

I can hear several heartbeats, faint to be sure, but somewhere ahead of us. Inside the suite, I see a number of tables and chairs, but nothing that could conceal an enemy. I've nae doubt they're outside the suite waiting for us to rush in.

Waiting in ambush.

Carl seems to have come to the same conclusion. He points at Andrew and Rolf and then indicates the box to the left. He mouths, "Fifteen, fourteen, thirteen ..." Rolf nods and continues the silent countdown. He and Andrew fly silently toward the left box. Carl starts to fly toward the box on the right, motioning me to follow.

I dinnae follow. I get up even with him. I will nae let him go in first.

We fly through the suite and wait at the door to the hall. It stands open.

Carl mouths, "Three, two, one." He flies toward the hall door, but I beat him through. I veer to the left. There are half a dozen vampires in the hall, three on either side of the door of the suite. Rolf and Andrew appear on the far side.

Rolf flies forward and skewers one of the enemy with his spear before I reach them. I put a sword right through the back of the closest man on my side. I withdraw the sword and relieve my man of his head. Carl's engaging one of them. Their combat takes them out into the open space of the hall, away from the rest of us.

I take on another man. He turns out to be a competent swordsman. It takes me a second or two to find an opening. He misses a parry, and I dispatch him.

I glance at Carl just as he kills his man.

I hear a cry of rage. "Nein!" Rolf has another man impaled on his spear, lifting him high. At Rolf's feet lie three bodies, two of them headless.

The third is Andrew.

He's nae headless, but his head is at an unnatural angle.

I drop to my knees and examine him. The neck is broken. He's nae breathing.

Rolf swings his spear, sending his man sliding off it. Rolf hews at the man's neck and sends him to judgment.

Andrew's lips move, but there's nae sound.

"Andrew," Carl says. He's kneeling beside me. Rolf stands near Andrew's feet, his eyes grim.

"Is he gonna be OK?" Carl asks.

I brush my fingers along Andrew's cheek. "I'm sorry, laddie." I dinnae know if I'm talking to Carl or to Andrew. "There's nae anything I can do." My tears fall on his face.

"He's not breathing," Carl says anxiously. "Shouldn't you be doing mouth-to-mouth? CPR?"

"'Twould only prolong the inevitable," I say. *Atlanto-occipital dislocation.* "'Tis internal decapitation. His spinal cord is severed. The Seed cannae repair it. We could keep him breathing and move blood through his veins for a bit, but he's dying and there's nae anything I can do to stop it."

The silent movement of Andrew's lips slows.

"Move away then," Rolf says. "Let me ease his suffering."

"No," Carl says. "I mean, *please* don't. It's not our place."

"You're joking, right?" Rolf says. "We've dealt death to a hundred to-night. A hundred who couldn't fight back. And I can't administer a *coup-de-grace* to a friend who's suffering?"

"It's not our place to . . ." Carl falters. "Mercy killing is . . ."

"It does nae matter," I say. "He's gone."

Andrew's face is still, slack. He does nae look peaceful. "He did nae suffer long. With nae oxygen to the brain, I doubt he was even aware of yer debate."

Rolf lets out a snarl and stabs at the corpses of the other vampires. "*Auch das noch!* And all for nothing! She's gone, isn't she?"

Three heartbeats. 'Tis all I can detect.

"Lilith got away again," Carl says. His voice raw, bitter as a cup of bile. "We should've left these and gone after her. Trouble is, they covered her escape. Now we don't even know where she's gone."

He slams his fist into the concrete floor. Dust and shards of concrete fly about. One of them scores my cheek. There's a small crater under Carl's fist. "Not again! How in the . . . ?" He looks up to heaven. "What am I supposed to do? I've done all You've asked of me! They're all dead! Seventy good people! They followed me. They trusted me. And we lost Tony *again!* And the kids . . . We lost the kids." Carl puts his head in his hands. "What am I doing wrong?" 'Tis almost a sob. "What am I missing? What am I supposed to do?"

I put a hand on his shoulder. "Laddie, we don't know that we've lost Tony again. Perhaps Lorenzo and Sergei got him to safety." Even as the words escape my mouth, I know they cannae be true.

Carl drops his hands and looks up. There's a grim set to his face. "Seventy-two."

Lorenzo and Sergei. Ach, nae! Nae them as well!

"They'd be back by now if they were able." Rolf has spoken the horrid truth.

I pull out my cell phone and quickly dial Lorenzo's number. There's nae answer. I dial Sergei. Once again, there's nae answer. It just rings and then goes to voice mail.

"And we don't even know where to look," Carl says. "We don't even know where to *start* looking."

There's something . . . something I should remember.

"Laddie," I say slowly, "just before the attack, ye shouted that she, Lilith, I mean . . . Ye said she had an army."

"Yup," is his only reply.

"How did ye know?" I ask.

He sighs wearily. "Tony was trying to warn us. He was pretending, acting like he'd lost it. He kept singing, 'Behold a royal legion,' and that bit about the pigs sinking into the sea. He got the word wrong. On purpose. It's 'army,' not 'legion.'"

"And the pigs drowning in the sea," Rolf says. "That was a reference to the Bible story, the one about the man possessed with a legion of devils, was it not?"

That's it!

"'Twas nae the words only, was it now?" I say.

Carl shakes his head. "No, the tune was off too. I didn't recognize it, but I know it wasn't the tune of 'Behold a Royal Army.' And he sang the same tune for the 'pigs is pigs' part too."

"Ye may nae recognize it, laddie, but I do. 'Tis an old tune. And though 'tis in our hymnbooks, 'tis nae often sung. The tune was an old Appalachian hymn called 'Prospect of Heaven.' But we use it today, when we sing it, that is, as a hymn called 'Adam-Ondi-Ahman.'"

He looks astonished. "You've got to be kidding me? Really?"

Nodding vigorously, I say, "Aye."

"What are you talking about?" Rolf asks.

"Adam-Ondi-Ahman," I reply. "It's one of the few phrases we know in Adamic, the language of Adam. It means, 'Where Adam walked with God,' or more likely, 'Adam with God.'"

Rolf looks completely confused. "You lost me. How would you know what anything means in the language of Adam? And what does that have to do with knowing where Lilith is?"

"'Twas revealed to the prophet Joseph Smith, and he was given to know what it meant," I say. "And he said Adam-Ondi-Ahman was located in Missouri, nae far from here."

Rolf smiles. "She's gone home, so to speak, to the place where she was born. So we know where she is!"

Carl laughs mirthlessly. "It's still a big area, but at least we know that general vicinity. From what I understand, it's mostly farmland up there. There's a site maintained by the Church, but I don't think there's any place at the site where Lilith could hide out during the day. Maybe there's a visitors' center or something. We'll have to get a map and . . ."

"Captain Morgan!"

I look behind me and see Colonel Evans leading a score or more of Marines up the hallway. They're running toward us.

Carl rises to his feet. "Sitrep, Colonel."

"Halt!" Evans cries. He and his men stop, holding their weapons ready. "We lost White Sox squad. All other Marines are present or accounted for. What's your status? Did we get her? Did we secure the civilian?"

"Negative on both counts," Carl says. "We wouldn't be standing here if Lilith were dead. When she dies, we die. Remember?"

Evans nods. "I guess I was hoping you were wrong about that part. And the civilian?"

"We assume she's got him *again*," Carl says. "Lilith escaped. And . . ." There's the slightest hitch in my husband's voice. ". . . we lost one good man and two more are MIA."

"I'm sorry to hear that, captain. At least we took out a whole buttload of vampires."

Carl nods. "That we did, sir."

"So, what's the plan? What can the Corps do to help?"

"We think we know where she's gone," Carl says. "At least we know the general area. I'll need to look at a map, though. Do any of your men happen to have a map of Missouri?"

"Doubtful, but we've got GPS units." Evans thumbs his throat microphone. "Brave, this is Mariner."

"Go ahead, Mariner." 'Tis Lieutenant Todd's voice in the colonel's earpiece.

"Secure me a GPS and bring it up to the third level on the double." Evans switches off his microphone.

"That'll help," Carl says, "but I kinda doubt we'll find the place name in a GPS."

"Are you kidding me, zoomie?" Evans smiles. "This ain't no namby-pamby Air Force GPS. Maybe you zoomies've got pisspoor GPS systems made in Taiwan, but in the Corps, we can do better."

Carl grins. "Much obliged, Colonel."

Evans nods. "When do we move out?"

"We, the three of us . . ." Carl points to Rolf and me. "We'll be on our own."

Evans opens his mouth, clearly to object, but Carl cuts him off. "We have to move out ASAP, and we need to fly. You'd only slow us down, sir."

Evans seems to accept Carl's logic. Then he cocks his head to the side. "You look like hell, Morgan." He points to Carl's chest. "What'd you do? Take one in the chest?"

Carl laughs once. "In the heart, actually."

Evans looks dubious. "In the heart?"

"I got better," Carl says. "It's a vampire thing."

Evans shakes his head. "I'll be damned. But you still look like hell."

Carl runs a hand through his hair. "Yeah, I'm beat. We all are. And Healing my heart . . . Well, that takes a lot of energy."

The Marine colonel looks Rolf and me over. "Yeah, you three do look the worse for wear." He turns to me. "No offense, ma'am."

I smile wearily. "None taken, laddie. Ye're grand."

Evans grins. "I think we can fix you up, though."

"And how do you propose to do that?" Rolf asks.

"We're gonna get you fed before you head out."

I blink at him, nae kenning what he means. "The only thing we can eat, Colonel, is human blood."

"Well, how much do you need?" the colonel asks. "I've got eighty-four strong men, including myself." He turns his head slightly and calls over his shoulder. "Any of you men willing to donate a cup of blood, take one step forward!"

As one, every single man behind Evans steps forward. There's nary a hint of hesitation. The colonel smiles in pride and satisfaction and takes one step forward himself.

He tilts his head to the side, pulling his microphone off his neck. "Me first."

'Tis a bizarre scene, to be sure. These brave men lining up to be bitten by a vampire. The Marines form three lines. As more of them arrive, the newcomers join the queues. Oh, aye, there are questions asked and explanations given, but, to a man, they line up.

It reminds me of all those souls who volunteered to donate blood after the nine-eleven attacks. They could nae go fight the terrorists, but they wanted to do something.

I take just a wee bit from each man.

Some of them *thank* me.

Eventually, I can drink nae more. The next Marine in my line actually looks *disappointed.*

Carl's still Feeding. His stomach's larger, being a man. Or perhaps he's taking less from each man. Rolf appears to be sated.

"Ma'am?" 'Tis Lieutenant Todd. He was one of the first in my queue, having claimed privilege. "Here's the GPS." He hands me a small hand-held device. "I've programmed in the target area. It took some doing. Had to try a bunch of things before I came up with the right place. It's about seventy-three miles to the north-north-east. That's driving distance, of course. You'll cut off a few miles in the air. If you press this button . . ."

My cell phone rings.

I hastily pull the phone from my pocket and look at the screen. My heart freezes in my chest, as I read:

Incoming call:
Lorenzo

Chapter 33

Tony

Where's Sergei? I can't see him. I can't hear him. And I want so much to please him.

He's dead!

That voice again. So distant. Less than a whisper. Soft. Weak. Irrelevant.

Sergei said to wait for the Queen. So I'm waiting for the Queen. I waited for her in the sports arena. Now I'm waiting for her in the farmhouse.

She's nearby. I can hear her. How I love the sound of her voice. I can smell her. I love her scent. I'd do anything for her. I love her. I worship her.

Where are you, Sergei? Command me. I live to serve you.

Dead! Dead! Dead!

"Sit." Her voice.

Ah, at last. A command. Something to fill the emptiness of my soul. A way to please her.

I sit.

"Bind him with these." Her voice again. Was that for me?

"Put your hands on the arms of the chair, lover."

That was for me.

Eagerly I put my hands on the arms of the chair.

A man—William is his name—stands in front of me. He wraps an iron bar around my left wrist and another around my right. The one on the right hurts. I hope it pleases the Queen. I would do anything to please her.

Fight this! Don't listen! Don't obey! Resist!

White noise. Static. Nothing compared to her voice.

"Not too tight, my love." Her voice again.

William loosens the iron around my right wrist. The pain eases.

She loves me. She cares about me.

I would do anything.

There she is. Right in front of me. Looking at me. Looking me in the eye.

Her eyes. So beautiful. So brown. So blue. So green. So black. The whole world in those eyes.

"Remember, lover." Her voice resonates through my whole being, matching the vibration of every molecule. How could I not obey her? "Remember everything."

And I remember.

A manic, shifting kaleidoscope of images and sounds, bouncing off each other like multicolored geometric bits in a rotating tube of memory, devoid of meaning or relevance, lacking attachment or consequence.

Sergei tells me to stay in the box suite and wait for the Queen.

The corpses of four heavily armed men, twisted into anatomically improbable shapes, littering the floor.

Gunfire and screams.

A fly alighting on the face of one corpse and then crawling into a nostril.

The Queen, beautiful beyond description.

Lilith's voice saying, "Carlos, Raphael, William, come with me. Raphael, bring the mortal. The rest of you remain behind and kill the rebels. He who brings me the head of the Unwilling or the Penitent shall be my First Husband. Do not fail me. Remember that I love you."

A man scooping me up and tucking me under one arm like a sack of wheat. Facing down, seeing the floor and the backs of his legs.

Lilith's blood red skirt.

A crash of shattering glass.

The cold night air whipping around me like a storm.

The flapping of many wings.

The lights of the city below me.

A man crying out.

The sound of steel on steel.

The lights of the city whirling as I'm spun around and pulled semiupright.

Lorenzo's face, filled with rage.

A flash of steel.

Lorenzo fighting with the vampire who's holding me. His name's William.

Another vampire, with sword drawn, flying toward Lorenzo from behind.

The voice in my head silently screaming, "Look out!"

Sergei slicing off the head of a vampire.

Sergei roaring, "No!"

Sparks flying in the night sky as Lorenzo's blade collides with William's.

Falling, tumbling.

William fighting Lorenzo.

Lorenzo falling.

The voice in my head wailing out Lorenzo's name.

Sergei flying toward me.

Another vampire behind him.

Sergei catching me in his arms, arresting my fall. "I've got you."

Looking up into his face, seeing the other vampire above him.

A flash of steel.

Sergei's head toppling from his shoulders, his blood spraying on me as his arms go limp.

Falling again.

Lorenzo plummeting past me.

The voice, so like my voice, silently calling his name again.

William catching me.

Flying up with him.

Lorenzo arresting his own tumbling fall.

Lorenzo flying up after us.

Lorenzo getting closer.

Lorenzo's hands empty. No sword.

Gray darkness enveloping me.

Clouds.

Lorenzo calling my name.

Lorenzo calling my name again, farther away this time.

Cold. Freezing. Wet.

Emerging from the clouds.

The farmhouse.

Lilith's eyes.

I'm free!

She's not staring at me anymore. Like waking up from a dream, a dream of being baptized in sweetness, drowning in honey.

I try to move my hands, but my wrists are held tight. My mind's free, though.

Persuaded. I must have been Persuaded.

Sergei's dead!

I don't get it. The succession of betrayals and counterbetrayals is dizzying, especially with my memories tainted by Persuasion.

Sergei flew with me across the arena floor, rescuing me from Lilith, but once we were clear, he looked me in the eye and . . .

That's when it must have happened. Persuasion.

He left me waiting for Lilith. She and some of her people came for me. Then Sergei and Lorenzo . . . Lorenzo's still alive! Sergei and Lorenzo came after me again. Lorenzo was injured. He fell. Sergei saved me again, but it cost him his life.

Now we're back in the farmhouse.

I see Lilith and William and one other vampire. I think his name is Raphael.

Only three of them left.

"What happened to the rest?" I ask.

"What's that, lover?" Lilith turns toward me again. Our eyes lock.

And she's transformed.

My pulse races. It's hard to breathe. So beautiful, like a fairy princess.

Fairy.

A glamour.

It's a *glamour* like in the old tales of fairies, this effect she has on me. One of the fair folk could have an enchantment, appearing more beautiful than she or he actually was, ensnaring and seducing mortals.

Maybe Lilith is the basis for those stories.

So it's fake.

I can fight this.

My breathing eases. She's still beautiful. It's hard to define the exact nature of her beauty, the color of her eyes, the color of her hair, her skin, but it's not real.

She murdered my children. She didn't do it herself, but she had her Children murder mine. She's a demon. Beautiful, yes, but in a way that is . . . manufactured. Promising pleasure, but not love. She tells her Children she loves them, and then she sacrifices them to save herself.

"What's that, lover?" she repeats.

"What happened to the rest of your . . . minions?" I ask.

She straightens her back, seeming to draw herself up in a regal pose. "They gave their lives in the service of their Queen."

William and Raphael exchange a furtive glance. They look worried.

Good.

Lilith smiles. "There is no greater expression of their love for me." She caresses William's cheek. He closes his eyes and trembles at her touch. It's as if he has cast all his doubts away, like a dog shaking water from its fur.

Lilith turns and caresses Raphael's cheek, and all doubt seems to vanish from his face too.

I begin to laugh. It starts out low, but it builds. And it builds. I close my eyes, squeezing tears of mirth from between the lids.

"Stop that." The Queen sounds annoyed.

I laugh all the harder.

"The Queen told you to stop, mortal!" Raphael snaps. He takes a step toward me, but Lilith holds up a halting hand. Raphael's face twists in a silent snarl. He bares his teeth. His fangs are extended.

He looks like a snarling dog.

I get my laughter under control. Mostly. "You're so pathetic. You two are the only ones left, right? Do you know how many of you she's 'sacrificed' tonight? How many last night? And you're still standing there like lapdogs being petted by your owner."

"Let me tear out his lying tongue, my Queen." William's voice, like the low growl of a wolf, is full of quiet menace.

Lilith holds up a hand, silencing him.

I smile. "Lying? You wouldn't know the truth if it bit you in the butt. What happened to the six you left behind? Shouldn't they be here by now?" I laugh again. "'He who brings me the head of the Unwilling or the Penitent . . .' Oops! No, wait! I get it. Another sacrifice!"

"Insolent son of a whore," Raphael says. "You dare . . ."

"I dare what, lapdog?" I say. "Speak the truth? Yeah, she'd sacrifice both of you in a heartbeat. *She* would sacrifice *you*. It wouldn't be your choice, would it, Raphy? Would it, Billy-Boy? You're her slaves."

"My Queen!" Raphael's expression flickers between rage and doubt. His fangs have retracted.

William looks worried. His eyes flit back and forth between me and Lilith.

"Why are you doing this, lover?" she asks. Her expression is cautious. "Are you trying to provoke me? Are you trying to get yourself killed? Because I can do far worse than kill you."

Why am *I doing this? Am I trying to get myself killed? Do I just want it all to be over? Abby and Little Tony are gone. Kathleen's safe, but she'll never forgive me for my failure.*

Why am *I doing this?*

Because sowing doubt is perhaps the only thing I can *do. That . . . and distracting her. Slowing her down. Keeping her here. Giving Carl and Moira a chance to decipher my message.*

Please, Heavenly Father. Help them figure it out.

"Why, lover?" she repeats.

"Stop calling me that, Lilith," I say, surprising myself with my own audacity. "I'm not your lover, and I never will be. That's why you're keeping me around, right? To consummate your seduction? Well, good luck with that. It'll be your grandfather Adam all over again. Although, after the last couple of nights of *epic* failure, what's one more botched seduction?"

She scowls.

I shake my head and sneer. "Face it, lady, you're no Kathleen."

Lilith's lovely face twists into a teeth-baring expression of rage. A scream starts low and builds to an ear-splitting howl. The house shakes. Lilith appears to grow, to fill the whole kitchen. She becomes a vast dark shadow, eyes blazing with fire, and with white wings spread from wall to wall.

On either side of her, Raphael and William shrink back from her in unabashed terror. Raphael exclaims something I can't hear above Lilith's scream and the groaning timbers of the house. William wails like a frightened child.

I feel like I'm about to lose control of my bowels.

In a flash, it's all gone. The shadow vanishes as well as the wings. The house stops quaking.

Lilith seems to collect herself. She tilts her head back until she's looking down her nose at me.

She's still lovely, breathtakingly beautiful. But the glamour, if that's what it was, is gone. *She's not trying anymore? Or have I broken her power over me?*

"Failure?" she whispers. After the howling and the house shaking, her soft, barely audible whisper is all the more terrifying. "Oh, no, lover. I haven't failed. And I won't. You'll be mine. You'll give yourself to me. This I swear. I'll just have to change tactics."

Why is this so important to her? Why is my seduction so important? A single failure six millennia ago? Could that have scarred her ego so badly that she cannot accept a second one? Or is it simply that she's not used to having anyone tell her "No"?

"But first things first," she says with a grin. "Let us post the guard."

"My Queen," William says, looking puzzled and still shaken by Lilith's temper tantrum, "there are but two of us. How shall we keep watch once the Sun is up?" William's manner of speaking and his very proper British accent make him seem to be older than most of the vampires I've met.

"Fear not, my pet," Lilith says, sounding more like her normal self. "I have other allies. Ones that can bear the Sun, don't I, *Helel?* I feel you here, Fallen One. So nice of you to drop by without my summoning you. Show yourself."

"Yes, Mistress?" Lucifer is standing in the living room.

Did he just appear, or did I simply not notice him before?

"Since you have come, Serpent," Lilith says, turning halfway to look at him, "since you are so concerned with my welfare, I have a task for you."

Satan's shoulders are slumped, his posture suggesting defeat. His expression is weary as he looks at Lilith. "Did I not serve you well, Daughter of Cain?" *Lucifer is whining!* "Did I not locate the rebels for you and spy on them as you commanded? What more do you want of me? Is it my fault you failed to kill them?"

"Know your place, Worm," Lilith snaps. "I want you to place members of your Host to guard this house. You will report to me personally if any of the rebels approach. You and your Host will become my new Honor Guard until such time as I can replace them with lovely, delicious mortal men. Men with bodies such as you will never have. Now go!"

The Devil bows low. "I exist but to serve you."

Lilith waves her hand in dismissal. "Go, Father of Lies."

Lucifer glances at me again. There is that same pleading look he has given me each time.

Deliver me.

Then he vanishes.

So what happens if Carl and Moira succeed in killing Lilith? What happens if they free Satan from his bondage to her? Will Satan become more powerful? Who is the greater enemy? Surely it's Satan. Will he be able to do more damage once he's free? Or does he simply want to escape her control, escape from the pain she can inflict on him? Or is there something more to this? He is the Father of Lies. Is he trying to trick me, to deceive me somehow into helping him? I don't know if . . .

"Bring him, William," Lilith says. "Pick up his chair and carry him into the bedroom upstairs. We'll make him *watch*." She runs her hands sensuously down her hips. Her eyes lock with mine, and she slowly licks her lips. "One way," she says, "or the other, lover."

♦ ♦ ♦

When I refuse to watch Lilith and Raphael writhing together on the bed, William holds my head stationary and my eyelids open. I try to look away, but William twists my head until the bed and its occupants are centered in my field of view. Sometimes I think he'll snap my neck. I roll my eyes up into my head to avoid watching, but I can't maintain it. Eventually, inevitably, I'm forced to observe them.

And listen to them.

After a while, William and Raphael switch places.

I try to tell myself that it doesn't affect me, doesn't concern me, but I know I'm lying.

The worst is when Lilith's eyes lock with mine. Then I have to wrestle with the sights and sounds, but also her glamour, her undeniable sensuality, and her pull.

I pray. I pray hard.

I try to hum a hymn tune.

"We're back to that, are we, Tony?" That's one of the few times Lilith hasn't called me "lover." With her doing . . . what she's doing, using my name is all the more unsettling.

As if she's reading my mind, she begins to call out my name in the throes of her passion.

Father in Heaven! Help me! She murdered my children!

"Tony!" Lilith cries out.

"Help me, Father!" *I said that out loud.* "Help me!"

Lilith laughs.

And something shifts inside me. At first, I don't know what it is, what has shifted, but I am certain *something* has changed. The first thing I can pinpoint is a building nausea. It's not so much that I think I'm going to be actively sick—especially since I haven't eaten anything in two days—it's more a growing sense of revulsion at what I'm seeing, at the thought of *her*, at the thought of me actually struggling with *attraction* to this monster. *She killed my children. She made Kathleen choose one child over the other. Kathleen. There is nothing . . .* nothing *about this woman-shaped demon that compares to Kathleen.*

And I begin to chuckle. And, to my mild amazement, it's not the laughter of someone who's lost his mind. It's simply a laugh of amusement and wonder.

Lilith and William pause. She locks eyes with me. The glamour's still there, but I feel *nothing* for this creature.

Nothing, that is, but disgust.

"Are we amusing you, Tony?"

I would shake my head, but Raphael holds it fixed. "No, Lilith. You *disgust* me. Aren't you tired yet? Aren't you bored?"

She stares at me, her confusion obvious. "Bored?"

"Well, I'm getting bored, Lilly," I say. "May I call you Lilly?"

"My Queen!" Raphael says, his voice filled with rage. "Please allow me to . . ."

He stops abruptly. Both William and Lilith are looking at something outside my field of vision. Raphael releases my head. My neck aches as I turn my head stiffly in the direction they appear to be looking.

Lucifer is there, the whiteness of his suit marred only by the black shoes and gold tie. The Devil looks as bored as I professed to be. He appears to be inspecting his nails as he makes a quiet throat-clearing sound.

"Light-Bearer!" Lilith cries. She shoves William off and scrambles to her feet.

She doesn't bother to cover herself.

"My apologies, Mistress, for interrupting your diversions," Satan says, his voice almost casual, as he now inspects the fingernails of his other hand, "but you did ask to be warned."

Lilith's eyes go wide. I see fear, then shock, then anger flit across her expression. "Speak!"

The two nude male vampires stand stock still, as if they've become rooted to the floor.

Are they afraid of attack, or are they afraid of Lucifer?

"As you command," The Devil drawls, bowing slightly. "Two rebels are engaged in a somewhat heated, if muted, quarrel in the sky above this . . . palace. One of them wishes to attack. The other insists they first confer with the Unwilling and the Penitent." He sighs as if completely disinterested. "Who will prevail, I wonder?"

Nobody moves. They seem paralyzed.

Lilith didn't think they'd be found here. Carl and Moira got my message!

Lucifer purses his lips and appears slightly annoyed. "I meant, who will win the argument? To attack," he waves his hand like a bored actor playing a world-weary Hamlet, "or not to attack? That is the question."

The bedroom window explodes in a hail of flying glass.

Lilith's mouth gapes open in mute shock.

There's a spear protruding from her chest. A spear with an ancient-looking iron head.

Rolf is standing behind Lilith, his eyes blazing with fury. "Für Sarah!" he snarls.

As one, Raphael and William leap for their swords.

Rolf holds the spear stationary, standing his ground.

He's waiting for Lilith to die.

Lilith makes a feeble, ineffectual attempt to pull the spear from her body.

Rolf draws Sarah's broadsword and glares at William defiantly. William evades Rolf's blade and thrusts his sword through Rolf's neck. Rolf slumps forward, releasing the spear and dropping his sword, his head at an unnatural angle.

Raphael drops his weapon and pulls the spear shaft from Lilith's chest. She too falls, landing upon the blood-soaked sheets of the bed.

She lies still, unmoving.

I hear the sound of laughter.

Lucifer is chuckling in the corner, his white suit untouched by the gore that seems to be everywhere.

No physical body.

Lorenzo comes flying into the room. He immediately lops off Raphael's head as the naked vampire bends over his fallen Queen.

William takes a wicked slice at Lorenzo, which my great-great-grandfather narrowly avoids. Lorenzo appears to slip in the blood, or maybe gets his foot tangled in the bedclothes. He stumbles, and William attacks again with a chop from above.

The Devil's laughter fills the room.

Lorenzo parries the blow and drives his left fist into William's midsection. William makes a woofing sound as the air is driven from his lungs. He weakly parries one blow from Lorenzo, but then misses the second. Lorenzo thrusts William through the heart. Wrenching the blade free, Lorenzo swings again, and William loses his head.

Lorenzo glances at me, and our eyes lock for a moment. Then he drops to the floor beside Rolf. He gently cradles Rolf's head in his hands, turning it so that the nearly severed neck is straight once again.

Will that be enough? Can he save Rolf?

Rolf's lips move silently. He mouths, "Sarah." Then he smiles.

His face goes slack.

Lorenzo says, "Go to her, my friend. She's waiting for you."

"Lorenzo," I say.

He doesn't look up, still staring into the dead face of Rolf.

"You're alive," I say. *Still alive!* "I thought that when Lilith died . . ."

"You thought me dead, lover?"

I feel sharp steel at my throat.

Lilith stands behind me.

And the Devil's no longer laughing.

Lorenzo looks up, but he's not looking at me. He looks past me and gasps.

He must be looking into her eyes.

"It's a trick," I say, but the sword at my throat presses deep. I feel blood trickling down my neck.

"Be still, or I'll kill him," Lilith says in that silken voice, sweet as honey.

Lorenzo looks at me. No, not at me. *Is he looking at the blood on my neck?*

"Do you think I care?" he says, licking his lips. Still focusing on the blood or the blade—I can't tell which—Lorenzo slowly begins to stand. "This mortal is nothing to me, not even a meal. Go ahead. Kill him." Lorenzo's now standing fully erect. He points his sword at Lilith, but he's still fixating on my throat. "I'm here to kill you, Lilith. If you take the time to kill the mortal, you will not have time to stop my blade from removing your lovely head from your shapely neck."

Lilith doesn't move.

Suddenly, I'm intensely aware of her nearness, her nakedness, the heat of her skin. I'm aware of it, but I force my mind to think past it.

"Do it," I manage to croak out.

Lorenzo's eyes flicker to mine. His eyes appear profoundly sad as if to say, *Forgive me.*

"Do it," I manage to say again.

"Helel," Lilith says. Her voice is harsh, imperious. Gone is the honey. "*Sever* him."

"What?" Lucifer sounds confused.

"Cut him off," Lilith says. "Now."

"I'm not sure that will work. It's never been done, but . . ." The Devil sighs. "As you command."

Lorenzo's confusion mirrors my own. Then his jaw drops, and his eyes go wide. The sword drops from his hand. He stumbles and puts a hand to his forehead.

The blade is gone from my neck. Lilith steps around from behind me. She places the blade on Lorenzo's shoulder.

Lorenzo falls to his knees. He gazes wordlessly up at Lilith in horror and shock.

"What have you done?" I whisper.

"I am the Mother of Night. I am Mistress of the Essence. It is mine to command. Mine to bestow and mine to remove."

Softly, Lucifer says, "Lilith giveth and Lilith taketh away."

Chapter 34

Moira

There! That house, laddie!" I point frantically to a large white frame house, sitting in the middle of dark green fields enclosed on three sides by a bend in the river.

"Are you sure?" Carl asks.

"It must be, laddie. 'Tis the only place with lights on in the wee hours. And 'twould have been along the path they'd have taken."

"Roger," Carl replies, and he wheels about. I follow right behind him.

'Rolf and I are going to investigate a house," Lorenzo said over the phone. Then he cried, "Rolf! No!" There was the sound of wind or air rushing and then the connection went dead.

Lorenzo must've dropped the phone. 'Twould seem that Rolf took off alone, and Lorenzo must've let the phone fall when he went after Rolf.

I pray we're nae too late. Ach, we're all about to die. If they're in that house, that'll be where *she* is.

And when we find her, it all ends. I can feel it in my ancient bones.

Aye, 'tis at last the end.

"That window on the north side," Carl says. "It's broken."

Aye, there's a broken window, and there's light and a moving shadow within.

Carl draws his sword, the claymore, and I draw my ebony blade.

The sword of truth, to fight demons.

Side by side, we dive toward the house.

As we approach, though, Carl slows and holds up a hand.

I can smell the blood from here. 'Tis vampire blood. At least for the most part. There's some mortal blood to be sure, but it does nae smell fresh.

There's nae longer someone moving around on the other side of the broken window.

I listen carefully. I can hear three distinct heartbeats, three people breathing, and nothing else.

I point to myself and then point at the window. *I should enter first.*

Carl shakes his head firmly. He points to me and points at the window with two fingers. *He means to take the lead and for me to follow.*

I'm about to argue when he starts toward the window.

So follow him I do.

He flies through with me right behind.

The room's in shambles. There's blood everywhere. Vampire blood. And three bodies. Two naked men and . . . Rolf!

Ach, nae!

Poor lad.

I want to weep, but there's nae time. He's with his Sarah now.

And we'll be joining them right soon.

Still hovering so as to keep from making noise, I move to the door. This time Carl has the good sense to let me take the "point."

We're in a hallway. The plaster on the ceiling has fallen in a number of places. Something heavy has been dragged through the white plaster dust on the floor. There's a stairway leading down. The heartbeats and sounds of breathing are coming from there.

"Show yourselves." 'Tis Lilith's voice. "I can hear you breathing. Show yourselves or I'll kill them both."

Both? She has Tony, but has she somehow captured Lorenzo as well?

I alight at the top of the stairs. Carl lands beside me. Together we descend, our swords leading the way.

At the bottom of the stairs is a short hallway and beyond that a parlor. And in that parlor, Lilith stands between two wooden chairs. On our left is Tony. His wrists are bound to the chair by twisted wrought-iron bars. Lorenzo's in the chair on our right. He's tied to the chair-back by strips of bloody cloth. *Scraps of sheet from the bedroom above?*

Why does Lorenzo nae free himself? 'Twould be child's play to rip those fetters.

Lilith holds a sword in each hand and she's holding them at the throats of our friends.

Why is Lorenzo just sitting there?

I can see two bodies, mortals, a man and a woman, shoved unceremoniously into a corner.

There's broken plaster in this room as well.

"We're here," Carl says.

Lilith smiles. "So you are." Her red dress bears but a few small spots of blood. Either she was nae a part of the fight upstairs or . . . Nae. There's blood on her hands and on her neck.

The naked men upstairs . . . Lilith was naked at the time.

"We have a stalemate here, don't we?" she says.

"What's wrong with Lorenzo?" I ask.

Lorenzo lifts his head. He looks utterly lost. "I'm mortal."

"What did you say?" *I cannae have heard him properly.*

"I'm mortal," he repeats.

"That's impossible," Carl says.

Lilith smiles. 'Tis the smile of a benevolent and long-suffering queen. "I have the power to grant immortality and to take it away," Lilith says. "I haven't stripped one of my Children of immortality in more than five thousand years. Would you like to be mortal again, Carl? Perhaps you, Moira MacDonald Morgan?"

For the first time ever, she looks directly at me.

I gasp in amazement. I have ne'er seen anyone so beautiful. I cannae breathe. I've nae e'er been attracted physically to a woman, but for the first time I can *understand* such attraction. She's perfection. I feel so small, so homely, so *lacking*, at least compared to her. I want to be close to her, to be like her. She looks like my mother, only my mother was ne'er so lovely.

Nae my mother; she looks like *me*, like me as I wish I were. As if I could be so bonnie . . .

And she's nae longer holding two swords. She's holding a bonnie wee bairn in her arms. Nae, 'tis *I*. I'm seeing *myself* hold a bairn with red curls. And I ken 'tis mine, my own flesh and blood. Nae, 'tis twins. A pair of bonnie bairns, a wee laddie and a precious wee lassie.

And they're mine. Mine and Carl's. The laddie has Carl's blue eyes. The lass, my green.

"All your life, you've yearned for a child, haven't you?" Her voice is honey and sweet, warm cream. "I can give you that, Moira. I can give you your heart's desire. I can make you mortal. Just think of it, Child. You and your beloved husband could have a family. You could grow old together."

"Moira?" Carl's voice. So harsh. I wish he'd be still. I want to listen to *her*. *How my arms ache to hold the bairns! My bairns!*

"Sever them, Helel." *Who's she speaking to?*

The air has been sucked from my lungs.

Dizzy.

I feel so strange.

So weak. I can barely stand.

I nearly drop my sword. I clutch at Carl with my free hand.

He's unsteady, as if he cannae stand either.

"What?" he says in a wobbly voice. "What did you do?"

"It's the Essence." 'Tis Tony speaking. "She's cut you off from the Essence."

The Essence? Gone?

So weak. I dinnae e'er remember feeling so weak, so powerless. Nae since I was . . .

"You're mortal," Tony says, "like me."

"I I-how?" I ask. *Lilith's still holding my bairns. I want my bairns! I know 'tis nae possible. 'Tis nae but a mental projection of some kind or something akin to Persuasion. It must be.*

Aye, but they're so bonnie!

"Show yourself, Helel," Lilith says, a malevolent grin splitting her face . . . my face. Nae. 'Tis nae my face.

So confused. I cannae think.

Suddenly I'm aware of a man. *Was he there before?* I dinnae remember seeing him. Dressed all in white save for his shoes and his necktie. I cannae hear his heartbeat or his breathing. *Another projection?*

"Yes, Mistress," he says. He looks at me.

His eyes. I feel . . . unclean. Weak and unclean and helpless . . . naked. So exposed. *Like being in Michael Beaumont's bed, waiting to be raped again.*

Carl and I lean against each other, barely keeping our feet.

"Who?" I manage to say.

Lilith puts one of the bairns, the wee laddie, my son—my son that could be—to her breast. *How did she expose her breast? Both her hands are full.* "Explain it to them, lover."

"You're"—Tony grunts—"cutting me." I drag my eyes away from Lilith and the bairns and look at Tony. I can see the sword again. She's holding a sword to Tony's neck and another to Lorenzo's. She's nae holding any children.

A trickle of blood runs down Tony's neck from beneath the blade.

Lilith pulls the sword an inch or so away from Tony's neck. "Is that better?" she asks.

Tony's blood smells delicious.

Glancing at Lorenzo, I see that his throat's bleeding too. Instinctively, I turn my head and sniff the air in his direction.

He still smells like a vampire.

"Satan," Tony says, drawing my attention back to him. "The Devil."

I look over at the handsome man in the white suit. He smiles.

I may vomit.

"The Essence," Tony continues, blood still trickling down his neck, "comes from Satan and the host of fallen spirits, the ones cast out of the premortal existence with him. When you draw energy from them, from the Essence, it causes them pain. It drains them, weakens them."

So 'tis demonic. Aye, as I always believed it to be.

"A fleeting condition, I assure you," the Devil says with a grin. He eyes me with that same malevolent lust and hatred I remember seeing in Michael's eyes.

Only 'tis a thousand times worse. 'Tis a hatred of all mankind, of all those with physical bodies.

"He's in bondage to Lilith," Tony says, "enslaved by the Covenant."

"So you see, my errant Children," Lilith says, drawing my eyes back to herself, "if you kill me, not only will you die yourselves, you'll also unleash Lucifer upon the world in all his malevolent might." She smiles and . . . she's holding and nursing my bairns again. "And we wouldn't want to do that, now would we?" *I can* hear *the babe suckling at her breast. My babe.* "You wouldn't want to be responsible for plunging mankind into a new age of wickedness. Perhaps the old man would have to send a second flood."

For an instant, her eyes harden and flash with raw fury. The image of Lilith appearing as me nursing my bairns flickers like a guttering candle.

"Deliver me," the Devil says. "Free me from a youthful miscalculation."

I dinnae want to look at him. *Let me gaze on my babes, even if 'tis only an illusion!*

"I . . ." Tony says. "I don't . . . She might be right. Killing her may make things worse."

"Walk away," Lilith says. "I'll grant you mortality and I'll leave you alone. I'll free Tony and your other friend here. Walk away, and I promise to leave you in peace all your mortal days. Walk away, and I promise that you and your descendants will be safe from me and my Children till the end of time. Otherwise, I'll destroy Tony, this other one, your mousy Kathleen, and everyone else you love. Consider . . . and choose wisely."

Choose? I cannae think! How can I choose?

She made Kathleen choose between her children. And then she killed them both.

Bairns of my own!

I wrench my eyes away from her, trying desperately to drive the image of my children from my mind.

My knees buckle. Carl catches me with his free arm, but he nearly topples with me. I push the point of my sword into the floor and use the weapon to steady myself.

Breathing hard, trying to clear my head, I concentrate on staying upright, on leaning on my husband, and propping myself up with the sword.

Black sword of truth.

To slay demons.

But, if I slay the demon, the Devil will be unleashed.

Black sword of truth. An emblem of power.

Powerless. I can barely keep my feet.

We're powerless. Bereft of the Essence.

But if we're powerless, why does she nae simply kill us and be done with it? We're at her mercy.

Or are we?

Why am I so weak? Even bereft of vampiric power, I should be able to stand on my own. Even if I'm mortal, I should nae be this weak. Is she making us think we're weak? Is it mere suggestion or Persuasion or something akin to that?

Concentrate, lassie.

I try to focus on . . . on anything but Lilith.

I close my eyes.

Carl's breathing is shallow, rapid. Tony's heart is pounding in his chest. The sweet blood pulses through his . . .

How can I hear his pulse? If I'm mortal, how can I hear his heart?

Very, very softly, I whisper, "We're nae mortal." I hope Lilith cannae hear me. "Laddie, we may be cut off from the Essence, but we're nae mortal. I can still hear Tony's heart."

"But," he whispers back, "we're powerless."

"Choose," Lilith says. If she can hear us, she gives nae indication.

"Nae powerless," I whisper. *Black sword of truth. Use the truth to fight demons. The truth.* "Ye're nae powerless, Carl. Ye have the priesthood. Banish the Devil. Then we'll deal with Lilith."

Carl stiffens at my words. He pulls himself up to his full height.

I let go of him and lean on my sword.

"Lucifer," Carl says out loud, his voice still unsteady. "In the name of Jesus Christ," he continues, gaining in strength and volume, "I command you to depart."

The Devil smiles triumphantly. "Farewell, Mistress," he says and vanishes. As if coming from a distance, his voice says, "And by the way, you summoned me without following the ancient forms."

What does that mean?

Tony begins to laugh.

What is going on?

"Silence!" Lilith says, turning her attention to Tony. She looks angry.

Tony laughs all the louder.

She pulls back the sword from Tony's neck. "You will be silent." She's going to strike.

And with her attention gone, I feel strength return to my limbs. I can stand.

Stand and more.

The Essence floods through me. After its absence, the power feels foul, like a raging river of sewage.

Lorenzo bursts his bonds and grasps Lilith by the arm. He yanks her away from Tony.

As one, Carl and I fly at her. My sword is aimed at her evil heart.

But she deftly dodges our blades.

I wheel about to strike at her, but I have to parry a thrust from one of her swords instead.

She's so fast! Faster than any vampire I've e'er faced.

Carl attacks, but she parries his stroke as well.

"Lorenzo," Carl cries, "get Tony out of here!"

Lorenzo moves to obey.

I hear a window shattering behind me, but I cannae watch their escape; I must contend with Lilith.

Carl and I are on either side of her, fighting furiously. She has nae technique as she flails about with both swords, combating two opponents at once. 'Tis as if she has nae fought before. But she's so fast! All my skill is nae match for her speed. 'Tis all I can do to hold my own.

Carl does nae fare so well as me. He takes a slash across his chest. He cries out, but fights on. Another slash almost severs his sword arm. He pulls back for a moment as it Heals.

Lilith attacks me with both blades. I parry one slash, but the second one catches my thigh. I stumble, trying to ignore the pain and the itch of Healing. She raises one blade in a killing stroke.

A figure bowls into her from behind, knocking her down. 'Tis Lorenzo! She hacks into his back and kicks him from her. He crashes into the wall.

Lilith rises to her feet, and Carl and I move in to attack.

Lilith roars, and the floor under me reels. I lose my footing, falling to my knees. The whole house is shaking.

An earthquake?

Carl, having fallen to the bucking floor beside me, struggles to get up.

Furniture topples, and ceiling plaster crashes to the floor, filling the air with a tempest of white dust. The air swirls around us like a hurricane. In the midst of the maelstrom, Lilith raises both swords. She seems to expand, a giantess filling the room. She opens her mouth impossibly wide. 'Tis filled with fangs, row upon row of them like the mouth of a shark.

"It's fake!" 'Tis Tony's voice. He's close, perhaps just outside the window. "Don't believe it!"

The horror before me snaps its head toward the window. The quaking of the floor ceases. I leap at the monster and aim low, guessing where her heart should be. My sword impales flesh. The illusion vanishes, leaving only Lilith, my black blade in her heart. She drops both swords and looks at her chest. She lifts her head and stares at me with stunned eyes, her mouth agape.

Carl's sword slices through her neck, and Lilith's head topples from her shoulders.

The head rolls, the mouth working in a silent scream.

We've but seconds.

I look at Carl, and our eyes lock. His eyes are so blue.

We throw our arms around each other in a desperate embrace.

"I love ye," I say.

He says, "I love . . ."

Blackness.

Chapter 35

Tony

Carl and Moira crumple to the floor. I can't see Lorenzo from where I'm standing outside, but nobody else is moving in the house. Even though the sill is only at about shoulder height, the window's too high for me to climb through in my present state, and there's too much jagged glass.

Find the door!

Where's the door?

To the left? No, the right!

I try to run, but I can't force myself to move quickly. Too weak. I haven't slept in days. Can't remember when I last ate anything. The vampires gave me water, but . . .

The door!

I scramble up the steps to the porch. I try the doorknob. Locked! I could ram the door with my shoulder.

No, it's too solid, too heavy.

Worthless!

I need to get in there!

Why? They're all dead.

I need to see Lorenzo's body with my own eyes.

The window. It's the only way.

I go back down the steps and hurry as fast as I can back to the window. I need some way to boost myself up there.

I look around for something to use for climbing.

The chair!

The chair I was bound to sits where Lorenzo left it. He unbent the rods that were used to manacle my wrists. I grab one of the rods. It's still twisted into a rough C-shape. I drag the chair over to the window. Even that's almost beyond my strength.

I climb on unsteady legs onto the chair. Using the rod, I knock the rest of the glass out of the window. From where I am, I can see my great-great-grandfather's legs. They aren't moving.

I climb over the windowsill and into the house.

Lorenzo is motionless, lying with his back to the wall as if he's just sitting up.

He obeyed Carl's order to get me out of the house, but he carried me only a dozen yards before setting me down. He tore off the iron rods that bound me, then he flew back to rejoin the battle.

I kneel next to Lorenzo. I don't know what I expected to find. I know the Prophecy by heart, both versions of it.

Thus sayeth the Lord: Mine handmaid Moira MacDonald shall marry in mine holy house. She shall be sealed to a worthy elder, the unwilling son of Lilith. And, if they are valiant in my service, it shall come to pass in the fullness of time that they shall be the sword of my vengeance to slay the daughter of Cain, and death shall fall upon all her children. In that day, mine handmaid Moira MacDonald and her husband, my servant, shall both die, but they shall see their Redeemer's face in the resurrection of the just.

". . . and death shall fall upon all her children," I say aloud.

Remembering the CPR training I took, I put two fingers to Lorenzo's throat. No pulse. Of course not. He's not breathing.

Dead.

I turn my head and look at Carl and Moira. Their arms are still wrapped loosely around each other. They could be asleep to all appearances.

At least they died together.

I sit next to Lorenzo and wrap my arms around him. A wracking sob shakes my whole body.

Abbey, Little Tony, Lorenzo, Carl, Moira, Rolf.

It's too much.

I let the grief wash over me like a wave and surrender to it.

I don't know how long I sat there, holding Lorenzo's corpse. At some point I must have fallen asleep.

I'm exhausted.

It must have been a while. The sun's up. Morning light streams in through the broken window. It falls on Moira's face.

She looks peaceful in death. Beautiful. She was a pretty woman. Beautiful in a way that Lilith never was.

Lilith.

Her headless corpse is still pinned to the wall, Moira's black sword holding it there like some monstrous, mutilated, red butterfly mounted on a plaque.

And I can see Lilith's head, lying in the shadows.

How did I ever think that creature was beautiful?

That's not honest, Tony.

She *was* beautiful, but only on the outside. On the inside . . .

I look back at Moira and Carl lying there in the sunlight.

In the sunlight.

Shouldn't they be burning? Sam Gallagher said even a dead vampire would burn in the sunlight. The Seed's photo-reactive, he said.

Well, they're not on fire. And I suppose that's a mercy. Otherwise, the house would be gone, and me with it.

A soft sound catches my attention. It sounds out of place in this chamber of death and carnage. It's a small sound, so ordinary.

Snoring.

Somebody's snoring.

Carl!

It can't be. He's dead.

I clamber to my feet, letting Lorenzo's body drop to the floor.

"Che?"

I stumble backward and fall painfully on my backside. "Lorenzo?"

He stirs. *A vampire rising from the dead.* He clutches his head. "My head hurts."

He's alive!

Lorenzo sits up. "Anthony? Why am I not dead? Did we . . . fail?" He looks at Lilith's corpse. "Isn't that she?" His eyes search the room until they locate her head.

"Lorenzo!" I scramble over to my grandfather and throw my arms a-round him.

"I'm alive?" he says, tentatively hugging me back. "How can this be? Not that I mind, really."

"You're alive!" I shout.

"*Sì.* So it would seem. What about Carl and Moira?"

I pull back from him, breaking the hug. "I thought I heard Carl snoring. That's why I . . . dropped you."

Lorenzo crawls across the room to where Carl and Moira lie. He avoids the sunlight at first, then hesitantly extends a hand into the light.

"*Mama mia!*" he mutters. "*Grazie, Signore!*" He continues into the light un-til he's kneeling beside them.

I crawl to the side to get a better view.

"I cannot hear their hearts," he says. "But of course not!" He laughs, a look of sheer delight on his face. He pats Carl's face. "Wake up, *capitano mio!*"

Carl stirs. "What? Lorenzo? What's going on?" He sounds groggy. Then Carl sits bolt upright.

As his arms come from around Moira, she wakes. Her eyes flutter open. They focus on Carl. "Are we . . . ?"

He scoops her up in his arms and holds her tight. "We're alive!" he says, kissing her face, her lips. "I don't know how, but we're alive!"

"Aye, laddie," she says, kissing him back. She hugs him close. Then her eyes light on me and she smiles. "Tony!"

"I'm here too," Lorenzo says.

"Lorenzo!" She beams at him. Then her expression transforms into horror. "The Sun!"

"It's OK," I say, laughing.

"The Sun's shining and we're alive!" Carl shouts. "We're alive!"

"I don't understand," Lorenzo says. He smiles and shrugs his shoulders. "And I don't care!"

"But the Prophecy," Carl says. "We killed Lilith. She's dead. *We're* supposed to be dead."

"Are ye complaining, laddie?" Moira asks. "Are ye so anxious to be rid o' me?"

"Never," he says and kisses her again.

"How is this possible?" Lorenzo asks. "The Prophecy says . . ."

"I think I know," I say. "The Prophecy states that you will die 'in that day.'"

"But we're not dead," Carl says.

"But you're mortal," I explain. "You *will* die. God said the same thing to Adam and Eve. 'In the day thou eatest thereof thou shalt surely die.' And they did die . . . in God's time. God's days tend to be a little longer than ours."

"Well, that leaves just one question," Carl says.

"What's that, laddie?" Moira's green eyes sparkle in the sun.

Carl grins. "How in the heck are we going to get home?"

Home?

Kathleen! Will she ever forgive me? Will she even want to see me again?

Moira digs her cell phone out of her pocket. As she turns the phone on, she smiles broadly. "Do ye think we might call in the Marines?"

It takes a couple of hours before the Marines arrive.

The names of the people who owned the house were Gary and Donna Whitfield, at least that's who the mail was addressed to. We didn't bury them. None of us had the heart or the stomach for it. Or the strength. Moira straightened their bodies and covered them with clean sheets. Carl and Lorenzo carried Rolf's body down to the living room, laid it beside the Whitfields, and covered it with a blanket.

Lilith's body they left where it was. I gave the head a kick and sent it rolling to rest at her feet.

While we waited, we ate cold fried chicken, cold mashed potatoes, and cold milk that we found in the fridge. We carried the food outside to escape the sight and stench of death.

Neither Moira nor Lorenzo had ever tasted fried chicken before. They even relished the taste of the tap water.

I did eat, but, weak though I was, I had little appetite.
I could think only of Kathleen.

Two large helicopters, painted in green camouflage, land in the field in front of the farmhouse.

A man wearing civilian clothes, but looking every bit a soldier, jumps from the first helicopter and comes running up to Carl. He salutes sharply. "Ready for evac, sir?"

"That's affirmative, Marine," Carl says, returning the salute and then shaking the soldier's hand warmly. "Good to see you, Ericson."

"And you, sir." The Marine turns to me and extends a hand. "Tony Lupescu?"

I nod. "That's me."

"Mr. Lupescu, I hope you'll forgive me. It's against the regs and all, but she insisted on coming along. Wouldn't take no for an answer."

"She?" I ask.

He points back to the nearer of the two helicopters.

Another Marine, this one wearing a green coverall and flying helmet, is assisting a woman out of the aircraft. Once she's on the ground, the Marine takes ahold of her arm and forces her to crouch until they're well away from the copter's rotating blades.

Once in the clear, the Marine releases her arm. She straightens up and begins to run.

Toward me.

Her hair is blonde, and although I can't see them from this distance, I'd bet my life that her eyes are blue.

Chapter 36

Tony

Nearly Nine Years Later

C an ye see, Sarah?" Moira gently pushes the little girl with the brown hair forward.

The girl turns her head and looks up at Moira with sparkling blue eyes. She holds a small finger to her rosy lips. "Shush, mama! They're going to pray!" She folds her arms tightly across her chest.

Moira smiles at the girl and nods. Moira hoists the toddler she's carrying a bit higher on her hip. "Fold yer arms, Sergei." The child obediently bows his head and folds his chubby little arms.

Dressed in white and standing waist-deep in the water, Carl holds the little boy with the wavy red hair by the wrist. Carl rests his right hand reassuringly on the child's back. "Ready, buddy?"

The boy nods eagerly and squeezes his green eyes shut. He pinches his nose with one small hand, and grips Carl's left forearm with the other, hanging on tight. The water comes up to the boy's chest.

Carl raises his right arm to the square. "Rolf Angus Morgan, having been commissioned of Jesus Christ, I baptize you in the name of the Father and of the Son and of the Holy Ghost." He closes the prayer, places his right hand on Rolf's back, and lowers him into the water.

Carl pulls the boy back to his feet and looks to Lorenzo who stands at one side of the baptismal font behind the Plexiglas splash shield. Lorenzo nods in confirmation. Then Carl looks to me on the other end of the splash shield. I nod as well.

Carl looks down at the beaming boy. Water streams from the kid's soaked red hair. "I guess we got it right the first time, buddy."

"Aye," the boy says. "That we did."

◆ ◆ ◆

Waiting for Carl and Rolf to change out of their wet clothes, we sit and listen to the teenage boy playing the piano. His dusky fingers play a beautiful tune. He's quite good, especially considering that he started playing the piano only a few years ago. But Daniel works hard at everything he does. *Carl says he's a whiz at computer programming.* Daniel nods and his mother, Esther, turns the page of the music book to the next bookmark. Daniel transitions seamlessly to the next song.

From human livestock to mayor of New Canaan, Utah.

Well, whom else would the members of the Tribe elect?

New Canaan is a young and tiny farming community south of Provo. Although she won't admit it, I suspect Moira purchased the land herself. I know she established the T.O.E. Foundation to help pay for the education of the Tribe and their integration into modern society. Tons of money poured in from all around the U.S., and this should've surprised no one, after all the media attention. When the Tribe was relocated there eight years ago, they naturally took up farming and sheep ranching. It hasn't been easy for them, but the Church has helped tremendously with food, clothing, training, and education.

Carl's web-design firm employs a number of Tribe members. Daniel works as a part-time intern there, after school.

Moira and Carl tried to get that Brotherhood of Tobias involved in supporting New Canaan, but, like all fanatics, by and large, they wouldn't give up their obsession with demons. Now that the demons were all mortal, the Brotherhood devoted their energies to tracking down and exposing erstwhile vampires. Most of the former Children of Lilith went into hiding. Many took their own lives rather than face life as a mortal or justice for their murders.

An older woman whom I don't recognize, a bit on the stocky side, but not unattractive for a woman her age, leans forward and taps Moira on the shoulder. Moira turns in her chair, and the two exchange a few whispered words. The woman arrived a bit late, so maybe this is the first chance that she and Moira have had to talk. The older woman extends her left hand and shows it to Moira. Moira, apparently spying the ring on the woman's finger, squeals with delight.

"Winnie!" Moira says. "When?"

"Jonathan proposed last night!" the older woman says. I notice the balding, silver-haired man sitting next to her. He grins and winks at me.

So that's Winnie Morrison? She's the director of the T.O.E. Foundation. I've never met her, but I know she's an old friend of Moira's from way back. Moira probably taught her in Primary or something.

Well, good for Sister Morrison. It always warms my heart when I see older folks finding romance.

I feel a tug on my sleeve. "Daddy, what's taking so long?"

I pat my little son on the knee. "Just a little longer, Lorenzo. Carl and Rolf are getting dressed." Little Lorenzo twists in his seat, his four-year-old body just too fidgety to sit still for long.

"I'll take him to get a drink," my great-great-grandfather says, standing and taking his namesake by the hand. "We'll be right back."

Sitting next to me and holding my hand, Kathleen lifts it and places it on her belly. I can feel the baby kick. It's risky having a child after forty, but Moira assures us that the baby's fine. Moira limits her practice to New Canaan, but Kathleen won't have another doctor.

Moira had to quit the hospital. Even though the publicity and the media attention dwindled after a while, too many patients refused to be seen by a vampire doctor, or at least a former vampire. Other patients were only too eager to be treated by the famous Dr. Moira MacDonald Morgan.

The baby's a girl. Kathleen wants to name her Moira.

I approve.

It took a long time for Kathleen and me to be ready to try again. It wasn't that Kathleen wasn't willing to forgive me; it was simply a matter of grieving for Abby and Little Tony.

This will be our last child, most likely. I'm so glad we're having a girl.

Kathleen leans toward my ear and whispers, "Moira's pregnant again. She's six weeks along."

I chuckle. "If anyone deserves to have a large family, it's her."

The door to the left of the baptismal font opens, and Carl leads Rolf out. Rolf's red hair is still wet, of course, but he looks quite dapper in his plaid vest and tartan tie. The vest, Moira tells me, is the MacDonald tartan. The tie is the Morgan tartan, of course.

Lorenzo and Little Lorenzo return a moment later. Lorenzo sits next to me and holds his great-great-great-grandson in his lap. My son folds his arms, but still manages to squirm a bit. Lorenzo kisses him on the top of his head. The boy tilts his head back and smiles at Lorenzo. "I love you, grandpa."

Lorenzo smiles back. "I love you too, *bambino.*"

Daniel finishes the song he's playing and moves from the piano to his seat. Esther, however, remains by the piano.

The man conducting the meeting, a man named Cornwall, stands in front of the closed baptismal font doors and says, "We'd like to thank Daniel Morgan for that lovely interlude music. We'll now have a short talk on the Holy Ghost given by Esther Polazhynets."

Half the population of New Canaan adopted the last name of Morgan. It would have been the whole town if not for the efforts of Carl and Moira. When Carl and Moira tried to convince them otherwise, the Tribe compromised by having half the town take the last name MacDonald instead. No amount of coaxing could dissuade them.

The mayor, however, changed her name when she married one of the Marines involved in the rescue of the Tribe. That romance blossomed years ago, but Esther refused to marry until her Marine joined the Church and was ready to take her to the temple.

"Dear brothers and sisters," Esther begins, "I am pleased that so many of you have come this day." She smiles at Rolf. "I am pleased, Rolf, to see that thou hast chosen to follow our Lord Jesus Christ into the waters of baptism."

I smile. *Esther never really has quite gotten the hang of modern English.*

♦ ♦ ♦

Carl stands behind Rolf's chair. "Lorenzo, Tony, Bishop," he says. He looks around searching for someone. His face splits in a grin. "Sam, would you join us please?"

I scan the room. *There he is.* Sam Gallagher stands up at the back of the room and comes forward.

I didn't know he made it.

I'm glad he did.

Sam's had a rough go.

I know how that is. Kathleen and I struggled for a while, but we made it. It was especially difficult since there were no bodies to bury. But we grieved and we got through it. Together.

Sam? Well, Nicole left him. He struggled for years. Even lost his job at BYU. Moira and Esther got him a job teaching science at New Canaan High School. I know he enjoys teaching there.

I hope someday he finds someone to love again.

"Glad you could make it, Sam," Carl says.

"Wouldn't miss it," Sam says.

Carl lays his hands on his son's head. We all join him. Last of all, Sam lays his hands atop mine.

"Rolf Angus Morgan," Carl begins, "in the name of Jesus Christ and by the power of the holy Melchizedek Priesthood, we lay our hands upon your head and confirm you a member of the Church of Jesus Christ of Latter-day Saints and say unto you, receive the Holy Ghost. And we give unto you a blessing . . ."

♦ ♦ ♦

"Congratulations, young man," Kathleen says, shaking Rolf's hand.

Everyone's enjoying punch and cookies (Scottish shortbread of course) after the baptismal service. Lorenzo's looking after his great-great-great-grandson.

"Thank you, Sister Loopy," Rolf says.

Kathleen smiles at the nickname the kid's used since he was very little and couldn't pronounce "Lupescu." She says, "I understand it's your birthday too."

"Aye." Rolf nods. "'Tis indeed."

It's so funny to hear the boy using his mother's speech patterns spoken in an accent that is unquestionably Utahan. I think it's adorable, but I bet some kids make fun of him. He'll grow out of it, assimilate, or be his own unique self.

I'm rooting for uniqueness.

"Baptized on your birthday, huh?" Kathleen asks. She winks at Moira. "Wasn't that eight years and nine months ago, almost to the day?"

Moira shifts Sergei to her other hip, leans in toward Kathleen, and whispers just loud enough for me to hear, "I can assure ye, lassie, he was conceived that very night!"

She means the night after Lilith died.

"Wasted no time, I see," Kathleen whispers back.

"I wasted two and a half centuries, lassie, but 'twas worth the wait!"

"What was worth the wait, mama?" Rolf says.

"Ye were, my bonnie wee laddie! Worth every century!"

"Aye," the boy says, "that I was!"

Acknowledgements

As I come to the end of a project such as this, into which I've poured so much love and energy and passion, I am acutely aware that none of this would be possible without the invaluable assistance of many, many people. Cindy Belt, Jeremiah Belt, Bryan Belt, Jacob Belt, Rachel Belt, Olha Polazhynets Goodrick (and, yes, that *is* where I got the name), Ryan Larsen, and Michael Young provided tremendous help with proofreading and critique. Dr. Steven Devenport and Bryan Belt assisted with medical expertise. Doug Myler provided pharmaceutical knowledge. Dr. Eric Huntsman, once again, invented the "Adamic." Rick Steadman, Michael Young, and Siegfried Hanuschick helped with and corrected my German translation. Olha Polazhynets Goodrick helped with the Russian translation. Luke Howard consulted about Australian slang. Malachi Hall, USMC-retired, was my source for Marine Corps procedures and lingo. Lloyd Newell advised me on network news procedure and journalistic ethics. Sam Newton provided tons of information on legal matters. I wish to give a special thanks to Nina Doxey for being such a good sport. Mable Belt and David Belt (once again, my father, not me) supplied encouragement and enthusiasm. And I must thank Elizabeth and George Bentley who *believed* enough in such a bizarre project to give it a chance.

I couldn't have done it without you.

Finally, I must acknowledge my Heavenly Father. Many nights I've prayed for inspiration and guidance to help me write my little vampire novels.

I know He has helped me.

About the Author

C. David Belt was born in Evanston, Wyoming. As a child, he lived and traveled extensively around the Far East. He served as an LDS missionary in South Korea and southern California (Korean-speak-ing). He graduated from Brigham Young University with a Bachelor of Science in Computer Science and a minor in Aerospace Studies. He served as a B-52 pilot in the US Air Force and as an Air Weapons Controller in the Washington Air National Guard. When he is not writing, he sings in the Mor-mon Tabernacle Choir and works as a software engineer. He collects swords (mostly Scottish), axes, spears, and other medieval weapons and armor. He and his wife have six children and live in Utah with an eclectus parrot named Mork (who likes to jump on the keyboard when David is writing).